Dragon Potatoes 

Dragon Potatoes

Evan Kvalvik

Dragon Potatoes

A Fantasy LitRPG

By Evan Kvalvik

Evan Kvalvik

First published in the United states of America by
DimeSquare Publishing, 2025.
ISBN: 979-8-9913976-5-0
First edition.

This is a work of fiction. Names, places, characters, and events portrayed in this book are fictitious and are a product of the author's questionable imagination.

This fiction is dedicated to my audio book narrator. Go ahead and say whatever you want.

Table of Contents

Chapter 1

"This stewed beef goes so well with these potatoes." Fin's mother said to no one in particular. "It's like they were meant for each other."

Fin shared an exasperated look with his father as his mother made another off-handed comment that wasn't subtle in the least.

"I agree," Hildred's mother said from across the table. "This would be the perfect dish for a wedding reception."

The two women began shamelessly planning a nondescript, hypothetical wedding that wasn't as hypothetical as they led on. Everyone knew what they were up to; it was why the two families met more and more frequently to share meals. They were trying to join the two farms by the bonds of holy matrimony, but Fin would never marry Hildred, not in a thousand years.

"It needs salt," Hildred's greasy opinion came from across the table as two greasier fingers bludgeoned their way into the salt dish. Most of the salt crystals stuck to her pudgy fingers, causing her to reach in a second time.

Fin was a seventh-generation potato farmer expected to take over the family farm and pass it to the eighth. The problem was there were few suitable options for him to marry within a day's radius of the farm. Still, there was Hildred with the Grober family farm only an hour away.

"I agree with Hildred," Fin's father said, picking up the salt dish and flicking out as many of the contaminated particles as he could. "I would spend a few years perfecting the recipe before trying to serve it at any wedding reception. It's good, but it needs time."

Fin suppressed a satisfied smile; they were clearly not talking about the food, and his father just told them all to back off for a few years. He was almost eighteen and could run the farm alone, but his father didn't need to rely on him anytime soon. His father frequently told him he could take off, explore the world, and return when ready to settle down. If he decided to come back with a wife, all the better. His mother, however, wasn't a patient woman.

"Nonsense," his mother protested. "If all it needs is a little salt, I don't see the problem."

"And butter," Hildred reached for the butter dish.

"Here, let me get that for you," her mother said, picking up the butter dish and putting a very conservative scoop on her plate.

Hildred looked accosted by the minuscule slab of butter her mom gave her. "More butter."

Fin glanced at his father, who was containing a laugh by meticulously wiping his face with his napkin.

"I think it's really good," Fin said quickly, finishing the last bite on his plate. "Can I be excused, please?"

"See?" Fin's mother said. "A match made by Frome."

"I was talking about the meal," Fin said off-handedly. "I should go grab some dirt before it gets dark."

"Very well," Fin's father said. "You better hurry."

Fin stood and bade farewell to their company. "It was a pleasure seeing you again, Mrs. Grober. Hildred, you too."

"Always a pleasure Finlay," Mrs. Grober said.

Fin stood and waited for Hildred to respond. Her mouth was full, and she made no effort to chew faster. A long, quiet moment ensued before she reached into her mouth, pulled out a thin piece of gristle, and said, "Bye, Fin."

Fin stepped outside and breathed in the warm summer air. He had ash-colored hair that he let fall around his shoulders in the winter and kept tied behind his head with a leather strap in the summer. He stood just a little taller than his father. His father had explained that each generation grew taller than the last. It was something to do with the potatoes.

Fin walked around the cabin, gripped the wooden cart holding a shovel, and began walking it down a well-beaten path through the tree line. As far as he was concerned, his chores were done for the day. He just needed an excuse to escape from the conversation about his marriage. He had told his mother he wasn't interested in marrying Hildred, but she ignored him. As soon as he was 18, he would take his father's advice and leave for a while. That should give his mother time to cool down.

The cart rumbled as it rolled down the secret road his great, great, great grandfather made all those years ago. The story his father told was that old Abernanthy was traveling through these woods when he saw movement from a clearing in the trees. He silently moved forward when he saw a grey dragon perched on a rock, just staring into the view beyond. He stood motionless behind a tree until the dragon finally jumped up and flew away. Abernanthy investigated the spot the dragon had been in only to find a massive pile of what he called "prime manure." He had found the dragon's favorite spot to sit and to do what one does in a quiet place with a relaxing view.

Abernanthy carted some of the manure out, experimented with it to grow potatoes, and found that it made the best he had ever produced. He started the Dragon's Throne Farm, and people still travel to buy and trade for the overpriced potatoes. People said they were the best potatoes ever, and some swore they had healing properties.

Fin came up to the clearing where the secret ingredient to their potatoes lay in a pile that still stood in a massive mound even though they had carted it off for years. Just beyond the hill of mythical dirt stood a wall of giant boulders with a perfect groove for a dragon to perch on if it was so inclined. Fin didn't necessarily believe the story. All he knew was one of his chores was to periodically cart the dirt back to the farm, and one day he would probably make his son do the same thing.

He rolled the cart next to the dirt and climbed the massive boulders. Here, he lounged in the crook of the rock and looked out, as he had done so many times before. Round hills curved up and down, crisscrossing each other and flowing gently to the next. He didn't know about dragons, but it was a nice relaxing view.

Chapter 2

The sun peeked through his window, and Fin opened his eyes. His blanket and sheet were lying on the floor next to his bed, and he was drenched in sweat. This happened occasionally; some nights, he needed a blanket, and other nights he needed a dip in a partially frozen lake.

He left the bed and walked outside to find his father splashing water on himself from the rain barrels. "Sleep well?" he asked.

"Slept hot," Fin responded, peeling off his shirt and stepping up to the rain barrel. "I woke up wet like I went to sleep swimming last night."

"I'm sure Hildred won't mind the extra warmth," his father joked and smiled.

Fin laughed. "Have you ever considered how our marriage would affect you? If she came here, you would have to see her every day. But, if I moved there, you would have to tend the farm by yourself."

His dad's face grew serious. "Good thing I don't need your help because there's no way I'm going to be able to see Hildred every morning. It's enough that only one of us has to suffer."

"I'm your son, and you're just going to banish me to the Grobers like that?" Fin asked in mock offense.

"Well, son," his father took a towel and dried off. "I suppose if you don't marry Hildred, everything should be fine. I just don't know how long you can hold off falling in love with her."

The two laughed together before the familiar sound of a horse-drawn cart froze them in place.

"Go get some clothes on and tell your mother to open shop," his dad ordered. "I'll go see what we have in stock."

Fin ran inside and told his mother. As soon as he had proper clothes on, he went back outside to see two soldiers driving a cart that looked like it was for carrying prisoners.

His mother greeted the two men from the potato stand. "Hello, gentlemen. What brings you to these parts?"

The men pulled the cart to a stop and began approaching before one of them answered. "War, ma'am. King Sevornand is calling in the draft."

"War?" Fin's father said, exiting the house. "We haven't heard anything of war, and we had customers from the Alam Kingdom just a few days ago. Rumors precede wars like a horse and cart."

The other guard spoke up quickly, "Ah, yes. Well, it turns out that the Kingdom of Rudford has been scheming to overthrow Alam for some time. The king just found out several days ago. But don't worry, his majesty doesn't necessarily want to fight a war, just accrue soldiers to show his force."

"How long ago did you find this out before the king dispatched you to gather soldiers for the draft?" Fin's father had keen eyes. "Last time I checked, King Sevornand's troops outnumber Rudford three to one."

"Not long," the first solder stated. "We're in a hurry, though. The king is only demanding one man per family to show his force. I recommend packing heavy; we have a lot of ground to cover. If it is as you say, we'll have you home before you know it."

Fin spoke out before his father decided to enlist himself, "I'll go."

"You can't go. We need you here. Hildred needs you." Fin's mother scolded.

Fin's face flustered with anger. "No, you need Father. Also, I'm not marrying Hildred. I don't care what you say. I don't like her, and that's all there is to it."

The two soldiers awkwardly turned away, pretending not to pay attention.

"Let the boy go," Fin's father said finally. "I think it'll be good for him to get some real-world experience. Alam has enough soldiers that they won't need him. Rudford isn't even a threat. Plus, it would be better for everyone if you parted with words of encouragement."

Fin's mother stood still as a stone until she finally relented. "Okay, but I won't send you off on an empty stomach. I'll run inside and make you something special."

"We would also appreciate something special before we leave too." One of the soldiers said before she went into the house.

"Fin, let's go pack your bags," his father said, ignoring the two soldiers. "I want to have a conversation with you before you leave."

Fin walked into his room and took out whatever clothes he thought he might need while his father left and came back with a large sack.

"It's not completely waterproof," he tossed the sack next to a small pile of clothes. "So try not to take it swimming."

Fin began stuffing clothes into the sack while his father spoke, "I was hoping you would have unlocked your first quest by now, but it seems you're going to have to do things the old-fashioned way."

Fin gave his father a puzzled look as he continued, "I know you never really believed me about the whole dragon thing, but I assure you it's real. I have proof, and before not too long, you'll have proof too. It started with your grandfather, who could see the window and got a few buffs but couldn't do much with it. I could not only see the window, but I could also allocate stat points. I just can't do anything with the ability points."

He raised his hands in defense, "Look, I was hoping you would have unlocked it before we had this conversation, so now you're just going to have to trust me. Through the generations, we absorbed something from the dragon. I don't know what it was, but each generation seems to get stronger. That will mean you will have more of the power than I had. The problem is the power was meant for dragons. The quests are hidden, and you can only reveal the quests or complete them by experiencing life... Well, by experiencing a dragon's life which is hard to do. Some quests aren't worth completing even though they will give you more power, and some are just not possible."

Fin tied the top of his sack and set it down. "You're saying we get quests, but they are hidden? And completing them makes us more powerful, but some of the quests aren't even possible?"

"Precisely," his father said. "And some are just too outrageous. Right now, I have a quest to battle all my children for. Hold on." He stared blankly up at the ceiling. "Battle your offspring for dominance. +1 Patriarch quest. +5 levels, +8 gold stat points, +2 ability points. Upgrade Sovereignty Quests to Patriarch Quests.

"Obviously, I'm not going to battle you for dominance," he laughed. "So you're safe for now. Usually, you can only see the quest after you complete it. Some quests reveal other quests. I once completed a quest after standing on the mountain and looking around. It said, "Quest complete: Survey the land, and then it gave me some perks. I'm glad it didn't require wings because I would have never gotten it if it did."

"Wait, are you just being crazy so I won't feel bad about leaving you to do all the work yourself?" Fin's face was somewhere between jovial and mock-serious.

"First of all, maybe," his father said. "But, whatever my reasoning, I need you to listen to this next part very seriously.

"There are six stat categories. Strength, Dexterity, Constitution, Intelligence, Wisdom, and Charisma. The first three can only be upgraded with basic stat points, but gold stat points can upgrade any six. All stats can technically be upgraded naturally, so think carefully about which one you think is best. Most importantly, upgrading any of the first three will make you very hungry, and the last three will make you tired. I put two into strength once and had to eat a meal big enough for a family. I put one into Charisma before I went to sleep and woke up in the morning a full day later!"

"First three food, last three sleep, got it," Fin said.

"Other than that," his father smiled, "Trial and error. You'll have to get creative to complete the quests you know about, and for the ones you don't know about, just try doing dragon things to complete them. If I'm correct, you'll have the first one completed before you get to the castle."

"What are dragon things?" Fin asked.

"The fact that you asked that question means you're on the right track," his father picked up the bag and led him out of the room. "I want you to ask yourself that question every morning. All I know is the more experiences you have, the more likely you'll complete a quest."

The two talked while their meal was being prepared. Finally, Fin's mother brought steamed potatoes, butter, fermented vegetables, and mushroom gravy. The sour crunch of the vegetables balanced out the rich flavors and textures. The taste of the potato skins transformed in the areas that were burnt. Fresh butter melted and mixed in with every aspect of the meal, making it an altogether pleasant experience.

When everyone was finished eating, Fin's mother gave him a sack of provisions, "That's a week's worth of food and a water skin that should last you four days if you ration it. It should get you to where you're going."

Fin hugged his parents and wished them farewell. One of the soldiers put Fin's pack on top of the cart and then held out his hand for the provisions. Fin opted to hold on to the food as he climbed into the cart.

"Looks more like a slave cart than a soldier recruiting cart," Fin's father muttered.

The soldiers looked at the cart as if noticing it for the first time. "I guess it kind of does. All I know is the king sent out every available cart, carriage, and wheelbarrow for the draft. I guess they were running low on options. Everyone ready?"

The soldiers climbed onto the cart and urged the horse forward. Fin waved to his family as they got further and further away. Minutes passed, and no one felt like talking much, so they traveled in comfortable silence.

Chapter 3

Fin had lost track of time when it happened. The thought that he wouldn't be sleeping in his own bed solidified when a small, flashing light appeared in the top left of his vision. He tried looking at it, and a screen appeared, floating in front of his face.

Level: 1 Class: None

Path: None

Strength: -19	Intelligence: 0
Dexterity: -11	Wisdom: 1
Constitution: -7	Charisma: 3
Basic stat points: 3	
Gold stat points: 3	
Ability points: 1	

Skill Atribute: None

His dad was right. He looked around to see if anyone noticed, and the window immediately disappeared. He looked up to the left, and the window popped up. Then he made it go away by simply looking past it. He pulled it up again to look closer.

Why are my first three stats negative numbers? He asked himself before focusing on the basic stat points. The basic stat points lit up, as did Strength, Dexterity, and Constitution. He knew his strength was the worst out of his basic stat points and decided that was the first one he would need to upgrade. Immediately, strength went to negative eighteen, and basic stat points went down to two. *That was treacherously easy,* he thought before a wave of hunger struck him like an arrow to the gut. His hands nearly shook, and he reached into the bag and pulled out and consumed seven hard-boiled eggs, four wheels of hard-tack bread, a lump of cheese, a jar of pickled minnows, and four strips of meat. He drank deeply from his water skin until it was less than half full. When his hunger was sated, he moved his arms around and felt them to see if anything had changed. His arms didn't feel bigger; they felt denser, and he felt stronger. He took inventory of his rations and found he only had one meal left; it was significantly less than he needed if he was going to upgrade his basic stat points again.

With a sigh, he sat back in his chair and noticed a blinking light to the top right of his vision. He looked at it, and a quest bar popped into his line of sight. It read: Sovereign Quest Complete: Flee the nest: +1 level, +3 basic stat points, +3 gold stat points, +1 ability point.

I guess leaving home is the equivalent of fleeing the nest, he pondered as he mindlessly chewed another strip of meat from his sack. He looked up to the left again, and the stat window popped back into view. He focused on the gold stat points, and all six categories lit up. Careful not to decide on anything, he made a mental note that the gold stat points could be allocated anywhere. He then selected the ability point, and a different menu popped up. It was a picture of a dragon on the left of the screen, and each part of it was selectable. He looked at the wings, and the right side was populated with descriptions in blue lettering. It read Wing Attack and Wing Shield. Knowing he would never need a skill for something he didn't have, he selected the head of the dragon and read, Jowls of Strength and Fear Howl. He chose the claws and read Crushing Grip and Strengthened Talons. He then pointlessly scanned over the tail attributes before selecting the body. On the body, he read Pain Resist and Piercing Resist.

On seeing Pain Resist, he decided that was the first attribute he would upgrade when he had more food. His father didn't say there were side effects to upgrading an ability, so he decided that as soon as he could, he would select it.

The Pain Resist attribute glowed and disappeared from the list. He quickly selected the status page and saw that his skill attributes now read passive attributes: pain resistance. Fin silently cursed himself for accidentally choosing a talent before being prepared for it. He preemptively held his strip of meat at the ready, but his hunger didn't return. Instead, he felt a cool tingling sensation spread over his whole body. He didn't feel tired or hungry; he felt invigorated.

"Hey," Fin got the attention of the soldiers driving the cart. "How much longer until we get to wherever we're going?"

"The royal armory won't take but maybe three or four days at the pace we're going," one of the soldiers said. "I would try to rest as much as possible. It's going to be a lot of hard work once we arrive.

"Oh, just one thing," the soldier continued. "Can I see one of your boots? We'll need to size you up for a uniform once we get there."

Fin pulled off one of his boots and passed it through the bars. The soldiers looked it over and held it up against their own boots.

"Looks about your size," one of them said.

"Yeah, that'll have to do." The other one said before passing the boot back to Fin.

After a brief conversation, Fin decided to allocate a single golden stat point and go to sleep for a while. He looked up at his menu, selected the gold stat point, and held it to experiment with mental control. As long as he didn't make up his mind, the stat point didn't allocate. He knew he didn't want to put it in Strength, Dexterity, or Constitution; he could use basic stat points for those. Instead, he looked at the last three, Intelligence, Wisdom, and Charisma. His father said upgrading one of these three would put him to sleep. Still, he couldn't recall the difference between Intelligence and Wisdom. Since his intelligence was zero, he decided he would put one there first, and then later, he would allocate one to wisdom and then compare the differences.

Immediately, Intelligence went from zero to one, and then Wisdom went from one to two. He laughed to himself as the realization came to him. The decision to allocate the point was all it needed. Next time he would hold off making any mental decisions until he was ready. Then he would even it out by putting his remaining point in intellige- He cut off his thought too late as intelligence went from one to two. He let out an exasperated laugh and said out loud, "Okay, now I've learned my lesson." Then he laid back and went to sleep.

Chapter 4

Fin awoke in the early morning. The cart was still plodding along, bouncing, and squeaking as it rolled forward. He was surprised to notice someone else in the carriage with him. The large man lay sleeping on the bench across from him.

He was hungry, but the pain of hunger seemed dampened. He figured it was the pain resistance he had acquired. A thought occurred to him, and he looked around for the sack of supplies his mother had left him. He knew the difference between wisdom and intelligence. Wisdom, brought on by experience, is the ability to read people, situations, and the world around him. Intelligence is the capability for problem-solving and the ability to acquire and use knowledge. The two seemed closely linked together but, in some ways, opposites. Wisdom was akin to instincts, while intelligence was for calculations and measured responses. He realized that this knowledge came from upgrading his intelligence, and he smiled at the irony of it.

He began looking for his food, when he couldn't find it, he noticed his boots were also missing. He felt mildly irritated at whatever prank was being played on him. After sitting up, he cleared his throat and said, "Where are my things?"

The soldier steering the cart startled and then nudged his sleeping companion. "Barnes, he's awake. I won the bet."

When Barnes woke up, the first soldier repeated himself.

"He's awake, is he?" Barnes asked in surprise.

"Yeah, I'm awake," Fin said, beginning to feel annoyed. "I can't find my boots or the provisions my mother left me."

"If by provisions you mean a couple of meager scraps in a bag you were holding, then I haven't seen them." Barnes looked over to his companion. "Did you see any provisions, Jack?"

"I certainly didn't see a week's worth of food if that's what you're asking. I might have seen a little less than half a meal." Jack said, and they both started laughing.

Knowing that whatever food was stolen would either be returned or it wouldn't, Fin asked about his boots.

"Boots?" Barnes asked. "Like what kind of boots?"

"I think he means these boots," Jack said, holding up his foot.

"Oh, those boots," Barnes said. "I haven't seen those either."

Now Fin was upset. "I'm not kidding. Give me my boots back."

"Sure," Jack put his leg down and held up his arms. "If you come out and get 'em, I'll even put them on your feet myself."

The two laughed so hard that the bigger man Fin had noticed earlier turned over and woke up.

Fin stood up and stepped towards the latched door. It was locked. He turned to his new neighbor, "I think they locked us in here. Help me get this open."

The bigger man sat up in his chair. "I've tried, and I'm sure countless other slaves have tried too. It's no use."

"Slaves? You mean recruits going to the castle or armory or whatever, right?" Fin looked at the two soldiers driving the cart. Through the dim light, he could see they weren't wearing uniforms anymore.

"Slavery isn't legal," Barnes turned and smiled. "So, I won't tell the king if you don't."

"I don't know what they told you to get you in here, but they had to beat me over the head to drag my limp body in here." The man said. "I thought they did the same to you. You've been out for days."

Fin's vision spun. "You're telling me this was all a trick?"

"I think I preferred it when he was sleeping," Jack reached behind him and took out a stick. "I'll give you ten seconds to sit down, accept your fate, and shut up before I pummel you with the smelly end of this stick."

"Sit down, lad," the man across from Fin lowered his voice. "We're not going to get out of here by losing our cool, you hear me?"

Fin sat and put his hands on his head. "This can't be happening. I'm a potato farmer, not a slave." He lowered his voice further and said with a quiver to his voice, "We have to get out of here."

"My name is Brando. What's yours?"

"Fin."

"Okay, Fin, here's what we're going to do," Brando's eyes flicked toward their two abductors.

"We're going to piss them off until they come in here, and then we're going to kill them."

"That's not going to work," Fin steepled his fingers. "He can just hit us with the stick."

"Do you have any ideas?" Brando's eyes were wide and frantic in the early sunlight.

"I think I've heard enough muttering from you two," Jack said from the front of the wagon before Fin could respond. He stabbed the stick through the bars multiple times until he managed to stab Fin in the rib cage and strike Brando in the head. "One more word from either of you, and I'll break your jaw."

Just then, a light started blinking in Fin's peripherals. He held up a hand in a way that said, "Wait, and we'll plan things out."

Brando gave a nod, and they both laid down on their respective sides of the cart. Fin checked his quest log and was surprised to find multiple entries. He read:

Sovereign Quest Complete: Get captured. +1 gold stat point, +1 quest revealed.

Sovereign Quest: Escape with your life and find a safe haven. +1 Wisdom, +1 gold stat point.

Path Quest Complete: gain an enemy. +1 ability point, +2 quests revealed.

Blood Quest: Death from Above: Kill an enemy with one swift strike from the air: +1 basic ability point, +1 wing ability point, forfeit all pain quests

Pain Quest: Paralyzing Fall: Drop an enemy from the air, paralyzing them to die a slow and painful death. +1 wing ability point, +1 body ability, Forfeit all blood quests

Upon looking at his quests, Fin surmised several things. First, his original quest, Flee the Nest, was no longer showing. This meant that after viewing a completed quest, it just went away. He would have to write down his completed quests to keep track of what he had accomplished. If all the quests were the same, he could compare notes with his father one day. He wasn't going to lose hope. He had something no one else had and hoped he could use it to escape.

Next, he noticed that some quests split off in two directions. He would have to decide which one he wanted to complete, if any. The blood quest seemed to refer to killing your enemies, while the pain quest meant making your enemies suffer. He searched his heart and found no qualms with killing the two slavers responsible for abducting him if that's what they were. The thought of killing the two slavers seemed comforting. He still hoped that this was just some sick prank. He didn't like the idea of making his enemies suffer. Though, he wasn't sure how he would dive in from the air to enact a single killing blow on anyone. Maybe that's what his father was referring to when he said that some quests were impossible. He was confident that if he found a ledge tall enough, and one of his captures was standing at the bottom, he could certainly try the lethal stunt of jumping on them with a knife. Or if they were all standing at the top of a ledge, he would try his hardest to push them off. But he knew better than to think he would be afforded any of those opportunities.

He searched for ideas and considered the possibility of him and Brando staging a fight. If the two soldiers were, in fact, slavers, then it would not be in their best interests for him and Brando to try killing each other. He played the scene in his head a few different ways. He would say something like, "Hey, you big fat oaf, stop touching my leg." Brando would say something like, "What are you going to do about it?" then they would have a fake but frantic brawl to the supposed death. Unfortunately, each time he played the scenario out in his head, they would just get pummeled with that stick until they stopped fighting.

Fin ran his hand over the wooden seating area he was lying on. The board was thick and riddled with nails. He quietly got up and tried to pry up the massive plank. It was no use; his fingers couldn't find any purchase. He searched the floorboards. They were equally unwavering. If he had a pry bar, he might have had a slight chance of unhinging the wooden beams. The cage bars were more significant than they needed to be to keep them in, and after attempting to twist and move each one, he gave up.

He searched his skills for anything that might help if he gained another ability point. He could have used a crushing grip to dislodge the boards if he hadn't allocated his only ability point into Pain Resist. He wasn't sure how strengthened talons would affect his human hands, but he would be willing to give that a try too.

He opened his quest log again to see if he had missed anything. Sure enough, his completed quests had disappeared after he looked at them. Now all he had was a quest to escape and two equally challenging quests for killing his enemies. All three quests were worthless to him. He would need to figure something else out, and he was still very hungry.

Chapter 5

The sun had risen to a late morning position when Fin noticed the landscape had changed. The massive green trees had been replaced by small brown shrubs, and the rolling hills were replaced by rough, grey valleys. The road looked more narrow and less trodden by half. He noticed a horse and rider approaching on the same lane ahead. He tapped Brando on the shoulder and saw he was already alert. The two stayed as they were, unmoving but poised to jump up like a loaded spring.

When the rider was close, he led his horse off the road and hailed the cart. He was bald with a scratch mark scar down his left temple. His chin thrusted forward in a greeting. He looked like he recognized the two men driving the wagon. "It looks like you two had a successful haul."

All hope of asking for help faded back into dread. Fin shared a look of concern with Brando as he got a better look at his fellow capture. He had long wavy hair that blended into a brown, braided beard. He wore animal pelts over his tunic that gave him a barbaric look. His hands were thick and stained darker than the rest of his body. Fin couldn't guess what could have dyed his hands the almost reddish color. His eyes were seething with a mixture of fear and rage.

"We aren't the lady's favorite for no reason," Jack said, resting his stick over his shoulders. "A little cleverness goes a long way."

The man rode past, glaring into the caged wagon with no subtlety. Fin caught a bloodthirsty look from his silent stare. The two held eye contact until they were too far apart to continue.

Slaves and slavers traveled the rest of the morning in silence until they came across two massive gates denying passage through a thick stone wall. Jack jumped off the wagon and struck the metal with his stick three times.

"What?" A voice from on top of the wall called.

"It's Jack and Barnes. We have business with Lady Marsha."

Silence engulfed them. Listening to the crackling wheels as they rolled through rough terrain for days on end made their momentary rest feel oppressively quiet.

Finally, the massive gates swung outward, letting the cart into the city beyond.

The cart lurched ahead, and Fin absorbed his surroundings. The word 'City' might have been a stretch. Wooden structures stood in rows between cave openings carved into the surrounding rock mounds. People moved on top of, into, and through the wooden frames, seemingly built at random. Some people stood and watched as other groups worked. Some groups carried water vessels, some stirred steaming vats of what could have been stew or laundry, and some worked together to lift and carry long wooden beams.

Fin noticed that more than a few of the people looked sick. Their skin had varying shades of green, and some were too thin or walked hunched over. Looking closer, the ones with green skin had pointed ears and noses. He realized that they weren't people at all; they were goblins.

Fin's father had told him once to stay clear if he ever saw goblins. "They're weak, but they fight something nasty. Nasty in theory and practice, mind you. A single scratch or bite from a goblin could give you the smirch." He didn't know what the smirch was, but he wasn't eager to find out.

The cart pulled up to a cave opening on the corner of two intersecting passageways and stopped. A young woman standing in front of the cave went inside and came out with her eyes lowered. Jack and Barnes jumped down onto the dirt road. They brushed the crumbs off their pants and walked around to inspect their two captives.

Jack poked the bigger man in the side. "Well, get up. Make yourself presentable." He then eyed Fin. Before Jack found another reason to stab them with the stick, a woman and two goblins walked out of the cave entrance.

"Hello, gentlemen," the lady said smoothly. She was an interesting-looking woman. She looked middle-aged, but her white hair made her look older than she was. She kept it up, shamelessly displaying a missing ear on her left side. "What have you brought me today?"

"Got a couple of big ones," Barnes gestured towards the two locked in the cart. "See for yourself."

The woman, Lady Marsha, sized the two men up. "I'll say you have a big one and a medium one, and that's me being generous. The big guy looks older, and it's harder to break the older ones in."

"Why don't you come in here, and we'll see who breaks first." Brando shot his arm out as far as it would go and grabbed at the empty air in front of the woman.

Lady Marsha raised an eyebrow at Barnes in a way that said, "See?"

Jack quickly brought his stick down hard on Brando's arm before addressing the woman, "We would be happy to accept your offer."

Lady Marsha nodded at one of the goblins who ran into the cave and came out with a leather pouch. He tossed it to Barnes, who snatched it from the air, reached inside, and pulled out two raw jewels.

"Always a pleasure doing business with you." He said, tucking the pouch away.

The goblin yelled out some incoherent words, and soon after, the cart was surrounded by goblins.

"Now, before we let you out, I feel like there's something important you should know," Lady Marsha addressed Fin and Brando. "If you make any problems, these good goblins here are going to do some very serious damage. You might be able to injure some of them, but eventually, you'll be overrun. There are only two of you, but there are always more goblins. Assuming they don't kill you, if you are too injured to work, you won't eat, and you will probably not survive.

"I understand you two have found yourself in a rather unfavorable position, and I can empathize with you. So, if you come quietly, without resistance, I will guarantee your safety and make sure that you are fed. I'm sure you are hungry from the journey, and who wants to fight off a bunch of scary goblins on an empty stomach? I'll give you a moment to decide between yourselves."

Fin counted the group of twelve goblins and realized that if there was a time to try to escape, now wouldn't be that time. He looked at Brando but couldn't read his expression. "Brando."

"Yeah?" he muttered.

"You want to go for it or not?" Fin asked quietly.

Brando searched each of their captor's faces for a long moment before coming to a decision. He did not want to fight on an empty stomach. "What are you serving?"

"Ah, an excellent question," Lady Marsha smiled. "I'll offer you two bowls each of Sophia's famous stew; she really is our best cook. Since it looks like you could do quite a bit of damage to my companions before they managed to break your ribs and bite your fingers off, I'll throw in a pint of my personal ale for your trouble. Keep in mind, you'll have to work for your next meal, so you should make it count."

Brando gave Fin a nod. "Okay, get us out of this thing."

Jack took a key ring off his belt and plunged it into the keyhole. He twisted the key until there was an audible click, then backed away behind the line of angry-looking goblins.

Fin pressed on the bars until the door swung outward in a controlled motion. The goblins lifted clubs, knives, and pointed sticks as Fin jumped out of the cage. Brando followed, bending his knees to test his legs. Something told Fin that Brando was still on the fence about fighting the goblins but restrained himself for the time being.

"Move," one of the goblins said, pushing the point of his stick into the small of Fin's back.

"Lady Marsha," Fin raised his voice. "Tell your men, or whatever they are, that if they poke me with their stick again, I am going to start getting angry."

"Vinny, that's no way to treat our guests," he heard Marsha address one of the goblins. "What have I told you about stabbing people that don't deserve it?"

"Sorry, Ma'am," the goblin replied with a gravely, high-pitched voice. "Stick gets restless." Some of the goblins nodded in agreement.

"My stick has a mind of its own, too," The woman said. "Do you want me to show you?"

Before Vinny could decide whether or not it was a trick question, after all, he did want to see her stick, the woman dismissed them. She shooed them away with more than several sweeping hand gestures before issuing one exasperated, verbal command, "I said carry on!"

The goblins led them through uneven, dusty streets until they reached a wooden structure. It wasn't more than four posts, a roof, and a table. An old woman was stirring a giant cauldron in the middle with a far-off look in her eyes. When she saw the goblins, she frowned. Her expression lightened up when she saw Fin and Brando.

"The lady said to give them two bowls each," Vinny said.

"Come in, sit down, you two," the lady dipped in a ladle and filled two wooden bowls with her steamy concoction. She set the bowls on the table. "I'm sorry, there doesn't seem to be any spoons here. I'm Sophia, and I've been making the best of this place for the last twenty years."

After introductions, Fin picked up his bowl and took a sip. It wasn't incredibly good, but he was hungry. "What is this place?"

"It's a mine," Sophia returned to stirring the stew. She didn't seem to want to talk about it, so the two finished their first and second bowls in silence.

"Let's go," a different goblin said, pointing with his knife.

"She said there would be ale," Brando said, wiping the inside of his bowl with his fingers and sticking them in his mouth.

"That's not my problem," the goblin tightened his grip on the knife. "It's time to go now."

"I don't think you understand," Brando set his empty bowl down and turned around on the bench.

"I'm not moving until there's a pint of ale in my hands. So, you can either stand there or go get my ale."

The goblins chittered between themselves before their language turned into yelling. Finally, the most diminutive goblin ran back in the direction they came. Time slowed to a crawl as the opposing forces glared at each other.

Fin took the time to view a notification blinking in his vision. He looked at it and read the newest quest entries.

Path Quest Complete: Gain over 10 enemies. +2 quests revealed.

Blood Quest: Hold the beating heart of an enemy. +1 basic ability point, +1 talon ability. Forfeit all pain quests.

Pain Quest: Deliver a hundred non-lethal cuts to a single enemy. +1 basic ability point, +1 talon ability. Forfeit all blood quests.

Fin cursed his luck out loud, causing everyone to jump.

"What happened?" Brando asked, not taking his eyes off Vinny.

"More worthless quests," Fin said, knowing the statement wouldn't mean much without context. "I'll tell you about it later. Maybe you'll be able to help."

Before Brando could respond, the small goblin came into view running with two sloshing mugs in his hands. By the time the mugs were set in front of the two, they were pitifully more than half full.

"She said a full pint," Brando sneered into his mug. "This is a very sad half-pint."

Fin poured his ale into Brando's mug topping it off and then finished the rest in two gulps. "I have some more enemies to make, and I need a clear head for it."

Brando frowned at his full mug. "It's the principle of it."

Fin inspected the bottoms of his bare feet. "I understand, but I have some things to consider, and I can't do it with all of these weird-looking green people watching us."

One of the goblins muttered something while leveling his spear. His arms were immediately grabbed from either side to prevent him from charging in for an attack.

Brando took a deep breath, lifted his mug, and didn't stop drinking until it was empty. "Okay, I'm ready," he set it down on the table and addressed the goblins. "Where are we going?"

"This way," Vinny said through gritted teeth, refusing to speak further.

As they were led away, Fin's eyes darted in every direction to gather as much information as he could. Teams of goblins in every direction stopped to sneer at the two newcomers as they passed. He had never fought a goblin before and had no idea how many he could fight off. He noticed Brando sizing them up too.

The group stopped at a metal gate. One of the goblins ran ahead and unlocked it.

"Go in," Vinny stabbed Fin in the back again.

Fin spun around, grabbed the stick from Vinny's hands, and pointed it back at him. "I warned you the first time-" his words were cut off when he heard the clicking sound from crossbows in every direction. He looked around to see more of the green creatures he hadn't noticed, holding crossbows, all trained at his head.

"I say we all take a breather," Brando gently took the stick from Fin's hands and slowly lowered it to the ground. "There's no reason to make any rash decisions in this heat."

Vinny slowly reached down and picked up his stick from the ground. "You both are very lucky one of you is smart. I've been waiting for a long time to sink my teeth into slave skin."

The two men walked through a gate that snapped shut behind them. The path led down into a grey and brown ravine that snaked between cliffs made taller by a surrounding wall. The stone walls were patrolled by more armed goblins.

"What now?" Brando addressed the group of goblins from the other side of the rusted iron bars.

"Now, you do whatever you want," Vinny said with a smirk. "If you get a mining pick from the bottom there, you can start digging for gems. If you want to eat, give the gems to the pit boss for food, or you can starve. The water is free. When the bell rings, return the equipment to the same place. Or don't. I'm sure you'll be fine either way."

The group of goblins started laughing and walking away.

The two said nothing as they made their way on the dirt trail. At the bottom, they found a large cave with wooden, retractable doors. Inside the cave sat an old-looking man behind a stack of crates. He solemnly greeted the two when they came into his line of sight. "A couple of new faces, I see."

"Are you the pit boss?" Brando eyed the man suspiciously.

"Oh, goodness no," the old man smiled. "He only shows up once a day or so. The big, ugly-looking sort. Hard to miss. I'm Leonard."

Fin greeted the man. "What do you do down here?"

"I'm in the same predicament you two are in," Leonard lifted his hands to indicate where they were. "Too old to mine anymore. They have me sitting in here, most days, handing out tools and ladling stew come mealtime."

"How long have you been down here?" Brando asked.

"You know, I'm not quite sure. Many years, I think." Leonard stood up and stretched his back. "Anyhow, it's pretty late in the morning. If you want to get any work done, I might as well get you situated."

The man rummaged around and brought back two rusty pickaxes. One of them had a handle. "Numbers ten and twenty-seven. These two aren't much, but they're the best I have right now. The pit boss will ring a bell before he comes down here. When you hear it, be quick to bring them back. This whole enclosure is one big circle. You're only allowed to mine on the inside, not the side with the walls. Keeps us from trying to tunnel out."

Fin accepted the tools curiously and handed Brando the one without a handle. "How do we get out of here?"

Leonard looked around cautiously before speaking. "I've seen a few successes in my day but even more attempts." He lifted his sleeve to display a pale brand in his skin. It was a simple 'x' of protruding skin on his forearm. "Tried so once myself. The goblins are pretty stupid, but they'll fight you to the death. You can do it, but you'll need to keep your strength up. For that, you're going to need some of these gems. It wouldn't hurt to gather a few extra to sell once you get out."

"What do they look like, and how do we find them?" Brando pressed his hand over the dull point of his handleless pickaxe.

"Have you ever seen a topaz? They're either light red, yellow, or clear." Leonard pulled out three dull crystals from his pocket. One was pink, and the other two were light yellow. "This is what you're looking for. I recommend finding a quiet place and start digging. This spot is riddled with gems. If you find a spot that has a lot of them, I recommend tunneling in and creating a shelter you can sleep in. It will protect you from the elements, and it marks your territory. Don't go too far in, or your tunnel might collapse. And avoid the fire ants. They're painful little buggers. I stepped on an ant hill once and got a bunch of welts down my right leg."

Fin thanked the man, and the two walked out to survey the valley. They soon discovered that goblins weren't the only ones guarding the walls. There were also humans walking around with spears and crossbows.

Fin felt more angry at the humans than he did the goblins. Everyone knew goblins were a savage race of grumpy green miscreants. The humans had no excuse.

Chapter 6

From Leonard, the road ran left and right. It took less than half an hour to circle the massive, fortified valley. They found other miners who eyed the two suspiciously as they passed. Around the halfway point, they finally met someone who didn't watch them cautiously.

A small man with a long beard stopped hitting a rock when he noticed them approaching. He greeted them with a thick accent that was hard to understand. "Aye, a couple of new ones. Great day for a dig, eh?"

"Sorry, I don't speak Dwarvish." Brando smiled and held out a hand in greeting.

"Dwarvish?!" The man guffawed. "Haven't spoken the tongue of my people for, let's see, it must have been about… A long time that. Ah, I'm getting old, aren't I?"

"Brando, he's speaking common," Fin said quietly before greeting the man. "Hello, I'm Fin, and this is Brando. Sorry, it's kind of difficult to understand you with your accent."

"The name's Heidle. Heidle the Hammer before I got locked in here..." The dwarf uncreased his frown and bowed deeply. "At your service. Can't do none about my speech."

"We noticed that a lot of the people here haven't been very enthusiastic about meeting us. Is there something we should know?" Fin asked.

Heidle waved a dismissive hand. "Don't pay them too much mind. The people on this side of the valley tend to want to keep to themselves. Sometimes new faces shake them up a bit. Which is their own damn fault if you ask me. The other side is a wee more crowded. Maybe a wee rude, but good people the lot."

Brando nudged him with his elbow. "What's he saying?"

Fin translated the conversation for him before Heidle looked at the sky. "Better get back to it. These rocks aren't going to hit themselves."

After they parted ways, Fin and Brando found a secluded spot to start digging.

"What's the plan?" Brando asked while chipping away at the valley's edge.

"You're going to find this hard to believe, but I think I need more enemies." Fin picked up a rock, looked at it, and then tossed it away.

"I think we have enough already." Brando rammed his useless tool into the hardened dirt. "Do you care to explain?"

Fin reluctantly began recounting the conversation he had with his father, the weird displays in his vision, and his system of quests. He also explained how certain things required either food or sleep to upgrade. When he was finished, Brando looked at him like he had expected - like he was crazy.

"I gave my father the same look when he explained it to me," Fin said, holding up two disarming hands. "I guess you have to see the quests for yourself before you understand. But I really think it's our best chance to get out of here."

"And what do these... 'quests' say?" Brando asked wryly. "Fly around in circles and blow fireballs out of your cheeky hole?"

"As soon as I complete a quest, it goes away, but right now, the ones that I have to say," Fin looked at his quests and began reading them.

"Okay, now read them again, word for word," Brando challenged.

Fin reread them all.

"Now read it backwards."

Fin read his quests backward.

"Okay, now read every other word."

After listening to Fin read his quests in every way possible, Brando relented. "Either you are very crazy or brilliant and crazy."

Fin shrugged. "Either way, I'm getting us out of here."

"How many slavers do you think live in the camp?" Brando traded pickaxes and started searching for gems again. "If you somehow met everyone, there could be more than a hundred enemies for you to draw your crazy power from. But you'll need to cut a goblin a hundred times without killing it."

Fin cracked the rock in half with his handless tool. "I don't think I'm going to take the pain route. I know it's the easiest to complete right now, but I don't like where it's going. I don't want to be the kind of person who tortures people or inflicts pain."

"And you want to be the kind of person who makes up crazy stuff about holding the beating heart of your enemies?" Brando pulled out another stone, inspected it, and then threw it away.

Fin laughed. "I want to see what happens when I get to a hundred. If it's more of the same stuff, I'll take the path of pain. Before I go around ripping people's hearts out, I need to unlock some more quests. Then I need to get enough food to upgrade my strength. Hopefully, I'll get a new ability that will help."

Brando asked for the list of abilities, and Fin read them aloud. After reading them several times, and then backward, Brando became thoughtful. "Okay, I'll play along. I don't know how the strengthened core will help, but the talon abilities might. Do you have any idea how the talons are going to affect your hands?"

"I'm not sure," Fin admitted. "But seeing how we have all this dirt to dig, it might be helpful to find gems."

"And you get the quests by doing dragon things, huh?" Brando blew the dirt off the wall and hit it. "Any idea what dragons do?"

"Besides flying around and blowing fireballs out of their cheeks, I have no clue."

"I'll start thinking of ideas," Brando said before dislodging more worthless rocks. "First, you need to give a good roar and see if that unlocks anything."

"I guess we should start somewhere," Fin said before bellowing out a loud roar.

"Now flap your wings and circle your prey!" Brando encouraged.

Fin began flapping his arms and jumping around in a circle.

Moments later, the dwarf ran up to them and yelled, "What in the Stones of Seger are you two doing?! I thought you were being attacked by a rock troll back there!"

Fin immediately dropped his arms and strengthened into a more dignified posture. "Sorry, I was trying to channel a dragon."

"Dragons?" Heidle asked seriously. "Out of all the lazy, good-for-nothing beasts… Look, if you want to find some gems, channel a dwarf, not an oversized lizard who sleeps all day. You nearly scared me to death back there with your yelling and hollering."

Brando nodded his head. He had only a small idea of what was being said.

"Sorry, I only had to try it once. I won't do it again." Fin said before the dwarf held his finger up for silence.

Fin and Brando stood motionless as the dwarf began listening for something. He lowered his ear to the ground. He then began slowly picking up rocks and holding them to his ear briefly before setting them back down and trying another one. The third rock was seemingly the one he was searching for. He gently held the rock up to his ear and nodded.

"This is it," he held the rock for a moment longer before gently offering it to Fin.

Fin lifted the rock, and as soon as he put his ear to it, Heidle made a crude noise and then started laughing. He clapped Fin on the shoulder and walked back to his spot.

"That was funny," Brando laughed. "Did you manage to unlock anything?"

Fin looked up and sighed. "Not yet."

The two chipped at the side of the cliff until the sun started setting. When they realized they wouldn't be able to recognize a gem if they were holding it in their hands, they started heading back.

"I guess some situations require a little bit of insanity to get out of," Brando said just as a bell rang out in the distance.

When they arrived at the gate, they returned their worthless pickaxes to Leonard and looked around and saw more people than they had expected.

The other miners were all covered in layers of various colored dirt and wore simple rags. They sat or mulled around in various groups, appraising the two newcomers with trepidation. Some of the larger miners gave them openly hostile looks.

"I'm not getting the feeling like these people plan on having us for tea any time soon." Fin noticed the dwarf was also standing alone.

The sound of metal keys, rusty locks, and stubborn hinges resonated through the valley. Fin watched as armed goblins followed a much larger, fatter goblin. They made their way through the gate, stood, and grouped up at the entrance until the gate was locked again.

The goblins moved in front of Leonard's cave while the fat goblin walked inside and inspected the tools. When satisfied that all the pickaxes were returned, he yelled out some commands to no one in particular then stood motionless.

Just when it looked like the goblins were going to grow impatient, a giant cauldron filled with what could only be the same stew from earlier lowered onto the valley floor with ropes and pulleys. The fat goblin began taking gems from people in exchange for loaves of bread and bowls of the watery substance.

"I'm hungry," Brando stood in line.

Fin rushed to stand next to him. "Didn't they say something about exchanging gems for food?"

"Only one way to find out," Brando's expression became determined. "Besides, the squeaking wheel gets the grease."

"I thought the squeaky wheel gets replaced. We had a wheelbarrow back home, and it didn't matter how much you greased it..."

Fin trailed off as Brando stepped in front of the fat goblin.

"Gems?" The fat goblin asked.

Brando began explaining how he didn't have any gems, but he would have some tomorrow, and he would do a much better job digging if he had food in his stomach.

The fat goblin yelled, "Gems!" which caused the other goblins to hold their weapons in a threatening way.

Brando held up his hands, "Okay, okay, gems. I get it, gems."

"Gems!" the fat goblin yelled again as Brando and Fin left the line.

"I didn't want any more of that flavorless stew anyway," Brando kicked a rock on the ground.

"We'll get some gems." Fin watched lanterns light up, one at a time, around the top parameter of the surrounding wall. It was getting dark. "Let's see how secure this place is at night."

They circled the enclosure in the dark. There was a goblin guard standing watch every ten paces or so. Some glared at the two as they passed; others were preoccupied with sharpening spears, picking their nose, or staring dumbly into the distance.

The pair whispered different escape ideas as they walked the loop. They passed shallow cave after shallow cave, where groups of miners set up their pitiful camps to tuck in for the night.

"Ever sleep outside before?" Brando leaned down and felt the terrain with his hands.

"I think I'll manage." Fin being without boots, he didn't need to search the ground with his hands; he could feel the rocks just fine.

"We should settle down before I get too hungry to sleep," Brando walked further down the deeply shaded road. "Should have done this while it was still light out."

"We hardly knew what they were planning on doing with us," Fin found an area that felt like it might be soft. Well, soft enough considering they were looking for a camping spot in the dark on rough terrain. "Over here."

Brando walked over, knelt, and brushed away a few sharp rocks and spare pebbles. "I guess this will have to do. Tomorrow we should find a spot when we can see."

As soon as they were lying down as comfortable as they could manage, Fin began thinking about Hildred, of all the people. He couldn't decide whether he would prefer marrying her or if he would rather spend his whole life digging for rocks only to end up like Leonard. His only regret is that his father might think he was dead or worse, that he decided not to go home.

Fin smiled. He was going to get out of here, and if he managed a hand full of gems first, he would be even better off. He wanted to review his status to get a clear idea of where to invest his points when they appeared. His status just popped into view when he decided to look at it. He considered what this feature said about dragons. He then shifted his thoughts toward what he would need to upgrade to get out of this place. He read his status:

Level: 1 Class: None

Path: None

Strength: -18	Intelligence: 2
Dexterity: -11	Wisdom: 2
Constitution: -7	Charisma: 3
Basic stat points: 3	
Gold stat points: 1	
Ability points: 1	

Passive Abilities: Pain Resist

Chapter 7

Fin woke up to the sound of abrupt movements, slapping, and whipping sounds. He opened his eyes to see Brando dancing around in his underclothes, whipping his pants through the air like a madman.

"Something bit me!" Brando dropped his pants and began wiping off every part of his body with his hands. "Check my back."

Fin got up and shook the blood into his tingling legs while trying to find anything crawling on Brando's back. "I don't see anything…" Then he noticed a new notification and exclaimed, "I got something!"

"Where is it?!" Brando thrashed around, trying to get whatever it was off him.

"You're fine; put your pants back on; I just got a new notification." Fin popped his status window into view and read out loud.

Path Quest Complete: Gain over 50 enemies +1 ability point +2 path quest reveal

Blood Quest: Devour your enemies: +1 level, +3 gold stat points, +1 eye ability. Forfeit all Pain Quests

Pain Quest: Swallow your enemies whole: +1 level, +4 basic ability points, +1 breath ability, Forfeit all Blood Quests

"I have over fifty enemies and a new ability point!" Fin yelped, drawing the attention of the parameter guards as he read the new entries on his quest log. "These quests are useless, though, there's no way I'm eating a goblin."

Brando looked concerned. "Hey, if I ever offended you, you would tell me before killing me in my sleep and roasting me over a campfire, right?"

Fin laughed. "You'll believe me after I get this ability. What should I get, Strengthened Talons or Crushing Grip? Those are the only useful ones I can think of unless Fear Howl can scare the goblins into releasing us."

"I don't know how effective you will be at scaring anyone into dropping their keys, and if all the talons will do is make your fingernails harder to bite off, then I would go for the grip." Brando offered his hand. "After you do, squeeze my hand as hard as you can. That way, when it doesn't work, you know that I know that you are completely insane."

Fin went to take Brando's hand, and a thought occurred to him. He voiced it out loud, "This is a bad idea; if I'm not lying, I'll probably break your hand. That's not worth proving that I'm not crazy. I'll think of something else."

A notification popped up, and Fin instinctually looked at it.

+1 Wisdom realized.

He went to his status page and saw that his wisdom was now three, but he wasn't feeling tired. It was curious. Fin interpreted this to indicate there would be no side effects when upgrading naturally.

"If you want to try crushing a rock or something, be my guest..." Brando's attention went to Fin's feet. They were covered in little red welts with even darker red ants crawling all over him. "You're covered in fire ants, you crazy bastard!"

Seeing the ants, Fin began frantically brushing himself off. Before not too long, he was the one jumping around in his undershorts. He noticed the bite marks didn't hurt but were the reason why his legs felt tingly. It was the pain resistance. There was a reason for pain; it prevented you from getting seriously hurt or killed.

Before Fin was fully dressed, a bell rang in the distance, and the two made their way toward the entrance.

Brando picked up a rock and handed it to Fin. "Something to practice on."

"I haven't upgraded it yet," Fin took the rock and inspected it. "I'll do it now." He pulled up his window and selected his single ability point.

The window showed the familiar dragon, and he mentally selected the talons. As soon as the display was visible, the words "Crushing Grip" glowed and then disappeared from the list.

He selected his status page and saw that his passive attributes said, "Pain Resist." Still, he had a new category called "Active Abilities," where Crushing Grip was located. He squeezed the rock to see if his hand strength had improved, but nothing happened.

They arrived at the gate to find two lines. One line ended at Leonard, issuing a pickaxe, the other at a barrel of water, and the lady from yesterday handing out little, white squares. The two decided to get some water first. They were both parched.

When they got to the end of the line, Brando dunked the large wooden ladle and drank from it.

Sophia offered him a white square while Fin drank from the barrel.

"What's this?" Brando inspected it in his hand.

"Breakfast," Sophia replied, handing Fin one as well.

"So, they're not trying to starve us to death?" Brando pondered out loud.

"You are the heart and soul of this operation," Sophia waved the two out of the way to keep the line going. "But that doesn't stop them from making you wish they would kill you."

Next in line was a lady nearly as old as Sophia. She gave a quivering thanks for the meal and slowly made her way to Leonard.

Fin stood behind her. When Leonard gave her the pickaxe, the weight of it made her arm sag. *How much longer will this woman last in here?*

She slowly walked off, not complaining but determined.

Fin got a sick feeling in his stomach. If he wasn't so hungry, he would have lost his appetite. After taking a bite of the sodden square, he did lose his appetite. It tasted slightly fermented and had a flavor that resembled rain boots.

Noting the look on Fin's face, Leonard interjected while handing him a broken-handled pickaxe. "You'll get used to it. Just give it some time."

"It tastes like a wet dog!" Brando stared at the bite he took, not seeing the proffered pickaxe in front of him.

"You know what, here," Leonard dropped the pickaxe in the box and replaced it with another one. "This one is slightly sharper. It's not much, but I hope it cheers you up."

Brando took the tool gently and recomposed himself. "Thank you, sir."

The sound of boots and feet on gravel filled the silence as the pair walked aimlessly toward their next mining spot.

"I don't know how I could swallow anyone whole," Fin broke the silence. "Assuming I wanted to swallow someone whole, dragons must have been huge to pull something like that off."

"Enough!" Brando bellowed. "I get it, you want to make me feel better by giving me some crazy notion of hope, but I don't want to talk about this dragon twaddle right now. I have to come up with a real plan to get out of here. I can't live off these wet dog, soggy squares, so I have to figure out how to get out of here while I still have the strength to."

The silence fell as abruptly as it had been broken. Fin wanted to figure out how to use his new ability so he could prove he wasn't crazy. He picked up a rock and willed his hand to have a crushing grip around it.

An odd feeling shot through his arm. It felt like pure power was vibrating rapidly through his body. It was almost like the wave that moved down a rope when you whipped it up and down. A loud snap echoed through the ravine.

Brando turned to see the final crumbs of rock fall to the ground. "What was that?"

"I just crushed this rock." Fin looked at his undamaged hand.

Brando picked up another rock and gave it to Fin. "Do it again."

Fin took the rock and repeated the same thing. The energy felt weaker than before, but it filled his body with intense power. He crushed the rock in his hand, producing another loud noise.

Brando stood disbelieving. "How did you do that?"

Fin smiled. "Crazy dragon twaddle."

"Can you do it again?" Brando asked, finding another rock to crush.

"The power was weaker the second time through," Fin admitted. "If I can, I don't want to waste it on crushing rocks."

Brando ignored him and handed him another one. It was slightly bigger. "Do this one."

Fin set down his pickaxe and wet dog bread and then took the rock in both hands. He willed his hands to crush the rock. The waves moved even slower than before, but his grip tightened. Cracks slowly split throughout the rock in tight webs. He knew that he had to concentrate to keep the power from dying out. The grip on his fingers slowly pulsed. He could feel when the waves of power were at a peak and when they were weakest. Timing the wave, he somehow caught it at its crest. Quickly, he loosened his muscles and sent the power to the rock. The rock split into two pieces.

Fin felt dizzy and sat on the ground. It wasn't that he overexerted his muscles, but he felt he had overexerted something.

Brando stared at him with wide eyes and an open mouth. "You can do dragon magic!"

Fin tried telling him that he had been trying to explain that this whole time, but instead, he had to, what? Catch his breath? No, he wasn't out of breath. What was he catching? A notification popped up, so he looked at his quest log.

+2 Intelligence realized.

+2 Wisdom realized.

+1 Charisma realized.

"I have a confession to make," Brando confessed sheepishly. "I didn't really believe you when you started saying all these crazy dragon things. I only pretended to because you were making so much effort to make your story sound true."

"I don't remember a single time when you pretended to believe me," Fin laid on his back and closed his eyes. "Also, you're still calling them crazy dragon things."

"Well, it is crazy!" Brando protested. "I mean, if someone came up to you and said, 'I have troll powers,' you would think they're crazy too. Anyway, are you okay?"

"I must have pushed myself too hard. I got some bonuses from the effort, though, so I think it was worth it. I might feel better after I choke down this fermented square." He reached over and picked up his now dust-covered square. He then tried to eat it as fast as he could. The squishy texture made it go down easier, though he wasn't sure how it could have been harder.

"I guess I'll start digging," Brando hefted his tool and began chipping at the closest bank.

Groups of miners passed them without a glance. It was as if someone lying in the middle of the road wasn't all that uncommon. Finally, Heidle walked past and remarked on Fin's ant bites. "I see you found the fire ants. Nasty little buggers, those."

Brando, understanding the words "ants" and "little buggers," absentmindedly responded, "It's his own fault that he's always trying to make new enemies."

Heidle grinned. "The best thing to do is to not scratch it when it starts itching."

Fin sat up. "What did you say?"

"Some say you can piss on it, but a dwarf would never!" Heidle spat on the ground. "Best just to leave it alone until it heals."

Fin wasn't listening. He bolted up, "I made new enemies! Don't you get it? To dragons, we're as small as ants!"

"Dwarves are even smaller than you," Heidle suggested. "That's probably why those lizard pests keep breaking into our mines and sleeping on our treasures."

"I can eat the ants!" Fin said before jogging off down the road.

Heidle watched him go. "It's a little warm outside, but I didn't think it was that hot. There's a reason dwarfs prefer living underground."

Brando, sensing a question was asked, shrugged. "He'll be okay. He's probably going to go eat some fire ants."

Heidle teetered on a thought. He didn't want to show these strangers one of his good spots, but if they were eating fire ants, they could use a few gems. Back home, he would never share his secret ore veins, not to his closest friends. But this was different; here, you weren't mining for greed; you were mining for survival. It pained him to lose something he had worked so hard to find, but he had other spots. Finally, he made up his mind.

"Do you see all the dirt here?" he pointed with his pickaxe. "It's got the wrong hue."

Brando looked quizzically at the dwarf.

"Come on, I'll show you a better spot." The dwarf waved the man to follow. "Eating fire ants when there's a whole mound of gems right there. A great way to get sick and die out here if you ask me."

Brando followed, unsure what the dwarf mumbled to himself when they reached a partially mined area. The dwarf gave him some verbal instructions, or at least he thought they were instructions. He asked the dwarf to speak slower.

The dwarf just pointed to a spot on the cliff and said, "Dig. Here."

Chapter 8

Fin found the spot that he slept in. He stared at the ground until he saw a red ant. After watching it for a while, other ants appeared, wandering aimlessly across the dirt. He watched them until he found their nest. Before he did anything, he checked his quest log.

Blood Quest: Devour your enemies: +1 level, +3 gold stat points, +1 eye ability. Forfeit all Pain Quests

Pain Quest: Swallow your enemies whole: +1 level, +4 basic ability points, +1 Talon ability, Forfeit all Blood Quests

He decided to take the blood quest path. The extra, basic ability point wouldn't help him here, not with the severe lack of food. The Talon ability seemed interesting, but he could only choose one path. The eye ability for the blood quest might prove to be incredibly useful. He wondered if it would make him see in the dark. If he could escape at night and still be able to find his way around, it would be worth it. He wasn't sure what he would do if the rewards were better for the pain quests, but he was glad not to feel like he was missing out on something.

He made the decision to choose the blood quest path. Now all he needed to do was make sure he didn't swallow any fire ants whole. He picked up one ant, popped its head off with his thumbnail, and tossed it into his mouth. He chewed the crunchy, acidic ant and then swallowed the best he could. He felt the grainy particles of the ant in his teeth, but nothing happened.

He grabbed another ant and chewed it without pulling the head off first. Again, there are no status notifications, gold stat points, or abilities. He went to the ant hill next to the rock and began agitating them.

He reached down, and they swarmed on his fingers, leaving tingling sensations on his hand. He licked them off of his fingers, trying not to clean the dirt off too much, and chewed the ants together. The flavor was enough to make him gag, but he pressed forward. He looked at his feet and noticed more ants were climbing on him. He took those, too, one at a time, and put them into his mouth.

Finding that he was collecting ants on his legs faster than he could eat them, he moved away. He repeated the process multiple times, moving closer, then farther away, popping them one by one into his mouth.

Finally, a status popped up, and he raised his hands triumphantly. Spitting the residual parts out of his mouth, he viewed the message:

Path Quest Complete: Gain over a hundred enemies +1 ability point, +2 Quests Revealed.

Blood quest: Defeat all your enemies. +2 levels, +8 gold stat points. Blood Halo. Forfeit all Pain Quests.

Pain Quest: Make all your enemies suffer. +2 levels, +8 gold stat points. Pain Halo. Forfeit all Blood quests.

He immediately stopped spitting out the ants. That wasn't unexpected. Not only was he not done eating bitter, sour ants, but he also received another impossible quest. How was he supposed to defeat all his enemies? *Not impossible,* he thought. *I just completed the most brutal-looking quest I had. I just need to come up with creative ways to outsmart the quest system. That's all.*

He still had questions. How was he going to kill every red ant that bit him? What about the ant's little friends who hadn't bitten him? Did they count as enemies he would need to defeat? And that was not counting all the slavers in the camp. Or was it just the goblin who poked him with a stick that he needed to kill? All he knew for sure was he was done making enemies.

Looking again, he noticed he was given a new ability point. He put the thought aside and began picking the rest of the ants off his skin. He was starting to feel like they didn't count as enemies until after they bit him. He thanked Frome, the farmer's deity, for his resistance to pain. All he needed now was to figure out how many more of these ants he needed to eat before it qualified as "devouring his enemies."

Another thought occurred, *do ants have hearts?* If he could figure out how to remove the beating heart of an ant, he could kill more birds with one stone or more ants with his... He left the thought alone and picked up another ant off his leg. He tried to crush it to find its heart but failed. It only took crushing four ants into paste until he gave up and started eating them again.

He was beginning to feel sick when another notification came up:

Blood Quest Complete: Devour your enemies: +1 level, +3 gold stat points, +1 eye ability. Forfeit all Pain Quests.

Ability: Discern Magic - locked until level 5.

"Okay, that's interesting," he said out loud. He was having a very productive day. He completed a quest, gained a new ability, learned how to use it, got some unique attributes, and then earned another quest, and the day was just beginning.

He checked his status to see what he had. There were three basic stat points, 4 golden stat points, and one ability point waiting to be used. There was no way he was going to upgrade anything that required food or sleep for now. He decided to come up with a plan before he accidentally allocated anything. He didn't know where to start on the plan, so he started walking back around the loop, keeping his eyes on the upper parameter guards as he walked.

His stomach was feeling sour. He wasn't sure if it was the fire ants or whatever he ate for breakfast, but he couldn't afford to toss up his sustenance. He tried keeping his mind on keeping his food down. His insides turned, but he kept walking. It was a slower pace, but he kept moving.

The farther he walked, the more he realized he should have seen Brando by now. *Oh well,* He thought, *it's not like he could have gone far.* His bare foot stepped on a shattered rock. It could have been the rock he crushed, but there were rocks everywhere, and they all looked the same. He clutched his stomach and continued on.

Chapter 9

Brando couldn't believe his luck. He wasn't finding any gems until the dwarf returned, picked up his unearthed pebbles, and congratulated him for his findings. He had mined three gems without knowing it. He tried offering the smallest gem to the dwarf, but he refused and went back to what he was doing.

He was chipping away for more gems when Fin came into view, said, "I did it!" then tossed his breakfast all over the road. The color was a rare mixture of white, red, and black.

Fin wiped his mouth and then viewed his new notifications.

Affinity Quest Complete (1 of 6): Purge caustic toxins from your body. +1 Breath Ability added.

Caustic Breath - Locked until Earth Affinity is realized. Forfeit all other affinities.

Fin smiled at his new accomplishment. "It's a good thing I got that out of my system. It looks like it could have burned a hole right through me."

Brando looked appalled. "Here he comes, trudging around the corner of the slave camp, proceeds to toss his pudding, and then smiles like he just won the award for the most colorful vomit? The first time I saw you, you were sleeping like a baby. Not in a hundred years did I think you could have been the cheery apparition of the dark underlord."

"I don't even know where to start," Fin tried to spit the bad flavor out of his mouth. "I completed some quests and have clues of what I need to do next. Most importantly, I have a new ability point."

"I was going to tell you about all the gems I found, but considering we're going to spend them on soup tonight, it doesn't seem half as important as new, rock-crushing abilities." Brando held out his hands to show the three gems. "Does this mean you're going to upgrade your fingernails?"

Fin took the gems and inspected them in the light. They didn't look like anything special. "Probably fingernails. There's nothing else to spend them on, especially since I don't have a tail. I don't think I'm going to do it until tomorrow. I'm still pretty spent from squeezing rocks. And even though I spent the morning devouring my enemies, I'm starving."

"Do you want the rest of my sog-square?" Brando pointed to his half-eaten breakfast sitting on a rock.

"I think I would rather starve." Fin handed the gems back.

Brando grew serious. "I think we might starve," he said, lowering the tone in his voice. "Do you know what I was doing when they took me? I was living in the woods. I had as much to eat as I wanted but had to continuously work for it. This bowl of stew that awaits us at the end of the day wouldn't give me the energy for an hour of hunting, and yet they expect us to chip away at this stone all day long on it? I'm telling you, it's impossible with a single bowl of stew each day. Because

I can't take more than a couple of bites of that white sog. I'm worried. More than I've ever been."

Fin looked his friend in the eye. After all, they were friends, right? They had only been thrown together a couple of days ago. But, in the few days they've known each other, they've already been through more than most people. Fin didn't really have much to base that on, but he felt that Brando was his friend and knew that his friend needed him to come through.

"What were you doing in the woods?" Fin asked sincerely.

"What does anyone do in the woods?" Brando considered possible negative outcomes of people's actions in the woods and then said, "I'm a leather worker in a large village." A few months ago, I decided to go hunting. I wasn't ready to go back to civilization, so I just stayed there. I kept going deeper and deeper into the woods. It was nice, you know?"

"I guess it sounds like it would be fun for a while. I don't know." Fin contemplated. "I think I would get lonely and want to see my family."

"The only family I really have is the village vicar," Brando creased his forehead at a memory he was having. "We both lost our families, and neither of us is very religious. Anyway, I'm ready to get out of here. You got a plan?"

Fin began drawing from his heightened wisdom and intelligence, "There are fewer guards on the wall during the day, and they won't expect us to make a break for it in broad daylight. I say we find a spot to use my magic grip to climb up, but we don't do anything until new slaves are dropped off. Then we climb the wall at whatever spot we decide, kill the assholes who abducted us, take their wagon, and ride off before anyone catches on. We might die, but I still have a stat point to allocate, so that counts in our favor. How many days was I sleeping?"

"Three," Brando answered simply.

"Three days," Fin considered. "Three days in and three days out. Give or take a couple of days. After today, we will have been here for two days. That means we have to be ready to go in less than a week. That means one week to find a way up and find a way out."

"We might need a rope," Brando offered. "Just in case."

"Let's walk around and see if there's anyone who has a rope." Fin started down the road and then had a small epiphany. "What did you mean, neither of you are religious? I thought vicars were supposed to, you know, be religious?"

"Most of them are low-born nobles who are placed in a parish out of necessity. Only having to run a service once a week, they'll usually spend their time doing more academic or recreational things."

The two talked and planned as they raced the sinking sun to clear a spot to sleep. After triple checking, there were absolutely no ant hills around. They walked to the entrance and inspected the gate that locked them out of the rest of the world.

"Do you think you can bend these bars?" Brando raised his hand to see if it could span two bars. They were too far apart.

Fin searched for a part of the gate that would have a favorable outcome if crushed. "I might be able to squeeze the lock, but it will only keep it from opening. Even with a key."

"With all the guards bunched up outside the gate," Brando considered. "It could cause some useful chaos. Hard to tell if it would be in our favor or not."

"With all the guards bunched up outside the gate, and some well-placed fire ants, there could be a great amount of chaos in our favor." Fin smiled mischievously.

"We'll need a bag or something to put them in," Brando put his hands through the bars and acted like he was dropping a sack on the other side. "A rope and a bag."

That night they lay under the stars and planned their great escape. The fact that they were two gems lighter was overshadowed by an almost satisfied feeling of having eaten. Finally, the stars winked out, and sleep swept them away from the mine, if only temporarily.

The next day, they walked around the loop, periodically stopping to ask a fellow miner how their day was going. The plan was to eventually ask about a rope or a bag, but most conversations didn't get that far. It wasn't until they found Heidle that they were met with a friendly face.

"How goes the dig?" Brando made a point of examining one of his scattered rocks.

"The dig is great," Heidle punctuated his sentence with the chop of a pickaxe. "How were the ants?"

Fin realized that Heidle was talking to him. "You heard about the ants, huh? Not good. I must have eaten a hundred of them. Luckily, I lost my lunch before they could do too much damage. Apparently, those things produce caustic toxins. I don't think the sog-bread helped much either."

"Sog bread!" Heidle bellowed out and laughed. "I heard it called many things, but not sog bread. Oh, that's a good one. I hope you don't mind if I use it?"

"Brando, I think you're the one who came up with it," After seeing Brando's blank face, he said, "Yeah, that's fine. Hey, where can we get a rope or a bag?"

"A rope and a bag, you say?" Heidle stroked his beard. "The only reason why someone would be looking for a rope is to…" he made a thumb gesture over his throat paired with a clicking sound.

"What? No," Fin tried waving away the miscommunication. "We were thinking more of..." he pointed his thumb over his shoulder with the same clicking sound. "You know, escape?"

"Ahhhh," Heidle stroked his beard. "The old gems in a bag technique, huh? I had the same idea once. It's not the worst I've had."

"We were thinking about putting fire ants in it," Fin admitted. "What were you thinking?"

"Oh, you put a bunch of rocks in a bag and have a conversation about all the gems you found. You just make sure one of the guards overhears you talk about it. Put it in your secret hiding spot and act like you're walking away." He winked when he said the word 'secret.' "Then, when the green bastard comes down to claim it, you club him in the head."

"How do they get down here?" Fin asked, looking at the surrounding valley made taller with the walls.

"You were looking for a rope," Heidle guided their eyes with his finger. "All the ropes are up there."

Brando glanced up at the roving parameter guards. "There's ropes up there?"

"That there are. I'll help, but you have to make an oath," Heidle grew serious. "If you get out, It would be a great service to me if you tell my people where I am and that there are enough gems here to sober the third king of Sonderfeltd."

Fin looked back down, "the what?"

"Tell them that Heidle the Hammer is here, and there's a great deal of gems. A great deal."

"I might be able to do that," Fin said honestly, "but don't you want to get out of here and tell them yourself?"

"I think about it every day," The dwarf threw a dejected rock at the side of the wall. "It's these little legs of mine. I wouldn't be able to run fast enough to escape. I'm too old to be swinging around a pickaxe in a fight. I need a walking stick, not a weapon."

"Assuming our plan works," Fin stared down at the dirt. "I don't know if I can get enough gems to support the journey, even if I survive."

Heidle waved a dismissive hand, "Bah! You have more of a chance than me trying to tunnel out of here without support beams. I can give you enough gems for a modest journey. What do you say?"

"You want to visit some dwarves when we get out of here?" Fin consulted Brando. "You know, get out of the forest for a while?"

"Better than hanging around here." Brando smiled. "I'm in."

Chapter 10

The dwarf went to great lengths to draw as detailed a map as possible on the dirt. He used pebbles for known villages, rocks for cities, and a slightly larger rock for the dwarven fortress. He then put an indent in the ground with his little finger for their current location.

"Go north," he walked his fingers to the first rock. "Rudford. Eat, drink, sleep, sell your gems, but don't stay." He made another walking motion with his fingers, "Northeast," when he reached a slightly smaller rock, he said, "Lokardale. Eat, drink, sleep, stay. Buy clothes, oil your beard, drink to my health." Again, his fingers were walking "Northeast" when they reached a pebble. "Small village. Eat, sleep, drink, stay. Don't leave until you eat the apple pie." His fingers set out towards the largest rock, "North." When his fingers arrived at their destination, he said, "Heidle the Hammer, lots of gems, build the map, walk with the fingers; it is the dwarven way."

"Got it," Fin went to stand, but he was stopped by Heidle's stony glare. The dwarf wanted him to repeat the finger-walking journey. After all, it was the dwarven way.

Fin placed his two fingers on the small indent. "We start here and go North." He walked his fingers up the map until he reached the first rock. He said, "Rudford, eat, sleep, drink-"

Heidle cut him off, "If you drink in the morning, you're going to be worthless for the rest of the day."

Instead of trying to explain that he had no intention of drinking in the morning, he started over, making sure to say the words "eat, drink, and sleep" in the correct order. He almost had to start over again when he forgot to try the apple pie before leaving the small pebble.

Satisfied with the finger journey, Heidle pointed to the biggest rock. "Remember, the biggest rock is for the dwarves, always."

Thinking they were about to leave, Heidle looked at Brando expectantly.

Brando wasn't as good at the memory map game. It took a while for his fingers to successfully traverse the journey.

Next, they were prompted to take the journey in reverse. Fin was scolded when his fingers reached the pebble; they were on official business, and there was no time for mandatory apple pie. The words, 'If there is time, maybe, try the apple pie,' gave Heidle a better feeling about the evolution.

Fin and Brando had only found a gem each when the bell rang. They still had the one left over from the day before, which meant that, ultimately, they had yet to make progress. The two gems would buy dinner. The dwarf had promised to fund their trip, but it would be nice to amass some kind of fortune before escaping. They shouldered their pickaxes and made their way to the front entrance.

When the fat goblin came into view, he pointed in their direction and yelled at them to hurry up. Responding to the raised voice, the other goblins attempted to make their features and postures more aggressive.

Once the pickaxes were returned, the goblins interrogated them about their tools. They both shrugged in confusion. They both explained that they returned their tools and didn't have any more of them hidden in their sleeves. Finally, the fat goblin attempted to snap his fingers. His motion didn't make more than a dry, wisping noise, but the order was understood. Three goblins went left, and three went right to search the loop for their missing pickaxe.

If the goblins were tense before, the other slaves in the camp became palpably more tense. Whispers drifted through the breezy silence like a rain cloud over a wedding. Balled-up fists and reassuring hands held the solemn mood that fell over everyone. Fin and Brando sank into the crowd, hoping for anonymity.

Grunts and soft cries slowly broke the sound of buzzing insects as six goblins dragged an old woman into sight. Fin recognized the old woman he had seen the day before, and she looked awful. Battered and bruised, she stumbled closer, pushed forward by the tips of three spears.

"Prepare the brand!" One of the goblins called ahead, waving the missing pickaxe.

"Fin, do you remember Leonard's cross-shaped scar?" Brando whispered. "I think they are going to try to do that to this old lady."

"I'm thinking the same thing," Fin responded without moving his eyes. "What do we do?"

Brando tore his eye off the limping woman to scan the crowd. "We can't rush them. You have to use your dragon magic."

Fin quickly pulled up his window and selected his stat point. He then read through all of his options: Wing attack, Wing shield, Jowls of Strength, Fear Howl, Strengthened Talons, and Piercing Resist.

"The only thing I can think that will help is Fear Howl," Fin stated, cautiously watching the old woman's life unravel before his eyes. "And I don't even know if it will work. I was going to invest this point in Strengthened Talons or Piercing Resist to help us get out of here."

Brando watched as the goblins threw the old lady on the ground into a heap. "Fin, we are getting out of here regardless of what you invest your points in."

Fin was frozen in place, staring at his options until a metal brand landed on the dirt next to the fat goblin. One side was wrapped in old leather tied down with fraying rope; the other had crossed metal, glowing with heat. A single spark jarred free from the impact solidifying the selection of Fear Howl. A tingling feeling crept up Fin's throat, and his voice rasped as he told Brando to plug his ears. He had no idea what effect this ability would have, but it was all he had.

The fat goblin smiled as he picked up the brand. He would teach these humans that when a goblin rings a bell, they should be honored to come running like dogs. It was their own fault that they acted so weak all the time. When a goblin was at his weakest, that's when he acted the most powerful and the most feral. When you show weakness, you only invite others to punish you. These humans made it all too easy for him.

Only allowing himself a brief smile of pleasure, he said, "Bring her."

The other goblins dragged the woman forward, propped her up, and held her arm out to receive the brand. It was easier than they expected. This one was as weak as she looked.

Just then, the fat goblin had an idea, wouldn't it be more fun to brand this woman's face instead? Before he had the chance to revel in his options, a loud and terrifying sound resonated through him. His memory flashed back to when he had stolen his mother's goat leg off the table. Just after he had taken a bite, the old hag walked into the room and leveled her ferocious glare at him. Mind blank with white-hot fear, he dropped the brand like he had dropped the goat leg all those years ago and stood frozen. Some of the other goblins dropped to their knees and whimpered for mercy.

Even though Brando had plugged his ears, he couldn't completely block out the sound. The loud yell sounded animalistic. It reminded him of all the predatory animals he had ever heard in the woods when it was too dark to see. He stopped breathing, hoping that whatever beast lurked in the shadows wouldn't sense him. He looked around and saw that everyone else looked like how he was feeling. Seeing the effect on the other miners, especially the goblins, restored his courage. He knew that whatever he had gone through, everyone else was experiencing it worse. He knew what to do.

He quickly approached the fat goblin and called, "Lower the soup!" No one moved, so he tried again.

Finally, one of the goblins on his knees lifted his head and shouted, "Just do it! Soup!"

With the sound of creaking, the giant cauldron swung out directly overhead of the four goblins holding the old woman.

Working quickly and soundlessly, Brando took the old woman and moved her off to the side. After another thought, he gently pushed the four goblins out of the way. There would be a time for crushing goblins under a giant cauldron, but now was not that time. They were operating on borrowed luck as it was.

The cauldron landed, followed by the crate of bowls. Brando walked through the unmoving crowd towards Leonard and guided him to the cauldron. He took a bowl and ladled stew into it. He handed the ladle to Leonard and gave the bowl to the woman. As soon as he thought her hands had a firm enough grip, he picked her up and moved her out of sight. When he returned, he noticed Leonard handing Fin two steaming bowls. He received two more steaming bowls and shouted, "Line up!" before following Fin out of the crowd.

Chapter 11

Fin and Brando sat in rapid silence while they ate their first bowl of stew. They had no desire to speak until they had consolidated their thoughts or finished their free meal or whichever came last. Brando was the first to set down his second bowl, breaking the stillness by standing up.

Surprised to feel full after finishing his meal, Fin spoke first. "Good job getting that woman out of there. I kind of froze up back there."

"Are you kidding me? Good job scaring the ever-loving senses out of everyone around! I had my ears plugged, and I was still too scared to breathe. I can't imagine how it affected the others." Brando spoke rapidly, abandoning his lookout position to face Fin. "That's how we're getting out of here! But you'll need to give me a secret signal before you do that again. You can't just say, 'Cover your ears!' because everyone else will too. You have to say something like..."

"Incoming?" Fin interjected.

"Yeah, say 'incoming.' Just give me a second to get situated first," Before Brando could continue, a group of miners came around the corner.

Fin gestured at the people approaching. "Incom... I mean, people are coming."

Brando turned to see two men and two women cautiously moving toward them. "Hello."

"Greetings," The man at the front waved his hand. "We don't know what you did back there, but we have come to thank you for your brave and heroic actions."

"He really s-" Brando was shocked into silence when the man took his forearm and bowed his head.

The next man, taller and thinner than the first, touched his forehead and bowed, hand over heart, toward Brando.

If Brando was astonished at the unexpected handshake, he was more so when the women both hugged him at the same time, complimenting and thanking him. "Guys, I'm sorry to disappoint you, but I'm not the one to thank," He pulled himself away from the group of embraces.

Before his friend could sell him out for his abilities, Fin spoke up, "He's right. As a Vicar's apprentice, Brother Brando means for you to thank Frome. He is too humble to take the credit for himself."

"It is fitting that you serve the one who causes the tree to grow out of season," The thin man bowed again. "I am a servant of the life that lives in that tree."

By the look on Brando's face, Fin could tell he had never heard of Frome or Deshon. It didn't surprise him; Brando had mentioned how he wasn't religious. Fin, on the other hand, was a seventh-generation farmer. It would be very difficult to be a farmer and not be a follower of the literal lord of farming, or Deshon, the lord of the harvest.

Fin spoke up for Brando, "You'll have to forgive him; his work in the orchards is unfinished. He wasn't expecting the unity of Deshon in the middle of his season. This comes as a shock to us all."

"Could this mean that Ruqa has fled the barren desert?" The thin man asked.

This one was lost on Fin. He had no idea who Ruqa was or what barren desert she would be fleeing. He was also growing tired of the theatrics. "We are humble farmers. What Ruqa does is beyond us. Anyway, I'm Fin, and this is Brother Brando."

"You are right, of course, and it is a pleasure meeting you Fin, and Brother Brando. I shall make introductions," The thin man gestured to himself and then to the rest of his group in turn. "I am Ethon. This is Garret, Cassidy, and Brenna."

"I am sorry we have been…" Garret searched for the word, "unwelcoming before. Sometimes people decide it is easier to rob gems from others rather than mine them out of the ground like everyone else. We also didn't know you were servants of Frome."

"It's okay," Fin replied. "It's good to finally have some allies down here."

"It's hard recognizing who you can trust. But I'm glad to have met you two." Cassidy gathered the four bowls on the ground.

Ethon held out his hands and received the bowls from her. "I will return these. You two have much to pray about."

Cassidy pointed in the direction Ethon had disappeared, "he's a little much at times, but he's a good person to have on your team. If there's anything we can do, just let us know."

"Do you know how we can get a rope or a bag?" Fin asked.

Brenna's eyes widened, "If you're breaking out of here, I want out too."

"The lord of all the plants has given us a secret orchard to water," Brando blurted out, trying to keep their covert plans covert. "When the garden needs rain, we will return on the clouds."

Trying not to slap his own or Brando's face at the wildly inappropriate use of religious jargon, Fin interjected, "What Brother Brando is trying to say is that we don't want to put your lives in danger over our reckless plans for a potential escape. But we feel obligated to return with an army to free you if we leave here alive."

Brenna's shoulders slumped slightly as the hope she had cultivated drained from her eyes.

Garret nodded and looked up at the holy man, "I don't know about a rope, but I can try to get you a bag. Frome is obviously with you, so I will help as much as I can. It's getting late. I'll look into it and discuss more with you tomorrow."

As everyone went in different directions, Brando finally said, "Brother Brando? Really?"

"I'm not trying to announce my abilities to the whole world," Fin protested. "How was I supposed to know that in all your years as the vicar's best friend, you didn't attend a single service?"

"I mostly only went over there for the meals," Brando smiled as he thought of the tables overflowing with food. "The village always gave him way too much to eat, so I mostly went to help him eat it all. It was me and the other kids without parents. All the vicar wanted to talk about was his antidotes to poisonous plants. I may have never heard of Desmos, but I know that if you get an ivy rash, you should rub the yellow loom flower over the affected area. If you get stung by a nettle, you should apply fir scepter. I also know that fir scepter isn't its actual name, but it roughly translates into that from old common."

"It's Deshon," Fin said flatly. "But thanks for covering for me. I don't know about the part where you return on the rain clouds to water your secret orchard, though."

Brando laid down on his spot of dirt. "Frome will reveal all to you in time, my son."

Fin laughed. "Are you sure you haven't been to a service? You're starting to sound like the real thing."

Brando's eyes fell shut, "Maybe one or two." With that, he fell asleep.

The following morning, Fin woke up to Brando shaking him. "Wake up. It looks like your secret rain clouds came early."

Fin opened his eyes in time to feel a raindrop on his face, "You mean 'your' secret rain clouds?"

"Whoever's rain clouds they are, they're coming for us," Brando helped Fin to his feet. "We should get somewhere dry until the sun comes out."

The morning was still dark and cold. They warmed up their joints as they searched for shelter. By the time they found an indent deep enough in the side of the ravine to keep the rain off, it began pouring. The two scrambled just outside the reach of the tumult and waited for the rain storm to dry up.

"I'm not going to be able to go back to sleep like this. Why don't you read me your dragon list?" Brando suggested. "It might help pass the time."

Fin pulled up his status sheet and read out loud.

Chapter 12

By the time it stopped raining, Fin still had a noticeable amount of mud covering his body. He put on his pants and walked barefoot, shirt in hand, with Brando to the front of the loop.

When they arrived, they stood at the back of the line for water and a sog-square.

Noticing them approaching, the woman at the back of the line touched her forehead and heart before stepping aside and bowing.

"It's okay, we'll stand back here," Brando said, waving at the woman to stop making a spectacle. He wasn't in a hurry for whatever was in the front of the line.

The rest of the line looked behind them with a similar response and moved to let the two pass.

"This is all your fault," Brando muttered to Fin before moving to the front of the line, telling each person to stop as he passed through. Fin, acting as if he didn't hear Brando, gave Frome's blessing to each of their fellow miners as he trailed after him.

Arriving at the front, Sophia offered them each two squares of the sour bread with a smile. "It is an honor serving a true follower of Frome."

After seeing her reject Brando's attempt to return one of the two squares, Fin took it and held a hand up. "We are honored by your gift, but the less attention we get, the better."

"As Frome wills," Sophia responded, then set Fin's two squares back.

"Uh, thanks," Brando muttered before moving towards Leonard's cave.

Leonard smiled brightly at them and handed them each a fully functional pickax. "These are the best we have, brothers."

"Frome be upon you," Brando said before speed-walking in the direction they came from.

"It's Frome be with you-" Fin corrected when he finally caught up.

"I don't care if it's Frome's flaming crack," Brando cut in. "With all this special treatment, it'll be the back of Frome's hand when the goblins catch wind of us and send us to bloody Frome himself. Then I'll have to explain what I was doing impersonating a priest farmer. It makes me uneasy."

"It sounds like you need a girlfriend." Fin pulled out his rock, kissed it, and tucked it away. "Can't have mine, though."

Brando's face creased with anger. He wanted to take that rock and throw it as far as possible. He wanted to take his pickax, throw it against the wall, and break it like the other mining tools. He realized that was probably why all the pickaxes were broken in the first place. People like Fin and his girlfriend rock. Then the absurdity of the situation dawned on him, and he started laughing.

Fin eyed him wearily. "Are you okay? Look, Frome isn't just for farmers. Some people would say that if you're lucky, you must have impressed Frome somehow. So, you aren't technically impersonating anyone. All things considered, you're better off than you could be."

Brando's hysteria subsided. "I've been in here a total of two minutes, and I'm already losing it. Just a few more days to go, right?"

"Just a few more days to go," Fin agreed.

The rest of the day was spent in silence and the constant clink of metal on stone. Brando chiseled away at the spot the dwarf had shown him, and Fin cleared away loose dirt from an area several paces away.

Their progress was interrupted a few times as the group they had met the day prior dropped off a crude cloth sack. Another time when the old lady they had rescued came to thank them. She offered a gem, but both declined the offering. They told her to use it to stay alive while they planned to escape and get help. When the woman finally left, they both continued their individual efforts.

Fin's efforts weren't completely worthless. As he reached into his tiny cave to remove a rock, he pulled out two small gems. His exclamation brought Brando over.

"What is it?" Brando asked excitedly.

"I just found these two little guys," Fin held up two clear gems as big as the tips of his index fingers.

"That's not bad, not as good as what I found," Brando smiled dumbly as he waited for Fin to ask what he meant.

"Let me see them," Fin relented, excitement growing on his face.

"There's only one," Brando corrected and then pulled out a Topaz, nearly as large as Fin's rock, and turned it so the light would catch.

Fin was about to exclaim at the size of it when he noticed movement coming from the wall behind Brando. "They're watching us," Fin whispered, taking the massive gemstone and trading it with the rock in his pocket.

"That's not a gem," Fin said loudly, showing Brando the rock he had spoken such sweet things to earlier. "You really had me going there." Fin casually discarded the rock.

"I'm going to get back to work then," Brando said softly, taking back his prized gemstone. "We'll talk later."

As Brando walked away, Fin completely ignored the goblin staring directly at him. He didn't want it to notice that he noticed the attention. When the goblin's attention finally drifted away, he walked over and picked up the rock he had discarded. Nearly convinced that the smooth, flat rock had nothing to do with unlocking his Earth quests, he tucked it away just in case.

Hours later, Fin's cave was complete. He crawled inside to test the comfort level. It was just wide enough for him to sprawl out and long enough that his feet could touch one wall without his head touching the other. Despite it being out of the sunlight, the earth seemed unusually warm. Still cooler than the summer heat, he closed his eyes and drifted off into a pleasant nap.

"The bell rang. We have to go!" Brando called into the opening of Fin's cave.

Fin opened his eyes to see a notification blinking in his peripherals. After crawling out of his cave, he brought his notifications into view as he started walking.

Instead of looking at a normal window, a spherical one surrounded his vision. Simply wanting to see what was beyond his scope, the circular window began rotating from right to left, displaying the windows he was familiar with and ones he had yet to see. There was his status page, abilities page, a blank page with two boxes he hadn't seen before, and his quest page. Stunned at how many quest notifications he had, he stopped and read through them.

Affinity Quest Complete: Earth (3 of 5): Earthen hovel. +1 Active Ability.

Active Ability: Stone Vizard - Locked until Earth Affinity is realized.

Hoard Quest Complete: Path of many treasures. +1 Active Ability. Forfeit all Bone Quests.

Active Ability: Lesser Stow.

Treasure Quest Complete: Sleep with your treasures. +1 Passive Ability.

Passive Ability: Treasured Sleep.

Shroud Quest Complete: Gain all parts to a complete halo set. +1 Passive Ability.

Passive Ability: Shroud Control.

Realizing he was walking alone, Brando turned to find Fin a reasonable distance away, just standing and staring off into space. "Fin! We have to go. I don't want to have another incident like last time. If you have to pull another stunt, I'm going to tell them who the real chosen one is."

Not wanting to close his notifications before memorizing his completed quests, the circular halo lifted out of sight and hung in the air above his head. Noticing it was safe, he ran to catch up.

"I just got a bunch of cool stuff by sleeping in the cave!" Fin announced as he drew closer to Brando. He pointed up. "Hey, can you see this?"

"Yeah, it's getting dark," Brando said blandly.

"No, this thing floating around my head," Fin drew the halo in front of his eyes and backed up, pointing directly at it.

"Did you find mushrooms growing in your cave?" Brando had an incredible idea. "We might be able to use them to escape! You didn't eat them all, did you? How many more do you have?"

Fin assured him that there were no mushrooms and decided that if Brando couldn't see the circle around his head, no one would be able to see it either. Making a mental note to gauge everyone's reactions when he reached the rest of the crowd, he read his new quests to Brando.

Chapter 13

"Just two more Earth quests, huh?" Brando pondered out loud, crunching rocks and dirt under his boots in rapid succession. "Lesser Sleep and Treasure Stow is interesting. Any idea what it does?"

"No idea, but you said it backward," Fin admitted, noticing the group of miners and goblins come into view around the corner. He discontinued the conversation while he carefully observed the surrounding reactions. Walking through the crowd, he noticed that most of the attention was on Brando, no matter how much he manipulated his halo.

The two returned their tools without incident and withdrew to an inconspicuous spot in the back of the crowd. Fin retrieved the two gems that he found and held them up. "Obviously, we're not going to trade the, uh, you know, for a bowl of soup. We'll just use these tonight."

Brando waved off Fin's offer and held up a small gem, "Hang on to it, for now, I have a backup."

Instead of tucking the gem away, Fin wanted to try something. He held the gem in his hand and whispered, "Lesser stow." He felt a brief cord of power through his arm, and the gem vanished. Excited, he pulled his rock out of his pocket and then caused it to disappear as well.

Curious about how to retrieve his items, he lowered his circular window and rotated it until he saw something interesting. The labeled representations of his two stowed items were displayed on the blank page he had not seen before. One was labeled "Unrefined Quartz," and the other, "Favorite Rock." Ignoring how his dragon magic marked his rock, he focused on the "Unrefined Quartz" description. Were all the gems in the mine quartz?

Wanting to inspect the unrefined quartz, the box emptied, and the clear crystal materialized in his hand. Quickly holding up his other hand, the other gem he held moved to his box with the now recognizable thread of power. It was also labeled "Unrefined Quartz."

"Brando, let me see your gem," Fin said, holding out his hand. With a shrug, the large man placed his soup gem into an outstretched hand. Stowing the gem and booting his favorite rock from his inventory, causing the rock to appear once again in his hand.

Brando flinched. Feelings of anger at losing his meal ticket and the surprise from watching it turn into a rock made Brando sputter until he realized what was happening. "The treasure stow!" Immediately regretting his outburst, he lowered his head and attempted to appear nonchalant in the growing looks of attention. "Can you make it change back?"

Ignoring Brando, Fin quickly looked to see how Brando's gem was labeled. Relieved at the words, "Unrefined Topaz," Fin explained his new ability quietly. "I didn't change it into a rock; I just stowed it away. I think I can only have two items at a time, though. When I tried to add a third, it unstowed whatever item was next in line. That's why it looked like your gem turned into a rock. Let me try something." Fin held up two hands, an empty hand and one holding the rock. With a little concentration, the rock disappeared, placing a quartz crystal in the other.

Before Brando could say anything, Fin handed him the quartz. "Use this instead. The ones I found were quartz, but I doubt the goblins will know the difference. If we're going to throw them away for food, we might as well toss the worthless ones first."

"How do you know it's quartz?" Brando polished the clear crystal with his thumb and looked closely at it.

After Fin explained how his two storage spaces cataloged his items, Brando insisted that he identified his large gem. If it was quartz, he was going to be disappointed. Handing it to Fin, he held his breath for the verdict.

Fin withdrew his rock and held the large gem. When it disappeared, he read out loud, "Unrefined Topaz."

Brando let out his breath, clutched the quartz in his hands, and came to a decision, "I think it will be safer if you hold on to it for now. Let's get some dinner."

When they arrived at the front of the line, the fat goblin accepted the crystals without hesitation, causing them both to immediately relax. Some of the other miners gave them greetings which were returned with a smile and a curt nod.

When the two men had eaten and discussed their plans, they retired for the night. Fin opted to sleep in his hovel.

Wanting to experiment with his Treasured Sleep ability, Fin brought out the two gems from his inventory and put them in the pocket with his rock. He assumed that since it was categorized as his favorite rock, it had to be a part of his treasure quest in a way. He wasn't sure what would have happened if he had accidentally fallen asleep next to bones, but whatever a Bone Quest was, it sounded disgusting. If he ever met a dragon with bones in his cave, he would have to ask about it.

The next morning came with the routine of his predicament. Brando woke up, cursed the rock that found itself under him while he was sleeping and walked over to see if Fin was awake. To his surprise, he found a pleasant look on Fin's face. This made him jealous enough to want to shake the boy out of his delightful little slumber. He hadn't slept as well as Fin appeared to be doing for a long time.

Opting to work the soreness out of his body, he moved his joints around and tried to work the soreness out of his muscles. He looked down and realized he was losing weight. He still had plenty of stored energy left, assuming their plan worked and was executed soon. He sat down and stared up at the surrounding cliffs and walls, going over their plan over and over.

When Fin woke up, he felt like he hadn't slept better in a long time. He found the two gems, and his rock snuggled next to him. He noticed that his status halo wasn't still up, but he felt like he could recite his quest log from memory now, so it didn't bother him. Throughout the day he brought it back up to experiment with.

Adding the gems to his inventory and the rock to his pocket, he crawled out of his cave. To his surprise, his body didn't feel as sore as it had the day before. He moved around to test out his body; he felt okay.

While watching Fin do lunges, Brando asked him how he slept. He seemed overly happy about the answer. "You haven't slept that well in years?! That's incredible! I'm so happy for you!"

"I think it has something to do with this Treasured Sleep ability," Fin added, unsure why Brando was so happy about how he rested.

"That makes so much sense!" Brando nodded like he was just given an obvious solution to a complex problem. "I'm going to want to hear more about how sore you don't feel later on, just don't let me forget to ask." His voice lowered, "I had an idea while you were resting, and I want to run it past you."

Before Fin could reply, Brando continued. "You know how we wanted to lock the goblins out? I was thinking, what if we locked them in? The more goblins trapped here, the less will be able to track us down when we get out. I don't know about you, but I don't know how far I can run after eating the bare minimum and sleeping on rocks every night. I say we spring our trap, and if it works, we'll sabotage the lock and trap them here."

"I was thinking about it too," Fin remembered. "When we do Heidle's rocks-in-a-bag plan, we're going to need a third person: two people to talk loudly, and when they walk away, we'll need a third person to club the goblin."

"Fair point," Brando agreed. "Let's catch up with the dwarf today and see what he thinks."

Chapter 14

Fin and Brando drank water, picked up their tools, and ate what they could stomach. They traversed the loop in search of Heidle. When they found him, he was already holding his first gem of the day.

"Congratulations on your find," Brando greeted. "Do you have a minute?"

"Have a seat," Heidle smiled, sitting down himself. "What's on your mind?"

Fin explained the changes to their plan and that they needed to be ready as soon as the new shipment of slaves arrived. That would ensure that they had a ride when they got out. He also explained how he planned on tricking the guards.

First, he selected a rock off the ground and secretly stowed it away. He then took out a cloth sack. "I'll say something like, oh, look at all of our gems. Then I'll place a gem in," Fin took the massive gem out of his pocket and put it in the bag, bringing out an empty hand. "Then we say, hey, let's hide this somewhere where no one can find it, and then we walk away." He handed the sack to the dwarf.

Heidle opened the sack, pulled the rock out, and tipped the bag over, dumping dirt and pebbles onto the ground. "Where did it go?"

"Oh, this?" Fin procured the gem and held it up for the dwarf to see.

"Magnificent trick! May I?" Heidle slowly brought his hands to hold the gem. "Where did you find this?"

"I found it in the place you showed me," Brando said, getting used to hearing the thick accent. "It's all thanks to you."

"This is a beautiful stone. When you leave, don't sell it. Take it to the dwarven fortress and show them." Heidle turned the gem in his hand one last time and then gave it to Brando. "They'll offer you more than you can get for it anywhere else." He opened the bag again. "That little trick of yours is really good. How do you do it?"

"It's all in the wrist. Anyway, I have a question that maybe you can help me with," Fin changed the subject. "What do you know about Earth Affinity?"

Heidle stroked his beard, still regarding the gem in Brando's hand. "Deep in the mountains are these round indents in the dirt and rock. Some say they're caused by sprites with an Earth affinity. I've never seen one, but we have a song about how they look like golden orbs. In the song, the dwarves who find them think they are some kind of gem. When they try to mine them, the things melt their tools, and as the song goes, 'the dirt eaters chased them away.'"

"Did you say dirt eaters?" Brando slapped his forehead. "Why didn't I think of that before? Fin, you have to eat some dirt! Oh, and you should put this away." He tossed the gem to Fin.

"Put it away, nice and easy," the dwarf commanded, slowly glancing up. Fin took the gem and stowed it, acting like he was putting it in the sack. As soon as his hand lifted out of the bag, he noticed two ropes tumbling down the wall in either direction.

"I think your plan worked a little too well," Brando said in a low voice as two goblins rappelled down the cliff.

The goblins were sparsely armored with leather breastplates and matching bracers. One of them had a metal helmet that was slightly too big that rested on his eyebrows. They both carried knives; the one with the helmet carried a short sword which he drew as soon as he landed. They ambled closer and stopped three meters from the slaves on either side.

"Why don't you give us the bag?" The goblin wearing the helmet suggested.

Fin held out the sack containing the rock. "You mean this bag?" He moved it left and right, watching their eyes track its movement.

"Which of you do you want him to give it to?" Brando jumped in with an idea to pit one against the other. He pointed a finger at each of them in turn. "You, or you?"

"I'll take it," Helmet announced quickly. When the other one didn't contest the claim, Brando frowned.

Fin considered his options. If he handed over the sack and they noticed there wasn't a gem inside, they would ask for it. When he didn't hand it over, it would be a fight to the death. There would be trouble even if they fought to the end and won.

"Guys, I think we're going to have to move our plans forward. I'm going to give them the bag." Fin looked at each of them in turn and gave them a slight, imperceptible nod. "I just can't decide who to give it to. I can't give it to one, because the other would get upset."

"Me, me, me!" Helmet shouted, lunging toward the bag.

Fin lobbed it high over the goblin's head. As Helmet turned to track it, Fin grabbed his pickaxe, dashed forward, and swung with everything he had.

Helmet sensed the movement too late. He barely raised his sword before the pickaxe crashed into him, knocking the blade from his grip. He swung again, and this time the pickaxe sank into his ribs. It felt like the goblin's body was made of wet paper.

The pickaxe stuck in the goblin's body, and Fin blinked. He was having trouble removing it. Before he was able to yank it free, the goblin pushed him, causing both of them to lose balance. They staggered like intoxicated dancers. Fin touched the ground near the fallen sword, which was close enough for him to reach out and take.

The second goblin saw where the bag landed and sprinted toward it. When he picked it up and found only a rock inside, he snarled. Spotting Fin grabbing his sword, he veered toward him with a scream.

Heidle reacted first, diving directly into the goblin's path. He curled up into a ball just as the goblin ran into him and tripped. It tumbled over and landed in the dirt. Heidle raised his pickaxe, ready to finish the raging creature, but Brando was already moving.

With a "There you go," Brando slammed a fist straight into the goblin's side. The blow crunched through armor and bone. The goblin gasped, twitched, and then lay still.

Heidle backed off, circling around Brando to help elsewhere if needed.

Fin, sword in hand, looked frantically between the goblins. Brando had the second one handled, so he faced the first one. Helmet was still standing.

The goblin reached up and yanked the pickaxe from his side. Blood poured freely, but he seemed unbothered. His eyes locked onto Fin with a cold, unflinching stare.

Fin didn't move.

Helmet wasn't charging. He wasn't doing anything at all. Just… glaring.

Footsteps approached. Heidle stopped beside Fin, watching. The goblin looked poised for attack.

Heidle bent, grabbed a rock, and hurled it. It struck Helmet hard on the helmet.

The goblin didn't dodge. Didn't even blink.

After the rock bounced off, Fin feigned an attack, trying to get a reaction, but there was none. He feigned forward again, nothing.

"This is ridiculous," Brando said, charging the creature. Before he got there, it fell dead before it hit the ground.

Fin stood over the body, chest heaving. "Is everyone okay? I'm okay."

"I've been waiting to throw a rock at one of those for a long time," Heidle said, breathless with excitement. "Nothing gets the blood moving like a good clean fight, eh?"

Brando gave a single nod. "I guess we kind of have to move our plans forward."

Fin's attention snapped back to the moment. "Yeah. We should move quickly." He turned to Heidle. "You sure you don't want to come with us?"

Heidle reached into his beard. With some twisting and maneuvering, he pulled out and gave Fin a small leather bag, bulging at the seams. "That should get you to where you're going. I'll wait here for your return."

Fin took the bag in his cupped fingers. "I'll try my best not to let you down. I swear it."

"Take as much time as you need. It'll give me a head start on my greedy, cave-dwelling brothers." Heidle smiled sincerely and then began stripping the armor off of the goblins.

"You'll need a disguise," Heidle said, wiping the blood off the helmet. "Every second you're not spotted will help."

"Heidle, we are going to try to climb directly over the wall and go South," Fin pointed at the wall. "As soon as we're safe, we'll cut around. Can you run ahead and make sure everyone's attention is down here?"

"I can lead everyone into singing 'Down in the Grey'" Heidle suggested.

"I don't think anyone will know that one," Brando countered. "Tell them to sing The Spice Merchant's Daughter. Trust me on this one."

Minutes ticked away as Fin and Brando quickly donned armor that was too small for them. Fin was concerned he wouldn't be able to get the helmet back off, while Brando was worried he couldn't keep his armor on. Brando's Chest plate barely went past his chest, and his arm guard straps were tied together with cloth from his shirt. If the disguises lasted at all, they wouldn't last for long.

The sword belt didn't fit Fin's waist, so he strapped it around his leg. Fortunately, it was short enough to just reach his ankle.

The goblin bodies were tied to the end of the rope so they could pull them out of the pit and not leave evidence to incriminate the dwarf.

Sparing a final farewell to the dwarf, they climbed the rope to the top of the wall.

Chapter 15

Arriving at the top of the wall, Brando quickly scanned the perimeter. They were roughly on the opposite end of the front entrance. Fortunately, none of the other sentries were paying attention. On the other side of a wall posed a new problem to their plan. The wall dropped into another ravine that offered no cover and no potential for escape. They would have to circle the perimeter and hope for a place to climb down or retreat.

Brando was pleased to see a loaded crossbow next to a quiver of ten bolts. He was even more pleased to find a loaf of bread, a wedge of cheese, and a jar of beer resting on a dingy cloth mat. Ignoring the loot, he reached down and helped Fin up the rest of the way. Both standing on the wall, they began hoisting the goblin bodies up. They hadn't decided what to do with them but didn't want the bodies to be spotted.

Declining to dump the bodies over the side, they settled on heaping them together. It occurred to them that maybe they should have kept the armor on the bodies; the goblins look like they were taking a shirtless nap together.

Quickly moving from one task to another, Fin pointed toward the direction he thought made the most sense. "If we go this way, there are fewer guards we'll have to get through."

Brando quickly loaded the food scraps into his sack and tied it to his belt. He strapped the coiled rope over his shoulders and the quiver of bolts around his head. Picking up the crossbow, he noticed one of the goblins looking at them from further along the wall. "We've caught some attention."

"Follow my lead," Fin waved for the guard to approach and then pointed at the two dead goblins. He then started laughing just loud enough for the approaching goblin to hear. He waved for the goblin to approach faster.

Brando, too let out a fake laugh and then repeated Fin's movements.

When he recognized who it was, the goblin broke into a jog, trying to see what the humans were laughing at. A feeling of terror gripped the goblin's chest just before a crossbow bolt quelled the feeling.

Brando reloaded his crossbow while Fin ran in the opposite direction. A song bloomed from the valley below as they sprinted along the uneven wall.

The next goblin they approached began loading his crossbow when he saw the two men, causing Fin to sprint faster. Just as the goblin placed an arrow on the track, Fin shouldered into him, causing the goblin to fall down into the mine.

Staggering back, Fin caught his balance in time to reach down for the quiver of bolts. He didn't have time to count the bolts before the sound of a wide projectile ripped past them. Not stopping to look around, he slung the bolts around his shoulder and continued forward.

They had been noticed. Whatever alarm system the slave camp was equipped with hadn't chimed yet; Brando knew it was only a matter of time before it did.

They ran forward, looking for targets and a spot to climb down. Outside the parameter, the ravine that blocked off escape from the South wall had ended. Still, the Southwestern route was an obstacle course of scattered gorges. There would be no straight path to freedom if they climbed down immediately.

"We need to run faster," Brando urged, loading another bolt into his crossbow.

Another bolt whistled by as Fin drew his sword. The goblins ahead had all clumped together. Three out of the five had a loaded bolt trained on them. "Cover your ears!" He called back before stopping dead in his tracks.

Brando stopped and set down his crossbow so quickly that he nearly dislodged the bolt. Instead of correcting Fin on the secret signal, he crammed his fingers into his ears and started humming. "Go!"

Unsure of the range of his ability and not wanting to take a chance on his mental selection of it, Fin called out "Fear Howl" and felt the vibrating energy pulse to his throat. When the ability was concluded, the goblins hadn't flinched or moved at all. He turned to see Brando plugging his ears and humming.

"I'm not sure if it worked," Fin said, turning back towards the goblins.

"One way to find out," Brando stood and then bellowed, "Drop your weapons!"

The goblins in front of them dropped their weapons so fast that a bolt discharged and shot one of the goblins in the leg. The sound echoed around them as other weapons and pickaxes were also dropped.

"Go!" Brando shouted as he retrieved his weapon from the ground.

Fin ran forward, sword in hand, at the goblins before him. The goblins stared dumbly at him as he pushed three off the wall and stabbed two others. Not waiting for Brando to catch up, he hopped over the scattered loot and continued forward.

As the wall curved to the North, Brando saw a good place to climb down and run for it. The path led West to a grouping of hills in the distance. They would take a chance by running out in the open for so long before reaching the hills, but it was their best chance.

"Fin, we should climb down now while we still have a chance," Brando removed the rope around his shoulders and dropped the unraveled end down the side of the wall.

Without hesitating, Fin jogged back and took in the surroundings as Brando tied the rope to the parapet. The remote slave town was visible from his vantage point, and he could see goblins running and forming groups.

Brando's armor fell off piece by piece as he climbed down the rope. When he reached the ground, he heard bells in the distance. "Hurry!"

Fin touched the ground, and they both started running. The distant bells gave them a jolt of energy, pushing them past their limits.

Just when their sprint eased into a jog, crossbow bolts broke on the ground around them.

Sparing a quick glance towards the encampment, Fin was relieved to see that no one was chasing them as the projectiles came from the wall.

The lifeless terrain proved difficult to run on. Rocks jutted up from the uneven ground, and deep ravines redirected them off course more than a few times. Finally, the hills grew in front of them until they were mere minutes away.

"I don't think they're pursuing us," Brando said in short bursts between breaths. "I think we can take a rest."

Fin looked to see how much the massive walls had shrunk since they escaped. The terrain had caused them to take a more indirect path towards the hills than they intended, but seeing how no one was coming after them made him overjoyed to be free.

The thought of being free made Fin realize that he still hadn't completed his quest, he read through it.

Sovereign Quest: Escape with your life and find a safe haven. +1 level, +1 Wisdom, +1 gold stat point, +1 basic stat point.

It made him feel better that the quest wasn't complete due to the stipulation that he needed to find a safe haven, but he still didn't feel like he was completely out of the woods. "We need to rest quickly and then go again. I don't want to take any chances."

Brando nodded and then fished out his jar. He drank half and then offered the other half to Fin.

Fin finished the contents of the jar. It didn't quench his thirst, but it helped. Before he could throw it, Brando stopped him and put it in his bag. "We shouldn't leave anything behind that will lead the goblins to us."

Sitting down to look at his feet, he was surprised to find them bleeding. The pain resistance had made it so he couldn't feel the pain of his punctured feet. "Look at this," he showed Brando.

Brando looked horrified at the sight. "Are you okay? You're probably leaving a trail of blood directly to us. We have to get those covered quickly!"

Fin looked around and found that the only thing he had was his shirt. "I can use this, but I don't think it will do it for both feet."

"This is what we get for laughing at those first goblins," Brando removed his leather jerkin and cut out two squares with his knife. Making several quick holes, he laced strips of Fin's shirt through. He put the sandal over one of Fin's Feet and tied the strips together until it was secure. "This isn't the first time I've needed to make footwear in a pinch. I would have-" He stopped and listened. Turning around, he couldn't see them, but he could hear the mob of goblins following their bloody trail. "On second thought, I have an idea. Do you think you can run with one exposed foot a little longer while we veer south? I should have your next sandal finished soon, and then we can cover our trail as we head West behind the hills."

"Like I said, I didn't even notice in the first place," Fin stood and began jogging, this time only leaving a single line of footprints behind. "I don't know if this is a bad time to tell you, but I also left the helmet and the other goblin armor on the trail as we ran."

Chapter 16

Brando quickly tied on Fin's other sandal. When he was finished, he walked further down the false trail and set the jar on the ground. It was past time to move behind the hills. Without hesitation, he turned and began jogging.

Fin felt like it was harder to run with the improvised sandals, but he was happy to not be tearing up his feet any more than he already had. He wondered if he could have bled out if he never noticed them. The pain tolerance was good, but it could also prove to be a dangerous talent. He would have to ensure he didn't accidentally cut himself and bleed out before noticing.

Reaching the base of the hill, they had to rest before moving on. Hungry, tired, and out of breath, they instinctively knew they would have to push themselves well beyond their limits to survive.

"Still better than eating sog-squares," Brando said, clutching his chest through the torn jerkin as if to keep his heart inside.

Fin nodded while he sucked in gasps of air. He was getting thirsty but put the feeling away and concentrated on catching his breath.

"I'm going to climb up and look around." Brando made a circular motion with two fingers and began climbing the slope.

When Fin got his heartbeat under control, he followed after. Each step sunk gently into the earth, knocking pebbles and dirt free. Giant, toothy boulders poked out from all around. Following Brando's footprints made Fin wonder how easily they would be tracked if goblins came this way. When he reached the top, he found Brando lying beside a boulder, unmoving.

"How does it look?" Fin asked, crouching next to him.

"See for yourself." Brando's voice was low and serious, "I think the goblins are reaching the end of our false trail now."

Fin got down to his stomach and crawled on his elbows until he could see where Brando was indicating. A group of goblins stood in the distance like a stain on an old canvas. There must have been forty or more of them. It looked like they were stationary, but he couldn't determine what they were doing. The residual sounds of loud voices rose to an audible level in scarce intervals.

"I think it's important for them to find us. If we escape, we will be able to inform the king of their operation and have the whole thing shut down," Brando pondered out loud as he watched. "Come to think of it, they might not let goblins return at all. They'll probably get locked out if they return empty handed."

"I hope they die out here looking for us," Fin mumbled with a focused determination on his face.

"I agree with that sentiment wholeheartedly," Brando smiled and then frowned. "They're moving again."

They split off into two groups, one traveling towards their location and one continuing forward.

"There's fifteen to thirty of them headed in our direction. Run or fight?" Brando instinctively put a hand on his crossbow. "At least we have the high ground."

"I think we should get farther away," Fin suggested in a hurry. "If the other group doesn't hear us fighting, we'll have more time."

A brief sound reached their vantage point that caused the group of advancing goblins to stop and run back toward the other group.

"They found the jar," Brando's smile was as sincere as it was smug. "And I casually placed the rest of your shirt a little further along. Come on, let's get out of here."

They moved North at a brisk walking pace. Both of them were thirsty and needed to conserve their energy in case they ran into another goblin patrol. As Brando put it, 'There's no use for us getting in fight to the death if we can avoid it.' So, they pressed on at a constant pace, traveling North.

When they cleared the hills, the valley to the east opened up, and they could see the walls they had escaped from. They traveled low, keeping as many bushes and other obstacles between them and the distant slave camp. It was a long way to travel without getting very far.

They both started to feel like all their work was wasted when Fin got a notification.

Affinity Quest Complete: Earth (4 of 5): Survey the land on foot. +1 Passive Ability

Passive Ability: Discern Earth - Locked until Earth Affinity is realized. Forfeit all other affinities.

After reading his notification, he explained what he gained to Brando and read his quest completion out loud.

"Remember how I was complaining about how we just walked in a massive circle?" Brando asked, finding it troublesome to talk with such a dry mouth. "That notification proves it. Anyway, I hate to admit it, but it is good news. Don't forget to eat some dirt when we find you water to wash it down with."

"Do any of these plants have water in them?" Fin gestured towards a cactus.

"They all do," Brando replied, trying to use as few words as possible. "Might kill you, though."

They walked in silence as the sun slowly drifted overhead. Looking up at the sky, Brando voiced his concerns about finding shelter. There wouldn't be much of a moon, so they scanned the terrain as they continued.

Finally, almost too dark to see, they settled next to a knee-high rock and hoped it would be good enough to hide them. They cleared the ground the best they could and hoped for the best. Then laid on the dirt listening for danger but only heard the slow churn of desert nature.

The next morning, Fin woke up feeling sore and miserable. After voicing his discomfort, Brando cheerfully led him through a series of movements and brief stretches. They scanned the area and collected their items, setting out North through the dry and desolate land.

A jolt of delight washed over Fin when a notification popped up, breaking up the monotony. He found another quest completion and read it out loud. As he read, his smile slowly dropped into a look of concern.

Path Quest Complete: Obtain at least -1 to all stats due to hunger and thirst. +2 Quests Revealed.

Strength Quest: Consume your body weight in food. +2 basic stat points. Forfeit all Power Quests.

Power Quest: Exceed your abilities in a reduced state. +2 golden stat points. Forfeit all Strength Quests

"I still have that food if you're about to die on me," Brando offered, pointing at the sack he was wearing.

"Thanks, but I don't think I would be able to swallow it." Fin declined, forcing each movement that brought him further away from danger.

They continued walking North, keeping an eye out for animals, green plants, or anything else that would signify that water was near. They hadn't found any by the time the sun set again. Instead of wasting their energy looking for shelter, they simply laid down and went to sleep.

Fin felt like he had just fallen asleep when he was woken up with a hand over his mouth. Brando whispered quietly in his ear, "Grab your sword, and don't make noise." Bleary-eyed from hunger, dehydration, and exhaustion, he drew his sword and drew himself up to a sitting position. Brando gripped his shoulder and pointed. There, in the distance, he saw a campfire.

"If they're goblins, we kill them in their sleep," Brando's disembodied voice sounded strange and husky in the dark. "If they're human, we give them one of our gems for water. We take our time. No noise."

Fin walked slowly and silently. The moon was light enough to make out vague shapes up close but not much else. Several times he had to step slightly further than he intended to dodge something in his way. He kept his eyes off of the nearing fire to maintain his eyesight in the dark.

It seemed to take forever, but the promise of a cool drink of water kept him moving indelibly forward. The sound of a horse snorting and blowing out air snapped him out of his trancelike state. Relief eased through his muscles as it occurred to him that he wouldn't be fighting goblins this evening. The goblins chasing them were not riding horses.

Brando caught his attention and motioned him to stay. He glanced at the area around the fire and noticed a person sleeping next to it. He was close enough to see a cooking pot with a wooden spoon sitting on top of it sitting next to the fire. It must be someone traveling alone. That was a relief.

He allowed his eyes to adjust to the dark while he waited. He could make out individual rocks on the ground by the time Brando returned.

Brando pointed to the left of the campsite and whispered two words that sent a wave of fear through his body, "It's them."

Chapter 17

Fin followed Brando at a frustratingly slow pace, towards the only people in the world who could be categorized as "them." They made a wide circle around where the horse was, not wanting it to sound an alert. Finally, Brando grabbed his shoulder and pointed to a caged carriage.

If it was a different carriage than the one that brought them into the Frome-forsaken wasteland, it was, at the very least, the same type. No one this close to a slave camp had any business driving a cart made for locking people up.

"If they're sleeping, club them," Brando pulled out his dagger and demonstrated clubbing them on the head with its pommel. "Or else, say incoming, not 'plug your ears.' If they are separate, you wait until I give the signal."

Fin nodded his head until Brando understood that he understood. Together, they crept into the camp like the things that belong in caged carriages.

When they found one person sleeping on a blanket in the middle of the campsite, Fin knew what to do. He stood ten paces away from the person's head and waited, sword hilt at the ready, while Brando searched the rest of the camp.

The adrenaline rushing through Fin's body was the only thing that kept him from falling asleep or passing out as the soft snores seduced him into boredom. He stayed vigilant and controlled his breathing, knowing that after this gruesome work was complete, there would be water.

Brando felt there might not be a second person after he searched the whole parameter. He was surprised that the sun hadn't started peaking over the valley for how long he had been searching. His intuition demanded that the man next to the fire was the second person, but something didn't seem right. The two bandits that captured them only had one horse between the two, but there were two horses. One was at the campsite with the fire, and the other was near the carriage.

Immediately he knew where the other person was. He had avoided the carriage because he didn't want to startle the horse into making noise, but what better place to sleep out in the wilderness than a protected cage without the risk of sleeping on rocks.

For the first time that night, Brando risked moving a little faster. He slowed down as he approached the carriage.

He saw that there was someone sleeping inside. He moved closer and gently tugged on the door. It was locked, but the person inside was unreachable due to the benches on either side of him. He set down his crossbow just under the carriage and moved towards Fin.

Fin was startled as Brando broke into sight. "I found him," he whispered, waving Fin to follow into the darkness just beyond the fire.

Drawing his blade and clapping a hand over the sleeping man's mouth, Brando cautioned the waking man against making any noise.

Keeping his dagger trained on the man's throat, Brando lifted the man to his feet and guided him to the carriage. As soon as they got close, the man called out a warning, earning him a swift blow to the head.

"Who's out there?" The man in the carriage asked.

"Toss out the keys, and we won't kill your friend and burn you alive in there." Brando managed to sound like an experienced highwayman.

"What do you want?" The man asked with fear seeping into his voice.

"One more word from you, and I'll pick up the crossbow at my feet and stick a bolt in your mouth," Brando warned the man, earning a loud snort from the horse. "Keys."

Fin watched as Brando slowly reached for his crossbow. When his hand hovered just above the weapon, the man threw out the keys.

"Make sure there isn't another key," Fin suggested.

"Remove your clothes and toss them through the bars," Brando commanded, beginning to strip the unconscious man at his feet.

When both men were stripped down to their shorts, Brando unlocked the gate and hoisted the unconscious man inside. Fin stood at the side with the tip of his sword hovering just inside the bars to prevent the man inside from trying anything.

When Brando locked the barred door, he was about ready to sit down and collect himself before searching the camp for water when an unexpected voice greeted him from behind.

"From one bandit to another, I applaud your style," the outline of a man spoke in a charming voice. "There isn't much you stand to gain by robbing us, but if you're looking for a job, you've more than gained our confidence in you. If you let my crew go now, we would be more than happy to have someone with your talents on our team."

"Incoming," Fin warned before calling out Fearing Howl. Nothing came out of his voice but gravelly air. Noticing his ability didn't work, he carefully moved forward, attempting to draw the man's attention and stall for time. "What kind of work do you three do?"

"I'm in the business of managing people," the man said, keeping his voice cool and level. "What I do is significantly more lucrative than petty theft."

"Let me guess," Fin tested the weight of his sword by moving it around in circles. "You capture people and then sell them to the lady at the goblin camp?"

"What? How do you know? She said she only does business with me," The man's confusion deflated his arrogance. "Who are you?"

Brando lifted his crossbow and pointed it, to the best of his ability, towards the man's dark outline. Unable to see the bolt or his target, he leveled his weapon, spoke some words, and pulled the trigger. "We're just a couple of escaped slaves."

Hearing the snap of the crossbow, Fin lunged in with his sword. In a wild fury, he stabbed, swung, and stabbed again. Not feeling the blows to his body or head, he kept hacking at the shadow before him as his consciousness grew foggy and drifted into a dreamless sleep.

Brando instinctively reset his crossbow and just as quickly drew a new bolt out. After a few tries, he blindly set the bolt into position. By the time he was ready to fire another shot, he couldn't see or hear his target.

"Fin?" he called out. There was no reply. He stepped forward; it was as silent as a graveyard. Not wanting to accidentally shoot Fin in the dark, he set his crossbow on the ground and held a bolt in his right hand. He moved forward until he saw what he thought was a body on the earth. Reaching down with his left hand, he touched a bare shoulder.

It was Fin. Relieved to find a pulse, he explored further, reaching past Fin's body. His hand met damp cloth over an unmoving chest. He followed the form until he reached the man's neck. Countless heartbeats pulsed in Brando's ear before he was satisfied that he could feel none with his fingers.

Casting away the bolt, he lifted Fin in his arms and moved towards the light of the dim fire. Nearly tripping and dropping his burden, Brando regained his balance and pressed forward on uncertain legs. When he finally reached the fire, he set him down on the recently occupied blanket. He checked Fin's exposed skin for deep cuts and stab wounds. Only seeing minor cuts and bruises, he left Fin's side to search the camp for water.

Chapter 18

As Fin woke up, he realized he wasn't stationary. He couldn't remember going to sleep. Light sprayed into his vision all at once, bringing the sounds and movement of traveling in a carriage. A powerful fear threatened to wriggle into his thoughts when a throbbing pain stole his attention. After letting out a groan of misery, all of the vibrations and noises stopped as Brando came to a halt.

"Fin, are you okay?" Brando's face finally hovered into his field of view. "You're pretty beat up."

"I think my head hurts," Fin managed to say. "And my body."

"Here, drink this," Brando held a waterskin out for him to take. "I tried to give you as much water as I could when you were unconscious. As you can imagine, making anyone drink when passed out cold is difficult at best. You've been out all night and all morning. I have some food, too, if you're ready for it."

A notification hung in his peripherals, but Fin was focused on the waterskin in his hands. He drank a quarter of the water before stopping to breathe. Not knowing how much water they had left, he corked the flask and set it down.

As quickly as his body would allow, he sat up and took in his surroundings. He was lying across the driver's bench on the wagon. Two horses adjusted their positions ahead, the reins of one attached to the saddle bag of the other. Digging through the pack of the front horse, Brando found what he was looking for and lifted out a small sack.

Green grass, plants, and trees were on either side of the dirt road. Weeds with flowers climbed vibrant green pastures and ran across the valley before them. Just behind, the mountains fraternized with round hills and intermingled in an unorganized line into eternity.

"Where are we?" Fin asked, imagining the blood in his veins moving more easily after drinking water.

"North, just past the mountains. You missed most of the excitement." Brando walked back and set a sack next to Fin. "It's dried meat. Eat as much as you want."

"We're hungry too," a voice from behind startled Fin. Looking behind him, he saw the two men who had abducted him locked behind bars. Their eyes had lost the haughtiness from before as they sat shirtless and defeated.

Brando reached into the space behind Fin without pausing for consideration and pulled out the dirty sack they had traveled with. He tossed it between the bars towards the men. "I got this at the goblin slave camp you sold us to. I was so hungry that I nearly cried tears of joy when I found it."

"This cheese has mold on it," the man, Fin remembered as Jack, complained. "Besides, there isn't enough for two people."

Fin motioned for Brando to hold a moment while he finished chewing. He reached down and untied the cloth strips that held his improvised foot protection in place. Peeling off the strip of leather and ripping open fresh wounds, he discarded the leather and looked at the sole of his foot.

The sight was worse than he expected, and he cringed at the state his foot was in. Black, brown, and bleeding, he lifted his leg over the backrest and showed the two men what they had ultimately done. "You took my food, stole my boots, and sold me to a goblin slave camp. If it was up to me, we wouldn't have given you that much. Where is that stick you used to keep us quiet with anyway?" Fin gingerly set his foot down and began untying his other sandal.

"It's right behind you," Brando answered with a grim face, calculating eyes trained on Fin.

After discarding his other sandal, Fin reached back and found his grip on the large stick. "Good to know. What are we doing with these two anyway?"

"Please have mercy," Jack begged. "I swear we've seen the error of our ways. If you let us go, we'll use what we know to help the orphans."

"We're bringing them to justice." Brando said with finality, "If their testimony helps save everyone in that desolate slave camp, then I don't care what the king decides to do with them."

"I swear I won't hurt another person for the rest of my life," Barnes cried.

Fin turned and made eye contact with the pleading men. "For some reason, hearing the sound of your voice has made me extraordinarily angry. I don't recommend saying anything else until I've sorted through these feelings."

"Fin, do you think you can take over for a while?" Brando asked with concern in his voice. "I haven't slept, but I don't think we should stop while there's still daylight."

"I can take over. You'll have to help me mount the horse, but I'll be fine from there." Fin slung the waterskin around his shoulders and attached the bag of dried meat strips.

"First, let's get you some clothes," Brando flipped open another saddle bag and took out a fistful of garments. Selecting a tunic and trousers, he tossed them over and put the rest back. "They're not much, but they're clean. The guy you took down had some extra clothes, too, and they fit."

Brando wore a black, low-cut tunic with silver threading and matching breeches. He wore his fur-lined boots that were still covered in mud from the mines, but he looked like a proper gentleman, if not filthy.

Fin pulled the loose tunic over his head and carefully slid his feet out of each leg of his filthy trousers. After some concentration, he was able to put on the new ones without scraping his foot wounds. After he tied his pants, he decided against covering his wounds with his old boots.

He checked the pockets of his tattered trousers. When he found what he was looking for, he pulled out the pouch the Dwarf had given him. After several tugs of the drawstring, he looked inside for the first time.

Twenty-four crystal clear gems spilled out onto his hand. Each had deep and varying shades of yellow except one. Mixed in with the other gems, like a ram among sheep, lay an icy blue gem. Instinctually, Fin knew that this must have been Heidle's most prized possession. He put the gems back into the leather pouch and tied it shut. He wasn't going to let Heidle's offering go to waste. He would find the dwarven city if it was the last thing he did.

Brando led the horse to the side of the wagon, and with some careful movements, he got Fin onto the saddle. "I'll lash my reins to your saddle bags. All you have to do is keep her going at a steady pace. I tied the crossbow to the saddle. In a pinch, just cut the threads with the knife on the other side."

Brando made sure that Fin had everything he needed and then lay across the bench. It didn't take long until the sway of the cart and the clopping steps put him into a deep sleep.

Fin chewed on meat and took sips of water as he led the horse behind him down the winding road. When he felt comfortable with what he was doing, he pulled up his notifications to read.

Strength Quest Complete: Defeat a mightier opponent in melee combat. +1 level. +4 basic stat points.

Power Quest Complete: Exceed your abilities in a reduced state. +2 golden stat points.

Quest Complete: Complete two opposing quests simultaneously. Strength and Power Quests available. Dual Affinity.

Class Quest Complete: Prove your strength in battle. +1 basic combat class. Class upgrades unlocked.

Basic Combat Class: Warrior. +1 Strength, +1 Dexterity, +1 Constitution.

Affinity Quest Complete: Shadow (1 of 5): Defeat an enemy in blind combat. +1 Active Ability.

Active Ability: Dark Sight - Locked until Shadow Affinity is realized.

He ate and drank as he read through each new entry. After stopping to relieve himself, he moved his halo out of the way to see if Brando was up. When Brando didn't stir, he resolved to tell him about it later. He only found it a little challenging to remount the horse, but when he finally made it, he let his feet hang in the breeze and moved forward at a steady pace.

Hour after uneventful hour passed until he saw two men walking on the road towards them. After several attempts, Fin finally managed to rouse Brando from his sleep.

"We have company."

"Oh, good," Brando yawned, "It means we're getting close to civilization."

Fin could see that underneath Brando's tired optimism, he had concern written on his face. After all, they were transporting two unclothed men in the back of a slave wagon. They decided that honesty would prevail and settled in while the two parties slowly approached.

"Hello! How are the roads ah-" Fin was cut off by a loud wailing behind him.

"Please help! We've been abducted. They're going to sell us into slavery!" Jack's voice was loud and panicked. "I was working on the farm when these two clubbed me over the head and took my clothes! I have a wife and four children at the home I'll never see again!"

Brando reached behind him and drew the stick. He jabbed between the bars and struck the irate slaver two solid times on his body, "I said be quiet!"

"Yes, master," Jack bellowed from the fetal position. "I swear I will do as you please, just don't beat me again!"

One of the men Fin had greeted drew his sword. The other nocked an arrow in his bow and drew back. The tip of the arrow swung up and aimed directly at Brando. "Drop that stick and come away from that cart!"

"These two are lying," Fin managed before the bow was trained on him, daring him to speak again.

"I said, step out!" The bowman yelled.

Brando stepped out of the carriage, but instead of raising his hands, he plugged his ears. In confusion, the bowman scanned his surroundings. The point of his arrow threatened every place the man looked.

Seeing that the charged arrow was pointed in a safe direction, Fin let out a Fear Howl. The arrow was released into an empty field, making Fin glad to have waited.

"Drop your weapons!" Fin demanded as he drew the knife and cut the leather straps holding the crossbow in place. He hefted the crossbow and trained the bolt on the man with the bow first.

The two men dropped their weapons and stood unmoving, with the exception of a slight quivering in their knees.

Brando moved to a standing position and quickly picked up the bow and arrow, and soon, it too was trained on the men. "What were you going to do? Kill us and let these criminals go free?"

"Criminals? You aren't the ones who are locked in a cage," the man said as bravely as he could.

"These two robbed us and sold us to a goblin slave camp," Fin said as quickly and as bluntly as possible. "We escaped and found them on the road. We are currently heading to Rudford to turn them in."

"There are no goblins in all of Eralind, let alone slave camps!" the swordsman spoke with righteous judgment burning in his eyes. "Besides, if you were going to Rudford, you're heading in the wrong direction. Rudford is West. Do what you will, but you aren't fooling anyone."

"I can tell you are honest people, if not completely deceived at the moment. But we aren't going to kill you," Fin reassured them. "Take it in good conscience that if we were slavers, we would put you in the cart along with these two. You can assume we are not, since we will not do that."

"Is this true?" The bowman directed his question to the men in the wagon.

"Let me prove it to you. My wife and children are back a ways. It's not more than a few days' journey." Jack's voice was that of a broken man. "My wife will tell you I'm an honest man. Maybe sometimes I drink too much."

The bowman's expression hardened at Fin, "Let this man prove his innocence."

"They kidnapped us and sold us to a slave camp," Brando said, exasperated. "So, no. We do not have to prove anything to anyone."

"The authorities will hear about this," the swordsman snarled.

"Do whatever you want. It's none of our concern. Take your packs and your money pouches and be gone," Fin's eyes were hot with anger. He wished that the travelers would just listen. "If you follow us, it will not go well for you."

"As you attacked us, you will not be getting your weapons back," Brando growled.

The two men started walking backward.

"Leave the arrows," Brando directed.

The quiver of arrows dropped to the ground, and the two men steadily ran faster as they got further and further from arrow range.

"I don't think bringing these men to justice will do us any," Brando admitted, picking the arrows off the ground. "What do we do?"

"What can we do?" Fin's posture was rigid as he looked toward the cart.

"I'm sorry, I was scared, that's all." Jack pleaded, "I won't do it again, I promise. The next time we meet people on the road, I'll tell them all my evil deeds."

"You'll look like heroes!" Barnes chimed in.

"Let's move further down before we get this wagon off the road," Brando said, ignoring the men. "I don't think we'll need it anymore. The world will be a better place without this carriage around. I'll go look for some dry branches."

A notification popped into view as soon as Fin pulled off the road.

Precarious Blessing Quest Complete: Spare a lesser being's life at your own peril. +1 Active Ability. Forfeit all Advantageous Curse Quests.

Active Ability: Violent Healing.

As soon as Fin read his quest completion, he read it over again several times to comprehend what any of it meant. The quest's names and abilities were getting strange.

When the carriage was a good distance off the road, Fin tied up his horse and walked out into the field. He wanted to try out his new ability. If the ability hurt, he felt he was more than prepared for the pain. He just didn't want the violent part to affect the horses by proximity.

He sat with his back against a tree and looked around to make sure he was alone. Then he curled his foot inward to try to violently heal it. Holding his right hand toward the bottom of it, he channeled Violent Healing. It took a long time to build up; it was nothing like using his other abilities.

As soon as the ability flared to life, he could tell something was wrong. His right hand was absorbing energy, and his left hand was dispelling it. He could feel a thick cord of power moving into his right hand and out his left. He switched them immediately.

At first, he could not feel anything out of the ordinary. He set his right hand on the ground for support, and a wave of energy radiated out of his other one. He moved his hand directly to the sole of his mangled foot and felt the restorative power course through him.

He was so enthralled by the process that he almost didn't notice the color change happening all around him. The green grass turned brown in a widening circle. A brown leaf dropped in front of him, followed by another. Finally, leaves danced toward the ground all around him. It wasn't until he heard a cracking sound and a branch fell to the earth that he stopped the ability.

Looking around, he noticed he was sitting in the middle of a massive circle of dead grass next to a brittle and broken tree. He touched the ground, and the grass crumbled like ashes under his touch. He hoped that it would be able to grow again. The tree, however, would never grow. It was as dry and fragile as the grass. He stepped away just as more limbs creaked and then snapped off.

Curious about the state of his foot, he sat down again and turned it upward. At first look, it still appeared to be in bad shape. He picked at it to check the damage. Underneath the layer of dirty scabs, he found fresh skin. His foot was mostly healed.

Wanting to compare it to his other one, he was surprised to find it, too, had been healed, though not nearly as much. Instead of a massive wound, he found fresh skin around partially healed scrapes. He could walk again without reopening his injury with every step.

He reached up to touch his head, hoping to find it had also healed. It was still tender and swollen. Excited at his new condition, he sprinted out on fresh feet to find Brando.

Chapter 19

"Violent healing?" Brando carried an armload of wood back to the wagon. "That's like saying, 'A soft kick in the plums,' or 'A loving stab in the chest.' What does it do?"

Fin explained the sensation he had when he used the ability and then lifted the bottom of his more healed foot towards Brando.

Brando set his branches down and gawked. "It's almost completely healed! I didn't want to tell you this, but I was convinced that they were going to have to cut your legs off. I just didn't have the heart to tell you."

"Cut my legs off because of a couple of scratches?" Fin shook his head, "That's the dumbest thing I've ever heard."

"It wasn't just a couple of scratches; your feet looked like they were a few days from getting the smirch," Brando picked up the wood and began filling his arms again. "I've been keeping my eye out for lungweed or any fruits to make vinegar with, I just don't know where lungweed grows, and I don't think the vinegar would be ready to clean your wound in time. That's also why I've wanted to get to a city so fast."

"I would have been fine. It didn't even hurt," Fin tried to shrug off the seriousness of Brando's voice.

"That's the worst part!" Brando raised his voice in frustration. "Any normal person wouldn't be able to walk because of the pain, which is a good thing. It makes it so their wounds can begin to heal. But you," he pointed an accusing finger from underneath his woodpile, "get the worst case of shredded feet I've ever seen and then go skipping around like it's your birthday!"

Fin laughed and slapped Brando on the back, dislodging one of his sticks. "You're so dramatic. Anyway, what are we going to do about Heidle's directions? We seem to be off track."

"According to his directions, if we continue North, we might hit Lokardale. If not, there's always the chance that we'll find a village that specializes in apple pies…" Brando cut off as a massive patch of dead grass came into view. A crumbling tree sat dead center in the circle of decay like a throne in the palace of death. "You weren't kidding. I see what makes it so violent. Do you think it would do this to other people if you pointed it at them?"

Fin knew exactly what Brando was thinking, having already had the same thought himself. He sighed deeply, "The only people that should benefit from those two's death are their future victims. I don't feel like it would be right to be in a position of justice and also the position to benefit from it."

"So, it might work on people?" Brando stopped walking and regarded Fin. "I guess we should talk about this then. By the way things went today, we both know we can't take them with us, but we can't set them free either."

"It's a judgment I'm willing to make," Fin looked Brando in the eyes. "Not out of revenge, not out of hate, but because there are other people out there who might not be as lucky as we were if we set those two loose. I'll make it quick and painless."

"We will make it quick and painless," Brando corrected, putting an emphasis on the word, *we*. He took one last glance at a dead and broken tree destined to become a burning pillar of justice. Its duty to destroy that which had trapped free will and to usher the disdainfully deceased into the afterlife was fast approaching. The pyre was ready, and the setting sun was already turning its back on what it was meant for.

Fin and Brando rode together in silence the next morning and throughout the day. Each on horseback, and each having their own share of thoughts to sort through. The words they spared were to discuss which direction to take at a fork, what to do about their dwindling food supply, and where to set up camp for the night.

When they came across a stream, they let their horses drink and graze by the water while they walked further down for a good spot to wade in. When they found a calm break in the water, they divested their clothes and washed the troubles of their journey from their souls and skin.

Brando tested their new bow but opted for the sturdier crossbow to hunt with. When no animals appeared, they finished their dwindling food supply and tucked in for the night. The silence persisted the next morning, but it was held by a weaker force than the day before. Upon meeting travelers on the road, that force that held the silence dissolved, lifting away like the embers from a burning slave carriage.

"Greetings," a man riding a carriage smiled at the two. "Beautiful day to be outside."

"That it is," Fin smiled back. "Can you tell us how far this road goes before it reaches any sort of civilization?"

"Not too much longer, and you'll reach a village with a nice little inn," the man replied, pointing directly behind him.

"We're looking for a city called Lokardale," Brando added. "Do you know where that might be?"

"Lokardale, you say? And it's big enough to be considered a city?" The man tipped his hat further up his forehead. "The only cities I know of around here are Clive Rae and Brax Fort. If you go forward a few hours and hang a left at the fork, Clive Rae is about a day's journey to the West. Brax Fort is at least ten days east of the village ahead, but I'm not familiar with anywhere called Lokardale."

"Thank you for your time," Brando nodded at the man. "If we had any coin, we would be in a better position to thank you properly."

"Oh, it's no problem," the man held his reins at the ready. "I'm happy to help."

The pair moved off the road to allow the old man to pass. When he was gone, Brando was giddy with excitement. "Well, come on then. Food and warm beds await!"

The excitement proved contagious, and soon they laughed and argued about who would take the longest bath. In spite of their high spirits, the short journey seemed to stretch on forever. When rooftops and a small wooden bridge came into view, they both let out a cheer.

"I just had a thought," Fin said. "If those men we met are from here, we should probably hide the bow and sword we got from them. If anybody recognizes it, we might find ourselves in trouble. Again."

"Good thinking." Brando removed the sword from his belt and paired it with his unstrung bow. After rifling through his saddleback, he pulled out a pair of pants and a crusty shirt and began concealing the weapons. After several attempts to make the bundle look natural, he lashed it to his horse. "Now, let's go get a pint!"

They had to ask several villagers before they found the inn. The fact that there wasn't a sign on the front made the place difficult to find. Fresh lumber mingled with withering wood to give the place a mismatched look. Brando felt that the place couldn't have looked more pleasing. They tied the horses to a support beam and went inside.

The door opened up into a thin haze of smoke that hung around rugged tables and the base of a staircase. Colorful sheets of cloth hung in front of the windows casting rectangular shapes through the milky air.

"Hello?" a quiet voice fought its way to where Fin and Brando were standing. It wasn't the welcoming greeting they were expecting, but more like the reaction to an unexpected guest.

"Hi, we were told this is an inn?" Brando explained, feeling uncomfortable. "There's no sign out front, so we weren't sure if everyone was just having a laugh by pointing us here."

A man no older than Fin stepped out into the lobby with a pipe in his mouth. "Oh, yes, come in. I've been meaning to fix the sign since my dah left me this place. There's just so much to do. Well, you know. How can I help you?"

"You're the innkeeper?" Brando addressed the man, unconvinced. "We would like a couple of rooms, a bath, some food, pretty much everything."

"Okay, great!" The man waved them over to the bar area. "Do you want me to run over and see what the butcher has now, or would you like to see your rooms?"

Disappointed that there wasn't already food cooking, Brando's words attempted to come out but failed to find a purchase.

"That sounds good," Fin jumped in. "There's one thing. We don't have the coin per se, but we can still pay you. It might be less conventional than what you're used to." He held up a defensive hand and continued. "We are miners, and all we have are the gems that we've gathered on our most recent expedition."

The innkeeper thought about it and then gave a nod. "I don't really know anything about gems, but I know someone who might. I'll go find him now."

Brando stopped the innkeeper before he ran off. "We could use a couple of pints while we wait, if you don't mind?"

The innkeeper hesitated but then picked up two mugs and filled them from a tap. "If I'm gone long, you can refill yourself here. Just tell me how many you've had when I come back."

Brando set down an empty mug at about the same time the innkeeper left. "You know, that's not a bad cider. You want another one?"

Fin looked at his half-empty mug and declined. "I think it would be better if we waited to see if he'll accept the gems first."

"I respectfully disagree." Brando refilled his mug and recited some words from memory, "The trick to a tap that is leaking is a mug in your hand while you're drinking. The more the tap leaks, the more mugs the tap needs until you're too drunk to know that it's empty."

"I don't think that applies to this situation," Fin held up his mug. "But I'll take another if you're offering."

"That's the spirit!" Brando swept the mug off the counter and held it under the tap. "Wait, I have an idea." Brando rushed out of the door and then came back a minute later, holding two handfuls of dirt. "Guess what we're about to try."

"You know, I've been thinking about it, and I don't really think I need to eat dirt," Fin produced his favorite rock from his pocket and held it up. "I feel like I'm getting somewhere with this. I can just feel it."

"Nonsense," Brando carefully set the dirt next to Fin's mug. "You have one more quest to complete before you get the Earth affinity. If your rock was going to give you anything, it would have done so by now. The cider will help the dirt go down."

Fin hesitantly reached forward and took a pinch of dirt between his thumb and forefinger. "I actually had another thought. What if I'm supposed to sharpen my nails on a rock or something?" Fin tried stalling for time. "Dragons, you know? They have to sharpen their talons on something. I think we should put off eating dirt until we've tried just about everything else."

"Just eat the dirt," Brando said in exasperation. "Think about all the cool skills you could unlock. Now that you have double infinity, you pretty much need to hurry this earth one up."

"Dual Affinity," Fin corrected, placing the pinch of dirt in his mouth and quickly washing it down with cider.

"Anything?" Brando asked.

"I don't think so."

"To be safe, you should probably just eat all of it," Brando shrugged. "I'm getting another one. Do you want?"

When the innkeeper walked into the lobby, he saw Fin pouring dirt into his mouth while Brando laughed and refilled his mug from the tap. Unsure about the kind of people he would be hosting, he cleared his throat. "Sorry to interrupt." He led a man towards them. "I found someone who knows something about gems."

"Hello, I am Eugal, this town's mercer," A tall and rotund man smiled easily with the predatory look, staple of professional traders.

"I'm Brando."

Fin had a mouthful of cider-flavored mud in his mouth. He held up a finger and swished more cider around before speaking. After the third swish and swallow, he felt he was in a good enough position to give his name. "I'm Fin."

"I understand you have gems you are looking to sell. May I see them?" Eugal asked, inviting them to sit at the counter with them.

"Cider?" Brando offered. When the cider was declined, he walked around to the tap and poured himself another.

When the attention was on Brando, Fin pulled out his pouch and slipped out two of the gems inside. He then unstowed a third gem, the smaller of what Brando had mined, and set all three on the table.

Attempting to be as aloof as possible, the mercer took one of the gems at random and held it up for a closer look. "Obviously, raw gems aren't as valuable as the cut ones; you understand that, right?"

"Yeah, that makes sense," Fin wiped the mud from his mouth and tried to envision how his father dealt with opportunist customers. "There is still a strong market for uncut gems, but you know that already or you wouldn't be talking to us."

"Oh, yes, quite right," the mercer smiled. "I hope you don't mind If I run a quick test on the gem. What did you say it was again?"

"Topaz," Brando managed to say without slurring, "and go ahead."

Eugal took out a glass marble from his pocket, put it in his hand with the gem, and abruptly threw them both at the ground.

Fin and Brando stood in post-shock as the man searched the ground for the gem and shards of the marble he broke. When he found them, he simply said, "It appears to be real."

Fin quickly tucked away his other gems before this insane person tried to break them on the ground as well.

"It's just a routine test," Eugal explained. "Most gems are harder than glass. Usually, it takes more than throwing them on the ground to break them."

"Usually?" Brando asked, incredulous.

"Yes, well, from time to time, there's always a chance of," Eugal smoothly shifted topics. "Well, anyway, I would be willing to take these three gems off your hands for the price of, let's say, your food and lodgings here for three nights?"

Fin saw Brando was about to protest and held a hand up to stop him. "How much do you charge for food and lodgings a day? Uh, I'm sorry, I never got your name."

"Felix," the innkeeper replied. "It's seven a day per person. With dinner, it comes to thirteen."

"How much does that come to providing the food, baths, and a stable for our horses?"

Felix quickly counted in his head and replied, "It comes to seventy-eight, or one silver and twelve copper pieces for the three days."

Fin pointed at the gem Eugal was holding. "Do you know how much those normally go for?"

"Maybe if you were in the city, you would be able to sell it for more," the mercer said. "Out here, you have to take what I offer you."

"I will sell you the gem you're holding for a silver and twenty."

"You're hardly in a position to negotiate," the mercer said in a matter-of-fact tone. "If you don't have the coin to pay for your stay, let alone the ciders you've already had, then I'm in a position to offer you whatever I want to offer, which stands at twenty-six each."

"I will sell you the gem you are holding and one more for sixty," Fin cut off the mercer's next words with a sharp gesture. "But you have to pay for our first night's stay. That includes all the ciders we've had and will have since we got here and all the food we can eat."

"How many ciders have you had already?" Eugal asked suspiciously.

"Five or six," Brando answered as honestly as he could.

Fin held up two fingers, indicating how many ciders he had.

"Forty for two gems, and I'll cover your costs for one night," Eugal said with finality and then held up his hand to shake on it. "Take it or leave it. If you don't like getting a low price, you can always go to the city for a better deal."

Brando just shook his head, so Fin held his hand out. "As much as we can eat."

Eugal shook Fin's hand and then peeled off forty copper coins with a satisfied smile. "Pleasure doing business with you."

"Why don't you join us for dinner, Eugal?" Fin set down six copper coins in front of Felix. "On me." He gave the rest of the money to Brando.

"I couldn't possibly say no to a free meal," Eugal accepted the invitation.

"Great," Fin smiled and directed his attention at the innkeeper. "Can you draw us four baths and prepare a meal for twenty people?"

"And my cider's empty," Brando added with a belch before walking around the counter to the tap. "This is six or seven. I hope you're keeping tabs."

"I said I would pay for the meals you ate," Eugal conceded, "but I'm not paying for dinner for a quarter of this town."

"Make that thirty." Fin finished his cider and then handed his mug to Brando for a refill. "I'll pay for all the food we don't eat, and Eugal will be here to witness what he'll have to pay. Either way, you'll get paid for feeding thirty people." Fin handed Felix a gem, "Hold onto this until after dinner."

"There's no way you can eat thirty meals. The portions here aren't the same as whatever backwoods village you came from," Eugal protested. After working out the prices, a serene look came over the pudgy man's face. "You know what, that's fine. If you agree to pay for everything you don't eat, that's better for me anyway. I was trying to help you before, but seeing how you want to play games, the price of your gems just went down to twenty copper pieces for each. Don't think that you'll be able to get away without paying, either. I recommend figuring out how you plan on eating thirty meals."

"The question should be, what are we doing with four baths?" Brando replied from the innkeeper's position behind the counter. "The answer to that question is, we're both pretty filthy."

Chapter 20

"How are we going to eat thirty meals?" Brando asked from the bathtub next to Fin. "I know you said you could eat a lot, but I'll probably only be able to help you with three of those."

"I have 9 basic stat points. The last time I used one, I ate about a week's worth of food," Fin recalled. "I should be fine."

"I don't know what you're saying, but if you can eat food like you can crush rocks, I'm with you. Can you pass me the soap?"

After a while, the two stepped out of their black bath water and into the two others that were prepared for them.

When Brando noticed Fin rinsing the rest of the dirt out of his mouth, he asked, "So eating dirt didn't work?"

Fin glared.

"Hey, at least you tried it, though," Brando pretended not to notice by cleaning his fingernails. "We have to try everything, you know? Anyway, I don't know what you're going to do while you wait for dinner, but I'm going to take a nap."

"I think I will, too. All that cider on an empty stomach has made me kind of sleepy," Fin leaned back in his tub and closed his eyes.

"Don't fall asleep now," Brando warned. "Normally, I would say that taking a nap in the bathtub is ideal, but there are warm beds up there, just waiting for us."

His eyes snapped open. "You're right. Warm beds await."

When Fin awoke to a knock at the door, it took him a moment to realize where he was. When he heard the innkeeper informing Brando that dinner was ready, he realized it wasn't a knock at his door that woke him up in the first place. His suspicions were confirmed when a louder knock followed by a similar message was delivered to him.

He stretched out on his bed, basking in the comfort of it. If he wasn't as hungry, he might stay where he was. A notification blinked in his vision, and he was pleased with what he saw.

Sovereign Quest Complete: Escape with your life and find a safe haven. +1 level, +1 Wisdom, +1 basic stat point, +1 gold stat point.

Ability Unlocked: Discern Magic.

He got out of bed and opened the door. Facing him from across the hallway, Brando stood looking as disheveled as ever. Bloodshot eyes, wild hair, and slight sway to his stance told Fin that Brando might regret his earlier choices.

"Are you alright?" Fin asked, understanding all too well the effects of cider.

"I don't feel as bad as I could, all things considered," Brando said, staggering through his door. "As soon as I have some food, I'll be fine."

"I completed my escape quest finally and reached level five," Fin bragged as he led the way down the stairs. "I wonder if there's one for getting captured a second time."

"Don't even joke about that," Brando said, gripping the handrails as he carefully climbed down each step. At the bottom of the staircase, the sight stopped both men dead in their tracks.

Tables filled with trays of food waited for them on large serving plates. Shrines dedicated to poultry, wild game, and bore decorated each table like spires on a temple. Steam from bowls of mashed, fried, and baked potatoes mingled with that of cabbage, carrots, and cauliflower. Gravies and sauces consorted with jams and glazes. Sliced loaves of bread sat next to blocks of cheese. Large knives stretched between serving spoons and smaller cutlery. Baskets of fruit decorated each table like the jewels in a royal crown.

"I hope you don't mind, but since we are having such esteemed guests such as yourselves, I took it upon myself to lend the aid of my kitchens and staff," the corpulent mercer said from in front of three serving assignees. "I also brought the town constable to ensure that both parties have equal representation."

"Don't mind me," a bulky man said from behind a tray of venison. "I'm just here to ensure a peaceful transaction."

"Please," Eugal gestured to two empty chairs. "If you're ready?"

When Fin and Brando took a seat, they were immediately greeted with a massive plate of food, a smaller plate with bread and cheese, and a mug of ale.

"I'm sure you understand that the ale is part of the meal," Eugal said with eyes all but laughing. "But you already knew that when you ordered thirty of them."

Brando looked at Fin for a sign of confidence and was not let down.

"I'm sure that won't be a problem," Fin winked at the man. "Before we begin, I would ask Brother Brando to give a prayer for Frome's blessings?"

Eugal's fork paused halfway to his mouth, a thick slab of pork dripping onto his plate. He lowered his first bite back and adopted an impatient posture.

"Uh, sure," Brando steepled his fingers and then orated the first approximation to prayer he had ever given. "When water is needed, who will be there on the rain cloud? Who can sway the trees or garden the gardens? Why Frome can, of course. And since trees and gardens all have one thing in common, we can all join in together to pluck the weeds together. That is unless weeds are a good thing in this case. Because even the weeds are a part of the circle of life. Frome wants weeds? He can have them, and we can all figure it out as we go along. Together."

Peaking up, Brando noticed that even though his prayer was over, everyone's eyes were still closed, so he added, "Let's eat!" for good measure.

"That was quite the, uh, prayer." Eugal adjusted a large cloth napkin around the front of his collar. "I was under the impression that you two were miners. Come to find you are also pilgrims? You are indeed honored guests this evening."

By the time Eugal was finished talking, Fin and Brando's mouths were full. All they were able to do was nod and grunt in the affirmative.

Eugal eyed them suspiciously but then found himself lost in the pleasure of the meal. When he finished his first plate, a server replaced it with a second.

Brando set his fork on the empty plate in front of him. "This is as far as I go, I think. My appetite must have shrunk somewhere on our journey. I'll help out when I can, but I think this is in Frome's gardening hands now."

A server approached to remove Brando's plate, but Fin stopped him. "Can you move the basket of fruit from the middle of the table and place our empty dishes there, please?"

The server bowed and pointed at the fruit for another server to whisk away. He then stacked two plates in the empty space.

"This is so I can keep track of how I'm doing," Fin explained, accepting a second plate in front of him.

"Confident until the bitter end!" Eugal praised. "I applaud your gumption."

Fin put one stat into strength and smiled. "I should be the one applauding your staff. That was a delicious first course." He dug in.

When Fin had finished his second plate, he waved for the servers to hurry with the third, causing Eugal to lift an uncertain eyebrow. The stack of plates in the middle of the table increased to three.

Brando leaned back in his chair and sipped his ale. "This is a delicious brew. Where did it come from?"

Eugal shifted his eyes between the two, not wanting to miss out on Fin's defeat. "I pick up several casks every time I'm in Clive Rae. I usually keep them for myself, but seeing as Felix needed to provide for you two, I donated a cask. It's unfortunate you will probably be too full to enjoy more than a taste of it."

A fourth plate added itself among the numbers. Fin drained his mug and held it up for a refill, "How are we keeping track of the ale?"

"Altogether, you are at three," The constable's voice materialized from his inconspicuous perch.

"I don't think there's very much room left for it right now." Brando finished his mug and held it up. "But I would be remiss not to take advantage of your private supply so graciously donated."

Fin snatched the last bite of potato from his plate before the server could remove it and stack it on top of the four others. The servers rushed around each other in a chaotic scramble missing collisions by a hair's breadth with each passing. Fin took small sips of his ale while he waited for his food. Eugal watched with a half-buttered slice of bread frozen between his plate and his gaping mouth.

By the eighth empty plate, Fin was starting to feel full. He upgraded his strength again and felt the comfort in his stomach return, followed by the discomfort of hunger. He dug in with renewed vigor, adding two plates at a time to the stack when the servers started doubling up.

"This is impossible! How does someone consume that much food?" Eugal nearly shouted.

Noticing Fin's preoccupation, Brando spoke for him, "Frome's fruits are plentiful."

Before Fin upgraded his strength again, he took a brief respite from dinner to stretch out. Feeling his muscles become even more tight and dense, he worked intensely to loosen up. He was surprised to find he didn't feel intoxicated. He must have consumed five ales with his fourteen empty plates on top of Brando's one.

Eugal let out a massive sigh of relief. "I have to hand it to you. I didn't expect you to get even this far. I was getting worried there for a second."

"Oh, were you?" Fin had his arm bent behind his head, and he was tugging on his elbow, stretching out the muscles in his arm.

"Yeah, this meal cost me a small fortune, but for twenty coins a gem, I'm still going to make out like a bandit, so to speak." Eugal's smile returned. "As it stands, you've more than exceeded expectations. It wasn't as good of a deal as I thought it was going to be, but I still turned over at least eight keystones, maybe more."

"What's a keystone?" Brando asked.

"It's how merchants set their prices," Eugal explained, leaning back in his chair. "If I buy a trinket from you for a silver piece and then turn around and sell it for two silver pieces, I've turned a keystone."

"We ate fifteen plates of food, and you're still making eight times what you paid us for the gems?" Brando asked.

"Approximately. We can settle up whenever you say the word, but for the most part, yes. Since the price has already been agreed upon, you can't go back on it now," Eugal pointed to the silent constable, "Hence why he's here to ensure both parties adhere to our previously set terms."

"That seems a little cutthroat," Fin pointed out, "How many keystones if we only ate one plate each?"

"Who's to say? Are you sure you're not still hungry?" Eugal laughed and wiped the sweat from his brow.

Fin swung his arms back and forth. "I just assumed your servers stopped bringing me food so you could talk. I never said I was done."

One of the servers straightened his back and quickly set another plate in front of Fin. To Eugal's pure astonishment, Fin started eating as if he had just sat down at the table.

Brando hid his own astonishment. Fin had told him about his appetite, but seeing it in person was nothing short of miraculous. He gestured for the men to replace Fin's cloth napkin and fill his cup.

Plate after plate added onto the wobbling pile in front of him as Fin devoured a feast made for a village. Between dishes, Fin flexed his arm and motioned for Brando to feel it. Brando reached out and squeezed his bicep. It was like squeezing a bent iron rod. He had allocated five basic stat points to strength and could already notice the difference.

"Eugal, what were you going to do with all this food when we inevitably didn't eat it all?" Fin asked, wiping his mouth with his third cloth napkin. "I mean, it's a lot of food to just throw away."

Distracted by his thoughts, Eugal turned to Fin before the question registered in his short-term memory. "Oh, um. Sell it to the townsfolk. Why?"

"Because I lost track for a while, I believe that's over thirty," Fin waved his hand towards the towering piles of plates and leaned back in his chair, patting his stomach.

"Thirty-nine," The constable said from the back of the room.

"I am impressed," the mercer declared. "But a deal is a deal, and since you've only finished 10 mugs of ale between the two of you, that counts for twenty unfinished meals. I hope you have enough gems to sell me at the agreed-upon price of twenty each. It's okay. We can do business whenever you're ready."

"Let me get this straight, we've eaten thirty-nine plates of food, but you're only going to count ten because we didn't drink enough?" Brando made a disapproving face.

"As I stated before the meal, the ale counts as part of the dinner." Eugal tore the cloth napkin off his neck. "As you are unable to consume twenty ales at six coins a meal, I will take the six gems you owe me and use one of them to repopulate my food stores."

"Will someone please bring whatever ale that is required to put this man at ease?" Fin asked the servers. "You guys are doing a great job, by the way."

Servers with mugs of ale lined up in front of Fin. When the servers were given empties, they filled them and returned to the back of the line.

Fin started feeling the effects of the alcohol by the third, but he pressed through. When it seemed that he was full again, he put another stat point into strength, and his stomach immediately made room for more. He was surprised to notice his head clear up as well. It was as if the effects of the ale got digested along with everything else.

"Constable, can you keep us updated on the count?" Brando directed his question toward the back of the room.

"Fourteen."

"Fifteen."

"Sixteen."

At twenty, Fin decided to allocate a basic stat point towards dexterity.

"Twenty-five."

"Twenty-six."

Seeing the determination on Fin's face, Eugal tried to break him. "I hope you're saving room for dessert."

"Dessert wasn't part of the deal," Brando protested. "We ordered thirty meals."

"And a meal comes with dessert," Eugal stated.

"Twenty-seven."

"Twenty-eight."

Fin looked up and saw something unexpected, a new notification. He pulled it up and squinted to read it.

Affinity Quest Complete: Water (1 of 5): Liquid diet: Allocate a basic stat point using a liquid-based meal. +1 Breath ability.

Passive Ability: Hydro Lung - Locked until Water Affinity is realized.

"Hey, if you had a passive ability called Hydro Lung, does that mean you can breathe underwater?" Fin asked the table with a wobble to his head.

Brando, watching Fin squint off into space, knew that he was both drunk and that he unlocked a new quest. He immediately covered for him, "I think I can take the next couple of ales."

The server placed a full mug before Brando and removed the empty one. Brando drained its contents, causing the constable to announce, "Twenty-nine." When he finished the final mug, he asked for one more to enjoy at his own pace.

"Thirty."

Chapter 21

Fin closed his window and looked unsteadily at Eugal, "Where's dessert?"

"It's at my estate. I will send my servers to retrieve it now," Eugal said with a defeated voice. The dessert would be a small investment to try to win back all his losses.

"I don't think so," Brando halted the room. "We asked the innkeeper to prepare thirty meals. If the innkeeper didn't include dessert with his meals, you have no right to thrust them upon us now. Constable?"

"I have come here to witness these two men eat thirty meals, and by the look of the empty stack of plates, they have more than achieved that goal," the constable said flatly. "If dessert wasn't presented at the start of the meal, I don't see why it would be fair to include it now. My job here is done."

Fin was down to two basic stat points. At the rate he was going, he would need to use his golden stat points to upgrade strength, which he did not want to do. When Felix gave the gem back, he tucked it into his pocket and asked the servers for their names. "Thank you for serving me this evening, Patrick, William, and Maddox."

"I call trickery!" Eugal shouted and rose to his feet. "You cheated, and you know it! Constable, I demand you arrest these men until we get to the bottom of this!"

"Calm down," Brando said after taking a sip, "A deal is a deal, remember? Anyway, all this was your idea. You basically forced this meal on him. Instead of increasing the portions, you could have made them smaller so you wouldn't have lost out on so much. I still can't believe you are willing to let this animal eat all your dessert."

Eugal looked under the table in hopes of finding where Fin had been stashing the food. He then circled the table. "It's not possible for one man to eat that much. I think these two are agents of the dark underlord!"

Fin stood and leveled his glare at the pudgy merchant. "I don't know what backwoods village you're from, but in the backwoods village I'm from, those are fighting words."

"Gentlemen, I think we should call it a night." The constable's voice was calm but stern. "Eugal, let me escort you home."

"I'll see you again." Eugal's voice dripped with venom. "When I do, you better watch your back!"

After the two men left, Brando slapped Fin on the shoulder, finding him much sturdier than expected. "That was amazing! I can't believe we did it!"

"All thanks to you and those last two ales," Fin laughed. "One day, they'll sing songs about those last two brews."

"Hold on, I think I got something," Brando said, looking concentrated. Finally, he nodded and sang out a verse, "The trick to a tap is Fin at your back, to drink all the ale with a mug in his hando." He stopped singing and said, "And so on. I set it up to rhyme with my name."

"I think you're onto something," Fin found the innkeeper cleaning up and asked, "You got that, Felix?"

"I'll start working on it forthwith," the innkeeper replied. "I think the song should be about the bottomless abyss you carry around in your stomach. At least, that's the tale I'm going to tell. And I will be telling that tale for as long as I live. I stood there watching the whole time and still don't believe it."

"Don't forget to mention how Brando heroically polished off the last two mugs," Fin added, "oh, you might want to mention the most beautiful, poetic, and heart-filled prayers to Frome you've ever heard."

"You're supposed to pray to Frome?" Brando asked. "I thought prayers were more of an inspirational thing."

"I felt inspired," Felix said, holding a bread plate and a fruit bowl. "I've never heard anything like it before, and it worked!"

"Felix, do you mind if we take some of that bread and fruit with us tomorrow?" Fin asked. "We're going to need provisions for our journey, and I don't think your mercer is too keen to trade with us anymore."

"As far as I'm concerned, you can take all of it," Felix answered, waving a hand over the bread, fruit, and cheese. "How many days' worth do you need?"

"We're trying to find the dwarves," Brando stated, "or Lokardale."

"I've never heard of Lokardale, but I'm sure there's plenty of dwarves in either Clive Rae or Brax Fort. Clive Rae is about a day of travel, so that's probably your best bet. Unless you plan on taking a significant journey to the East?"

"By the looks of Heidle's map, we shouldn't need to go too far in that direction," Brando stated. "Since Clive Rae is so close, maybe we should see if anybody there has any information."

The innkeeper gave them similar directions to the ones from earlier that day. Then he wished them a good night as they climbed the stairs to their beds.

The next morning Fin woke up, stowed his two favorite gems to sleep with, and tucked away his favorite rock. His muscles seemed more relaxed than they did the night before, which he attributed to his Treasured Sleep ability. He checked his status page to see how he had progressed.

Level: 5 Class: Warrior

Path: Blood, Treasure, Strength, Power, Precarious Blessing.

Strength: -10	Intelligence: 4
Dexterity: -8	Wisdom: 7
Constitution: -5	Charisma: 4
Basic stat points: 2	
Gold stat points: 8	
Ability points: 1	

Passive Abilities: Pain Resist, Treasured Sleep, Shroud Control, Discern Magic, Earth Resistance - Locked, Discern Earth - Locked, Hydro Lung - Locked, Dark Sight - Locked.

He had forgotten about the Hydro Lung quest he completed for the water affinity. The idea of being able to breathe underwater was exciting, but he didn't like the thought of growing gills. He would need to ask around to find out if water dragons had gills and consider holding off on committing to an affinity until he was certain that was the one he wanted to choose.

The Discern Magic ability he unlocked at level five was interesting. If it was a passive ability, he should be able to see magic now. He looked around the room and didn't notice anything. He imagined magic looking like vibrant colors that moved around like smoke from a fire. When he was dressed and ready, he took his belongings and went to find that colorful smoke.

When he walked downstairs, he saw Brando drinking a steaming cup. Wondering if it was a magic potion or just hot, he ordered one for himself. He sat down and greeted Brando, "Good Morning."

"Almost," Brando replied, blowing on his drink. "Felix says that this is his secret family recipe and that it's supposed to cure hangovers."

"It tastes awful, but it works like magic," Felix said, mixing herbs into a cup of hot water.

"So, it's magic?!" Fin asked excitedly.

Brando flinched at the sound of Fin's outburst. "Not so loud."

"No, it's not magic." Felix waved the idea away with his hands. "Mostly just herbs, salt, a little lemon, and butter. It'll put lead in your paint."

"Oh," Fin regretted ordering the drink before asking what was in it. "Are you going to be ready to go soon?"

"If you left now, you should arrive before nightfall," the innkeeper set a steaming cup in front of Fin. "I've packed the fruit and bread you've asked for. I even added a couple of water skins."

Fin reached out his hand. "Thanks for all your help, Felix."

"Don't mention it," the innkeeper said, taking his hand and firmly gripping it. "Here, I'll help load your horses."

After they were finished, Fin removed the bundle of procured weapons and handed them over. "On our way here, two men attacked us because they thought we were bad people. We managed to get the upper hand and took their weapons so they wouldn't attack us. Can you hold on to these and return them if they ever come back?" Fin described what they looked like and what they were wearing.

"I think I can do that," the innkeeper said, taking the pack. "I don't care what Eugal says about you. You two are as decent as they come, and you're always welcome at my inn."

"We might not be able to find your inn if you don't put a sign up," Fin said, only half joking. "What's the name of it?"

"The Village Inn," Felix said proudly.

"No offense, but you might consider naming it something more eye-catching. My family farm is called, The Dragon's Throne Farm," Fin explained, "but I suppose 'The Village Inn' is better than nothing."

When Brando had finished both his and Fin's tea, they mounted their horses and moved South. When they reached the fork in the road, they took a right and raced the sun to Clive Rae.

The mundane motions of moving across unremarkable terrain lulled both of them into introspection. The sounds of Fin grunting and slapping his forehead broke Brando out of his thoughtful state, and he asked what it was.

"I've been so excited to use my Magic Sense ability that I didn't think to just create it myself," Fin said excitedly. "I'm going to run through everything I have and see what it looks like."

He held out his hands and mentally channeled Crushing Grip. A colorless light materialized in his arms and shot toward his fingers. He could see a strand of light in each arm rise and dive into uniformly arching waves. At his hands, the strand broke off into five smaller strands that ended at his fingertips. He canceled the ability, and the light faded.

"Anything?" Brando asked, riding next to him.

When Fin explained what he saw, Brando asked if it looked like lightning.

"Kind of," Fin said. "Lightning is shaped more randomly, and it thins out the farther down it goes. What I'm doing looks more like the trace a fish would make swimming up and down. Hang on, I'm going to put some gems in my inventory."

Fin pulled out his sack of gems and took one out. Holding the gem in his hand, he activated Lesser Stow. A small tendril of power sprung out towards the gem. It retreated just as quickly, snapping the gem out of existence. Having a full inventory already, Fin was surprised when one of his gems didn't dislodge. He pulled his inventory up and noticed there were still only two boxes, but one of them had two gems inside.

"I think my inventory got bigger," Fin said, looking at the invisible window.

"How big?" Brando asked.

"Let's find out." Fin stowed one gem after the other, watching as tendrils of power snapped the rocks out of his hand. When all the gems were stowed, he noticed that fifteen of them were neatly displayed in the inventory slot that included the large gem, and ten gems were stowed in the blue topaz slot. "I think it's up to thirty-five. There's only one way to tell. Can you give me six copper coins?"

Brando carefully set down his apple and produced six copper coins. Riding closer to Fin, he handed them over.

Fin tried to stow all of them at once, but only two disappeared. When he stowed the sixth coin, the large gemstone popped into his hand. "It must have something to do with my increase of strength."

"What, like five or six per level?" Brando asked.

"I don't think so," Fin said after doing some quick calculations. "It doesn't really make sense. If it was five per level, then it would be at around forty items. If it was four per level, then I would be at thirty-four. No other number really makes sense."

"What if it's increasing, like one, two, four, eight, and so on?" Brando conjectured before trying to add it all up.

They both silently added numbers to themselves while the horses trotted forward. Finally, Brando shook his head. "It's not adding up."

"I have an idea," Fin finally said. "We take into consideration that before I gained eight points of strength, I could stow two items. Now I can stow thirty-five. When I upgrade my strength again, we'll see what it is and go from there. I still have an ability point."

"Going for the nails?" Brando asked, trying to re-secure his money.

"I could spend it on a wing ability, but since I don't have wings, it might be risky," Fin reasoned.

"Just get the nails. You've been talking about it non-stop," Brando said. "I say you just do it and get it over with already."

"I've been talking about it this whole time?" Fin asked ironically. "You've been talking about it this whole time. But you know what? I'm just going to do it so I don't have to hear about it anymore."

"It's your best option," Brando declared. "Anyway, if you're going to stand a chance to rip the heart out of someone's chest, you'll need it."

"Just because I have a quest for that doesn't mean I have to do it, but fine. I'll upgrade the nails." Fin selected his ability point and mentally attributed it to Strengthened Talons. The ability disappeared from his list, and he felt a tingling in his fingertips.

He channeled the ability and saw a thick, colorless glow form around his fingers, forming sharp tips at the ends of his fingers. He couldn't feel the power until he touched his fingers together, creating a sharp clicking sound.

"This is cool," Fin said, holding his fingers up in the air. "It's like I'm wearing finger gloves that make my fingers pointy."

"Are you sure?" Brando asked, looking at Fin's bare fingers. "It just looks like hands to me."

Fin clicked his fingers together loudly, "Can you hear that?"

"Can I hear you slap your fingers around like a bunch of sausages? Yes, I can hear that." Brando said with a grin. "Why do you ask?"

Fin got off his saddle and then stabbed his fingers into the dirt. They passed through the packed earth like a fork through bread dough. "I think this was a good choice."

When the sun began setting, and it was finally out of their eyes, they saw a black outline of the city against a dark orange sky. Not wanting to run out of daylight, they charged their horses forward until they arrived at last at the gates of Clive Rae.

Two guardsmen halted them at the gate and asked what their business was. Once they were satisfied with the jumble of answers they received, one of the guards held up a hand, "That'll be two copper per person. The money goes towards keeping the street lamps lit for you latecomers. Don't need you running into things and breaking stuff this late in the evening."

Fin held up a hand to tell Brando, "I'll take care of this," and pulled out four coins from an otherwise empty leather pouch. He handed it to the guards and asked where they could find a good inn.

"If you go straight down this road and take your second left, you'll find yourself at the Hornblower. Good place, decent prices, and soft beds. There are others, but I wouldn't go near them with a ten-foot polearm."

Fin tossed the guard a coin and thanked him.

As quickly as he caught it, he tucked it away, "Thanks, but we aren't allowed to accept tips; we're on official duty."

Noticing that the guard made no effort to return the coin, Fin smiled and led the way into town.

Chapter 22

Square buildings stood shoulder to shoulder with other taller or shorter square buildings. A single torch placed at each intersection gave the impression that the roads' grid was also square, but it was getting harder to see with each passing second. When they turned left down the second street, the area around the spaced-out torches showed the only visible sight.

They trotted along slowly, looking for the Hornblower in the dark. The signs in front of shops, or what they thought were signs, proved impossible to read. After fifteen minutes at a slow pace, they heard muted noises from ahead.

"Sounds like there might be a tavern ahead. Let's get directions from there," Brando suggested.

"You need directions?" An unexpected voice asked from the dark.

"No, we're fine," Brando assured the invisible voice. "Just enjoying a nice quiet stroll."

"I think he thinks you're some kind of rogue," Another voice said with a laugh.

Laughter from someone else joined in. "As far as your wife's concerned, you are."

"Calm down, you lot. We're the city watch. Come into the light, and we'll point you in the right direction." The second voice said before a man wearing a plated uniform stepped into the lantern at the next intersection. A second man followed close behind.

Brando took a deep breath to try to get his heart rate under control. In his experience, strangers looking to make introductions when it was too dark to see never turned out well. After a few calming breaths, he stepped into the light to join the men. When Fin pulled up next to him, he said, "We're looking for the Hornblower."

"Then you're going the right direction, just one more block down." The watchmen said, pointing in the direction they were headed. "It's the door on your right just before the next intersection."

Before they reached the next intersection, two young men ran outside with lanterns. "You staying at the inn, sir? Do you want us to stable your horses?" One of them asked.

"Uh, maybe. Fin, if you want to talk to the innkeeper, I can wait with the horses," Brando suggested, glancing dubiously at the potential horse thieves.

Fin dismounted his horse and made for the door.

"Here, take this, sir," one of the boys spoke, holding out a wooden coin. "It has your number on it."

Fin accepted the token and walked inside. Candles and lanterns lined the tables casting pearls of light dancing off puddles of spilled drinks. Groups of people huddled or lounged around, adding low voices to the chorus of low conversations.

"What can I do for you, young master?" A large man with a beard as round as his body asked from behind the counter.

"My companion and I are looking to stay for the night, maybe longer," Fin said after stepping around two people having a conversation in the middle of the walkway. "He's outside with the horses."

"It's twenty a night per person." the innkeeper gestured for the door. "If that works for you, my boys can take care of your horses and bring your bags to your room."

Realizing that the price of this inn was beyond their budget, Fin hesitated. "I don't think we have that kind of money tonight. We have some business in town tomorrow. Would it be okay to pay you after?"

"Most of the people that stay here are in town for business, with similar circumstances," the innkeeper assured him. "In the worst-case scenario, I'm also a horse merchant. With this," he held up the wooden chip, "You would be able to stay a month or so, depending on how much you drink. We can square up the costs whenever your business is concluded."

Fin thanked the man and went outside to tell Brando.

"Alright, let's do it," Brando handed the reins of his horse to the young man. "Let me grab my things."

"We can take your bags to your room, sir," One of the boys said, handing him a wooden chip. "This has your number on it."

After they got their room keys, Fin pointed towards a dwarf in the back of the common room. He was sitting by himself. "We should ask him where the dwarven city is."

"The dwarves might be secretive about their city. It might be safer to ask about Lokardale." Brando held up his hand. "If you buy him a round, leave me out of it. I'm never drinking again."

"Excuse me," Fin approached the dwarf. "We were given directions that we can't make heads or tails of. Do you know where Lokardale is?"

The dwarf frowned and then looked up at the stranger who so rudely interrupted his thoughts. "The oldest joke in the book, and you can't even tell it right. You twicelings don't have a humorous bone in your body."

"Uh, what?" Brando asked. With a more mellow accent than Heidle, he could comprehend what the dwarf was saying significantly easier. He just couldn't understand why he said it.

"The joke goes, have you seen Lokardale?" The dwarf shifted his eyes back and forth between the two men.

"That's what we're trying to find out," Fin stated, confused.

"You're lokarn at it! Hahaha!" The dwarf slapped his knee.

"I don't get it," Brando admitted. "You're lokarn at it?"

The dwarf sighed and then pointed to the chairs adjacent to his. "Please, have a seat." He then raised his hand and motioned for the bartender to bring a round for the table on the two men. "When the dwarves discovered this town, we named it Lokardale, but when the humans arrived, they decided to rename it. Hence the joke, a dwarf and a human walk into a tavern. The barman asks what they're having. The human says, 'I'll have the Clive Rae.' When the dwarf asks what that is, the barman turns and says, 'It's your town's new name!' There's more versions of the joke, but you get the point."

"So, this is Lokardale?" Fin pointed in a circle. "All of this."

"That's right," The dwarf said, taking three new mugs of ale from the innkeeper and distributing them out. "What brings you to town?"

"Have you heard of a dwarf named Heidle the Hammer?" Brando asked.

"Heidle the Hammer, you say?" The dwarf asked more to see if the name would jog his memory. "I can't say that we've ever met. Why?"

Brando set his untouched mug in front of the dwarf. "It's a long story; you're going to need this."

The two began telling their story, switching back and forth between speakers. Fin described the fake soldiers that picked him up from his house, the goblin slave camp, and the map Heidle had shown them. Brando talked about their escape and their run-in with their previous captors. They did not talk about Fin's abilities.

When they were finished with their story, the dwarf leaned back in his chair. "That is quite the tale indeed. I believe that the dwarves would be more than happy to secure such a mine. Especially if it meant saving one of our own. May I see one of these gems?"

Fin reached his hand into the leather pouch and unstowed one of his gems.

The dwarf reached out and took it. "Very nice. My name is Kaper, by the way. I want to see you succeed in rescuing this Heidle the Hammer. I'll help with what I can in my limited capacity. Where are you planning on selling the gems?"

"We didn't have a specific place in mind," Brando admitted just as the innkeeper set another mug in front of him. "Do you have any recommendations?"

Kaper returned the gem and offered names and directions to three precious stone merchants. "It's better if you get several quotes, but sometimes merchants will offer you less for leaving and then coming back. They can be temperamental."

When Kaper was finished explaining what prices they should expect, he gave one last recommendation, "If I don't see you before you leave, you have to try the zim zamaroni."

"What's that?" Brando asked.

Kaper slapped his knee and bellowed, "It's your town's new name!"

Chapter 23

On the following day, the sun had vanished behind a thick layer of midafternoon clouds before Fin and Brando set out to explore the streets of the city with two names.

"Eat, drink, sleep, stay. Buy clothes, oil your beard, drink to my health, Lokardale." Brando said to himself as he explored the sights.

"What did you say?" Fin asked, walking beside him.

"It's what Heidle said. Eat, drink, sleep, stay. Buy clothes, oil your beard, drink to my health, Lokardale." Brando repeated the words like a chant. "It's like the longer we're out of the goblin camp, the more I forget how important things were to us back there. I mean, when Heidle told us to eat the apple pie at the village, I felt like there was nothing more important I could do in my life than eat that apple pie. Now that we're here, I think we should do everything in our power to buy clothes, oil our beards, and drink to Heidle's health."

"Gems and then clothes?" Fin asked.

"Gems, bath house, and then clothes." Brando amended. "I also might get a pipe. Who knows?"

"I bet a copper coin I can guess where you got your boots!" A gruff voice from a timeworn man announced as he approached them.

Brando looked at Fin and then back at the man. "I bet you can't."

"You got your boots on Richman Road!" The man bellowed his answer in triumph.

Fin and Brando shared a similar look of confusion. Finally, the man pointed at a road sign that read Richman Rd.

Brando's honor led him to instinctively pull out a coin, but then he hesitated and then pulled out another. The play on words barely qualified the man for a win, but another play on words would even the odds. "Double or nothing. I bet you can't guess where you'll pick these coins up from."

The man knew Brando was up to something; he just didn't know what that something was. "Uh, Richman Road?" he guessed the obvious answer.

"I guess we'll see," Brando threw the coins up and behind him as hard as he could. The sound of scrambling legs preceded the clinking of copper coins.

"Double or nothing, huh?" Fin asked offhandedly.

"The guy was being intentionally deceptive," Brando said with a shrug. "At least this way, I feel better about losing on a technicality. If he would have guessed where you actually got your boots, I was prepared to give him everything I got."

"Come and find what secrets the future holds," a woman with bandages over her eyes said from the side of the road. "The cards show a secret passage to treasures unknown."

"I don't know how she's supposed to see the cards with her eyes covered like that," Brando blurted out.

"I am blind, not deaf, you bonnet-wearing bastard," the woman said, pointing directly at Brando.

"If you're so blind, how did you know I was wearing a bonnet?" Brando chimed back, winning a look of pure awe from Fin.

"You're on a roll today." Fin shook his head in wonderment. "We should hire a bard to follow you around and play a tune whenever you piss someone off."

"They would be playing nonstop." Brando jested. "Where did he say this gem dealer was again?"

Fin pointed at a statue of who could only be assumed to be Clive Rae himself. They walked beyond the statue, following Kaper's instructions. When they found what they were looking for, they headed to the storefront that matched Kaper's description.

A yellow awning protected two large men from the overcast sky. Fin and Brando cautiously moved past and entered the door between them. Glass cases displaying jewelry, gemstones, and ornamental knives surrounded them. Walking sticks with animal heads featuring colorful and glittering eyes peered disdainfully at the other accoutrements of status. Fin noticed another large man sitting unobtrusively in the back corner.

"Good afternoon," a woman with a voice dripping in extravagance greeted them. "What can I help you find today?"

"Hello, we have some raw gems that we might be interested in selling," Brando told the woman, prompting Fin to start the unstowing process.

The woman held out her hand. "In that case, I might be interested in seeing them. My name is Cynthia."

Fin offered his name and the pouch of gems. Brando quickly offered his.

Cynthia tisked at the sight of the leather pouch earning a self-conscious feeling from Fin. She unrolled a black, velvet-lined mat and carefully poured twenty-three gems. "Decently sized, varying tones, and most appear to have a nice clarity. May I assume these are all topaz?"

"Yeah, good eye." Fin complimented.

"I'll have to do an inspection before I can quote you a price, but I am confident that both of us are going to walk away satisfied with this transaction." Cynthia picked up and admired the largest of the gems. "I'll have to run some tests."

"You're not going to just throw these gems at the ground, are you?" Brando asked, pensive. "I'll tell you right now they are real."

Cynthia covered her mouth and let out a laugh. "Please, I wouldn't do anything so barbaric. Mostly I just need to check them for quality which requires looking at each of them very closely. It shouldn't take too long. I might need to verify a couple of them. For all you know, some of them could be quartz or something else entirely."

Brando pointed his thumb over his shoulder. "He can identify any gem, so we know we're good on that front. But, by all means, do what you need to."

"Oh yeah? You can identify any gem, huh?" Cynthia reached under the counter and brought out two red gems. "Which one of these is real?"

Fin took them in his hand and stowed them into his inventory. Each of them read "Cut Glass Marble." Fin unstowed the fake gems and set them on the countertop. "They're both fake."

Brando picked one of them up to try to see if he could tell. He couldn't.

"Okay, then what's this?" Cynthia set down a black stone.

Fin picked it up, seemingly held it in his hand, and then set it back down. "Onyx."

Cynthia walked to the back of the store and quickly opened and shut a drawer. When she returned, she set another black stone on the counter.

Fin picked it up and then set it back down. "Jet."

Cynthia set one precious stone after another in front of Fin, and he accurately named each of them.

Finally, she set two nearly identical clear gems in front of him. "Okay, try these two."

Fin picked them up, under the watchful glare of her security guard, and then set them back down. "Diamond and sapphire, though I would have never guessed it was a sapphire just by looking at it."

A look of pure astonishment passed over Cynthia's face as a notification appeared.

Ignoring the jewelry woman's high praise and complex description of white sapphires, Fin pulled up his notification.

Path Quest Complete: Attract a potential mate. +2 path quest revealed.

Sovereign Quest: Battle your potential mate for ascendancy. +2 levels, +4 gold stat points, +1 ability point. Forfeit all Patriarch Quests.

Patriarch Quest: Spread your seed throughout the land and battle your offspring for dominance. +4 levels, +8 gold stat points, +2 ability points. Upgrade Sovereign Quests to Patriarch Quests.

Upon seeing the words, 'attract a potential mate,' he blushed and raised his window out of sight. There were too many words to read, and he had already missed half of the woman's conversation. He started listening, trying to catch up.

"...And I've seen them in all different colors, but it's hard to tell someone, 'Yeah, this might look like an aquamarine, but it's really just a cornflower-blue sapphire.' You know?"

Fin nodded his head like he was listening intently the whole time. "I have this blue topaz that you wouldn't expect to see from a place that mostly has yellow and orange ones."

"May I see it?" Cynthia asked while running her fingers through her hair.

Fin reached into his pocket, unstowed the blue topaz, and held it in front of him. "I don't really want to sell it because I feel like it's important."

Cynthia reached out and took the gem, hand lingering on Fin's for a half measure longer than necessary. "I completely understand! Sometimes, when I come across a gem, I fall deeply in love with it and can't bring myself around to selling it. I'm a hopeless romantic that way. If you want, I can show you my private collection sometime. Just us, of course."

"Yeah, maybe we should do that. I'll let you know when I have some time," Fin felt the awkwardness of knowing she was attracted to him based on his quest completion. Fortunately, the quests only tended to pop off a single time, and he wouldn't have to worry about it again. "What do you think?"

"Are you sure this is a topaz?" Cynthia asked, looking closely at the gem. "I hate to sound like a hypocrite, but this looks more like an aquamarine."

Brando was looking at the assortment of jeweled rings and bracelets when he noticed the tone of flirtation in the woman's voice. Fin must have really impressed her with his ability. She was leaning across the counter and looking up at him with feral eyes. If there wasn't someone else in the room beside him, he would have left for a while and returned after the two of them had sorted through their feelings.

He tried to imagine if they were a good match or not. She was a little older, sure, but she was beautiful by anyone's standards. More than enough to overlook the age difference. The problem was she reminded him of his first wife. The two had a lot of similarities. If this woman was anything like his first wife, Fin was in for some serious trouble. It would be something he would have to learn on his own. Who knows? Maybe they would work out after all. He felt like it wasn't his place to worry about it.

Brando walked over to the walking sticks and picked up the one that looked like a snake, two red gems for eyes. He marveled at the craftsmanship that went into it. He tried it out and walked back and forth with the assistance of the viper staff, tapping his progress across the stone floor. Deciding he wouldn't like carrying around a stick everywhere, even one as interesting as a snake-headed staff. He gently put it back and listened for any cues that he should leave for a while.

"This one has several small bubbles around the edges, which is fine. Those will disappear through the cutting process. This next one seems big, but with its odd shape, a lot of it will have to be taken off." Cynthia spoke excitedly, moving from one gem to the next.

"If you two want me to take off for a while, It's no problem," Brando suggested. He wasn't sure what they were talking about anyway.

"I'm almost done pricing your gems," Cynthia said, dropping all pretenses from her voice. "Hang on, okay?"

Brando had looked at every item in the store twice before Cynthia was finished pricing the gems. She had gone off on tangents about how well she could cook and made off-handed comments about how lonely she's been since her husband left her, but she diligently sorted through all twenty-three gems and came up with a price.

"Five gold, two silver, and ten copper coins for everything," Cynthia said, placing the final gem on the black velvet mat.

"We'll take it," Brando said before Fin could ruin his chances with her by bartering.

At Fin's prompting, Cynthia replaced a gold coin with ten silver coins and added them to the two separate piles. She slid a stack of coins toward each of the men.

When Fin was about to put his coins into Heidle's leather pouch, she stopped him by placing a hand on top of his. She then walked over to a display case and returned with a new coin purse. Taking Fin's money, she tucked the coins inside and handed Fin the pouch.

Fin looked at it. It was a soft leather with a golden embroidered eagle across the side. The drawstring was a brown braided rope with interwoven silver strands. Inside of the pouch was lined with red fur. "Thank you, this is really nice."

"Stop by again soon," Cynthia said before the two left. "I'll try to get some more gems for you to identify. We could make a date out of it."

Chapter 24

"I think she likes you," Brando said when they were far enough from the shop. "I mean, she didn't give me a new money pouch, and she kept fluttering her eyelashes at you. You noticed, right?"

Fin looked around to see if anyone was listening. "Oh, I noticed. I completed a quest there."

"What? Like identifying all of Cynthia's gems for free?" Brando asked with an accusatory look. "I'm pretty sure you saved her a week's worth of work in there."

"No, I mean, it said that she was attracted to me," Fin stated, embarrassed. "It felt like I knew something I wasn't supposed to. Especially when she started going on about how she could tell how good of a kisser someone is based on their handshake."

"She said that?!" Brando exclaimed and then held out his hand. "Try it on me."

Fin recoiled from Brando's outstretched hand. "Get that thing away from me. I'm not shaking your hand, Brando!"

Brando laughed and lowered his hand. "Your loss. What did the quest say?"

Fin read his quest notifications out loud. "Weird, right?"

"Battle your potential mate for ascendancy? Dragons must have had some strange courting rituals." Brando deepened his voice and mimicked a stern father, "What are your intentions with my daughter?" He pitched his tone higher and said, "Well, sir, I really like her. I know it's soon, but one day I would really like to kick her ass." He mimicked the father again, "You seem to be a decent dragon, so when it's time, watch out for her left hook."

"This quest seems familiar. I think this is the one my father told me about!" Fin exclaimed. "Except, he only mentioned having to battle his offspring. He never mentioned anything about sowing his wild oats everywhere."

"It's probably best if you don't mention that one to your mom right away," Brando suggested. "At least not until you first straighten out the story with your father. Which one are you going to choose?"

Fin looked at Brando incredulously. "None of them. I'm not going to fight the girl I like, and I'm not interested in planting a family forest."

"But you would fight a girl you don't like?" Brando asked, glaring at Fin with mock disappointment.

"I didn't say that." Fin protested.

"Mm-hmm." Brando crossed his arms.

"Anyway, don't we have things to do?" Fin changed the subject.

"I mean, we could stick to the plan, but if you're more interested in challenging Cynthia to a duel, it's up to you," Brando said before lifting his hands to thwart any potential attack. "Okay, okay, let's go find a bathhouse. You can pick a fight with Cynthia later."

When they found a bathhouse, they were each given a white bathrobe and a brief rundown of the establishment's rules. They were offered a wide variety of soaps, scrubs, and creams for purchase which they each splurged on. The attendant asked if they had any questions before he left.

"Do you have beard oil for sale?" Brando asked, instinctively running a hand through his facial hair.

"Yes," the attendant answered. "We have an assortment of oils for sale after you are finished with the baths. If the oil gets in the water, it's nothing but bad news, so we don't offer it until the end. The hot spring that supplies the water would wash it away eventually, but if everybody oiled their beards in there, well, they would get out looking like a well-oiled pig. No offense to the pig, of course."

After washing himself in the private but musty-smelling stall, Fin found himself in a rather awkward predicament. The bath robes provided by the establishment covered enough for the bare minimum amount of comfort. However, the public part of the public bath loomed just ahead, and he didn't quite know how he felt about disrobing in front of everyone. As far as he could tell, no one in the public bath seemed concerned. If becoming culturally diverse meant soaking in a hot spring bath with a bunch of other naked men, then so be it. He gritted his teeth and pressed forward.

Before him, a circuit of water bubbled up from a square bath that could fit seven people uncomfortably. He could tell by the steam that the smaller bath was significantly hotter. From there, the water ran in a trench to a larger bath that could fit around twenty people. He couldn't tell where the free-flowing water went from there, but he assumed there was a path somewhere inside the pool.

He spotted Brando, who was soaking in the larger bath, talking to an old man. Sounds of their conversation echoed a thousand ways inside the large stone chamber, disguising their words behind a rich texture of tones. He walked past them, quickly doffing his robe and getting into the smaller bath. Mostly because no one else was in there.

"You sure the water isn't too hot in there?" Brando asked with words nearly indistinguishable. "The man said that the water is running a little hot today, and if we didn't want to 'Boil our eggs,' we would be safer in here."

Fin started to notice a tingling sensation on his skin. It was almost like the tingling he felt when the ants bit his legs. Deciding not to let his pain resistance trick him into melting his skin off, he quickly exited the smaller pool. Not wanting to stand around naked, he jumped into the larger one.

"Hey, take it easy," Brando admonished. "No jumping in. If it's not a rule, it's at least a common courtesy."

"Sorry," Fin said, lowering his body until only his head was exposed.

"Glad you could join us," The old man said, wiping the splashed water out of his eyes. He had long white hair that he kept neatly tied behind his head. He had matching hair covering his chest that moved around in Fin's wake. "I accidentally got into the hot side once. Down to my knees, anyway. Nearly jumped in here myself to cool off."

"Fin, this is an actual priest of Frome," Brando lifted his hands out of the water to gesture towards the man. "While you've been taking your sweet time getting out here, we've been discussing the ethical dilemmas of posing as an official of Frome. He said that the dirt in my fingernails makes me a priest already!"

"I said no such thing," the old man stated. "I was alluding to the fact that Frome uses everyone for his purposes, not unlike the refuse in a compost pile. So technically, you don't have to pretend to be his servant when you are already serving in one capacity or another. I just pointed out the dirt in your nails so you wouldn't forget to clean them."

"I might have a question, too," Fin found a seat along the ledge of the pool. "Uh, how should I address you?"

"You may call me Your Holy Eminence," the old man said with a serious look before breaking into a smile. "Just a little joke. My name is Gerome."

Fin laughed and continued, "My question is about dragons. Let's say I grew these potatoes that somehow absorbed dragon magic, and it gave me dragon powers. I know that Frome battled a dragon once, so does that mean Frome wouldn't like me?"

"Out of all the theological questions I've been asked in this bath, this one might be the most unique," Gerome chuckled to himself and then pondered out loud. "I might see where you're getting at. If you accidentally eat, let's call them, medicinal potatoes, and they make you think you are a dragon and see fairies and the like, I believe Frome would completely understand. As long as you don't abuse these potatoes. There's a time and a place, my boy."

"You are saying I should only use my powers for good and not selfish reasons?" Fin extrapolated. "And I'll stay in the good graces of Frome?"

"Precisely!" Gerome exclaimed. "Now, if you two will excuse me, it appears my mid-afternoon bath time has expired. It has been a pleasure talking with you two. Stop by the church and see me any time."

When the naked priest was thankfully out of sight, Fin turned to Brando. "Speaking of ethical dilemmas, do you think that by not telling the authorities here about the slave camp, we are holding out for selfish reasons? I mean, Heidle told us to go to the dwarves, but there are other people in there besides him. I know I would want us to tell everyone possible."

"He funded our trip," Brando said, holding the bulk of his beard in the water. "It's our duty to tell the dwarves after we oil our beards. You might want to opt for a shave, though. I couldn't grow a proper beard until my late twenties. I also think we should tell everyone who will listen. Including the king."

"And if something happens to us, we would be a lot happier that someone else knew about it," Fin said, feeling his sparse facial hair. "You don't think I should keep my facial hair when we meet the dwarves? I think it's a sign of respect or something."

"You should follow your heart on that one," Brando offered. "I know that if I looked like you, I would try to cover my face completely."

"I think Cynthia would argue otherwise," Fin parried.

Brando smiled and slapped Fin on the back, splashing water everywhere. "That she would."

When Brando's beard was properly oiled, the bath attendant offered Fin a shave. Fin took it as a sign and resigned himself into the chair.

Brando paid three extra copper coins to keep wearing the thigh-high robe and placed his dirty clothes in a bag. Appalled at the prospect of walking outside in nothing but a robe, Fin donned his old clothes. After a brief conversation with the attendant, the two had an idea about where to go next. They thanked the man, tipped him well, and left the bathhouse.

Chapter 25

A bell rang over Brando's head as he pushed open the door. Fin followed behind, taking in the large room. To say the least, it was underwhelming. Four racks of dangling sets of clothing sat in four neat rows, sparsely decorated with hanging pants, tunics, and jackets. Several boxed-in shelves held more garments, but other than that, the place was empty.

Fin looked at Brando in a way that asked, "Are you sure we are in the right place?" when a voice startled both of their attention from each other.

"Hello, and welcome to Kris and Bert Apparel," A woman standing in the center of the barren shop greeted. She was elderly with a slight hunch to her stance.

A man holding a pair of large scissors walked out, and when he noticed how Brando was dressed, he led the woman reluctantly away. "Hello, my name is Bert. How can I help you two gentlemen today?"

"For starters, I need pants," Brando waved his hands over his legs. "After that, we'll probably need to find somewhere with more of a selection. We were told that this place would have everything we need."

"I suppose that poses the question, what do you need exactly?" The man tucked his scissors into one of his many pockets and gestured toward one of the four racks. "Feel free to browse our wares. If you find something with the fabric or style you like, I will be able to produce a fitting pair in no time." He cleared his throat, "Would I need to recommend some undershorts before we begin?"

Brando nodded and then pointed an accusatory finger toward Fin. "He needs some too."

Bert led them to one of the shelves that held a single style of undershorts in various colors, prints, and fabrics. When Fin and Brando selected their preferred pairs, Bert disappeared in the back and returned in a quick fashion with two neatly folded piles in his hands. One of them was a dark gray, and the other had a jaguar print.

"How much are these?" Fin asked, taking the small stack of dark gray undershorts.

After Bert ascertained they were paying separately, he pointed towards the stack Fin was holding and said, "Forty for the gray ones and a silver ten for the others."

"We'll take them," Brando said, disregarding the fact he was paying nearly triple the cost for his. After slipping a pair on under his bathrobe, he untied his drawstring to see how they looked. "If Cynthia saw me wearing these, I don't know, Fin. I might have been the one who has to fight her."

Surprisingly, Bert didn't seem affected by the comment. "I'm assuming you two are here to try your hand at the mine. If you direct yourselves to the farthest rack, we have a sturdier selection for you to choose from."

"The sturdier, the better," Brando said, walking towards the rack with his jaguar shorts peeking through his open robe. "But we've already done the mine thing. Somewhat successfully, I might add."

"You cleared the mine?" Bert asked, incredulous. "I apologize. I figured there would be celebrations, fanfare, and reckless parties in the street."

"These two cleared the mine?" The elderly woman, presumably Kris, reentered the room.

"I think there might be a misunderstanding," Fin said. "We don't know anything about a mine around here."

"It's a dwarven mine, or at least it used to be," Kris started, drinking in Brando's figure.

"I'll tell them about the mine," Bert said, handing Kris his pair of scissors. "You have things to cut in the back. The city's mine has been overrun with these creatures," Burt said, following Kris with his eyes. "The mine has been unusable for over four generations. The king made a royal proclamation that whoever clears the mine could have whatever he or she wanted."

"Is there a limit to what you can ask for?" Brando asked, holding a pair of leather pants up to him. "Also, do you have these in a bigger size?"

Bert pulled out a rope with lines on it and quickly assessed Brando's size. He wrapped the rope around Brando's waist several times and held it lengthwise down his legs. "It's funny, you should ask.

The king more than implied one could ask for his daughter's hand in marriage. He mentioned it in one of his more famous proclamations. Since then, mercenaries have flooded in from all over. Can you imagine going from mercenary to royal consort? Once word got out, the city hasn't been the same."

"How does she feel about that?" Fin asked, inspecting his own rack of clothes. "The princess."

"I am not sure. Excuse me one moment," Bert took Brando's pants and walked to the back. He returned a moment later with empty hands. "She shouldn't take long. Anyway, with the influx of travelers coming to try their hand at the mine, businesses have grown more than ever. Sometimes I wonder if we're better off if the mine isn't conquered."

Fin found some clothes he liked and gave them to Bert. Bert took some measurements and whisked them away.

Kris came out holding two pairs of pants towards Brando. "I couldn't help but notice you might fit some pants that I've embroidered. I do it for fun mostly, but I think this might suit you."

Brando took the pants and inspected them. As skilled as he was at leatherwork, the quality and detail astounded him. "This is incredible!" Brando praised, holding up the stitch work for Fin to see. "I'll take them both."

Kris curtsied and ran off into the back, avoiding eye contact.

"Do you want to check out the mine?" Brando asked before tossing Fin the pair of pants he thought he had been interested in. "There could be a princess involved. I know how much you love high-maintenance women."

"My parents tried to arrange a marriage for me back home. Well, my mother did anyway. If the king's daughter feels anything like how I felt, marrying her would not be an act of love." Fin looked at the pants Brando had tossed to him. They were a dark red fabric inlaid with a soft, cool material. "These look a little too..."

"They look perfect," Brando said, finishing Fin's thought. "I married for love twice. It doesn't work. You should marry for something more practical, like money. At least you know what's going to happen when it runs out."

"Brando, that's probably the most depressing and jaded thing I've ever heard you say." Fin looked at the pants he was holding. "Fine, I'll get the pants. You've crushed my soul into not caring anymore."

"That's the spirit," Brando said, picking up his pile of clothes. "You should probably get a matching tunic."

When they each had two sets of clothing they brought them to the counter. Bert folded the clothes and tied them off into neat, little packages.

"It comes to three silver and fifty-five for the young sir and five silver and ten for the gentleman who got my wife all excited by coming in wearing a bathrobe," Bert said cheerlessly.

"My name is Brando."

"I'm sure she will be delighted to know."

Fin pulled out his and Brando's coins and set them on the table.

When Bert returned their change, they both took their wrapped packages and walked out of the shop looking like new men.

Fin wore simple gray pants and a blue tunic. The clothes felt light and easy to move in. His matching-red outfit was wrapped in a cloth bundle neatly tied under a twine bow.

Brando wore black leather pants with a brown horse stretched out in a running pose over his pelvic girdle. He tucked his white tunic in the front, covering the tips of the horse's nose and tail.

"That was fun," Brando said, walking out into the middle of the street. "Do you want to go see if the castle is taking visitors?"

"Sure," Fin replied. "Let's go drop off our packages first."

"Just stow them away, and let's go," Brando said, offering Fin his bags.

"It doesn't work like that," Fin admitted. "I think it has to do with size, not weight. If I rolled up the undershorts into a ball, I could probably stow them. I just can't do anything with the rest."

Brando stood motionless as Fin's words sank in. Finally, he let out a sigh, "Fine. We'll go to the Hornblower first. I'm going to start considering how we can upgrade your lesser stow to a full, pack-mule stow. How did you get this one again?"

Fin explained how he wasn't quite sure how he got the ability, but it was after he slept with the gems in his hovel. Brando came up with multiple ideas on how to achieve 'pack mule status' while they walked to the Hornblower.

After dropping off their packages, the castle wasn't hard to find. They followed Castle Road until they got there.

The castle's spires stabbed through the tops of buildings like sharpened lances. When it came into view, the castle looked like delicate art carved from a broad fortress. Surrounding the castle, stone sculptures stood in junctions that connected thick metal bars protecting the royal palace in decadence.

The gardens surrounding the castle marked the first circular landscape they had seen since arriving In Clive Rae. Multiple flagstone walkways encompassed the castle on which pairs of guards marched slowly in even intervals around.

"Fin, I'm concerned," Brando said with a small voice. "I've never been to a castle before."

"And I have?" Fin's voice was equally small. "I'm a potato farmer. One of us has to take the lead on this, and I don't think that person is me."

"Okay, I have a plan," Brando said, determination overcoming his disquiet. "I'll try taking the lead, but if I give you the signal, it's your show."

"Okay, what's the signal?" Fin asked.

"I'll elbow you in the arm."

When they reached the first of what seemed like multiple checkpoints of entry, an official standing between two sturdy guards hailed them, "Mercs can only visit the first of the week."

Brando nudged Fin's arm, so he spoke, "We are not mercs. We have a pressing issue that the king will be most interested in hearing."

"If you want to report an offense, the office of the city guard is in the town square," the official replied stoically.

"This is not an offense," Fin said, speaking about how he felt his father would in this situation. "We have a pressing mission that requires his majesty's support."

"We are a diplomatic envoy coming to address delicate but pressing matters," Brando blurted out.

Fin looked at him, astonished at the lie that could probably get them both killed.

"Diplomatic envoy, you say?" the official's face didn't show a hint of surprise. "Where, may I ask, where are you a diplomatic envoy from?"

Fin looked at Brando in a way that said, "Yeah, where are we diplomats from, you giant dunce?"

"Rudford," Brando said with a straight posture.

"Ah, you'll have to forgive me," the official said, mirroring Brando's posture. "I wasn't briefed on your arrival. I am Taddus, and I can escort you in."

"Please," Brando gestured towards the locked gates.

With a nod from Taddus, the gates opened, and the two followed him through.

Chapter 26

Fences, gates, and large doors opened before Fin and Brando as Taddus led them deeper into the castle's inner sanctum. Quiet halls came to life under the sound of footsteps on cold, swept floors. Paintings of unknown nobles offered glares of judgment as they passed by. Fin and Brando knew there would be no easy escape if their lie was discovered.

Taddus ushered them into a sitting room lined with lamps and bookshelves with a table in the center. "Will you take tea?"

"Yes, please," Fin said, happy for anything to take the tension off.

"Very well, I will have someone bring it up while you wait," Taddus said before taking his leave.

Long, quiet seconds crept through the room. Neither Fin nor Brando spoke, worried their conversation would give them away. In one sense, the wait was good. Before not too long, Fin's posture relaxed, and Brando's fists unclenched as they became more acquainted with their surroundings.

The door clicked, and three servants entered the room, causing the tension to return. A young man sat down a tray holding a kettle and four cups. Next came an assortment of round dishes with lids. Behind him, a young woman set down a tower of pastries. She poured the tea as the other two left the room.

"The honey and cream are over here. Help yourselves," The woman stated, pointing at a separate tray. She looked up, taking in the two men for the first time.

"Thank you very much," Brando took the honey jar and rolled the honey dripper around.

The woman hesitated, "You two don't look like diplomats."

"We are trying to stay unnoticed," Brando said simply. "That's why we're dressed like this."

"Trying to stay unnoticed with a horse etched into the front of your pants?" The woman asked, unsatisfied with Brando's answer. "Also, diplomats are trained in high tea etiquette, but there you are, stirring your tea with the honey dripper."

Brando looked down at his hand. Then he looked at the assortment of small spoons he hadn't noticed before. He was in too deep; the only way out was forward. "I find it adds the most unique flavor."

"Finally, diplomats are trained to stand when a princess enters the room," The woman said, bright green eyes slightly squinted. "But here I am standing, and there you are sitting."

The woman was not dressed like a servant. She wore a simple but elegant white dress. Braids of golden hair cascaded gently to either side of her slender neck. Her green eyes shot mixed feelings of wonder and terror down their spines. The two men bolted to their feet, muttered a jumble of apologies and excuses, and bowed multiple times.

"I am going to give you one chance to speak," the princess said, leveling her gaze at the two men. "I caution you to be honest with me, or I will have you dragged out of here wishing we hadn't met. Let's start with you." she pointed at Fin. Her other hand rested firmly on the door handle. "Who are you, and why are you standing in my home under false pretenses?"

The words spilled out of Fin like water through a broken dam. He told her their names and where they met and described the slave camp. The princess stood there and stared at them.

"That's why we want to tell the king," Brando filled in the gaps. "We are heading down to the dwarven city or fortress or whatever it is. We just stopped here to sell our gems and resupply. We want only to inform you so we can be on our way without the guilt of all those currently enslaved by a bunch of money-hungry goblins. One of the prisoners there made us promise to tell his people, and that's why we are seeking out the dwarves."

"Do you have one of these gems?" The princess asked, loosening her grip on the door handle.

"I have two," Fin said, reaching into the collar of his tunic to unstow the largest gem. He set it on the table.

The princess picked it up and looked at it, unimpressed. "If this is a gem, it's the ugliest I've ever seen. It just looks like a see-through rock."

"That's how all gems look like before they are refined," Brando said, trying not to sound disparaging.

"Guards!" The princess yelled, startling Fin and Brando.

The doors immediately slammed open, and five guards surrounded the princess. They stood at the ready, weapons drawn. Fin raised his hands, and Brando placed his hands on his head.

"Your majesty?" One of the guards asked through gasps of breath.

"Who knows anything about gems?"

There was a brief pause before one of them spoke, "Sir Jeffcoat might."

"Go get him."

The guard sheathed his sword and ran out of the room. The other swords slowly adjusted themselves until they were all at a uniform height.

Minutes passed as the princess slowly turned the large gem around in her hand. She eventually grew bored of it and held it loosely to her side.

Brando was the first to drop his hands. When Fin saw that none of the guards had moved, he followed suit.

Finally, the guard reentered the room, followed by a tall, well-built man. He had thin brown hair, a well-defined jaw, and calculating eyes. He bowed to the princess, "Sir Jeffcoat at your service, Your Highness."

The princess handed him the large gem. "What can you tell me about this?"

Sir Jeffcoat took the stone and inspected it with awe. "This appears to be one of the biggest gems I've ever seen. By the light orange color, I could assume it is a topaz. A large topaz if it's real."

"Is it real?"

"I'll do a quick test," Sir Jeffcoat began saying when Brando interrupted him.

"Wait, don't drop it." Brando lurched forward, causing the guards to startle.

Before the words got out, Sir Jeffcoat dropped the gem. It landed on the stone floor with a loud crack.

The guards startled more, bringing the points of their swords to Fin and Brando's necks.

"By the elements, you are a jumpy lot. Stand down, men." Sir Jeffcoat picked the gem and inspected it. "It's real. Is there anything else I can do, highness?"

"That will be all." The princess dismissed the man.

Sir Jeffcoat bowed toward the princess and returned the gem. He gave Fin and Brando a nod and then left the room.

The princess bounced the gem in her hand while she tried to decide what to do.

"The king is-" Taddus began to announce from the open doorway when he saw the guards and their drawn weapons. "His Majesty is in the study unless there is a change of plan?"

The princess took one more look at the gem before handing it back to Fin. "We are finished here, Taddus. I will show the diplomats to the study."

Fin and Brando walked gingerly past the guards and out of the door.

They took deep, calming breaths as they followed the princess through the castle's silent corridors with all five guards in tow.

The princess stopped at a door, knocked three times, and then opened it. "Sir Finlay and Sir Brando," she announced.

"Ah, Dezi, what a pleasant surprise," The king's voice came from within. "Won't you join us?"

"I would be delighted to join you," Dezi said, glaring at the two men and entering.

Fin and Brando walked in and greeted the king with a bow.

Tapestries of jousting knights hung from stone walls. A blue and gold desk sat at the far end of the room, holding jars of ink, writing quills, and piles of neatly stacked papers.

"Thank you for seeing us on such short notice, Your Majesty," Fin said.

"Of course. How is old Sevornand doing these days?" The king asked, gesturing towards the rectangular table in the center of the room. "Please sit."

Fin stood behind the closest chair, "He is well, your majesty."

Brando stood behind a chair next to Fin.

The princess walked at an infuriatingly slow pace toward the table, causing a trickle of sweat to form on Fin's brow. She stood behind one of the chairs as if considering if she wanted to sit at all.

Fin didn't know if he should sit down because the king told them to or wait for the princess. It was one of the rules they broke that got them exposed in the first place. A casual glance at Brando showed that he was in a similar state of mental turmoil. They could tell that the king was growing impatient, waiting for them to sit down, which made matters worse.

"Dezi, will you please sit down. These men are clearly too chivalrous to sit in your company, even when directed to do so by the king," The king said, frowning at his daughter.

"Why should I care about chivalry when you offered my hand to any unchivalrous commoner with a strong enough sword?" Dezi asked, feet firmly planted on the floor behind her chair.

"You refused everyone else," The king said. "My hands are all but tied."

"I refused them because they were a bunch of crusty old men," Dezi said with a slightly raised voice. "I'm not marrying any of your old friends, and I'm not marrying the first bloodthirsty fighter who kills a bunch of mindless creatures in a cave."

"Leave us. We will talk about this later," The king said with finality. "We have honored guests with us."

"They're not honored guests," Dezi said, causing Fin's heart to stop. "I want to talk about this now. It's always 'later' with you."

The king stood and walked to the door. He opened it and stood there. The princess finally walked towards him and exited. The king shut the door with an audible click. "Will you take some tea?"

Fin and Brando politely but adamantly refused the tea.

"That's Dezi. She takes after her mother mostly." The king sat in his chair, signaling the others to sit as well. "Not the usual diplomatic welcoming, I'm afraid."

"A charming one none-the-less," Fin offered, hoping it was the right words to say.

"What news do you bring from my allies in the West?" The king asked, jumping subjects.

"Not great news, I'm afraid." Fin began. He described the slave camp and the goblins as if they were reported by multiple people. He also explained there were reports of people being abducted and taken to the slave camp.

The king lounged back and listened. When it was finished, the king asked, "Where is it?"

"South," Brando said, producing coins from his pocket and placing them on the table to represent landmarks. "If we are here, we travel a day to the East and then head South."

"You don't have to draw a dwarven map with me," The king said with a smile and then called for a servant. "We haven't been a dwarven city since my father was sitting in this chair. Which is for the best; those bearded children are the bane of my existence."

Fin froze at the insult. Brando looked astonished at the brazen comment. They hadn't met many dwarves, but the ones they had met, they really liked.

"What are those looks for?" The king looked under the table. "Is there a dwarf hiding under my table somewhere?"

A young woman entered the room and bowed.

"Bring me a map of Clive Rae," The king ordered.

The woman left and returned shortly after with a roll of parchment. She gave the map to the king, bowed, and retreated back through the door.

The king unrolled the map showing the castle in the center, the city, and acres of farmlands and grasslands around. He turned the map to Brando, "Okay, where is it?"

Fin was the first to understand the layout. He pointed to the far-right side and said, "South on this road until you reach the mountain range. Then about three days further."

The king shook his head. "I'm afraid it is completely out of my domain. You will stay for a while and sample my hospitality, won't you?"

"They are mining jewels there," Fin said, placing his large gem on the table. "Just think of all the riches you could accumulate by liberating the place."

"My main concern is clearing out my current mine," the king said, rolling up the map. "Besides, I already have a steady supply of Topaz coming to my kingdom already."

Fin was about to state that the gems he was accumulating probably came from the slave mine when Brando put his hand on his arm.

"Thank you for your time and your offer of hospitality, your majesty," Brando said respectively. "Unfortunately, we are pressed for time and will be returning forthwith."

The king stood. "It is always a pleasure receiving visitors from my allies at Rudford. I am sorry I can't be of more help. Goblins and slavery, nasty business, that."

Fin and Brando found Taddus waiting for them when they exited the room. They silently followed him when the princess flanked them in the halls. "I'll take it from here, Taddus."

Taddus bowed, and when he was out of sight, the princess said, "This way."

Fin and Brando exchanged a cagey look as they detoured through corridors they hadn't seen before.

"How did it go with my father?" The princess asked.

"He's not going to help," Brando said, speaking softly in the hall.

"Not unexpected," The princess said before coming to an unexpected stop. She looked around and then entered a dimly lit room. "Hurry."

When the door shut behind him, Fin asked, "What are we doing?"

"You're getting me out of here," she stated.

"Can't we get in trouble for that?" Brando asked, hesitant to go along with any of this crazy girl's crazy plans.

"Only if we get caught," The princess said, moving deeper into the room. "It's about the same amount of trouble as you would get in if I told everyone who you really were."

The threat hung in the air like the executioner's ax. Not for the first time that day, Fin and Brando regretted coming to the palace.

Chapter 27

"A bird cage?" Brando asked, incredulous. "Why don't you just wear a servant's outfit and walk out of here like a normal person?"

"I'm the princess; everyone knows what I look like," the princess said like she was talking to a child. "Bird cages are expected to be covered, so no one will see me inside."

"I'm sorry, uh, princess," Fin stammered. "Why don't you order the guards to just stand aside."

"My name is Dezi." The princess folded her arms. "Also, my father has ordered everyone not to let me leave. He says that all I could ever want or need is right here. If I want to spend some time alone in the gardens, I have to do it with a party of twelve."

"Won't it look weird if we are struggling under the weight of a birdcage?" Brando asked, looking down at the cage that could have been meant for a baby bear.

"I might be able to do it," Fin said, sizing up the cage. "I'm a lot stronger now."

"If we do this," Brando leveled his gaze at Dezi. "We're even, right? If you get caught running around outside of here, you won't tell them about us, right?"

"If you get me out of here, I'll act as if I've never seen you before," Dezi replied and then trailed her eyes down. "And that's saying a lot because you have a horse on the front of your pants."

"Do you have a plan once you leave?" Fin asked, somehow concerned for her.

"Yeah, I'm going to run away," Dezi stated like it was the simplest concept in the world. "I'm not going to stick around while my father controls every little aspect of my life. Any other questions?"

"Let's just do it so we can be done with it." Brando turned towards Dezi. "Do you have everything you need? Like money or a dress that won't get dirty the second we step outside?"

"I'm not a half-wit." Dezi held up a black satchel. "Everything I need is right here."

"Okay, get in," Brando demanded, pointing towards the cage, earning him a distasteful look from the princess. "Look, either you want to leave, or you don't. Being blackmailed into smuggling you out of the castle wasn't my idea."

Dezi crawled into the cage. She sat cross-legged in the center and leaned back against the thin iron bars. "Okay, pull the curtains across."

Brando drew black curtains around each side and overlapped them together. "Fin, you ready?"

Fin rocked the cage back until he could get his fingers underneath. When Brando had done the same, they counted to three and lifted it into the air.

"It's not as bad as I thought," Brando said, loosening his grip.

Fin looked around. "How do we get out of here?"

"Through the door to the right and left at the intersection. It's a straight shot from there." Dezi's voice came from inside the curtain.

The two left the room, took a right, and followed her instructions. When they took a right at the intersection, they found themselves at the base of a staircase with nowhere left to go.

"Something's wrong," Fin said, looking around. "We've reached some stairs; we didn't take any stairs to get here."

"I might have meant a right instead of a left," Dezi's voice rang out from the cage significantly louder than a whisper.

"That's it, we're going to die," Brando said, losing his nerve. "There's going to be a guard nearby, and our chatty little princess is going to start chatting it up. Then, oh no, where did my head go?"

"It's fine, Brando," Fin said, turning in a half circle. "We'll just turn around and walk straight. We'll be fine as long as our giant bird shuts her giant mouth."

"Or we can kill two birds with one stone and see if there's a balcony up these stairs," Brando said, daring the princess to talk again. When no reply came, he shook his head and continued walking.

The two kept walking until they saw familiar paintings giving them familiar looks of judgment. Finally, they reached the front doors of the castle. A doorman and a doorwoman started moving when the two came into sight, opening the path ahead. They walked outside without a word in exchange.

"Steps," Fin warned.

"I see them," Brando said, taking the stairs in rhythm with Fin.

As they approached the front gate, Taddus approached them with a greeting. "I see things went well with the king. What did he give you?"

"It's a gift from the princess, actually," Fin corrected. "It's a bird of some sort."

"May I see?" Taddus asked, approaching the cage.

"It's nocturnal," Brando quickly said. "She said only to open the curtains at night. It's one of those birds that gets all grumpy and starts killing people when things don't go its way."

"I see," Taddus said, disappointed. "Do you want me to get someone to carry that for you?"

"No, it's fine," Brando said, struggling under the cage's weight. "Just open the gates, and we'll carry on."

"Very well," Taddus said before signaling his men to open the gates. "Travel well, both of you."

"Thanks," Brando said, instinctively adding, "You too."

When the gates swung open, Fin got a notification as he carried the suspiciously heavy birdcage through the castle gates. He looked at his quest completion, bewildered.

Treasure Quest Complete: Abduct a royal princess. +1 Active Ability.

Active Ability: Greater Stow.

Quest Complete: Upgrade an ability two tier levels with one achievement. +2 ability points.

"I think I got it!" Fin exclaimed as soon as they were in the clear. "I have a better stow ability now. I think it's the best. It's called Greater Stow anyway."

"You got the pack-mule?" Brando asked, sharing in the excitement. "I thought you had to sleep in a vault for that."

"I guess all I needed was to procure a princess," Fin said, opening his screen. "I still want to try sleeping in a vault, though."

Brando nodded his head towards a perfectly despicable-looking alleyway, and the two disappeared into it. When they were certain that no one was watching, they set the cage down and quickly assisted Dezi out of it.

"I did not appreciate you making jokes about dropping me off the balcony," Dezi scolded the two while vigorously brushing the wrinkles out of her dress.

"What about when you told the king that we weren't honored guests?" Brando countered. "We are trying to free a whole community of slaves, and you were trying to destroy our lives because you were throwing a tantrum. Dropping you off a balcony was a viable option as far as I'm concerned."

"Okay, everyone, calm down," Fin demanded. "We're all alive, the princess is free, and our heads are still on all of our shoulders. How about we part ways on good terms? I'll go first. Princess, you are a beautiful person on the outside. How you made it all the way through life with that attitude of yours is truly a feat of mastery. I know that one day you'll learn how to deal with your issues instead of running from them like a child. Who wants to go next?"

Dezi's face glowed a bright red. She looked like she was eager to spit venom. She only managed to make a frustrated sound before stomping off, leaving the alley.

"I had no idea you were so good with words," Brando praised after watching Dezi disappear out of the alley. "I think we need to get you a bard."

"It's all about diplomacy." Fin shrugged and walked over to the bird cage. He placed his hand on it and said, "Are you ready to see if this works?"

"Yes!" Brando nearly shouted. "If it does, I'll never have to carry another bag!"

Fin channeled Greater Stow; nothing happened. He lifted the cage and tried again. A massive tendril of power snatched the birdcage out of sight and into his inventory. He blinked at the empty area, not believing his eyes. "I did it?"

"You did it!" Brando cheered and then joined in a celebratory jig.

They danced around, kicking their legs and pumping their fists. When they were facing the entrance of the alleyway, their victory dance came to an abrupt stop.

The princess was standing in plain sight with a wide-eyed look of bewilderment. "How did you do that?"

Brando mumbled a disappointed word under his breath and looked at Fin.

Fin snapped out of his surprise and gave the first response that came to his mind. "Do what?"

"I saw what you did," Dezi replied, walking slowly towards them. "There was a bird cage, you put your hand on it, and it disappeared. How did you do it?"

"It's a busker's trick," Brando jumped in. "It's just smoke and mirrors. We're buskers."

Dezi walked past the two men and stood where the cage was just moments ago. She looked around and stomped on the ground. There was no smoke and no mirrors, but she did not need to tell them that. She could tell by the look on their faces that there was something more to this trick than they were letting on.

"Look," Fin said, holding up his hands. "You have your secrets, and we have ours. We've only just met you today, and so far, you've done nothing but build distrust in an already rocky relationship. If there was a secret to share, you would be the last person we would trust it with."

"I feel like we got off to a bad start," Dezi said, sounding soft and genuine. "I was not very kind to you today, and I am sorry. If I felt we could start over, I would reintroduce myself and learn both of your names all over again. I don't blame you for not trusting me. After my behavior today, I would not trust me either. You are welcome to keep your secrets, and I promise not to pry. I just have one favor to ask you, and I will be out of your hair forever. Can you retrieve the satchel that was in the cage, please? That's all."

Brando looked at Fin and imperceptibly shook his head.

Fin let out a sigh, held his hand out, and unstowed the cage.

"I knew it!" Dezi's voice lost every ounce of meekness it had just moments ago. "I honestly didn't believe it the first time I saw it. Are you two wizards? I've never met a wizard before."

Brando pushed past Fin, opened the cage, and retrieved Dezi's satchel. He quickly tossed it to her. "Here you go. Have a nice life."

Fin hesitated and then restowed the birdcage. As far as he was concerned, the damage had already been done. Besides, he could probably sell the cage at a decent price.

"I've decided that I'm going to go with you," Dezi stated, taking note of the blank stares she got in return. "To the dwarven city. It's where I want to go, and since you're already going there, I will come with you."

The words "No" and "Absolutely not" shot at Dezi in unison. Statements like "One day was more than enough" and "I would rather eat a thousand fire ants" convoluted in the air.

"The thing is, Dezi," Brando tried to channel Fin's diplomacy. "You are way more trouble than you are worth. I'll put this in perspective for you. Today you told us that if we didn't tell you the truth, you would make sure we wished we had never met you. We told you the truth, yet here we are, wishing we'd never met you. The answer is no."

"You're going to get us killed," Fin said candidly. "You'll probably complain all day, tell everyone you're a princess, and get taken and sold for ransom. They won't abduct you until after they slit our throats. You've probably never saddled a horse, and I'm not going to saddle your horse; Brando probably won't."

"It's true, I won't saddle your horse," Brando cut in.

"The biggest reason I can think of for not taking you," Fin took a deep breath. "You're used to a certain level of pampering. In a few days, you're going to realize that normal people don't get treated very well out here. You are going to get homesick, and then you are going to walk back through those gates and return home."

"And if I promise not to complain or get homesick and all that, I can come, right?" Dezi asked, making her face look innocent and pleading.

"We are not having this conversation in an alleyway of all places." Brando started walking at a brisk pace toward the road. "Good luck out there, Dezi. Also, you should probably go by a different name."

Fin took one last look at the hopeless princess. Feelings of guilt and pity tried to weasel their way into his gut. He rejected the feelings and focused on the path ahead. He quickly caught up with Brando, leaving the princess in the alley.

Chapter 28

"I think I'm done for the day," Brando said, ignoring a gaudily dressed man juggling oranges. "I'm coming to find that life and death situations really take it out of me."

"I have an idea," Fin said, tossing a coin and missing the juggler's basket. "Let's go back, have a few drinks, and leave first thing in the morning. They'll probably lock the gates and shut down the place when they find out you-know-who isn't you-know-where."

"In that case, we should settle our bill at the inn."

It was late afternoon, and the inn was sparsely populated. The innkeeper sat at a table finishing a meal with his two boys. Fin and Brando gestured for him to take his time, but the innkeeper got up and concluded his meal.

"This rabbit and venison pie is really good," the innkeeper said, setting the dishes in a large wooden bucket and handing it off to one of his boys. "Are you hungry?"

No sooner were large mugs of ale placed on the table that an unwelcome shadow fell over their meals.

"You said you didn't want to talk about it in the alley, so we can talk about it here," Dezi said, taking a power stance. "How much for your services?"

Brando's face grew red. "It's not what it sounds like!" He looked at the innkeeper, who immediately started acting busy.

"Will you sit down and stop making us sound like we offer our services in an alleyway?" Brando spoke in a harsh whisper. "Also, I'm never standing for a lady ever again, so if you're waiting for me, don't."

Dezi smoothed her dress and sat in a chair across the table. "So, how much?"

"Dez-, uh, Della," Fin quickly renamed her. "Della, why ever would you think that we have services to offer? We can barely take care of ourselves."

"If you don't want to travel with me, I will just have to follow you to the dwarven city," Dezi stated and then looked around. "Is this where you two are staying?"

"Nope," Fin lied. "We are staying across town at a secret location. We just popped in for a bite."

"Innkeeper," Dezi asked, drawing the man's attention. "How much are these men paying for their rooms?"

"Forty a night, ma'am," the innkeeper answered with a smile. "Shall I prepare you a room as well?"

"Yes, please," Dezi replied sweetly.

Thump! Brando's head landed on the table. "I'll just turn myself in. Maybe we can use your dragon powers to escape before they dangle us from a rope."

"Dragon powers?" Dezi asked, raising an eyebrow. "Is that what you used to vanish the birdcage?"

"Okay, what do you want, Della?" Fin squared off. "The reason why you're escaping is because you don't want to be forced into a relationship, right? If we clear the mine really quickly, you'll have no reason to want to leave, am I right?"

"I guess," Dezi replied slowly.

Fin stood up. "Okay, I'll clear the mine really quick and be done with you." Fin sat back down. "As soon as I finish this delicious meal."

"I don't think that is quite necessary," Dezi explained. "Who's going to take me to the dwarves when you get killed in there?"

"It will be a good death," Brando said before plopping his forehead back on the table. "I don't think I have much of an appetite anymore. Fin, you can have mine."

Fin slid Brando's dish closer to himself.

Brando sat up and slid the plate back, "I'll just take a couple bites first."

When their meals were finished, and their bill was settled, Fin and Brando collected their weapons from their rooms. Upon Brando's insistence, Fin stowed all of their belongings. One by one, their bundles of clothing, weapons, saddle bags, and one very large crossbow disappeared.

"Do you feel heavier?" Brando asked, holding out a forgotten bundle of clothing.

Fin jumped a few times and moved around. "I don't think so."

He pulled up his inventory to view the items. Instead of only two rows of item slots, there were now four. Curiously, there was a single, larger item slot on the right side. None of the items ended up in that box. Instead, they were placed in one of the four rows of thirty-five slots. He figured it must be for very large items.

"This is great!" Brando exclaimed. "Too bad the princess is going to get us killed before we can enjoy it."

The two of them took one more look before setting out for the mine.

On the street, Fin turned and noticed they were being closely followed. "You should wait in your room. It'll probably be dangerous if you come with us."

"I've waited in my room long enough, thank you," The princess said, walking quickly to catch up. "Besides, I've never been to the mine."

"Probably because it's too dangerous," Fin explained. "Where is this place anyway?"

"How am I supposed to know?" Dezi asked like it was the dumbest question she had ever heard.

"Hang on, I'll ask," Brando said and then walked off to talk to the people who were around. After receiving three sets of vague directions, he had a decent idea of where to go.

"Follow me."

The three walked through the streets in silence. Dezi soaked in her surroundings, Brando mentally prepared himself, and Fin looked over his stats.

Fin had two ability points to allocate, so he blindly followed along while he looked over his options. He read Wing Attack, Wing Shield, Jowls of Strength, Strengthened Tail, Piercing Tail, and Piercing Resist. There wasn't a lot to choose from, and he didn't want to break his teeth. He selected Piercing Resist and felt his skin tighten and then return to normal. He felt the skin on his arms and neck, but it still felt normal.

"Brando, I need you to do something for me," Fin said, lifting the halo from his sight. "I need you to stab me in the arm."

"You're starting to sound as crazy as Destiny over here," Brando said, gesturing towards the princess.

"If you're trying to get out of this, all you have to do is say so, and we'll turn around."

"No, I just have this feeling like I am immune all of a sudden," Fin said, hoping Brando would get the hint. "Just stab me in the arm and see what happens."

Brando stopped. "Okay, but who knows where this knife has been? Don't blame me if you get the smirch."

Fin held out his arm, and Brando stabbed his arm just enough to break through. It came in contact, but it didn't pierce through. Brando tried again, harder, with the same outcome. Finally, Brando raised the knife high into the air and sliced it down with an aggressive strike.

Fin quickly moved his arm out of the way. "I said, 'Stab at me,' not try to cut my arm off. Anyway, I think it works."

Dezi held her hands to her mouth in shocked silence.

"Dobby, you're sworn to secrecy from this day forward," Brando quickly said, adding for good measure, "Also, you're not coming with us. So that shouldn't be a problem."

They approached an old wooden sign that read, 'Lok le Mine' and knew they were in the right place.

Tents, shanties, and carts lined the path to the miner's entrance. People shouted their wares out, but most of the calls were the same; they were weapons dealers.

Brando walked up to the first cart he saw. Knives and swords glittered in the cool sunlight. When he saw a sword he liked, he picked it up. It felt good in his hands. After a few smooth gliding swings, he asked how much it was. He then placed the sword back as gently as possible and moved to the next stall.

"Don't you already have weapons?" Dezi asked before Fin could join in the hunt. "I thought you were professionals."

"We aren't. I'm a professional farmer, and Brando works with leather," Fin admitted and then unstowed his small sword. "I took this from a goblin I killed in the mine. It's the first time I've owned a sword, as small as it is. Brando got his knife from a goblin too."

"Fine, but you only get one weapon each, and I'm not paying more than two gold per weapon," Dezi said, drawing a hard line. She would have considered going to four gold each, but she had been taught at an early age how to negotiate.

"No more than two gold each." Fin slowly nodded, trying to hide the excitement he was feeling. "I will tell Brando."

He walked at what he considered to be a casual pace. When he reached Brando, he spoke in a low voice, "Princess just offered to pay two gold for any weapon of your choice. We can only get one, so make it count."

Brando gave a wide smile and turned towards the first stall he had stopped at, "Come with me."

Brando lifted the sword he first looked at and handed it to Fin. Half of the hilt was wrapped in leather, and the lower half was bare steel, fanning out into a simple pommel. The long blade gently glided into a wide, sturdy cross-guard. There were no lavish designs, only simple, deadly steel.

"Ah, I see you've come back for the Soldure Longblade. It's a great two-handed choice for the more discerning swordsmen," An old merchant said, speaking smoothly and effortlessly. "How about you, young master? Do you see anything you like or have any questions?"

"What's the best weapon for the mine?" Fin asked, inspecting a set of daggers. They were matching, single-edged blades, a hand's length from point to hilt.

"Some say a mace, and some say a sword. The only thing they all seem to agree on is a short length and a strong blade," The old merchant said. "I hear there can be some tight quarter fighting down there."

"What kind of monsters are down there?" Brando asked, feeling concerned that his favorite sword might be too long.

"I'm not even sure myself. I've heard there are cave trolls, rock beasts, and sprites. It seems there's a whole mess of evil down there." The merchant selected a sword hanging on the wall and handed it to Fin.

The thick, double blade widened out into the cross-guard and slowly narrowed into a triangular point. The square pummel matched the square cross-guard, and the black leather grip fit perfectly into Fin's hand.

"It's a little heavy for a single-handed sword, but it won't break. And the balance is surprisingly nice. You should see the scabbard." The merchant dug around for a moment and then set a beautiful black-leather scabbard on the table. Its wide mouth was encased in a ring of metal with simple designs etched around in an unbroken line.

"How much for these?" Fin asked, worried that it would be too expensive.

"Three gold and six silver pieces," The merchant said.

"We'll do four gold for the two swords and the two matching daggers," Brando offered.

"The best I can do is four and five," The merchant said with finality. "Those are good knives."

"It's going to be difficult to split a silver between the two of us," Fin said, pointing towards Brando. "If you give it to us for four gold and four silver, we'll take them off your hands right now."

"You got yourselves a deal," The merchant smiled and reached his hand across the counter.

Brando and Fin each shook the man's hand when Brando waved Dezi over.

"She said we could only have one weapon each," Fin said out of the corner of his mouth.

Brando picked the knives up and handed them to Fin. "Quick, stow these."

Fin quickly turned, placing his hand behind his back. Brando slipped the knives into his hand, and they disappeared just as Dezi greeted them.

"I found some really great weapons just a few stalls down," Dezi announced. "They're significantly less expensive, and they come pretested."

"I wouldn't trust a used weapon with my life," The merchant spat to the side. "It's just reckless."

"We found some weapons already but thank you." Fin set four silver pieces on the counter. "It's just four gold more."

Chapter 29

Fin's sword felt good hanging from his belt. He had never owned a real sword before, aside from the one he pilfered from the goblin, but that one was more like a large knife. He rested his left hand on the pommel while he walked, feeling powerful for the first time in his life.

The sword on Brando's back irritated him. He would need to adjust the shoulder straps if he somehow managed to survive the week. He tucked his thumbs into the straps and pressed forward to the mouth of the cave.

"Torches for sale!" A thin merchant called out from just ahead. "Sweet-smelling torches! Each torch burns for over an hour! Gives a sweet-smelling smoke!"

"How much are they?" Fin asked.

"Ten coppers each."

"We'll take ten," Fin said before looking at Dezi. "Will you please pay the man?"

Dezi sighed and then dug through her satchel. She produced a silver coin and held it out. Fin took the coin and gave her as many torches as she could carry.

"Don't worry, you won't need to hold them long," Fin assured her, only carrying two torches himself.

The merchant lit one of Fin's torches and wished him luck.

The mouth of the mine swallowed their group as they passed through thick timber support beams. The solid, dirt-packed ground replaced soft green fields as tufts of grass grew scantily apart.

They turned a corner, and the ceiling shot up as the walls gradually opened. Fin was surprised to find that the torches' smoke did actually smell pleasant. The smell of sweet, burning wood drifted up into the growing cavern like a prayer for more headroom.

Fin picked up Dezi's torches and stowed them one by one. When her arms were empty, he handed her the lit torch and lit another one off of it. Their visibility increased, revealing a clear path ahead.

Brando drew his sword, causing a startled gasp to exit Dezi's lips. Brando regarded Dezi, "Sorry, it's just uncomfortable to wear on my back. Also, why are you still here?"

"I'm not waiting outside with all those brutes," Dezi declared. "They're all creepy and weird."

"Careful not to say that too loud," Brando admonished. "One of those creepy brutes is probably your future husband."

A sound like someone clearing their throat resonated through the cavern.

"Did you hear that?" Dezi asked, reluctantly ignoring Brando's comment.

"Yeah," Fin whispered. "Shh."

The group moved on without incident. Periodically, a gentle crunching sound echoed across the walls causing Fin to test the grip on his sword. Old mining gear sat vacated between rocks and on small mounds of gravel.

Brando leaned down and collected a pickax off the ground. He gave it a look of appreciation and handed it to Fin.

Fin stowed the tool and whispered, "That's nice. Can you find me one too?"

The princess ignored the exchange, opting to locate where the crunching sound was coming from. At times she felt like it was coming from behind her. She banished that terrifying thought and remained vigilant.

Dezi noticed movement from ahead and rapidly tapped Fin's shoulder.

Fin produced a third torch, lit it, and placed it in her free hand. The extra light revealed a pile of rocks. Just as Fin was about to maneuver past the rocks, they started vibrating under his hand.

The group slowly moved backward. Round arms pushed against the ground as legs formed under the rough shape of a torso. It stood less than shoulder height and moved laconically towards them at a slow, walking pace.

Fin stopped and held his ground. "It's moving kind of slow. I think I can take it."

The others continued moving backward as Fin met the creature. When it was in range, he swung towards its center. The sword struck with a jarring noise and bounced ineffectively off.

The creature swung its arm with an unexpected speed, hitting Fin's arm and dislodging the sword from his grip.

He jumped back, trying to lift his arm. He found that he couldn't. He glanced down and saw that it swung uselessly at his side. He ran back.

"I can't move my right arm," Fin shouted, approaching the two.

Brando grasped Fin's hand, turned it, and rotated his arm about the shoulder. A small popping noise indicated that the arm was back in place. "It's probably going to hurt for a few days."

"It feels fine," Fin said, testing out his arm and running back towards the rock monster. "Thanks!"

The creature continued walking towards Fin, blocking off the path to his sword.

"Plug your ears!" Fin called. He waited a moment and let out a Fear Howl. When the monster kept moving forward, unaffected, he grew concerned.

The creature stepped into range and swung.

Fin caught the attack to his chest and stumbled back on his feet. He activated Crushing Grip and Strengthened Talons in unison. He stepped forward and stabbed with his hand as fast as he could. The attack slipped between several of the rocks in the creature's arms, dropping inert stones to the ground.

"I think I'm doing it!" Fin called out after dodging the creature's counter strike. He could still hear his own words echo through the chamber when the fallen rocks started reattaching themselves to the creature's body. "Never mind!"

"You've got this!" Dezi's cheerful voice echoed through the dark cave.

A more masculine voice called out, "There are worse things than death if you don't beat this thing!"

Fin acted as quickly as he could with another strike to the creature's body. His glowing fingers ricocheted off, merely scratching one of the many stones that made up its body. He would have to dislodge each rock individually or in groups of rocks if he could. Suddenly an idea struck him, and he called for more light.

A torch bounced and rolled to a stop just behind him. He pulled out two more torches, lit them off of the first, and spread them out.

He stabbed his hand between the rocks with his claws and activated Greater Stow. Two of the creature's rocks disappeared into his inventory. He moved away too slowly and was struck across the face hard.

Fin wavered on his feet. When his sight steadied, he jumped back in, cautious not to make the same mistake twice. He fell into a rhythm of lunge, attack, stow, and jump back over and over again. The light grew dim by the time the creature was whittled down to nothing more than a helpless pile of rocks.

He walked over to the three remaining pieces of the creature and inspected them. They wormed on the ground, still trying to fight. The rocks piled up into a small mound and then snapped down at Fin, missing his foot by the smallest of margins.

Exhausted, he quickly snatched up the rocks and stowed them. A message popped into view.

Treasure Quest Complete: Capture an Elemental. +1 Level. +1 Active Ability.

Active Ability: Sense Treasure.

Earth Quest Complete: Capture an Earth Plane creature. +1 Passive Ability.

Passive Ability: Earth Commune - Locked until Earth Affinity is realized.

"I won!" Fin Shouted. He selected his saddle bag from his inventory and started rifling through it. He pulled out a loaf of bread, squeezed it, smelled it, and then took a bite.

Dezi and Brando approached him and crouched down.

"We think someone else is in here," Brando whispered.

Dezi nodded and pointed in the direction they came. She spoke in a soft voice, "We heard a noise, and a man cursed. I'm concerned."

Fin dropped his bread and saddle bags into his inventory and looked around for his sword. It was still on the ground where the elemental dislocated his shoulder. He started walking towards it when he heard a terrifying noise. He turned to see two drawn bows step into the light. One of them was pointed directly at him.

"Now!" A voice called out.

Brando saw the threat and advanced with his sword raised. He was mid-stride when an arrow shot into his gut. He cried out in pain and collapsed on the ground, sliding to a stop.

A second arrow shot towards Fin. The impact pushed the air out of his lungs and doubled him over. He fell to his knees, gasping for air.

A man grabbed Dezi from behind. She thrashed wildly in his arms. He finally turned her around, punched her in the face, and dropped her in a crumpled heap on the ground.

"I thought we would have to wait all night," A man said from the back.

"By the way, they were spending money out there," Another voice said, "I would have waited all week if I had to."

Fin raised his head as a man reached down to pilfer his pockets. He activated Crushing Grip and Strengthen Talons and struck forward.

The man dodged away, landing on his side and taking a scratch across the shoulder. He rolled into a prone position and began to get up.

Fin picked up a large rock with both hands and threw it at the man's head as hard as he could. It struck with a sickening noise, pinning the man to the ground. The stone did not roll away.

Another arrow struck Fin's chest, puncturing a hole in his tunic and falling harmlessly to the ground. He glared up and saw one of the men dashing for him with a sword.

Fin quickly let out a Fear Howl and retrieved the arrow. He pierced it through the top of the charging man's chest. Fin gripped the man's arm as he fell, taking his sword and falling momentarily off balance.

The third and final man stood motionless, bow in hand. Fin knocked him out and dragged his body towards Brando. He checked to see if Brando was still alive; he was at least still breathing.

Fin activated Violent Healing and rolled Brando over, revealing the arrow shaft protruding from his back. It did not look good. He immediately broke the shaft of the arrow and pulled the rest of it through Brando's stomach.

The activation time was taking too long. He held the bleeding at bay with his healing hand and gripped the unconscious man's wrist with his other. Finally, the ability jolted into action. He felt the life force flood into Brando, swiftly stopping the bleeding and closing the wound.

Dezi stood up and drew a discarded weapon. She watched as the bandit's body slowly shrunk into a lifeless husk of a man. She turned away from the sight to look anywhere else.

Brando coughed and spat blood off to the side. "Did you get them?"

"Yeah," Fin replied. "How are you feeling?"

"I think I'll make it." Brando's voice cut off. He looked behind Fin and said, "Watch out!"

The bandit with an arrow sticking out of his chest, lifted a large, bloody rock over his head and arched back to throw the stone at Fin and Brando. Dezi's sword swung through the air and passed through the man's forearm. The rock fell to the ground, clipping the side of his head.

Fin stood and tackled the man, keeping his right hand around his neck. Brando was too far, so he filled himself with healing energy. When the healing stopped, Fin ended his ability and checked on Brando's wound.

Brando sat up and pushed Fin away. "I'm fine. We have to check for others."

Dezi picked up a bow and nocked an arrow. "I'll go." She turned and silently disappeared into the darkness.

Fin took a brief moment to look at his notifications. "Brando, you're never going to believe this."

Brando was stretching his body, trying to see if he was still injured. "Believe what?"

Fin's body and clothes turned into a stone sculpture that matched the walls of the cave. He looked at his hands. "I finally got the Earth Affinity."

Chapter 30

"That's really great news," Brando said, holding a torch towards the path behind them. "Do you think we should go help the princess? I mean, there's no way she knows what she's doing out there."

Fin ended the Stone Vizard ability. He was sure the dragons meant to label it "Stone Wizard." His body lost its stony appearance as his skin took on the appearance of a dirty cave crawler. He shrugged. "If she runs into any trouble, she'll probably scream. Do you want to be the first to witness what stone spire wings look like?"

Brando agreed excitedly, and Fin activated his long-awaited wing ability. He had no idea what it would do or if it would even work. He held out his arms, activated Stone Spire Wings, and felt the raw energy through his back, searching to find purchase. As if unable to decide where Fin's wings were, the energy dwindled out and died.

"It's not working," Fin said, disappointed. "I think I was right to assume that I need preexisting wings."

"When we get out of here, we'll figure it out," Brando said, picking up one of the torches and walking away. "I'll go see what kind of goods these Bandits left for us."

Fin moved away from the carnage and sat down on the ground. He ate several pieces of fruit and finished his loaf of bread. Finally, he pulled out one of the rocks associated with the elemental. He turned it around in his hand. There was nothing spectacular about it. He tried talking to see if his Earth Commune ability would work.

"Hello," Fin greeted. There was no response. He tried again. Failing to commune with the rock, he set it down and took out another. The second rock didn't respond, either. He set it next to the first. They were just normal rocks.

He looked at his inventory and found the problem. Most of the rocks were labeled "Unbonded Rock." There was only one with the label "Earth Elemental Core." To be safe, he put the two unmoving rocks away and pulled out the core. It glowed in his hand with a golden hue. He instinctively knew he could see the glow because of his Discern Earth ability.

"Hello," Fin tried greeting again. The stone hummed deeply, giving the impression that it was very old.

"How many friends do you have down here?" Fin asked the rock. The stone didn't reply. Finally, it gave off a short vibrating grunt. It was clear that it did not want to have a conversation. Fin persisted.

"I don't think there's anyone else out there," Dezi said, approaching with a bow and arrow in each hand. She stopped and watched Fin. "Are you talking to a rock?"

"Trying to," Fin said, frowning. "It doesn't seem to want to talk."

Brando dropped a pile of weapons, money, and random supplies next to Fin's feet. "Don't judge him based on this one occurrence. Usually, he has a way with the rocks. You should have seen him seduce the last one.

He gave it a kiss that would make your grandmother blush."

"He's exaggerating," Fin explained. "I gave it one tiny kiss. It was four seconds tops. Nothing crazy."

Dezi ignored the conversation and pointed. "If that's part of the monster you were fighting earlier, it's dead now."

"Technically, it is the monster we were fighting," Fin corrected, holding it towards her. "It won't listen to me. Do you want to give it a go?"

Dezi reached over and took the rock in her hands. "I think this goes without saying, but this is a bad time for jokes."

"It's not a joke," Fin said, exasperated. "Just tell the rock that you're a princess and start demanding answers. You know, like you normally do. Oh, specifically ask if there are any dragons with a bone quest."

Dezi lifted the rock and shook it. "Are there any dragons back there?"

After a breathless moment, Fin shook his head and began stowing the pile of loot off the ground. There were two sets of flint, a whetstone, two water flasks, and thirty copper coins.

"I don't blame the thing," Brando smiled and gestured with his dagger. "If I was the rock, I wouldn't want to talk to her either."

"I'll give you a gold coin right now if you tell Brando to shut his filthy, rotten mouth," Dezi growled at the rock. The stone rumbled in Dezi's hands. She yelped and dropped it to the ground. It started rolling, picking up speed as it tumbled deeper into the cavern. "It moved!"

"If that thing just insulted me, I'm going to drop it in an outhouse," Brando claimed, rising to his feet.

"Quick, it's getting away!" Fin picked up his torch and ran after it. The others followed suit.

The path split off into different abandoned tunnels, most of which had visible dead ends. Fin saw the golden glow of the elemental rolling just ahead, so he pressed onward.

The curve of the ceiling abruptly dropped, causing Fin to crouch low. When he could fully stand, the passage had grown into a bulbous room. He charged and threw himself on top of the escaping elemental, pulling it towards him and stowing it. He realized too late that he had darted past a large, ugly creature lurking next to the entrance.

The creature stood and roared a challenge for combat, lifting gangly arms. Its cry was cut short as Brando's massive sword drove through its back and pierced through its chest. Dezi ran up beside the creature and rammed her sword through its ribcage.

Brando pulled his sword out, kicking the monster's back for leverage.

Dezi tried to pull her sword free, jerking the falling creature towards her. She scrambled to get out of the way, tripped, and landed in the direct path of its falling corpse. It landed on top of her with a dry, slapping sound.

"Help!" Dezi called out from under the lifeless monster. "It smells! It's awful! Get me out!"

Fin and Brando lifted the creature allowing Dezi to roll out from underneath. She stood and tugged her sword free.

"Nice work, you two," Fin said, handing his dagger to Dezi. "Take this. Next time, just let go of the sword and use it if you have to. I think you need it more than I do, anyway."

Dezi reached out and accepted the weapon. After looking over it, she attached it to her sword belt with a rare word of gratitude. "Thanks."

"Here." Brando shoved his dagger into her hands. "They're a matching set." Before the princess could respond, he added, "I just don't want anyone thinking we have friendship daggers."

Fin advanced and inspected the tunnel ahead. "Uh, guys. I don't know about this."

Brando moved to where Fin was standing. He could see just through the room's exit, the walls opened up again, but he couldn't see anything beyond the wall of dim torchlight. "What is it?"

"I think it's a large room," Fin whispered, looking at multiple golden, glowing orbs punctuating the darkness like dots on a canvas. "There has to be at least twelve elementals in there."

"How can you tell?" Dezi asked, not able to see anything beyond the pitiful ring of light. "All I can see is darkness."

"This is why it's so important to build trust. If you had said something like that, I would walk in knowing you're a liar and probably get myself killed." Brando said, matching Fin's volume. "Okay, what's the plan?"

"Now that we know there's only a single, controlling rock on each elemental, I think I can probably snatch it out in one go," Fin said, giving an example by grabbing at the air in front of him. "I think I'll need a distraction to get close."

"We can put the princess back in the cage," Brando suggested. "That might distract them."

"I'll put you in the cage," Dezi threatened.

"We could put the elemental core in the cage," Fin said off-handedly. "We can see if it draws any of the elementals towards us. I might need your help, though."

The group discussed the plan. Fin would stand just inside the passageway so that when they lured an elemental in, it would hopefully walk by without noticing. They would distract the creature, and he would stow its core. Everyone agreed.

When they were in position, Fin unstowed the cage in the center of the cavernous room. He then placed the elemental core inside and waited. The stone emitted a deep, rumbling sound that vibrated the bent metal bars. Another rumbling echo answered the call from just inside the passageway.

Fin was starting to second guess his plan. What if the caged elemental attracted all of the elementals at once? He began moving towards the cage to stow the creature so they could reassess their plan. He took one step forward when a giant foot formed from dirt and rocks stepped next to him.

He backed up and hugged the wall, hoping the large monster would keep its eyes fixed ahead.

As planned, Dezi pulled the cage back, and Brando prepared to stab at it with his long sword. A second foot emerged, and Fin spotted his target. One of the rocks that made up the elemental's left thigh had a bright golden glow.

Brando ran onward to distract the creature. It stood a head taller than him. It was nearly twice the size of the first one they had encountered. He waved his sword in haphazard arches, drawing the creature's attention.

Fin took the opportunity and acted. He ran up behind the creature, activated Strengthen Grip, and pulled as hard as he could on the glowing rock. It wouldn't budge. Fortunately, the thing hadn't noticed him.

Brando hadn't been able to swing at the creature as planned. Fortunately, his running around and dodging constant attacks was working well enough, giving Fin time to work.

Fin gripped a rock in the elemental's leg just above the glowing one, and with an ability-powered squeeze, he crushed it into dust and small shards.

The creature lost its balance and tried to shift its weight. When it found its footing, it wheeled towards Fin.

Brando jumped forward and thrust toward the elemental. The tip of his sword clashed against its right shoulder, causing it to pivot away from attacking Fin.

Fin quickly grabbed the elemental core, pulled as hard as he could, and activated his stow ability. The rock moved slightly under his effort and then disappeared entirely. The creature fell to the ground and scattered into a hundred deadly projectiles.

Before anyone could celebrate, another elemental entered the domed space just as quickly as the first one fell. Its glowing core sat on top of its torso like a neckless, off-centered head. Fin crept around the room as Brando moved in the opposite direction shouting taunts. The creature seemingly ignored Brando, opting to follow Fin with its assumed gaze. It reached back to swing at Fin when a rock flew through the air and hit the creature's left arm.

Dezi yelled, throwing a second rock. The behemoth changed targets again, turning towards Dezi. Fin immediately jumped up and climbed on its back. He gripped the elemental's core fiercely as it hurled a rock at Dezi.

Brando stole the creature's aggression with a wild strike, landing a blow to its arm and breaking several rocks free.

Fin held on for dear life as the monster wound up and swung at Brando. It missed its target but carried through with its swing, hitting the side of the cavernous wall with a thundering noise.

Fin's legs swung out and around, but his hands held fast. When the spin came to an abrupt stop, he kept swinging with increasing momentum. The motion twisted off the core, sending him flying. He landed against the wall and dropped to the ground with a bounce.

Stalactites broke free and fell to pieces on the ground, followed by the crumbling pieces of the elemental's body. The elemental body joined the scattered rocks and cave formations on the ground extinguishing all but one torch.

"Fin, are you alright?" Brando asked, dashing over to him. He set down a dim torch next to Fin and checked for injuries.

"I need a few moments," Fin said in a pained voice. He stowed the core still gripped in his hands and took out a torch. "I think I broke something. If I die, don't get lost here."

"You're not going to die," Brando said, lighting a new torch.

"Just use your healing-"

"We have another one!" Dezi cut him off as another Elemental entered their domain.

Fin channeled Violent Healing. As he waited for the ability to come to life, he looked for a weak spot in the approaching enemy. "Right knee!" He called.

Dezi caught the elemental's attention by throwing rocks at it.

Brando steeled his nerves and moved into action. He ran forward and slid under thick, pillar-like legs. He slid to a stop, landing in the perfect position to get stepped on. He rolled away, got to his feet, and swung where Fin had told him to. Small chips of rock came free, stunning his grip. He swung over and over again, hacking at rocks and dulling his blade.

The monster took slow but constant steps, turning towards Brando.

When Dezi's rocks failed to regain its attention, she decided to go with a version of their original plan. She darted for the birdcage and opened it. "Are you looking for this?" she said, lifting out the rock.

The elemental kept turning and swiping long pendulous swings toward Brando, so Dezi lifted and smashed the core on the ground as hard as she could. She picked it up again and again, smashing the rock repeatedly. Finally, it multiplied into a dozen pieces as it broke on the ground. She looked up to find the elemental had stopped turning. It regarded her stoically and prepared its next attack.

"Run!" Brando shouted and drove his sword on the Elemental's knee over and over again. Dezi ran and dove. The ground erupted where she had been standing, spraying wicked shards of stone all around.

Brando jumped forward and swung with all of his might. The sword hit the monster's knee with a clang, spreading a web of cracks throughout the pinnacle stone.

The elemental took several uneasy steps, placing too much weight on its bad knee, blowing it out. It fell down and broke into pieces spreading out on the floor like the others.

Brando ran over to Fin. "How's it going?"

"Not good," Fin coughed. "I can't find vegetation anywhere. I also tried these cores; they're no good."

"What kind of vegetation do you need?" Dezi asked, beginning to accept that Fin had unorthodox needs. "I saw some tree roots back there about a hundred paces or so."

"Perfect. Take me there." Fin ended his ability and stood up on shaky feet. After several uneasy steps, Brando wrapped his arm around him for support and followed Dezi back through the cave.

Fin gripped the thick, white roots growing from the damp, gray walls. Healing energy flowed through him, knitting broken bones and calming angry wounds. He could tell that his body was badly damaged under his dirt-brown tunic. His body would heal, but his tunic was a lost cause. At least it wasn't as bad as Dezi's dress.

What was once the stark white symbol of purity was now the macabre representation of ruin. Dezi's dress was an intricate combination of dirt, blood, and viscera; every part of it was corrupted by the mine. She didn't seem to notice, or rather, she forced herself not to. Her introspective eyes remained parallel to the ground as she never lowered her chin.

"Guys, I have an apology to make," Dezi said, licking her lips and then spitting out dirt. "A real one. I was selfish, and I almost got us all killed because of it. Instead of taking 'no' for an answer, I kept forcing my will upon you. I thought that, eventually, you would see things my way and stop caring. It's selfish, I know. It's not much, but if you want to turn around now, I will find my own way from now on. This mine be damned."

"I think I want to finish it out," Fin finally said. "Besides, there are a few abilities I still haven't tried yet. Brando, if you want, we can meet back up at the inn."

Brando shrugged and checked his sword for any places that weren't blunted by rocks. "I suppose I have a few sharp spots left on my sword that need dulling."

"Do we have enough torches?" Dezi asked.

"What do you mean 'we'?" Fin asked. "I thought you said you were going to find your own way."

"I said that if you wanted to leave, I would find my own way," Dezi explained. "As it stands, we are all going to the same place. Besides, I paid for those torches."

"If we run out of torches, we can always use your dress," Brando replied, moving his eyes upwards to meet hers. "It needs to be burned anyways."

"I can't believe you said it!" Fin yelled and then burst out laughing. "I was thinking it, but I wasn't going to say anything."

The two laughed together, making references to bards and blind fortune tellers. Whatever tension was haunting the princess in the blackness of the cave did not evaporate with the laughter at her expense. She gave a terse smile, a sneer, and then some unbreakable oaths for violence if they didn't stop making fun of her dress. After all, there had been enough human deaths for one day.

Chapter 31

The cool cave tirelessly sapped the heat off their skin as Fin, Dezi, and Brando made their way deeper into the cavernous mine. In the round room, they found the carcass of the monster that had landed on Dezi, precisely as they had left it.

"Ugly thing probably just wanted to warn us about the elementals, and we slew him for his troubles. I guess no good deed truly goes unpunished," Brando said, kicking the monster's corpse. "What do you think it is?"

"It's probably a cave troll," Dezi said, keeping a wide berth.

"Fin, do you think you can stow this and identify it?" Brando asked. "You know, like the gems?"

"If I pick it up," Fin said. His tone of voice suggested he was not about to pick it up. He clarified any ambiguity by saying, "I'm not doing that."

Brando brought his sword down on the creature's hand, severing several fingers. He picked one up. "What about a finger?"

Dezi audibly gagged. "Drop that this instant! That's utterly disgusting!"

Fin smiled and reached for the finger. If he had the stomach for it, he would devise creative ways to further disgust Dezi. Instead, he stowed it and looked at the item in his inventory. It read "Cave Troll Finger."

"It's a cave troll," Fin said, opting to keep the finger just in case. If the princess decided to act up, maybe he would pull it out. It might not ward off evil, but it might work for a self-entitled princesses.

Brando gave a questionable look at the torch, "How many torches do we have left?"

Fin cast a brief glance at their dwindling supply. "We only have four, and we'll need one of them to get out. So, we should have about three hours to lure the rest of these elements out. If we can't do it in under three torches, we'll just leave."

"Maybe if somebody didn't light all of them off at once," Dezi scolded with her hands on hips, "We wouldn't be in such a hurry."

"How many of these things did you and your father kill before we showed up?" Brando asked her, waiting for the reply he knew wouldn't come. "What's that? In all your time as the princess, with all of your torches and all the king's men, you couldn't kill a single one of these rock creatures. You know what, Fin? You should light another torch. You owe it to yourself."

"We should hurry," Fin said, maneuvering around the pieces of elemental remains scattered throughout the room. "Same plan as last time, but as soon as one of them starts moving toward us, I'm going to stow the core."

Fin stood at the passage that led to the elemental's room and looked inside. There was a myriad of golden orbs dotting the darkness. He removed the core and added one more light to the others.

The group sat and listened while they waited. They were primed like traps, ready to run at any hint of an approaching enemy. Their ears became acclimated to the quiet, much like their eyes had adjusted to their dark environment. A water drip splashed against a wet surface somewhere beyond the umbra of darkness.

"Hey," Brando prodded with a hushed voice. "I don't think it's working, and our torch is about to die."

"We should stash one in here somewhere," Fin said, pulling out two torches and handing one to Brando. "If something happens, we'll at least know where the light is."

Brando tucked the torch under the cave troll's arm and placed a flint stone in its good hand. "If it's too dark to see, we can smell our way towards the light."

"Smart thinking," Fin commended. Before Dezi could argue about the torch placement, he lit his own and set out. "I'm going in."

"I'll go with you," Brando said, offering Dezi his dwindling torch.

Dezi refused the gift. "I'm coming too."

The light opened into a massive cavern as the group drew cautiously in. Sundial shadows counted backward as Fin's torch passed giant stalagmites. The smooth-looking ground gave excellent traction as it rose and fell like the rolling farmland hills.

Brando pointed towards a shredded piece of cloth on the ground. It had either been long lost or torn from its owner in a futile, last-stand skirmish.

They continued until they found the person the cloth could have belonged to. Fin's torch illuminated clean bones scattered in a semi-circle. More of the matching and mangled shreds of cloth lay among them. Fin stepped around the dry and dusty carnage, drawing closer to the nearest globe of golden light.

Fin crouched behind a group of blunt stalagmites and waved for the others to do the same. Fin slowly crept to the end and peered around the corner. He was startled to find there wasn't an elemental on the other side of the jagged boundary. Instead, there was a massive, stone-scaled worm. Its head ended in a four-toothed hole suctioned to a grey rock. The lazy way it fed on the rock produced the same affinity light as the elemental cores.

Brando crept up behind Fin and peered behind the corner. He then picked up a rock and gestured his intention to throw it at the creature. Fin shrugged and then readied his sword.

Brando hurdled the rock. It arched through the cool air and struck it with a thump.

The golden glow died as the worm slowly moved to reposition itself. It slithered around the rock and reignited its golden orb.

Brando felt comfortable enough to whisper. "I don't think it cared that I threw a rock at it."

"It moves pretty slow," Fin handed his torch to Brando. "I'm going to get a closer look. I can see just fine with the light it's emitting."

"What light?" Brando asked, standing up and looking around.

"I think it's an Earth affinity glow," Fin said.

"Be careful," Brando cautioned. "It could spit acid or something."

"Whatever that thing shoots, I think I have a resistance to it," Fin said, standing up from a crouched position. "If I can see it and you can't, it's because of the Sense Earth ability. I also have an Earth Resistance ability. So, if I can see it, I can resist it."

"Can't you also sense magic and treasure?" Brando asked, noticing Dezi had started listening in. "It's possible you're just looking at gold or magic."

"Sense Treasure is an active ability that I am not actively using," Fin explained. "Magic looks more silvery. I'm assuming Earth is gold. I don't know what treasure looks like, but I need to conserve energy. I'm still feeling fatigued from the healing ability I used earlier. I'll be careful."

Fin walked cautiously toward the cave worm. He heard Dezi ask where he was going in a quiet voice; Brando ignored her. He approached the worm and stood close enough to touch it. The worm didn't notice he was there, so he gently reached out and petted it. Its texture was rigid and grainy, with minor bumps and ridges set into its composite shell.

The worm was oblivious, so Fin reached towards the glow and put his finger in it. He could feel the coolness of the golden light on the tip of his finger. He withdrew his hand and found his finger was undamaged. He was relieved his theory wasn't wrong, but he would need more evidence to prove it was right. The golden light seemed to be safe.

He withdrew the severed cave troll finger from his inventory and pressed it into the light. Immediately the light flickered out and disappeared. Unable to see what the worm was doing, Fin darted towards Brando's torch.

"What happened?" Dezi asked, panic rising in her voice. "Are you okay?"

The golden glow appeared again. The worm had shifted to another spot.

Fin held up the remains of the troll finger, noting that it had been reduced to a nub. "I don't think it will chase us, but if it does, stay away from its mouth. I think it's eating the rock, but the glow went out after it took a bite of the troll's finger. I don't think it wants to eat us."

Chapter 32

"I don't want to touch it," Dezi protested, standing four paces away from the hideous, rock-eating worm.

"Brando did," Fin said, clapping him on the shoulder.

"Years from now, how can you tell people that you are the queen of this cave when you didn't even pet the rock worms?" Brando asked, nearly sounding sincere.

"First of all, it's a mine. Secondly, I'm not touching it and won't tell you again." Dezi said, crossing her arms. "If that thing can melt a finger off, I'm not putting my hand anywhere near it. Also, the fact that you are carrying around a severed finger is beyond my comprehension. It's sick and psychotic."

"I don't have it anymore," Fin said, wounded. He looked around for the next area to investigate. "But, now that you mention it, remind me to get another one on our way out."

Fin ignored the disgusted noises Dezi made and started moving forward. "If all that's left here are more worms, I would say this cave is cleared."

"It's a mine," Dezi said, catching up to Fin. "And I would say the worst part is over. These worms shouldn't be too hard to kill."

Fin stopped dead in his tracks, turned, and faced Dezi. "You're not planning on killing them, are you?"

"Yeah, they're almost cute," Brando added from outside the purview of the torch. "All they do is lounge around and eat rocks."

"My cat Chelsea is cute; those worms are an abomination," Dezi proclaimed. "Besides, they're dangerous. You said it yourself."

"Only if you put your finger in its mouth, but anything is dangerous if you put your finger in its mouth," Fin said, lowing his voice again with effort. "Brando threw a rock at it, and it just moved out of the way. It didn't hiss, it didn't attack, and it didn't shoot acid at anyone. If I threw a rock at Chelsea, it would probably attack me."

"You wouldn't dare throw a rock at my special girl," Dezi hissed. "And she's a she, not an it."

"Well, George is a boy," Fin claimed, not knowing if his statement was correct. "He's my special boy. Besides, I rescued you from the castle and cleared the mine so you wouldn't have to marry some random mercenary. I think I've earned a favor. Spare my pets, including George."

"Fine," Dezi relented. "I'll do everything in my power to ensure your pets are spared."

"Swear it," Fin demanded.

Dezi gave her word of honor, and Fin's lips curled into a wicked smile. "I'm going to name them all."

"That's cheating!" Dezi's voice echoed throughout the cavern.

"Not so loud," Brando chided. "I'm going to name the next one Terry."

"That's a great idea," Fin said, pointing the way forward with his torch. "The next one is this way."

Dezi ran after Fin and Brando, worried she would be left in the dark. "Come on, we don't have that much time."

"Then you better hurry," Brando said behind his shoulder.

"You are Terry," Fin proclaimed at the next worm before darting forward again.

After naming the fifth worm, the names started getting creative. Two worms were called "Cobble Kisser" and "Brick-lips." After the twentieth worm, titles were handed out like candied apples at the Autumn Festival. Worms were dubbed "Sir Knight of the Cave," "Captain Troll Finger," and "Duchess of the Mine." There was an especially large worm that Fin gave the title of "Queen Golden of Lokardale, The First of Her Name."

They had not explored the whole cavern, but they explored enough to deem it reasonably less dangerous. They stumbled across more than several piles of bones. Fin assured everyone it was fine as long as the bones weren't gathered in one place. Dezi wasn't convinced, but the confidence was enough to give her the courage to continue forward.

The third torch dimmed by the time the worms had all been named. Some of them were named twice. A quest notification appeared, and Fin halted to read it.

Insight Quest Complete: Impact a life by bestowing the power of a name. +1 Active Ability. Forfeit all Frenzy Quests.

Active Ability: True Name.

"What is it?" Brando asked, surprised at the abrupt stop. He was breathing heavily from their efforts.

"Apparently, running around naming worms was a quest," Fin said with a smile. "I just got a new ability."

"What kind of ability?" Dezi asked, between breaths.

Fin turned towards Dezi and said, "True Name." He was about to say more but noticed a small window hovering over Dezi's head. It read Desiree Rae.

"That doesn't sound very helpful," Dezi said. "It would have been better if you got something that made torches last longer."

Fin ignored her statement and asked, "Your name is Desiree Rae?"

"Yeah, Princess Desiree Rae. Everyone knows who I am," Dezi claimed, shaking her head. "What's your point?"

"My point is, I just came up with a fun little nickname to give you," Fine smiled mischievously.

"I'll bet I can guess what it is," Brando mused.

"If you say it, I will not deign to protect a single one of your pets, on my word," Dezi warned. "Now, what were you about to say?"

Fin held up a hand to stop Brando from saying whatever he was thinking. He had worked too hard to have all his efforts thrown away. "I was going to say we should get out of here and be rid of you once and for all."

Dezi hmphed and walked ahead.

Fin and Brando followed in contemplative silence. They passed the first shamble of bones they came across. They stepped over the bones and scraps of cloth, keeping up with Dezi's brisk pace. The spoils of the dead lying forgotten once more.

Fin approached the entrance to the round room and halted Brando by the shoulder, terrified. Fin's torch caught the reflection of two beady eyes standing deep inside the room. It was too late to tell Dezi to stop, come back, or run.

Dezi stepped into the cave troll room with a determined stride. She had never felt so disrespected in her life. Usually, people would step all over themselves just to fawn over her, but not these two. How did her usual charm not affect a simple potato farmer or a big ugly oaf? They should be so lucky to even grovel in her presence.

She removed the torch from the cave troll's carcass. They could have put the torch anywhere, so why had they thought it was a good idea to tuck it under the arm of a dead, smelly troll? The smell had seemed to get worse since they were in here last.

She heard the potato farmer tell her to come back. At last, her charm had broken through. She turned to say something coy when she noticed something in the room wasn't quite right. Realization struck as she found herself face to face with a bigger and uglier version of the creature they had killed earlier. She only let out half a scream before something struck her, and her vision became as black as the unlit mine.

Fin charged in as the cave troll swung a meaty hand and struck Dezi's face. He stabbed forward, sinking the sword deep inside its back. The troll spun for an attack, tearing the sword grip from Fin's hand. Fin dove to the side, barely dodging the troll's flailing fist. The dim torch fell next to him, causing the shadows in the room to grow.

Brando arced his sword toward the creature's neck. The blade sliced through empty air as the troll pivoted towards Fin. Brando regained his footing and swung again, this time lodging the sword halfway through the monster's forearm.

The cave troll roared in pain, backhanding Brando with its limp claw. The swing connected with Brando's jaw, momentarily jarring his senses. Brando could feel unbidden tears form in his eyes. He staggered dizzily away, willing his senses to return.

Fin landed on scattered rocks and had trouble regaining his balance. He pushed away a jumble of unseen rocks and pressed against the ground. He raised himself up to his feet just as the creature lunged for him with a giant hand. Fin rolled away from the attack, but the creature grabbed him by his sword arm and lifted him effortlessly in the air.

Face to face with Fin, the cave troll opened his mouth for a bite attack. The torchlight painted a clear picture of what was to come. Fin let out a Fear Howl and felt the reverberating magic thrum to life in his throat.

The cave troll closed its jaw briefly before shaking the Fear Howl's effects off and redoubling its efforts. This time it was determined to bite its prey's head off.

Not expecting Fin to use his ability, Brando found himself stuck deep in the shadows. He had experienced this ability multiple times to lesser degrees. It was a simple trick of the mind; he could overcome it. He had to. Squaring his shoulders, Brando let out a warrior's yell and gripped his sword as hard as he could. He took a step and broke free.

Fin panicked as his face drew closer to the open mouth of the cave troll. Sticky breath brought the smell of rotten meat through brown and yellow teeth. Fin squirmed and struggled, but his wrist held firmly in the creature's massive hand. Without a moment to spare, he yelled, "Caustic Breath!" and took a deep breath of noxious air. He blew as hard as he could, trying not to gag.

Brando's sword hit the side of the cave troll's knee with all his strength. The critical blow made a satisfying pop from the monster's joint, but the blade failed to sink in. Without skipping a beat, Brando pulled his sword back and swung again.

Golden mist filled the cave troll's mouth, corroding its innermost parts. Teeth and skin disintegrated, mixing together in black pools of saliva. The monster dropped Fin and jerked sideways, hands held to its mouth.

Fin unstowed one of the bandits' swords from his inventory. His strength failed in his right hand, so he gripped it with his left and began hammering the blade into the cave troll.

Fin and Brando hacked and stabbed the creature relentlessly. It swung an arm out multiple times, tripping Brando and snuffing out the light.

Darkness enveloped their world.

"Just stab it!" Brando yelled. "Try not to hit me!"

The pair blindly sank their swords into the cave troll over and over. It felt like stabbing through a mud pit with multiple rocks inside. Finally, it stopped moving.

"Are you alright?" Fin asked, panting for air.

"I don't know," Brando managed to say between gasps of breath. "How are you?"

"I don't know either. We have to find the torch Dezi had." He pulled up his inventory and unstowed the other flint stone. "I have a flint stone."

"See if one of your abilities can help you find our way around," Brando suggested. "I'll see if I can find the old torch. It might spark back to life."

"Already on it," Fin said, looking over his options. First, he tried True Name, but nothing happened. He probably needed to see the person for it to work. Then he tried Sense Treasure, and his word blazed to life. It was still too dark to see, but the outline of the room came into sight.

Specks and veins of gold lit up in the walls and ceiling like he saw them in broad daylight. Below him, he could see other sporadic veins a great distance downward. He still couldn't see his body, but it felt like he was hovering over a deep ravine. The feeling was surreal.

He pulled his eyes upward and found what appeared to be Dezi's coins. They sat stacked together in a perfect cylinder of gold. He hoped she was still wearing her pouch as he took one unsteady step after another. When he finally got there, he felt Dezi's cold skin.

"I found Dezi," Fin said, feeling for a pulse, but his hands were shaking too hard. "I can't tell if she's alive or not."

"Checking on her won't do us any good without light," Brando said. "Just find that torch."

They each searched for a torch. Fin felt around the princess for the new one while Brando searched around the cave troll for the old.

"Aha! Found it!" Brando erupted, followed by his blowing on any possible coals left.

Fin touched a smooth handle of wood. He took hold of it and felt it with his hands. "I found the other one!"

Fin crawled back toward the princess and drew her dagger. He was about to use it on the flint stone when the room came into view.

Brando ran over to Fin and lit his torch. "She's in bad shape."

Fin looked down at Dezi. On one side of her face, she was bleeding from three long gashes and one large developing bruise. Her blonde hair was dark red above her forehead.

Brando lowered his head and placed his ear to her mouth. "She's alive, but we have to hurry. You have anything left?"

"We'll find out," Fin offered. "Can you carry her?"

"I guess we'll find that out, too," Brando tossed aside his dying torch and scooped Dezi into his arms. "Lead the way."

Chapter 33

Fin dashed ahead through stone tunnels carrying the torch. He had to slow down, stop, and sometimes backtrack to avoid losing Brando. He held the light low, illuminating Brando's cautious footsteps. The terrain periodically shifted from flat to treacherous without notice. No matter how he held the torch, Brando had difficulty seeing his footsteps while carrying the unconscious princess.

They passed recognizable features like unique stone formations, mining tools, and a pile of dead bandits. They also found themselves looking at places they did not recognize. Still, they continued forward, lungs burning from exertion.

Finally, Brando called for a halt, "I need to rest for a minute. Do you think you can take this thing for a while?"

"It's not a thing; she's a she," Fin mimicked the princess. He immediately felt a tinge of guilt threatening to rise in his chest. He shoved it down with the rest of his troubles and followed through with the joke, "She's a special princess."

"She's a special pain in the ass, is what she is," Brando said with a smile hidden behind exhaustion and shadows.

"Give her here. I'll try to take her for as long as I can." Fin set the torch down and scooped his arms under her. She was lighter than he expected. He wasn't used to how strong he had grown over the last few days. He was still tired and hungry but felt he could carry her the rest of the way out if needed.

With Brando in the lead, Fin fell into a rhythm of steps and breathing. His heart pounded at a steady pace, somewhere between elevated and erratic. The drooping weight in his arms bore down on him. Still, he persisted in the mindless march through the endless tunnels. The crunching of rocks and echoes of heavy breathing occupied his thoughts.

"I think we're close," Brando said with an uncertain whisper. The spoken words directed their minds back to the present.

"Okay, here's the plan," Fin's words betrayed his drowsiness. "As soon as we reach the mouth of the cave, I'm going to kill all the grass I can and try to revive her. I don't know if I have much energy left, but try my best."

"Let me take her then," Brando hoisted the girl out of Fin's arms. "Take the torch."

Fin thought he had stepped into another large cavern when the wind blew on his skin. The pitch-black night offered rustling trees, distant voices, and other evidence of their freedom from the mine. But he had more pressing issues before he could bask in the open air.

Violent Healing came to life with a colorless haze of light. Fin placed his filthy hand on Dezi's equally dirty face and pushed life into her from the surrounding foliage. The flow of healing started weakly and slowly degraded into a tiny trickle. Still, he held fast to the ability until it was gone entirely.

"That's all I have," Fin said drowsily. "You'll have to take her from here. I'm completely spent."

Brando picked the princess off the brittle grass and started for their inn. He didn't need to turn around to know Fin was following him. The disheveled sound of feet dragging behind him was enough.

"Halt in the name of the King!" Brando heard from behind him mere steps from the inn. "What's going on here? What's going on with that young lady?"

Brando knew he should have circumnavigated the street lantern's light, but he got greedy for his bed. He stopped and turned towards the authoritative voice as two stern faces came into the light. One of them sized them up under bushy eyebrows, and the other glared at them over a pointed nose.

"We just got out of the mine. No one told us how rough it would be," Brando said as nonchalantly as he knew how.

"You're mercenaries then?" eyebrows asked, approaching closer. The other stood back and watched silently. "What happened to the girl?"

"She just got a little bruised up in there," Brando responded. "All she needs is a good night's rest."

"She looks like she needs a physician," The guard responded. "Where are you going?"

"The Hornblower," Brando said, pointing ahead.

"To bring her to your room?" Pointy Nose accused.

"She has her own room," Fin explained, caught off guard by the brash implication. "We are not thugs. Follow us if you want, but we've all had a long day, and no one has the energy for your bottomless pit of questions."

"You would be wise to mind your attitude, boy," Nose warned. "We'll escort you to the Hornblower, but if your story doesn't check out, we'll lock you up until her story does."

Eyebrows opened the door to the Hornblower and gestured Fin and Brando inside. The common room was empty, except for a boy sleeping in a cot behind the bar.

The guard cleared his throat and dropped a heavy fist on the counter, startling the boy awake.

"I was just closing my eyes, sir." The boy rushed to stand before the guard. "How can I help you?"

"Does this young lady have a room here?" The guard asked.

"I don't know, sir. I've never seen her before," The boy replied honestly.

The guard furrowed his eyebrows at Brando, waiting for an excuse. "I thought you said she had a room here?"

"She spoke to the innkeeper." Brando held back any further remarks.

"Shall I wake him?" The boy asked, eager to resolve whatever conflict there was.

"I don't know," The guard said, eyes trained on Brando. "Should he get him?"

"Yes, just get him," Fin jumped in. "The sooner you get the innkeeper, the sooner we can all go to bed."

When the innkeeper came out, he didn't look happy. But he smiled regardless. "What can I do for you, gentlemen?"

"Does she have a room here?" the guard pointed at the unconscious girl.

The innkeeper wiped the fog from his eyes and looked closely at the young woman. "Aye, she paid for her room in advance. What happened to her?"

Dezi's face looked beaten and bruised. A light scratch mark drew a red line across her left cheek to the top of her upper lip. Three deeper gashes paralleled the line to the bridge of her nose. Dirt and dry blood crackled around her face from chin to temple.

"She was struck in the face by a cave troll," Brando replied. He faced the guard, "Are we good here?"

"She's going to need someone to look at those wounds," the guard said, giving the oddly familiar-looking girl an appraising look. "If you leave her like that, those wounds will fester."

"Just take her to her room. I'll have Martha come up and see to her face. It will probably leave a scar, but that's not bad for a mercenary, ey? The more scars, the more money, is how I understand it," The innkeeper tried lightening the mood. He turned to his son and gestured for him to wake his mother. "Can I offer you, gentlemen, anything else? Ale?"

"None for us, thanks," The guard said sadly. He clapped his hands together and made for the exit. "The night is still young."

"Water, please," Fin croaked, watching the guards leave.

"Water for me, too," Brando said, walking toward the stairs with the princess in his arms. "I'll be right back."

The following day, Fin woke up with a square patch of sunlight in his eyes. He tried looking at the dirty clothes he was still wearing, but his neck wouldn't allow it. His body was sore, and his mobility was restricted to only slight movements. He slid his feet out of bed, dropping kernels of dirt and rock on the wood plank floor. He needed a bath, but he settled for the cloth and washbasin sitting in the corner of his room.

When he was clean, or at least less filthy, he donned his red outfit. He wandered out of his room to check on Brando.

"How are you feeling?" Fin asked, looking down at the bedraggled man.

"My muscles are sore, and my body hurts. I want to stay in bed," Brando complained. "Is the princess dead?"

"I haven't checked." Fin unstowed Brando's second set of clothes and placed them on the bed. "If she is, we'll need to get out of town before anyone finds out."

Brando sat up in bed with more grunting and groaning than was probably necessary. "Order me breakfast; I'll be down in a minute."

Brando finally appeared on the staircase, taking one step at a time and firmly gripping the handrail. He approached Fin's table and sat down slowly in a chair. "I feel like I've been beaten with a bag of rocks."

"As soon as we get out of town, I'll heal you up, but if we don't leave soon, we might not be leaving at all," Fin cautioned.

The innkeeper brought two plates of food just as a guard stepped through the door. The guard stepped up to the bar and stood, scanning the common room.

"I'll be with you in a moment," The tired innkeeper said, setting two plates on their table.

"It seems the princess has gone missing," The guard stated, not waiting for the innkeeper's attention. "Has anybody seen her? She's about nineteen years of age, blonde hair, and about this high." The guard held his hand up to his shoulder level.

Fin and Brando shared a look. Both held their breath.

"There is a girl upstairs that roughly matches that description, but I don't believe she's the princess. She's with these two." The innkeeper nodded toward Fin and Brando. "You're mercenaries, am I right?"

Fin cleared his throat. "Yes, we're mercenaries."

The guard shook his head. "We're checking all shops, inns, and alleys. I'm sure she'll show up somewhere. I'll just take a look."

"She was attacked by a cave troll last night in the mine," Fin quickly said. He only needed to buy some time to settle the bill and leave. "She needs the rest. Can you come back later?"

The innkeeper nodded. "Martha was up until all hours seeing to her wounds. She's got some pretty nasty thrashings."

The guard hesitated and said, "Alright, I suppose I can come back."

As the guard turned to leave, the innkeeper, in all his ignorance, said, "Wait, here she comes now. See for yourself."

Fin's heart stopped as he saw the dainty princess walk down the stairs. She wore a black gown that looked nothing like something she would own. It was probably lent to her by the innkeeper's wife. She wore a yellow scarf that veiled the left side of her clean face. When she saw the guards, she stopped and turned her face away. She then began going back to the direction she came from.

"Stop!" the guard demanded, but the princess ignored him and fled to her room.

The guard opened the front door, leaned out, and summoned two others inside.

"Something is going on. Make sure nobody leaves." He waited for the guards to acknowledge, and then ran up the stairs.

Fin shoveled eggs, potatoes, and sausage into his mouth. Whatever he was up against, he didn't want to do it on an empty stomach. He could hear the guard bang on the door and demand it be opened. Finally, he heard the click of a latch and the creak of a door swinging open.

"What's the meaning of this?" The guard's voice boomed from the second floor. "Princess? Is that you? What happened to your face?"

Shock and horror overcame the faces in the common room. The innkeeper's expression shifted from concern to surprise and then back to concern.

"She never said she was the princess!" Brando said with false confusion. It was a pitiful attempt at self-preservation. He looked at the stern-faced guards and sighed. Their lives rested on the balance of Dezi's caprice, which wasn't a good place to be.

Chapter 34

"She's here, but her face is badly damaged," The guard told the others as he walked back down the stairs. He pointed a finger toward Fin and Brando. "Arrest these men on charges of abduction, treason, and conspiracy."

Fin set down his fork and raised his hands. His mouth was too full to say anything. He had shoveled the remainder of his breakfast into it.

"We didn't do anything," Brando protested as three guards approached him. "She just started following us. What were we supposed to do?"

"Arrest the innkeeper, too," the guard said with an intense look in his eye. "Harboring, aiding, and abetting criminal activity."

"Stop this at once!" Dezi's voice filled the room from on top of the stairs. She slowly climbed down, speaking order into the chaotic space. "You will arrest no one."

"Your Highness, we need these men for questioning. We have to get to the bottom of this," the guard who gave the orders explained.

"You need no such thing," Dezi stated, walking towards the men as if she was a head taller and not the other way around. The cuts and bruises on her face became more apparent as she approached.

"These men saved my life." Dezi pointed at Fin, whose mouth was still stuffed. "He rescued me from a cave troll and countless elementals and single-handedly cleared the mine. He carried me out of the mine and got me to safety while I was unconscious." She pointed at Brando. "This man helped." She pointed at the innkeeper. "The only thing the innkeeper is guilty of is running his inn. His wife saw to my wounds while I was still incapacitated. You will not be arresting anyone, but I believe some congratulations are in order."

The room fell into an uncertain silence. The innkeeper looked relieved; Brando looked upset. Fin took a drink from his mug.

The door burst open, and a young guard rushed in. He looked like he had something important to say, but after one look at his tense surroundings, his words choked up in his throat.

"Very well, Your Highness," the guard replied, moving his hand away from his sword grip. "It will be as you say."

"The carriage is ready, sir," the newcomer said. He correctly assumed that he wanted nothing to do with whatever was going on and retreated outside

"The carriage awaits," the guard repeated, waving his men to attend to the princess.

Fin and Brando stood up and followed after the princess. They each paid the innkeeper and turned toward the door.

The guard stood in front of the door, blocking their exit. "You two are coming with me."

Fin and Brando walked and limped to the castle, surrounded by a complement of guards. The sound of metal on metal accompanied a chorus of tight leather seams stretching out and compressing together to the rhythm of marching. The gates of the castle opened in tandem, swallowing them into their barred shadows.

The paving stones lead them through a different path this time. Instead of passing through the front entrance, they walked around the castle to the left, where they were led down a stone staircase into its unknown depths. There, they were escorted by a different set of guards through a wood and cast iron door.

The damp walls and stale air were not the warm welcome they expected; it was the welcome they feared. Fin and Brando repressed their base instincts to run or fight. When they heard the heavy sound of a door closing, followed by a thick sound of a lock, they knew they had no other choice but to be led further into the fortified labyrinth.

The new guards escorted them through the damp corridor and finally stopped before a row of small prison cells. Each cell had just enough room for one man to sit uncomfortably when he grew tired of standing.

"In you go." The man in charge gestured toward two adjacent cells.

"We're supposed to wait in there?" Fin asked, wondering why they weren't led to the tea room. "Is this some kind of joke?"

The guards said nothing, but when Fin heard the sound of a sword sliding out of its scabbard, he stepped into the cell. Brando shook his head and stepped into his. After the two gates were shut and locked, the guards turned and walked away without a word.

"Hey!" Brando called after them. "How long are you going to leave us in here? Hey!"

The guards ignored Brando's questions and left without a word.

"Don't worry. Did you hear what Dezi was saying?" Fin asked, trying to calm the storm in his own gut. "She told them we saved her life."

"She said that you saved your life," Brando corrected. "She only said that I helped. What a royal piece of work she is, huh? I helped? I saved her useless, unconscious life, and this is the thanks I get."

"I don't think she meant for this to happen," Fin said honestly. "We need to think of all the possible outcomes and make a plan."

"Possible outcome one." Brando held up a finger. "We rot in the dungeon forever."

"If that's the case, I can probably get us out." Fin put his back against the wall and used his Stone Vizard ability. His body blended into the wall behind him and disappeared in a protrusion of rock and stone. "All you have to do is tell them I escaped through a loose rock somewhere. When they come in to investigate," Fin's ability melted off him as he struck forward with clawed fingers, "Bam, we're out. I also still have swords and a dagger."

Brando lightly applauded. "And if the princess makes you marry her?"

Fin pondered the question with mock solemness. "I'll take her cat."

The two sat in contemplative silence for an indistinguishable amount of time. They were sealed off from the light outside, unable to tell time. Each dozed off and slept uncomfortably for an uncertain span of time.

"What are we doing in here?" Brando asked in frustration, causing Fin to wake up. "They should be putting up statues of us, not locking us away in a dungeon. When I get out, I'm leaving and never coming back."

"I could probably melt these locks off," Fin considered, giving the locks a few experimental taps with his finger.

"You mean with your sog breath?" Brando tapped on his lock too. "Wait. Are you sure you want to do that? What if the king wants to reward us for clearing the cave and saving the princess?"

"Do you think he would throw us in the dungeon if he was going to reward us?" Fin asked, waving a hand towards their surroundings.

"He might just be talking to Dezi to make sure we weren't holding her under duress," Brando noted Fin's blank look. "You know, like telling her we would kill her if she doesn't do what we say. She'll clear things up as soon as he talks to her."

Fin thought about it for a while. "And if she tells him everything?"

"Yeah," Brando agreed. "You should hurry and melt the bars."

Fin activated Caustic Breath and inhaled. He blew a golden stream of air onto the lock in front of him, causing the metal to smoke and simmer. Black metal dripped away, opening a small hole in the back of the square lock. Fin breathed in again and blew into the hole, opening it further and melting the inner mechanisms that locked the cell door shut. He pushed on the bars, and his cell opened, dropping several pieces of metal on the ground.

"Now do mine!" Brando shouted in excitement.

"Hang on, I'm feeling lightheaded." Fin held the bars of his cage and took slow, steadying breaths. Finally, he stepped out into the passageway and stretched out. "You might want to move to the side."

Brando moved as far as possible, and Fin lowered his mouth to the keyhole. Before he breathed in, the sound of a distant door slammed open and then slammed shut. Fin and Brando looked at each other wide-eyed.

Brando pointed to Fin's cell. "Go back, go back. Just act normal."

Fin dashed into his cell and closed the gate. It immediately swung open and came to a rest with a cockeyed gap. He shut it, and the gate opened again. Finally, he put his foot between the bars, pulled the gate shut, holding it fast with his boot.

Two guards rounded a corner into sight. "It looks like it's your lucky day," One of them said, selecting a key from his keyring and bringing it toward Fin's broken lock. "What's this?"

Fin shrugged. "It was like this when they put me in here. I assumed you did it on purpose."

"Aye, Yarve, aren't you the one that put these two in here?" The guard accused. "The lock is broken."

"The lock worked just fine when I used it. He must have tampered with it." Yarve looked from the lock to Fin.

"With what?" Fin asked, turning his empty hands upward. "The smithy I have in here with me?"

"I saw what happened," Brando said, drawing the attention to himself. "His breath was so bad it melted the bars."

"That's a funny joke, Brando," Fin attempted a fake laugh and faced the guards. "Some people just can't be trusted with a secret."

"We can sort this out later," The guard brought his key to Brando's lock and twisted. "We have to get these two up there."

The guards escorted Fin and Brando out of the damp dungeon into the sunlight. They squinted at their surroundings as they turned toward the back of the castle. They were led up a small set of stairs into the castle, through undecorated halls. Finally, their trip ended at the familiar tearoom where all their princess problems began.

The guards stationed themselves just inside the door and stared blankly ahead, holding their weapons. Fin sat in the chair he was used to, and Brando followed suit.

"Does any of you know what's going on?" Brando asked the guards. They responded with silence, holding their eyes firmly forward.

A familiar-looking man walked into the room. He turned towards the guards and excused them with a single wave of his hand.

Fin couldn't remember his name, but he remembered he didn't need to. He activated True Name, and a box appeared over the man's head. It read "Sir Adrian Jeffcoat."

"It is quite the tangle you two are in," Sir Jeffcoat said, halting any responses with a lifted hand. "I have been instructed to take you to the king for a private hearing. As you can imagine, this is an extremely rare event, and I'm not sure how well it will go for you. If it goes bad, it will likely spell your death. However, if you somehow manage to find the king's favor, I want to help you so that you will return the favor one day."

"Thank you, Sir Jeffcoat," Fin sat forward on his chair. "I will not forget your help for as long as I live."

"We don't have long, so pay attention," Sir Jeffcoat looked around the room conspiratorially and lowered his voice. "We all know the princess has a proclivity towards stretching the truth. I know it, the king knows it, but if anyone says it…" Sir Jeffcoat brought his thumb across his throat. "I had the good fortune of overhearing Dezi's story. She said a lot of things that you're just going to have to agree with. She said she helped you kill five stone creatures and two cave trolls, where in reality, you probably did it all yourself. Whatever you do, do not challenge her version of the story. What she says is truth even though no one believes it."

"We can do that," Brando said, bouncing his leg nervously. "Anything else?"

"My best recommendation is to be as silent and as still as possible." Sir Jeffcoat explained, "When the king couldn't find his daughter, he was in a very bad way. It was the worst I've ever seen him. The fact that he has an opportunity to butcher a scapegoat and give an outlet to his rage should not be taken lightly. When you go in there, walk to the center of the room, and keep as quiet as possible."

"Thank you," Brando said with a sigh. He was ready to be done with politics, prisons, and princesses.

"Collect yourselves." Sir Jeffcoat stood to his feet and adjusted his jacket. "It is time."

He led them down a familiar path to a set of familiar doors. He knocked three times and grasped both door handles at once. The doors swung open to reveal a semicircle of armed knights, guards, and the king standing at the focal point in the middle. He gently nudged Fin and Brando forward, then took his place next to another knight on the left.

Fin and Brando walked to the center of the room and faced the king. He looked tired and on edge, like a man called out of bed in the dead of night by the sound of glass breaking in the kitchen. He wore simple garments that would make the situation feel less official.

"These last few days have been troubling." The king said with an unmoving stance. "You can't imagine the horror I felt to discover my daughter had gone missing. There is nothing in this world that has frightened me more. When she returned, my relief was short-lived. After I saw her in her battered and bruised state, I ordered the ones responsible to be drawn and quartered." The king paused, letting the idea sink in. "The only reason you are standing before me right now is because she stayed my hand. I made her tell me everything. It should come as no surprise that your offenses had doubled by the end of her little tale. Do you know what she said?"

The urgent expectation for Fin or Brando to say something weighed heavy in the air. Every second of silence compounded into the next until Fin finally spoke, "I'm sure she told you the truth, Your Majesty."

The king's brow furled. "Of course, she told me the truth!" He yelled into every empty space of the room. He drew the sword at his belt and stalked toward them. "My family's honor is supreme!"

Fin prepared to use Fear Howl, but the king's sword was not primed for an attack. Instead, it hung at an arbitrarily threatening angle.

"After listening to her story, there was just one thing I couldn't quite understand." The king began pacing back and forth. "Why come into my house under the pretense of a diplomatic envoy and lie to my face about some fictitious slave camp run by goblins?"

This time there was no reply. If they told him the truth, there would be no proving their story. The king would call them liars and probably strike them down where they stood. Also, neither of them could think of a single reason why they would risk their lives to lie about something so serious.

"I know why you did it." The king stopped pacing and looked squarely at both of them. "I kept asking myself why anyone would do such a brash, bold, and reckless thing? Then, the answer came to me like a vision. It was love, wasn't it? Love makes us do crazy things. You pretended to be diplomats in order to win Dezi's heart before you won the right to marry her. Tell me I'm wrong."

"It is as you say, Your Majesty," Fin said, looking at Brando to make sure he didn't try to argue. "I only wanted to impress her Royal Highness."

"Of course, this was your idea." The king looked at Fin. "In this case, fortune favors the bold, and I believe your plan succeeded, and I can tell that you won her over. And you," the king said, turning to Brando. "Your loyalty and selfless determination have paid off. Dezi told me how you helped in the mine. Your contributions might have been small, but they had a big impact. You have done this kingdom a great service."

Brando had never wanted to choke someone more in his life. However, he gritted his teeth and bore it. At least he didn't have to pretend to love Dezi. That, at least, made him feel better.

"Finlay, is it?" The king asked. "Where is it you hail from?"

"Dragon's Throne F-." Fin cut himself off. He did not want the king's men to find him after he left. If he never made it back home, he didn't want them harassing his parents. "Finlay of Dragonthrone, Your Majesty."

"Take a knee, both of you," The king ordered. After Fin and Brando hesitantly took a knee, he placed his sword on Fin's shoulder. "By my power as King of Clive Rae, I absolve you of all your crimes and bestow upon you the title of Lord Dragonthrone. Arise, Lord Finlay of Dragonthrone."

Fin stood as the king placed his sword on Brando's shoulder. He saw a notification and read it to himself.

Path Quest Complete: Gain a royal title. +1 Charisma. +2 quests revealed.

Royal Advantage: Defend a kingdom. +1 Passive Ability, +2 Charisma. Forfeit all Royal Conquest quests.

Royal Conquest: Attack a kingdom. +1 Passive Ability, +1 Active ability. Forfeit all Royal Advantage quests.

Fin stopped reading through his quest completion when he heard the king say, "Arise, Sir Brando of Dragonthrone."

The room burst into applause.

Chapter 35

The king signed two sheets of parchment and handed them to Fin and Brando each. "These certificates prove your titles. You may not give them away or sell them. Ordinarily, a new title would mean expanding the kingdom. But, under the circumstances, you may want to focus on your courtship with Dezi. I will assign you some guest rooms and a chaperone. We can discuss the future of Dragonthrone at another time, but for now, I need some rest."

"Thank you, Your Majesty," Fin said, accepting his title. He thought he might hang it on his wall one day when he returned to a life of farming. "There's just one thing I feel I should say."

"Speak freely," The king said, showing only a slight hint of impatience.

"We killed all of the major threats in the mine, but it's possible there might be a cave troll or two hiding in there somewhere," Fin confessed under the exhausted gaze of the king. "I recommend sending in some swords before opening it up to the public."

"A wise plan," the king said. "Is that it?"

"There is something else," Fin hesitated before continuing. "There are these worms in there…"

"Ah yes, the worms." The king smiled. "Dezi told me all about them. I will take care of that now." He turned his attention toward the rest of the room and spoke in a loud voice, "We will need to do a clean sweep of the mine to verify that it is safe. Lord Walters, I am entrusting you with this responsibility."

"It will be done, Sire," An old man said from behind.

"Station guards at the entrance. Since we won the mine, I am claiming it from here on out. I do not want us to admit any dwarves. Today, Clive Rae becomes an independent kingdom!"

The room broke out in cheers and applause. The king waited for the cheering to die down and said, "Also, leave the giant ugly worms alone. They are under my protection. Now, I have pressing things to attend. Please stay and celebrate in my absence. I will send someone up shortly."

The king left, and immediately, the other nobles gathered toward Fin and Brando, offering congratulations paired with hearty slaps on the back.

"You'll have to duel me sometime," A tall noble said, swinging an invisible sword. "I want to see how I pair up with the champion of the mine."

"Me too," Someone else said from behind him. "I would like to try my hand at the champion."

"I don't know how well I would do in a duel," Fin began saying with the intention of backing out.

"If you want a real competition, you should try challenging him to an eating contest," Brando said quietly enough to not expect anyone to hear.

"What's that? An eating contest. How dastardly appropriate." A man from the crowd responded. "If he can outdo Sir Goyder, he truly is the champion. Do you think the king would mind too terribly much if we commandeered the kitchens?"

"It would be a shame if we came all the way up here and didn't stay for lunch."

"Who's Sir Goyder?" Fin asked, looking around the room.

Sir Jeffcoat set a hand on Fin's shoulder. "Someone you would have to be a fool to bet against. Congratulations, by the way. That went better than even I expected."

"Thank you for your help. I owe you one." Fin smiled. "Now let me return the favor. I wouldn't bet against me on this one."

The room erupted in laughter, but Fin held steady eye contact with Sir Jeffcoat. He gave a slight nod, signifying he had an extra fork up his sleeve.

Sir Jeffcoat laughed with the group but kept a keen eye on Fin. There was something about the man's confidence that shook him. "Who said anything about betting?"

"I'll bet ten bottles of my brother's wine on Goyder," Lord Walters bellowed.

"I'm afraid I can't back that bet." Sir Jeffcoat lifted his hands in surrender.

"I can." Fin reached into his tunic and unstowed the large, uncut topaz. He held it up for the old man to see. "It's a raw topaz."

"You carry that thing around with you?" Lord Walters asked, dumbfounded. "Where do you keep it?"

"In my pocket." Fin bounced the heavy stone in his hands to take the attention off his fictitious pocket. "It's a good luck charm."

The door to the room opened, and a grey-haired man with long arms entered the room and cleared his throat, "Drinks will be served in the Great Hall presently."

Conversations grouped off into pairs as everyone started filing out of the room. Fin and Brando followed behind until the man at the door stopped them personally.

"You must be the new Lord," The man bowed slightly. "You may call me Pike. Do you have a moment to spare?"

Fin and Brando stepped out of the doorway and waited for the man to continue.

"The king has informed me that you may want to get cleaned up," Pike said in a low voice. "I have assigned you temporary rooms in the east wing. I took the liberty of drawing you some baths. I am working on having a selection of clothes brought to you." He clapped twice, and a young man ran around the corner and stopped in front of them. "This page will help you navigate the palace, daily schedules, and the like. He will escort you to your rooms."

"This way, my lords," The page said, walking ahead.

When they reached their rooms, they found them side by side, each with a steaming bathtub in the center.

"Does every room have a bathtub?" Fin asked the young man.

"None of them do, My Lord," The page chirped. "We carry them up and fill them with pots of hot water."

"And when we're done with them, you just take them out?" Brando asked, glancing out the unending passageway in either direction.

"That's right, My Lord," The boy beamed. "Water first."

"What's your name?"

"Brixton, My Lord."

"Well, Brixton, you may call me Fin." He said, flipping Brixton a silver coin, hoping to buy the kid's favor.

"Thank you, Lord Fin," Brixton said, standing in the passageway. "I'll be out here if you need anything."

Brando hesitated at his door and cast a cautious glance around. "Fin, how long are we going to, uh, stay in these temporary rooms?"

Understanding that Brando was asking when they were leaving, Fin answered, "Let's eat and rest, then we'll take a trip into town. I'm sure the excitement will have died down by tomorrow."

They separated and went into their respective rooms. Fin's room was less ostentatious than he expected from a palace guest room, but it was still grander than he was used to. A four-post bed covered nearly a third of the room with its gaudy red, yellow, quilted blanket. The tub that sat in the middle of the room beckoned him from on top of water-splattered stone tiles.

Fin stripped his clothes off and stepped into the copper tub. The lukewarm water was wonderful in contrast to the cold stone floor. Fin sank into it, splashing water inadvertently adding to the shallow puddles around him. He was getting used to bathing in a proper bath. He wanted to incorporate it into his life outside the city of baths.

When he felt sufficiently clean, he looked around for a drying cloth. He was certain there was one lying around. When he couldn't immediately locate one, he decided to inquire with Brixton. The boy seemed eager to help, and he had already tipped him a whole silver coin.

"Brixton, is there something I can use to towel off?" He called from his tub. When the door opened, he started to repeat his question when he noticed it wasn't Brixton who entered.

Just inside his room, an elderly woman stood cross-armed, looking at him with an imperious glare. "I have retired your page and assumed his duties of looking after you. I am Isabel, your chaperone."

Fin thrashed in the tub to lower himself as deep as he could. "No, thanks, bring Brixton back. As you can see, I'm a little indecent right now."

"It's nothing I haven't seen before," Isabel walked unconcerned toward a large wardrobe and produced a towel from a drawer. "You'll have to get used to it, the king has ordered me not to let you out of my sight, and I don't intend to."

"Surely the king didn't mean to rob me of every measure of privacy." Fin's face was flushed, and he squirmed in the pool to find modesty through the translucent water. "It's not like you can watch me day and night."

"I take this responsibility very seriously. After all, the princess's honor is on the line." Isabel held up the white fabric. "I take it you don't want me to give you this?"

"I can get it myself."

"Suit yourself." Isabel tucked the towel back into the drawer and walked toward the exit. "I'll be just outside."

A knock came at the door just as she reached it. She swung it open humiliatingly wide and bid whoever was out there to enter.

A thin man stepped into the room carrying three sets of clothes. "The tailor sends his best with a selection of dinner wear."

Isabel peeled each set of clothes into her hands and scrutinized each. "He'll take this one, thank you."

"Wait, I want to see." Fin was beginning to feel upset with the woman. Who did she think she was barging into his room while he was bathing and assuming to select what he wore?

"Then come take a look." Isabel's wrinkly face creased in a smile, giving the slightest hint of jagged teeth. She didn't wait for Fin to respond before solidifying her selection and bidding the man farewell. She placed the yellow garment inside the wardrobe and left without another word.

Fin waited for the door to click shut before jumping out of the tub and creating a trail of water toward the drawer with his towel. Whatever escape plan he and Brando had, he was confident that Isabel would confound it.

Brando laughed when he saw Fin walk out of his room wearing yellow tights and a matching yellow tunic draped over his powder-blue, bunched-up, short pants. Fin mentioned how Isabel had picked it out and made a motion to convey she was likely the type of person to listen in on other people's conversations. They began speaking in code, or at least Fin hoped Brando understood his hidden implications as they were led through the palace corridors.

"She says she's here to keep an eye on me day and night," Fin whispered. Meaning, '*If we're going to get out of here, we have to figure out how to lose her.*'

"We had a chance to speak while you were getting ready. She's quite charming." Brando lifted a fist and feigned a punch forward. "Though, surely you don't need a chaperone when you aren't actively visiting with the princess, do you?"

'*I just met her, and I already hate her. If her only job is to make sure you don't seduce Dezi, then she should just as well go home.*'

"She took over Brixton's job of helping us find our way around and assisting us however we need," Fin spoke, moving forward with his eyes fixed on the woman's back. "We'll have to sort out a small problem of privacy. Other than that, I'm grateful for the assistance."

'*She's going to follow us everywhere. We'll need to sneak out of the watershed window if we have any chance of losing her.*'

"I was thinking about going into town after lunch," Brando pondered out loud. "Would you care to join me?"

'*Have you considered just walking out the front door?*'

"That might not be prudent, as you are a Lord who is courting the royal princess" Isabel raised a wrinkly, judgmental eyebrow over her shoulder. "Can you imagine? Stirring up intrigue so early in your career? I don't think the king would look fondly on the matter."

'*To answer your question, no, you cannot just walk out of the front door.*'

"Perhaps I will stay as well. There seems like a lot to explore here," Brando addressed Isabel, "I noticed a lot of naked statues around. Are they just for decoration, or are they in honor of someone specific?"

'I have an idea. It's a long shot, but it's not like we have many options.'

"Some are for decorations." Isabel gestured toward a chiseled statue of a woman in what appeared to be a nightgown. "Clive Rae the Second was especially fond of the more provocative pieces. Some statues outside are of well-known scholars, athletes, and some, the spiritually enlightened. Most of the statues are dwarven-made. I can take you on a tour if you are interested enough."

'Clive Rae the Second was a philanderer, something I suspect is a quality you share with him. I dare you to accept my offer to ogle the statues and prove me right.'

"A tour sounds like a great idea." Brando clasped his hands behind his back. "I would hate to waste a perfectly good opportunity to learn from someone so knowledgeable."

'I hope you have strong legs, you old hag. I have a feeling we'll be walking everywhere together.'

Chapter 36

Isabel led Finn and Brando inside a large room and departed to watch them from among uniformly standing servants. An older, sleek-looking man, dressed slightly differently than the other servers, tried handing her an empty tray. She swatted it out of his hand and admonished him with hissed whispers. Isabel would not let anyone disrupt her from her primary job of glaring at Fin from the back of the room.

They made their way toward the end of a great table opposite of what they assumed was the royal chair. They were about to sit down when Lord Walters called them toward the head of the table near the plush red chair. The two walked the length of the table, passing elegantly dressed nobles who whispered conspiratorially at seeing them.

Sitting down, Brando asked, "Did we miss dinner?" while a server filled his and Fin's glass with a deep red wine.

"Certainly not, but there has been a lot of talk about the new lord's challenge," Lord Walters gestured to a large man sitting opposite Fin. "Let me introduce you to Sir Goyder. He is especially excited to meet you."

Across the table, a large man raised a glass toward the two newcomers. Even sitting down, they could tell he was tall. His muscular arms bulged under his clothes like an overstuffed sausage. His belly, partially hidden by the table, held him snugly in an otherwise oversized chair.

"I can see why no one wanted to bet on you," Goyder greeted with a smirk. "Did you really stake a large gem on beating me?"

"It's just a friendly wager. Were there any other bets?" Fin looked around and noticed everyone at the table was craning their heads to listen in on the conversation; Sir Jeffcoat looked away.

"You might be a champion of the mine, but in here," Sir Goyder spoke, lifting his palms upward. "This is my domain. You would be hard-pressed to find someone to bet against me in the dining room."

The fifth bell vibrated the stone walls around them, causing the servers to exit the room in a single file.

"I'll bet against you." Brando leaned back and untied his coin purse. "How much?"

Goyder laughed. "Let's make this a gentlemen's bet. How about one month of guard duty? There's nothing like guard patrol to get a protector of the realm acquainted with his new surroundings."

Brando agreed, and the food was served. Round lids lifted off steaming plates displaying portions of lamb, venison, and poultry next to colorful vegetables, boiled potatoes, and a thick brown gravy. The smell was intoxicating.

Fin and Goyder finished their first serving at the same time. At Fin's direction, their empty plates went to the center of the table to track their progress. As Fin waited for his next plate, he looked at his stats. He had four basic stat points to distribute. His strength was at -10, Dexterity -8, and Constitution -5. He realized that his fight in the mine would have gone a lot smoother had he been lighter on his feet. So, after his second plate, he distributed a point toward Dexterity.

A server approached him with a third plate and lifted the domed covering. Instead of food, a letter was addressed to Lord Finlay of Dragonthrone. Fin thanked the server and handed the letter to Brando. He was too hungry for the correspondence.

Brando took the letter and opened it with his fork. The modish lettering was difficult to read but not impossible. When he finally deciphered the creatively shaped letters, he frowned. "It looks like you have tea with the princess at the sixth bell."

Lord Walters misinterpreted their shared look of sheer horror for something else entirely. "Ah, I remember the stresses of courting over tea. Just take a spoon of sugar, offer her cream, and you'll be alright. Remember that not all personalities match, so it isn't necessarily your fault if it goes awry."

"He's going to need more than a scoop of sugar to get him through this one," Brando mumbled, knowing exactly whose fault it would be when it went awry.

"I wouldn't do that," Lord Walters warned. "In love and war, how you take your tea speaks volumes about who you are. More than two spoons of sugar will announce a proclivity toward instant gratification. No sugar announces that you are perhaps stern and boring. One spoon will suffice. If you offer her cream, it shows that you are considerate."

Listening intently, Fin asked between bites, "How do you take your tea at war?"

"That could depend on any number of things," Lord Walters considered. "My favorite move is to take the cream. They have to work with me to get it if they want it. It shows that I hold my ground boldly but am also easy to work with. Consequently, if they take the cream, I eat the citrus."

None of this made sense to Fin or Brando, so Lord Walters explained, "The lemon is a cultural courtesy for those with a sore throat. But if you had a sore throat, it isn't likely you would feel well enough for tea. Regardless, it's there to show the host is caring. Eating a slice of lemon, rind and all, shows you have grit. You must keep a straight face, mind you, or it will have a reverse effect."

"How do you tell someone that you are unimpressed with them?" Brando asked eagerly.

Lord Walters laughed. "This is a fun move. Look at the honey, then opt for the sugar. Take a sip and then add more sugar. My mother perfected this one. She could make you sound unimpressive just by listening to you speak."

By the time Fin turned back toward the table, he noticed that Goyder had gotten a plate ahead and was waiting for his next one.

"It appears I have an appointment in less than an hour."

"Does that mean you are throwing in the napkin, so to speak?" Goyder scoffed.

Fin looked around. "I was going to recommend they bring the food out faster."

Listening intently to the conversation, Lord Walters summoned a servant and whispered in her ear. Moments later, a line of serving staff stood behind Fin and Goyder, each holding a covered plate.

Fin placed his fourth plate on his pile and dug into the next with haste. He added another point into

Dexterity and felt his joints and tendons loosening up. He realized he should have been upgrading Strength and Dexterity in pairs this whole time. He also felt more control over his knife and fork. He could eat faster.

Plate after plate stacked in tandem before Goyder had to loosen his belt. He did this as an intimidation, more than to relieve the pressure on his midsection. The move had the opposite effect on Fin; he took it as a sign that Goyder was reaching his limit.

Fin had two more basic stat points to allocate and wanted to use both. He began taking the lids off his new plates, dumping the contents on the plate in front of him, and sending the empty ones away. He brought his Dexterity to -5.

Goyder wiped his face with his fourth napkin. He had begun sweating profusely. He was slowing down. Fin leaned back in his chair and began enjoying his ever-refilling wine.

"Just because you're leaving soon doesn't mean that I can't catch up with you while you're gone." Goyder pointed a turkey leg aloft. "No one said anything about a time limit when we started."

This bit of information startled Fin. Given enough time, surely Goyder would be able to catch up a meager two plates. "What if I'm ten plates ahead by the time I leave?"

"I'll bet my roof it can't be done!" Lord Atrium shouted from several chairs away.

"If you get ten plates ahead of me by the time you leave, I'll concede," Goyder announced loud enough for the whole table to hear. "I'll even add twenty gold to the pot. You're already slowing down."

Fin procured two gold and two silver from his inventory, along with the blue gem. Brando dug out two gold and three silver from his pouch and added it to Fin's pile on the table. Goyder took out his money pouch and dumped it on top of the pile.

Fin used his last basic stat point to bring his Constitution to -4 to see what would happen. Aside from feeling like he hadn't eaten in two days, he felt life flow to his cheeks and behind his eyes. It felt like he had taken an afternoon nap in the shade. To the shock of everyone at the table, he began devouring his meal anew.

When he reached seven plates ahead, he had no option but to upgrade his basic stats with golden stat points. When he was about to do so, he noticed that Goyder's next plate had significantly smaller portions, and his own plate had larger ones. He realized the food on his plate had been steadily increasing for some time. Someone was clearly cheating, but it made no difference. He decided not to mention it and put a golden stat point to Constitution, bringing it to -3.

Relaxation and calmness came over Fin's body as he stacked another plate on his pile; Goyder did as well. Fin was still leading by seven plates, but he was also still hungry. Goyder's next plate was even smaller, while Fin's was larger yet.

Brando was about to say something when Fin stopped him, "This works out better for me."

The sixth bell rang, and everyone looked at Fin as if expecting him to accept defeat. He shrugged and said, "We didn't put a time limit on it. We just agreed on whenever I left."

If anyone was upset they didn't say anything as Fin started devouring his overfilled dinner plates. When he reached nine plates ahead, he was already stuffed. He had no other choice except to use another golden stat point. He brought his strength to -7 and didn't stop eating until his plates reached eleven over Goyder's.

Fin plucked the blue gem out of the pile of coins and slid the rest to Brando. "I have to go. Don't get stabbed."

Chapter 37

Fin tried testing out his body, but Isabel led the way slower than her usual gait. He wanted to run, jump, and walk on his hands, but he was stuck moving at Isabel's sauntering pace. It was as if she was intentionally trying to make him more late than he already was. The two had passed several guards before stopping at an ordinary door. It was typical for the castle but still stronger and sturdier than his front door back home.

Isabel knocked and said, "If we are too late, we can try again tomorrow."

The door swung open to reveal a nominal glare from a newly bandaged face.

"I specifically said "tea at sixth bell," but here you are at a quarter past," Dezi clipped her words. "Can I assume all farmers are as punctual as you?"

Fin shouldered past both Dezi and Isabel and entered the room. It was decorated with light blue patterns against a golden trim. Plants, tables, and tapestries decorated the corners of the room. He was surprised to find a row of instruments lining the wall.

Isabel voiced her horror at Fin's intrusion, but he ignored her and turned toward Dezi. "It appears you and I are courting now. I don't suppose you had anything to do with this?"

Dezi's anger melted instantly, and she offered him a chair. "That's what I wanted to talk about. Will you take tea?"

Fin sat in the chair next to the one Dezi gestured to and waited as she poured tea into two cups.

As soon as Dezi finished pouring the tea, she sat down and watched, astounded at Fin's firm grasp on conveying disappointment, tactical strength, tenderness, and something else she had never seen before. She feigned an air of polite patience as Fin took the cream and set it next to himself, out of her reach. Furthermore, he took a slice of lemon and put the whole thing in his mouth. He chewed the entire thing while looking under each lid for the honey. When he found it, he added a scoop of sugar into the jar of honey.

He looked as if he was making up his mind about something and then took a spoon of sugared honey and added it to his tea. He then offered her the cream he had swindled. She accepted, completely thrown off guard.

Dezi cleared her throat. "Do you want to see my scars?"

Fin looked up from his tea as Dezi began unbandaging her face. She revealed three raw scratch marks across her cheek.

"That will probably scar," Fin said blandly.

"That's what I'm afraid of," Dezi confessed, still unraveling the bandages. "At least no one will try to take me from you."

This time Fin was caught off guard. He sat speechless between the remarks, "If anyone wants you, I will gladly give them written permission," and "I don't think your face is the problem here." Even with the scars,

Dezi could be considered beautiful, an aspect that was hard to see behind her treacherous personality. Fin felt she was also pure evil, which was enough reason to leave as soon as possible.

"It wasn't my idea," Dezi said, sipping her tea. "All I did was tell my father how much of an asset you would be to the kingdom. You are brave, a strong fighter, and you rescued me. He took it for something else."

Fin drained his tea and set down his empty cup. "I'll tell you what. I will pretend to court you, whatever that means, but I'm still leaving. I have a goblin-run slave camp to liberate, no thanks to you or your father. If that is all, I wish you a good night."

Fin stood up, but Dezi grabbed his arm and stopped him. "Can you stay for a little longer? It gets so boring in here by myself. Do you want to play a game or hear some music?"

"You have musicians on staff?" Fin asked, eyeing the neat row of organized instruments.

"I do if you want me to get them," Dezi said, walking towards a medium-sized harp. "Or I can play something myself?"

Fin looked longingly at the door but resigned himself to his chair. "I can stick around for a song if you want to play something."

Dezi sat on a stool and leaned up against the harp. She tested several of the strings and then began to play. Her fingers started weaving patterns of sound together, slowly at first, plucking a single string at a time. Her song became more intricate without changing the cadence as she grasped at two, three, and four strings at a time. The pastel melody bounced cheerfully to a simple rhythm.

Fin's defenses slipped, and he found himself smiling. When the song ended, He clapped genuinely. He wondered if it was possible to appreciate someone you despised wholeheartedly. He wondered if the Dark Underlord was a woman that could also play the harp.

Dezi stood and curtsied. "Sometimes Father has me play for his guests. Will you stay for one more?"

Fin shrugged off his earlier rush and waved her on. She replaced the larger harp with a smaller, simpler one she called a lyre. This time, the song was less intricate but deep and haunting. She played through a melodic loop several times, and to Fin's great surprise, she started singing.

Her voice was pure and inviting, which stood juxtaposed with the evil in her heart. Her song spoke of planting in the autumn and asked if the winter wine could still melt her heart? Fin knew that once grapes froze, they would be less than useless. If you weren't planting snap peas, some leafy greens, or asparagus, you were better off planting mid-spring. Some seeds could preserve through the winter, but there would be a small chance of survival. Potatoes, maybe, but not grapes and not from a newly planted vineyard.

The haunting music continued, but instead of basic farming, Dezi sang about a lover departing for the winter and their hearts freezing. Fin imagined he and Dezi were the people she sang about. She was the one crying and telling him not to go. Then he brushed the hair away from her cold face, revealing old, tear-streaked scars. Just before his lips touched hers, he snapped out of it. He sat petrified of his disloyal imagination.

Dezi played the song's last note and then stood and bowed playfully. "What do you think?"

Fin's heart was in his throat. He knew that if magic was involved, he would have been able to see it. He just couldn't think of any other reason why his emotions would directly oppose his mind. All he knew was he needed to get as far away from her as he could and never return. At least not until he upgraded his wisdom. He quickly checked to make sure he hadn't upgraded his wisdom. He hadn't.

"I am nearly speechless," Fin said, trying to shake off the spell he was under. "I had no idea you could do that. Can you play every instrument?"

"My father won't let me learn to play the lute," Dezi frowned. "He says it's below me."

"I really enjoyed myself tonight," Fin smiled, casually rushing for the door. "Thank you for inviting me."

As soon as he left her room, his smile dropped to a scowl. He cursed his emotions as he walked. He would be leaving tomorrow, regardless of the circumstances.

Chapter 38

Fin woke up earlier than usual. He opened his eyes, expecting the light to pour into his small window. Instead, it trickled in like a leaking gutter on a misty day. It was still mostly dark, but for whatever reason, he felt well-rested.

He stood up and donned yesterday's clothes. On the farm, he would have needed to wash the caked mud off his shirt from the day prior, but he hadn't been around dirt or anything else that would soil his clothes. He paced his room, considering waking up Brando, but decided against the idea. Brando would probably get upset. Instead, he considered his plan of escape.

After four laps around his room, Fin decided to pace the halls of the castle. As soon as he stepped outside, he heard the pattering of feet running away from him. It was strange, but he realized that Isabel had most likely hired someone to wake her if he showed his face. He made a mental note to leave his room sporadically throughout all hours of the night. That is if the plan he was scheming didn't work.

After wandering around for a quarter of an hour, Isabel rounded on him. "What are you doing up so early?"

"I'm an early riser," Fin guessed before turning the question back on her. "What are you doing up so early?"

"I'm up to tell you to go back to your room," Isabel snarled.

"Not going to happen," Fin stood his ground. "You go back to your room."

"I'll tell the guards."

"For what?" Fin asked before continuing his morning exploration. Isabel must have decided it was a futile battle and didn't reply. She remained quiet and stalked silently in tow.

When the sun had risen to a decent hour, Fin visited Brando. Two knocks and he opened the door to find the man completely submerged in blankets and pillows. After waking him, he told him the plan. He then repeated the plan when Brando was fully awake.

Brando shot out of bed and put himself together. In a matter of minutes, he was dressed and out the door. Fin returned to his room and waited.

Hours later, a knock came to his door, and he answered. He opened it, expecting Brando, but found Brixton instead.

"I have a letter for you, my lord," Brixton announced, holding out the folded white parchment.

Fin opened his door and invited the young man in. "Did Isabel hire you to follow me around?" He asked, taking the letter and breaking the seal.

"No, my lord," Brixton said with an honest tone. "She has Todrey and Phillip following you."

"Brixton, I might need a favor. Can you hang on a moment?" Fin asked, unfolding the letter and reading it. It was a summons from the princess to take a stroll around the garden at noon. His new time limit to leave was noon. "Actually, I might have to ask you for two favors."

Brando entered the room to find the young page waiting patiently while Fin drafted what looked like his fourth letter, or maybe his fifth, by the look of the crumpled papers around him.

"Please tell me you're not, uh," Brando hesitated at the sight of Brixton eavesdropping. "Informing people of... certain things?"

"I've been invited for a light stroll at noon," Fin said, lifting up his feather quill so it didn't drop ink on his sixth letter revision. "I am rescheduling for a different day."

Brando leaned down to inspect one of the failed letters, and Fin snatched it from his hands. "I can't let you read this."

"Why?" Brando asked, moving toward another.

Fin started snatching the scattered papers and feeding them to his inventory. "I'm not very proud of some of these."

Brando relented and held up his hands in surrender. "Okay, you win. Anyway, I brought the goods."

Fin walked over and looked out of the door. In the hallway stood a cheerful looking dwarf guarding a hand cart. There was a sheet of fabric covering the load it carried.

"Do you think you can get the cart inside?" Fin asked, holding the door open.

"I think it'll fit. I've gotten bigger things into tighter spaces" The dwarf chuckled. "The name's Rosby."

Fin introduced himself and, after a brief hesitation, introduced Brixton.

The dwarf nodded to the boy. "It's a pleasure meeting you, young sir."

"My Beloved Dezi, I regret to inform you that I will not be available today…" Brando read from a crumpled piece of paper in his hands. "What is this? She didn't turn you, did she?"

Fin's face flushed red. At least Brando hadn't been reading one of the others. He wanted to give the impression that he was still interested in the courtship, so no one looked for him for the rest of the day. Hopefully, that would buy them enough time to escape. He couldn't explain why leaving on good terms or even with false romantic words was important. Surely the princess would understand that he didn't mean any of the heartfelt things he inscribed in his letter.

"It's all part of the plan," Fin finally said, and then added for the sake of the loose ends in the room, "To surprise her with this secret thing that we aren't talking about."

Fin went to his unfinished letter and made several more entries. When the ink was dry, he folded the paper and gave it to Brixton, along with some coins. "Please give this to the princess just before midday. The timing is important."

"And the other favor?" Brixton asked, tucking the letter in his jacket.

"If you see me running, tell whoever is chasing me that I went the other way."

When the boy left, Rosby pulled a hammer and chisel from his satchel. "I appreciate the job and all, but I have to warn you, I've never sculpted a thing in my life. I'm an accountant. Are you sure you want me to do this?"

"We don't need you to be a sculptor." Brando ripped the canvas sheet away from three stacked rocks. "We need you to look and sound like one."

"Are you saying that just because I'm four feet tall, I automatically look like I know how to carve stone?" Rosby huffed.

"Yes," Fin and Brando said in unison.

Fin knelt down in front of the dwarf. "No one would believe a human could build a perfect sculpture in under an hour, but they'll believe in you. Now, can you please start making chisel noises?"

After a long period of the constant ping of hammer on chisel, a knock sounded from the door.

Brando took the blanket off the bed and threw it toward Fin. "Pretend that you're naked. It will make the story more believable, and they'll be too embarrassed to stick around."

Without hesitation, Fin stripped off his tunic and undershirt and wrapped the pale green comforter around his waist. As soon as he was covered, Brando opened the door.

Isabel stood at the doorway with a guard on either side of her. "What is the meaning of all this noise?" She asked the pond of guilty faces.

"We are making a sculpture of the hero of the mine, your ladyship," Brando recited his rehearsed lines. "It should be done shortly."

Isabel stomped in the room while the dwarf covered the messy mound of small boulders. She towered over the dwarf and shot Fin a disapproving glance. "You three are up to no good. Also, by the look of it, you aren't nearly finished with anything."

"I carve the stone from the inside out, ma'am," Rosby patted the canvas-covered rock. "It's an ancient dwarven technique."

"Will you please get out? I'm not decent." Fin said to the crusty old woman. "Who gave you permission to barge in here anyway?"

The guards began shuffling their feet. Finally, one said, "Let's go," but waited for Isabel to follow.

"I'm keeping an eye on you," Isabel warned as she walked toward the guards. She mumbled some curses and slammed the door behind her.

"That went better than expected," Brando said cheerfully. "Carving the stone from the inside out, huh? Rosby, you're a genius."

"My price just went up three silver," Rosby said, continuing his arbitrary chiseling. "You're lucky you long leggers can't tell us apart."

"You get us out of here as planned, and we'll give you an extra gold for your trouble," Fin stated, looking through his inventory. He didn't have more than twenty-three copper coins on him. "Brando, please tell me you have the money from last night?"

Brando left the room and then returned with an overstuffed coin pouch in his hands. "She's still out there. Waiting," He said, tossing the bag in the air.

Fin caught the bag and flipped Rosby a gold coin. "That's your bonus." He removed half of the coins and tossed the bag Back to Brando. "We'll pay you the rest when we're out of here."

"Are we ready to go now?" Brando asked, attaching his coin purse to his belt.

Fin took a deep breath and then let it out slowly. "I'm ready if you are."

Chapter 39

Fin stepped out into the passageway and found Isabel a reasonable distance down the hall. He pretended not to see her and turned in the opposite direction. He walked casually at first, brushing the dust off his tunic and seemingly taking his time. As soon as he rounded a corner, he broke into a run.

He could hear rapid footsteps approaching the corner as he turned down another corridor. He also heard Isabel curse and call for her helpers. At the end of the hall, he turned again. He had almost made a complete loop. Just when he was about to make his final turn, a pair of guards appeared around the corner in the direction he was running. He forced himself to slow down and walk with a nonchalant gait.

"Good morning, guards," Fin greeted with a nod of the head. "Beautiful day for a walk, wouldn't you say?"

"It is my lord," One of them responded as they passed Fin. They both began talking about wishing to be outside in the warm weather. Their conversation persisted while Fin rounded the last corner in the loop and broke for his room.

Brando and Rosby stood at the ready with an empty hand cart and canvas sheet. Fin stepped on the cart and covered himself up with the canvas.

Brando cleared his throat. "Erm, shouldn't you get undressed first?"

Fin pulled the sheet off his head and looked incredulous at Brando. "Why?"

"When Isabel came in, you made her believe you were creating a nude statue." Brando pointed out, looking uncomfortable. "Wouldn't it seem strange if your statue was fully clothed?"

"It was your idea for me to strip down in the first place!" Fin flared with anger.

Rosby had no interest in seeing Fin naked any more than anyone else, but he saw the logic of it. "I hate to say this, but I can't help but agree with the lad. You have to get naked."

"Quickly now," Brando looked at the door. "We don't have much time."

Fin visibly deflated as defeat settled on his shoulders. "Don't let anyone peek under the sheet."

When everyone had turned around, Fin began undressing and stowing his clothes. He found Dezi's invitation in his tunic. After a moment of hesitation, he threw it to the ground. It was best if he left her and her invitations in the past.

He activated his Stone Vizard ability. The color of his body morphed into that of a textured stone. He hastened for the protection of the dingy cloth and the cart.

Brando reached for the door just as it burst open. Isabel stormed inside with a face red from anger and glistening from effort.

"Where is he?" Isabel shot an accusing finger at Brando. "I knew you were up to something the moment I saw you."

Isabel noticed the sheet covering a person on the cart. "Do you think this is funny?" She ripped the sheet off Fin's head, revealing an intricately carved statue with no shortage of detail and every shortage of censorship. "Oh my!" She gasped.

"I don't know where Fin went off to, but if he was in here, you would see him," Brando floundered the statement's delivery.

"Wherever he is, I intend to find him," Isabel proclaimed, moving further into the room to search every possible hiding place.

Fin remembered Dezi's invitation. If Isabel thought he was having a private meeting with the princess, surely she would start looking elsewhere. He subtly pointed to the letter on the floor in front of him.

Brando noticed Fin was trying to catch his attention, but he refused to look down. The incessant moving of his hand was way too close to other things he didn't want to look at, rock colored or not. Rosby, on the other hand, was at eye level with Fin's pointing finger. It was the worst part about being a dwarf. He made a sound like, "Achh!" when he looked directly at Fin's hand and noticed what was beyond.

Isabel moved to the front of the room and investigated the outburst. She found the dwarf picking up a letter on the ground.

"What is that?" She asked.

"I'm sure it's nothing," Rosby hid the letter behind his back. He wasn't sure what it was for, but he knew Isabel shouldn't see it.

"Give me that!" She commanded, trying to snatch whatever it was the halfling was holding. Finally, she showed an unnatural strength by picking Rosby off the ground. That was the second worse part about being a dwarf. Brando stepped forward to stop the bullying mad woman, but she got to the letter first.

"A walk with the princess, huh?" Isabel said, reading the note. "Is this where he went?"

"It's not even midday yet," Brando started building a story of a secret rendezvous. "What could they possibly be doing so long before their date?"

Isabel didn't need to think about it for very long. After another thorough appraisal of Fin's statue, she left to catch Fin red-handed.

Fin wasn't sure if his face would show him blushing, but he didn't care. He put the sheet back over his head. "Let's hurry."

Leaving the castle was easy for everyone but Fin. On more than several occasions, guards demanded to see what was under the sheet. More so than not, they ironically joked about the cold weather. Still, Brando pushed his naked friend towards the exit. When they were free, they paid Rosby two more gold coins and gave him the cart.

In town, Fin bought and changed into more common-looking clothes. He also bought a light jacket with a hood to disguise his features. Brando kept his rich guise. He didn't want to spend any more time in Clive Rae than was absolutely necessary.

Fin waited outside as Brando went inside the Hornblower to retrieve their horses. It took longer than expected, but soon enough, they were saddling them up in a dimly lit alleyway. They were about finished when a disheveled-looking man approached them.

"This is an odd place to be saddling horses." He said, moving closer.

Something in the man's soft and eerie voice conveyed that he was not an upstanding citizen. Without talking, Brando stepped forward and punched the man square in the jaw. The man fell backward on the ground and didn't move.

The man hadn't said anything wrong. An alley was, in fact, an odd place to be saddling horses. He wasn't sure if it was the slimy way the man looked, talked, or approached them with his hands hidden away; Brando could not say. He felt like it was the right thing to do and didn't have time to mull around about it.

Fin looked at the unconscious man and whistled, "This guy really set you off, huh?"

"Frome be with him," Brando replied.

Fin slipped a silver coin into the man's shirt and got on his horse. As he rode toward the city gates, he considered the man. Did he deserve to be knocked out cold? Probably not, but he would have never approached someone in a dark alley. Maybe some lessons needed to be learned the hard way. Like courting a princess. He should have never answered Dezi's letter in the first place. There are no good options with princesses. But the one with the greatest chance of a continued life expectancy is to run. And keep running.

Chapter 40

Nobody stopped them or gave them a second glance as Fin and Brando rode through the front gates of Clive Rae. Finally, they were on the open road. As soon as the city disappeared behind them, a sense of freedom hung in the air like a bird in flight resting on a tremendous gust of wind.

"I'm hungry," Brando stated. "Please tell me we brought something to eat."

Fin searched his inventory and then his saddle bags. He produced the last of the bread and fruit he had saved. After tossing some questionably colored bits by the roadside, he gave Brando one of the two nearly empty water skins.

"It looks like this is it. It should be enough to get us to where we're going." Fin pondered out loud. He thought he had become accustomed to going long periods without eating or drinking, but it seemed his body had forgotten. He wondered whether it was all he had eaten recently or if his newfound strength needed more sustenance.

"We should be fine," Brando said before breathing the air loudly through his nostrils. "Look at us; it's just you, me, and a massive bag of gold out in the wild with sparse provisions. We've come a long way since we were doing the same thing, poor."

When Fin had finished his half of his provisions, he traded his worries of hunger for his favorite rock.

"Have you given any thoughts about what you're going to do after this is all over?"

"A few," Brando spat a seed into the rolling brush. "With your ability to procure infinite wealth, I was thinking I would stroll into town and throw coins around like I pilfered the royal treasury just to see the looks on my first and second wife's faces. Then, I don't know. Maybe check out the giant hill of dragon manure that is our family secret. You know, now that I'm part of the family."

"There may be a royal decree saying you are part of the family, but you'll always be an orphan to me." Fin joked.

Brando smiled and shook his head. "Any plans yourself?"

"I have no idea," Fin guided his horse back on the trail. "Like you said, I have the possibility for infinite wealth, but I haven't really decided what I want to do."

"You don't suppose killing some goblin slavers would make you feel better?" Brando asked with a half-cocked eyebrow. "You could pull the beating heart out of one of their chests. It would make a great story for the grandkids."

"I mean, these quests aren't going to complete themselves," Fin shrugged. "I guess that sounds like something that would make me feel better. After that, I wouldn't mind seeing the look on your ex-wives' faces watching you throw money around, either."

A large smile bloomed on Brando's face. "If we're going to do this thing, we need our swords sharpened. And we need some armor. We'll fire the crossbow at it to see if it's strong enough!"

The two made battle plans as the sun and road moved orthogonally apart. Their village destination peeked over the road when the silver sunset began dimming. Once inside, the few people still left moving around the streets shot them repeated glances and muttered to each other softly. Fin and Brando, transfixed over finding the unnamed inn, hadn't given it a second thought.

Brando pushed open the door to the village Inn and made his way around the bar. He took out two mugs and filled them with the cider cask.

"You shouldn't be here," Felix greeted them with a nervous look on his face. "There's a bounty on your heads."

Brando slid a mug to Fin from the other side of the bar. "What does that even mean? Like, just our heads? As if the rest of me holds no real value?" He took a drink.

"Easier to carry around," Fin guessed before drinking himself.

Brando turned to refill his empty mug. "Felix, would you mind explaining what has everyone so excited about my head?"

"The Brayburn brothers returned and started telling a story about the two slavers that attacked them on the street. They described you." Felix's eyes twitched towards the door. "I returned the weapons you gave me as you asked, but it just confirmed their story. Eugal said he witnessed you hiding the slave cart before you entered the town, but I saw how angry he was when you beat him at his own game. I know he's lying, but everyone else believes him. They'll come for you; they probably already know you're here."

"It looks like we're sleeping in the woods tonight." Brando frowned, setting down his empty mug.

"Is there any way we can-" Fin started before the door was thrown open, spilling in a mismatched brood of armed men.

"There they are!" Eugal yelled in an overly excited voice. "Don't let them escape!"

Before Fin could set his empty mug on the counter, he was surrounded by sword points, spear points, and one rusty, triple-pointed pitchfork. He raised an empty mug parallel to his other hand.

"Don't think you can get away with leering at our women and children in hopes for your slave cart and get away with it," Eugal declared bravely from behind a proverbial fence of weapons. "I saw everything, you slimy bandits!"

"What are you talking about?" Brando asked, incredulous. "We haven't leered at anyone."

"The village elder will listen to both sides in the morning," the constable said calmly. "Eugal, may I ask you to draft your first-hand account of everything you witnessed these two doing?"

"I will go home and do that now," Eugal smiled coyly and exited the inn.

Fin and Brando were led out of the inn and down the street. They walked silently forward, guided, and followed by spear point until Brando gently nudged Fin's arm. When he had Fin's attention, he imperceptibly motioned towards Eugal, entering a house, presumably his own. It had to have been his house. It was more significant than the surrounding ones and separated from them with large sections of meticulously groomed property. Matching trees formed a single line through the property, only broken by a stone path to the front door. Fin nodded. The message was clear, and they both memorized where the house was in case of an opportunity to confront the man later.

Chapter 41

There was only one prison cell. It was large enough for five people with a bench that seated two. The rest of the cell was a droll combination of bricks, bars, and an old drunk sleeping it off on the bench. When Fin and Brando were ushered in, the cell door opened and shut without so much as a grading screech.

"I'm going to kill him," Brando said as soon as they were alone. He sat on the cold stone floor, folded his arms, and fumed.

Before Fin could reply, a voice startled him from behind.

"Water?" The man asked, tinging the atmosphere with the smell of fermented berries.

Fin, nearly to his feet, stood up the rest of the way and called for the guards. "Hey, this guy needs some water."

From the lack of response in clear view of the lantern light outside the bars, Fin could tell no one was in the building. "Sorry, I don't think anyone is coming," he broke the news to the drunk, who was already sleeping again.

"You know, I have been detained more times in a week than I have my entire life," Brando considered out loud. "Kind of makes me feel like I've fallen in with the wrong crowd."

"Hey, we're the good guys here." Fin said with the same breath, "How long are we waiting until we break out of here and beat Eugal's face in?"

"I just hope we don't break into the wrong house," Brando considered, leaning back on the cool brick wall.

"This guy might know," Fin threw his thumb over his shoulder to the sleeping figure on the bench. "Let's just ask."

Brando got up and moved towards the bench. "Hey," he reached out and shook the man's shoulder, "Where does Eugal live?"

"I'm not allowed," the man lamented. "He seems to think I owe him money."

"His house is the big one, right?" Fin asked. "Lots of property?"

"Yes, now leave me alone," the man grumbled. "I'm trying to sleep."

"Last question, and we will go away," Brando promised. "What does he have in front of his house?"

"I don't know," The man rolled over, opened his eyes, and squinted angrily at the too-curious strangers. "A walkway? A bunch of trees? A pissing dog? This is the one night I have without my nagging wife yapping my ear off, but now you two are asking me basket case questions about landscaping! Can I please have peace for one night in my entire life?"

"I'm sorry," Fin offered a solemn apology. "We'll leave you alone."

Without another word, the man rolled over and huffed.

Brando walked toward the gate and waved Fin away from the man. "I think we have the right house.

I'm so mad I don't know what I'm going to do. Eugal is going to pay for this."

Just to be safe, the two waited and listened in silence. After a sufficient period without hearing any voices or sounds, they agreed it was time to leave.

Fin stood up and inspected the lock. A basic skeleton key-operated latch was lowered between the frame and the gate. Fin didn't necessarily want people figuring out his secret, so he tried to keep the damage to a minimum this time. He activated Caustic Breath and briefly blew the golden mist onto the latch. He then tried pushing on the gate.

"What are you doing?" Brando asked, watching Fin's attempt at escape fail.

"Just trust me on this one. I'll explain later," He said and gently blew again on the lock. After the fourth time, Fin pushed, and the gate opened with a snap. They both paused and looked at the sleeping stranger in unison. He didn't stir, so they opened the gate the rest of the way and walked out.

Exiting was easy; the door leading outside was unguarded, and the night was sufficiently dark to hide their escape. They took the lantern with them and used it to retrace their steps. Brando followed Fin at a distance. They decided they would be less recognizable in the dark if they weren't directly next to each other.

The empty streets eventually led them to the house they saw Eugal enter earlier that night. The rows of trees cast uniform shadows that they crept through. The soft crunch of grass masked the sounds of their heartbeats as they approached the front door.

Brando tried to open the door, but it was locked. A few hand gestures later, they walked around the house for a different entrance. They found a side door and a back door, both locked.

Brando left to investigate their surroundings. Fin stayed and looked around for another option. There was a balcony at the back of the house. He covered the lantern to the best of his ability. Still, he knew that if anyone looked out from that balcony, they wouldn't have a problem finding him sneaking around, half glowing.

Brando returned sometime later with a ladder in both hands. It looked well-built, but the wood squeaked and rattled as they leaned it against the balcony.

"We should hurry," Brando said, knowing that if the sound of the ladder drew any attention, the best thing they could do was get out of sight. So, he went first, climbing quickly and as quietly as the ladder allowed. Fin followed behind.

On the balcony, Brando was already trying the door. When it cracked open, he faced Fin and nodded. He tried opening the door quietly, but he might as well have opened it with a hatchet. The door groaned as it opened.

"Who's there?" A tired and concerned voice asked.

Brando ran in, and Fin followed, closing the door on the way inside. Shuffling noises twisted around like sheets, and a voice was stifled mid-exclamation. Fin uncovered his lantern to see he was standing in Eugal's bedroom. Brando clapped a hand over the man's mouth.

"Is there anyone else in the house?" Brando asked in a deep whisper.

Eugal shook his head. Or at least he tried to, considering the hands encompassing his face.

Fin closed the curtains and inspected the room with the light. There was a messy bookshelf holding just as many trinkets as books, a large closet, and a writing desk with a written letter of some sort. Upon further inspection, it wasn't a letter but the statement Eugal had promised to deliver in the morning. He picked it up and began reading.

"Brando," Fin interrupted. "This is the witness statement. It says he saw us following young women around and overheard us saying, and I quote, "These girls will be perfect for the slave pits." It also says he saw us robbing people on his trip to Clive Rae but didn't recognize us until after we left."

Brando let out a huge sigh. "Eugal, I'm going to release your mouth so you can explain why you wrote these things about us. I really hope you scream, I really do, because if you try to weasel your way out of this when I was giving you a chance to explain yourself, I'll kill you."

He slowly removed his hands, and Eugal began talking. "I'm sorry, I've been under a lot of pressure lately. I made a mistake, and I was wrong. I'll never do it agai-"

Brando put a hand back on his mouth. "What are we going to do? If we were found guilty, they would have hanged us for slavers and all for what? These blatant lies? Not to mention the damage to my reputation. Our reputations. Fin, how are we going to make this right?"

Fin lowered the parchment and considered the question. "As far as our lives go, there's no making that right. I mean, I wouldn't trade my life for all the gold in the world, but he ultimately tried to get us killed with this statement. Let's ask him what he would do."

"Well, Eugal, what would you do if you were in our position?" Brando asked, lifting his hand off the man's mouth.

"I would understand that sometimes we make mistakes, and I would forgive you," Eugal made his best effort to put on angelic features. "If you forgive me this grave error, I understand that your lives are priceless, so I will give you a priceless gift. I will also swear my loyalty to you from now until forever."

Fin sighed. "I don't know, this is a pretty nasty letter. I guess I just need to think about it. Eugal, do you have any rope to tie you up while we consider this?"

"In my storeroom," he said helpfully. "Downstairs, first door on your left."

"I'll be right back," Fin said, alighting the lantern on the desk and leaving the room. He followed the staircase down and found the door. Inside, he found tools, gardening equipment, and the rope he was looking for. Before exiting, he noticed six crates filled to the brim with green apples. It reminded him about the apple pie.

He left the storeroom and searched the house until he found what he was looking for. On a wooden shelf stacked to the ceiling sat rows of the apple pies Heidle the Hammer had told them about. Some sat on receipts showing they were already sold, awaiting delivery. Fin took a pie and a receipt and ran upstairs. He had an idea.

Chapter 42

When Eugal was properly bound and gagged, Fin pulled Brando off to the side and explained his idea. Brando's frown lessened with each passing word until, finally, he was nodding his head in agreement. They immediately started searching the house for supplies.

They gathered bread, dried fruit and meat, cider, wine, salt, herbs, frying pans, lanterns, and other items they would need on their journey forward. They also found blankets to bundle everything together for easier stowing. Fin added several more pies to their collection, all gathered near the desk.

"Eugal, we have decided that we are going to be merciful with you," Fin said, pulling off the man's gag and untying his ropes. "However, you have to figure out how to clear our names while we're gone and promise never to do it again."

"Yes, I will tell everyone the truth," Eugal said eagerly.

"I wouldn't do that," Brando warned the man. "You've lied so much already that you'll probably need to do some more lying to even start clearing things up."

"Sage advice," Eugal stated humbly. "I will consider how to clear your names in the most delicate way possible."

"I believe you," Fin said honestly before gesturing toward the gathered items. "I know it's late in the evening, but do you mind if we buy these items from you? I hope you don't mind too terribly."

"You can take them," Eugal brushed his hands upward. "They're yours."

Brando winced. "We just don't feel comfortable taking things from you after tying you up like that. It would ease my conscience to know we bought them at a fair price from you."

"By all means, you can have them all for one copper," Eugal gave a slimy smile.

"Let's negotiate each item individually; we have some coin," Fin suggested. "Can you make us some receipts and do this transaction over the table?"

"I will need my logbook, but I have everything else I need right here."

Eugal informed Fin where the logbook was, and Fin was happy to get it for him. Soon enough, Brando was holding up items, and Eugal was giving a price for each. In some cases, Brando was too surprised at the low cost and insisted on paying more. Fin walked into the closet and started browsing the man's wardrobe. Periodically, he would come out of the closet holding up a set of clothes and ask if he could purchase them. Eugal was more than happy to add the items to the growing list.

Finally, Eugal held the finished receipt up for Brando's inspection. Brando looked over it, and when he agreed, both men signed the receipt, and Brando produced a single gold and a single copper coin.

Brando gave the receipt to Fin, who scrutinized it.

"Now I want you to write a receipt for two slaves bought from someone named Jack and Barnes," Fin stated, holding their receipt in his hands. "Let it specify that it's for a woman and a child for the price of three gold."

Eugal's eyes went wide. "I can't do that! That would imply I was buying slaves!"

Fin procured a knife from their pile of items and handed it to Brando. "That's the point. I'm sure you can understand we would be apprehensive to trust you will keep your word. So, we need insurance. Hence, we have receipts for all these items. Now, you can't say these items were stolen. Who would believe robbers came into your house to pay for everything they took?"

Brando took the knife and held it to Eugal's throat. "A woman and child. Jack and Barnes."

Eugal scribbled out the receipt and slammed his quill on the desk.

"You need to sign it," Brando pushed the point of the knife into the man's neck.

Eugal signed, and Fin wrote 'Jack' and 'Barnes' at the bottom. He then lifted the paper and compared it to his own receipt. "Your signature isn't the same."

"Make another one," Brando smacked Eugal on the head with the side of the knife and then placed the tip back against his throat. "This time, two men."

The cycle went on and on. Eugal would make a receipt, Fin would sign it 'Jack' and 'Barnes' and then stow it away. Finally, they had him start a new series of receipts.

"Now I want you to sell these two slaves to someone named Goblin Chef," Fin shuffled through his stack of papers until he found the first one. "A woman and a child, but this time, we're going to sell them for more. What was that concept you taught me? A keystone? Since you bought them for three gold, you're going to sell them for six and turn a profit."

Eugal resigned himself to making the false receipts. He made one after the other, not even trying to convolute his signature. When they were all finished, Fin paired the pieces of paper in his hands and stowed them.

"Are we done now?" Eugal asked, defeated.

"Not quite," Brando smiled. "Now is when you hold up your end of the bargain. We have taken your advice to heart. I understand that sometimes we make mistakes, and I forgive you. Since our lives are priceless, you have promised a priceless gift and to swear loyalty from now until forever."

Eugal began talking, but Brando raised his hand. "Him first. We are two different people, after all."

Eugal faced Fin, inhaled, and swore his loyalty. "I swear loyalty to you from now until forever."

Fin noticed and pulled up his notification the moment it appeared.

Minion Quest Complete: Gain one minion. +1 Active Ability, +1 Level, +1 gold stat point, +1 basic stat point.

Active Ability: Lesser Control Minion

Fin closed his notifications just as Eugal finished swearing his loyalty to Brando. "It looks like I already got my priceless gift."

"And what's that?" Brando asked.

"I don't exactly know yet; let's find out together," Fin activated Lesser Control Minion. "Eugal, dance a jig."

Eugal immediately started dancing, a frown growing ever prominent across his brow.

"What is this?" he asked, swinging his legs around, rocking his arms back and forth, and kicking in every direction.

"Whatever it is, it's entertaining," Fin smiled.

Brando wiped the knife he was holding on his pants and then cut into one of the pies. He pulled a piece out and ate, still watching Eugal.

"Having him dance is genius," Brando said with jealousy. "I wish I would have thought of that."

Fin asked for some pie, and they both ate in silence as they watched a very sad man do a very joyful dance.

Eugal began sweating and swearing. "Make it stop!" he shouted.

Fin reacted to the yelling like a physical blow. "Okay, stop dancing." He said, not wanting the shouts and stomps to attract any attention.

Eugal stopped dancing, put his hands on his knees, and bent over, fighting for breath.

"The pie is delicious. Do you make it yourself?" Brando asked, inspecting the rare jewel in the lamplight.

Eugal just nodded, unable to get the words out.

"For my priceless gift, I want a lifetime supply of pies," He took another bite and reveled in the flavor of it. It was sweet and sour, creamy and crunchy, and his hunger made it the most magical thing he had ever tasted. "An endless supply of pies. I want my oldest to inherit the wealth of pies if I decide to get married a third time and have children."

Eugal reluctantly walked over to his desk and wrote yet another receipt for an endless supply of pies. He signed it and wrote, 'Paid in full.' He begrudgingly handed the paper to Brando.

Fin busied himself with lighting their new lanterns and stacking everything on their new blankets. When everything was ready, he lifted the bundles and stowed them. Eugal looked astonished, but the two ignored him.

"It's been fun, Eugal. Don't forget to clear our names while we're gone," Brando said, gathering the rope together. "I'll tie him up now."

"Wait, if he's tied up and someone finds him like that, it might serve to prove his story," Fin considered. "Let me try something."

Fin took his lantern and opened the back door a crack. He then activated Lesser Minion Control and spoke, "Eugal, go to sleep and don't wake up until morning."

Eugal walked to his bed, lifted his sheets, and got in. Brando stared in disbelief as the man's breathing slowed until he was making a soft snore.

"I'll explain later," Fin whispered and motioned Brando onto the balcony.

Chapter 43

Fin and Brando walked through the streets with only one of their lanterns lit. They navigated toward their horses at the inn only to discover a group of men with torches surrounding the place. They both realized they spent too long at Eugal's, and it was apparent that someone had noticed they were missing. Fin immediately extinguished the lantern, and they slipped down an alleyway to watch the group. They watched for a long time, but the group did not look like they were about to move.

"Should we just cut our losses and go on foot?" Fin asked, feeling exhausted.

"I'll take care of this," Brando whispered confidently. "Just get these lanterns lit and keep them covered. Then get ready to run for the horses."

Brando left his lantern beside the other and moved farther into the alley. Fin did his best to cover them behind a stack of broken baskets before lighting them. He then sat and waited for whatever Brando was going to do.

"They're over here!" Brando's disguised voice shouted from across the building.

The men jerked toward the direction save for one who shouted back, "Who are you?"

Brando responded, "Hurry! They're getting away!" The men all charged in that direction, throwing caution to the wind.

Fin grabbed his covered lanterns and raced for the inn. The horses startled at his approach, but he quieted and saddled them as fast as possible. Just as Fin had climbed on his horse, Brando ran around the corner and followed suit. They set out Northward with a hurried clip.

Too dark to ride without a light source, they held their lanterns high, revealing as much as possible. There was no use hiding the light anyway; the horses were making enough noise to make finding them easy enough. The glow kept them on the right path and signaled others to follow.

Two men ran out with swords in hand. Brando pointed to the right and yelled, "They went that way! We're riding around to cut them off!" The two men bolted toward where Brando had pointed without another word.

"I can't believe that worked!" Fin remarked, trying to keep up with Brando's horse.

"I was a part of a manhunt once," Brando explained. "There was so much confusion that we gave up. Later, we found the person we were looking for was helping us search the whole time. You should try it."

Fin noticed three men with farming tools standing off the road just ahead. Fin pointed left and said, "They just went in there! After them!"

The three men ran in the direction Fin indicated. They hit a dead end and had to turn around. Fin used the trick again on a larger group. He yelled and pointed people in the wrong direction, and they complied.

Despite the danger, the two couldn't help but laugh at the absurdity of their life-and-death situation. Fin noticed a notification blinking in his peripherals but ignored it until he was out of danger.

The village took longer than expected to traverse. Still, the dirt road that signified the end of the village borderline came and went. They rode by lantern light for yet another sleepless night. Tired arms carried heavy lanterns that shined daggers into heavy eyes. They kept it up until they were far from the village and still kept going.

When the gloomy light was sufficient to see by, Fin stowed his lantern and looked at his notifications.

Malevolent Quest Complete: Give intentionally wrong directions to 10 lesser beings. +1 Active Ability, +2 Charisma. Forfeit all Benevolent quests.

Active Ability: Detect Lies.

"I don't believe it," Fin said, causing Brando to startle awake and fall off his horse.

Brando shuffled to his feet and took the reins before his horse could run off. "What happened?"

"Tell me a lie, anything, I don't care. Just lie to me." Fin demanded, ignoring Brando's mishap and activating Detect Lies. The world around him tinted blue and began twisting ever so slightly. It was enough to give him an uneasy feeling in his stomach.

"I miss the princess," Brando said flatly, brushing himself off. "Why?"

Hearing the lie, Fin noticed a soft orange glow centered on Brando's chest. He deactivated the ability and restored the world back to normal. After explaining his new achievement, he also explained the Control Minion ability he got back in the village.

Brando shook his head, "You are telling me that you can see gold hidden in rocks, tell if someone's lying, and control anyone you want? You realize that puts you in the position to make both of my ex-wives dance a jig, right?"

"I don't think it's that easy," Fin tried explaining. "I only got this quest after Eugal swore loyalty to me forever. But, if I can somehow get someone to swear to me, then, yeah. It will be dancing time."

"Marriage is technically swearing loyalty for life, regardless of whether or not they plan on leaving you," Brando digressed and remounted his horse. "If you got one of them to marry you, you could do it."

"Brando, I'm not marrying one of your ex-wives just to get them back for leaving you," Fin drew the proverbial line. "Besides, we're family now, and family don't marry family's ex-wives."

"They did," Brando said with a bit of hurt. "They are sisters, so if we are speaking in terms of technicalities, it's only fair for us to do it since they did it first."

"You married sisters?" Fin asked incredulously.

"Twins, actually," Brando explained. "Their fault, not mine. Though, it did make the transition easy for me. 'Easier,' I should say. It still hurt."

At a complete loss for words, Fin did the only thing he could think of. He pulled out a stick of dried meat and handed it to his friend. He didn't know if he wanted to hear the rest of the story. Nevertheless, he was still intrigued. It made him want to carry out Brando's original secret plan and see the look on their faces when he threw money around like a careless noble.

Fin went rigid when he considered the implications of his own marriage. He decided he did not want to marry someone he had complete control over. This would mean that the woman he married, whoever she was, definitely not Hildred, would have to understand his ability and consider using creative vows when the time came. But definitely not with Hildred or Dezi.

Chapter 44

After Brando fell off his horse the second time, Fin recommended they pull off the road and set up camp for the night. The two found a secluded area near a mulberry tree where they hid behind a row of bushes. They peered over them and tried to listen for anyone following. The echoes of their travels still rang through the silence, but they pushed through the phantom noises only to hear the sounds of nature. Finally, they threw their blankets on the grass, collapsed onto them, and were asleep before noon.

Fin woke at dusk, collected fallen branches and twigs, and made a fire. He prepared sausage links and toasted bread, which Brando got up for, ate, and promptly passed out again. Unable to go to sleep so readily, he tended the fire until the embers turned to ash. Then he lay, gazing at the stars until the starlight glow was extinguished behind his eyelids.

The two woke at the same time to the sounds of a struggle. Fin instinctively unstowed two swords and gave one to Brando. They crouched low against the battlement of bushes and cautiously stood to see over the top. What they saw mesmerized and froze them in a half-standing crouch. Fin stowed his sword and wordlessly reached over to take Brando's, too.

Three tiny people climbed on each other's shoulders, pushing up against the tree for balance. They could have been gnomes or young dwarves by the look of their short beards. Several attempts and failures sent the small people tumbling to the ground, but they got back up and tried again. They were trying to make a three-person tower. Fin's leg started cramping, but he disregarded the feeling. He would not allow anything as trivial as leg and back cramps to ruin this perfect moment.

The tower wasn't working, so the one on top moved to the bottom. He braced the tree in front of him while another climbed his shoulders and, in turn, also braced against the tree. Finally, it was the last one's turn. Cautiously, he climbed, using braced arms, shoulders, and heads as handholds and footholds. Then, in a glorious feat of strength and agility, he reached the top, placing each foot squarely on the shoulders below.

Then came the hard part. The one on the bottom turned around and deliberately took one tiny footstep after another, adjusting for balance at each step. When the top gnome and or dwarf reached up and plucked a berry from the tree, Fin's heart mushroomed with pride for the little people. Deep down, he forced an involuntary outburst of praise as another berry was picked and traded off to the hands below. In time, a third berry got plucked from the tree, and the three dismounted from each other's shoulders, landing on their little feet and butts.

Brando stood up and, with a big grin on his face, yelled, "You did it!"

The three startled and jumped so high they could have almost picked the berries themselves. They scrambled to their feet and ran as fast as their little legs would take them.

"Brando, you scared them!" Fin chided, picking up his blanket off the ground and stowing it.

"At least I waited until they were done!" Brando defended himself, reaching down to pick his own blanket up. He handed it to Fin, who glared at him.

Brando began picking berries off the tree. Fin finally came over to help. Without mentioning it, they only took the higher-hanging fruit. The berries were sweet and delicious. Soon, they were back on the trail, riding their horses with handfuls of berries.

The road began sloping upward between towering pine trees. The further the path stretched, the steeper it became. The warm air turned crisp as the two dismounted to lead their horses on foot. Soon, Fin, Brando, and the horses breathed heavily as they climbed.

Respite came as the path leveled off before twisting downward and around the mountain-studded valley. A bowl of trees, farms, and stone structures populated the valley below, with roads coalescing in front of a structure as magnificent as the mountain it was built into. At a distance, eight uniform pillars that appeared as large as Fin's little finger propped up an entire mountain. Through the pillars, he could make out the vague shape of a courtyard.

Traveling closer, the pillars grew to a mammoth proportion, and the courtyard a bustling marketplace inhabited by dwarves, some humans, and sparse others. Brando appeared to be a mixture of awestruck and discomfort. Fin felt none the better.

"We finally made it!" Brando exclaimed in little more than a whisper. "First order of business?"

"Let's get cleaned up and dressed and go tell the king everything we know," Fin suggested, unsure if horses belonged in such a metropolitan area. "Then, I suppose, we get our swords sharpened and look at armor for when we," He made a few stabbing motions with an invisible knife.

"Skewer some goblins?" Brando guessed and added, "Maybe the king will give us everything we need just for agreeing to help. We are nobility now, after all."

Fin agreed and they both set off for the first order of business.

Chapter 45

Having grown up on a farm, Fin had never really considered how he felt about crowds. When Brando started discussing his opinion about the matter, or rather, against it, Fin looked around and tried to decide his own opinion.

The air was warm, with varied currents of cooler air blowing in from outside. The noise level was perhaps loud, but not 'the chickens are under attack again' loud. The sounds were a concurrent murmur, shuffling of feet and clothes, and various sharp sounds of glass, coins, and cutlery.

Being able to see over all the tops of heads in his surroundings, he could locate where each sound was coming from. Some shops sold trinkets, and others sold clothing. The smell of a wood fire made him look for the shops selling food. It wasn't long before he found what he was smelling for. He got Brando's attention and gestured toward a stall selling something skewered and roasted on a stick. Even though he stood more than several feet above the normal height, no one seemed to pay him any attention. While walking, he decided he didn't share Brando's views on crowds; he was pretty comfortable.

"Rewbies on a stick, five coppers a piece," an older-looking dwarf sang out behind his booth. "Good for a strong, healthy beard!"

"Excuse me," Fin said, placing ten coins on the counter. "I'll take two. Also, can you tell me where we can find a good inn?"

The dwarf handed out two sticks with the mysterious-looking food speared through the middle. They were shaped like a twisted tear drop with a rough surface where it was rolled in nuts and herbs before roasting. Brando took a bite and blew residual steam from his mouth.

"You're looking for The Traveler's House. It's a decent inn with a stable," The dwarf pointed over his shoulder with a skewer. "It's over there a ways. Big sign with a horse; you can't miss it. They have running water most days and beds for you long leggers."

Brando, seemingly oblivious to the conversation, blurted out, "It's a potato."

Fin, remembering the stick he was holding, took a bite. The outer crust tasted sweet and bitter. There was almost too much flavor until his teeth sank further into something similar to a potato, allowing the flavors to spread out. It wasn't a potato. However, there were some distinct similarities.

"It's a rew-bee," the dwarf said slowly, annunciating the word as if he were talking to a child. "It takes twice as long to grow, has diamond-shaped leaves, and makes your beard shine better than any potato."

Fin held up his stick. "I bet I can grow a potato that's shaped like this."

"It's not a potato!" the dwarf bellowed, causing a stunt in the flow of traffic around them.

Noticing how serious the dwarf had become, Brando changed the subject, "It's called The Traveler's House, then? Got it. Thank you for your time and this delicious vegetable on a stick that is certainly not a potato."

The two walked in the direction the angry dwarf had given, and before long, they were standing in front of the Traveler's House. The outside of the building offered no insights into what was inside. The building matched the surrounding ones in all but size. It could only be described as square, grey, and having several windows, which were indeed being used to spy on their disappointed expressions. Fortunately, the establishment did seem prepared to handle horses, notably by the hitching post outside. After their horses were secure, Fin leaned down, reached for the knob, and opened the door.

The inside of the building only made sense after thinking about it. Dwarves were universally recognized as among Erland's best miners, craftsmen, and builders. The massive stone pillars built inside and out of the mountain were a testament to their abilities, but rumors of dwarven interior decoration had never circulated, and Fin could see why.

The common room was bare of any decorations save for a light brown blanket folded neatly on a chest. The short reception desk, though made of rich and marbled stone, had nothing on top of it. The walls were bare, the floor was bare, and the tables and bar were square, plain, and also bare. Nothing attempted to create a cozy environment.

Behind the reception desk, a female dwarf looked up at the men. "Welcome in. I'm not going to break my neck looking up at you, so take a knee if you want a conversation." Despite the rumors, her round face was completely without a beard. Her walnut-brown hair lay neatly over her shoulder in a series of braids. Her smile might have been charming if it had been genuine.

"We're looking for," Brando started before the desk clerk's words registered. He stopped, crouched in front of the desk, and started over. "Hi, I'm Brando, and this is Fin. We are looking for a room and stables for a few nights."

"I am Velamy, and it is a pleasure to meet you two," she said matter-of-factly. "The tall-folk rooms are a silver a night, but I only have one left. The stables come with the room. I assume those are your horses?"

"Yes," Fin considered, crouching next to Brando. "Will we have to share a bed?"

Velamy laughed. "Only if you squeeze really tight. The beds are big but not big enough for the both of you, so I recommend getting your cuddles in before going to sleep."

Relieved at the implication that there was more than one bed, Fin ignored the quip and nodded.

Brando needed clarification. "There are two beds, right?"

The room did, in fact, have two beds. It also had a dresser, a bathing room with running water, a clothesline, and no decorations. The walls were a textured mixture of white and brown paint that matched the blankets and pillows on the beds.

Brando collapsed on the bed and closed his eyes before jumping to his feet. "We have to go see the king."

Fin, transfixed with the lever that made water come out of a spout, agreed without looking up. "Let's get cleaned up then."

When Fin and Brando exited the inn, the streets were even more busy than before. After asking for several sets of directions they found it. Near a thick grated gate stood guards between two defense towers. The towers featured dark and vacated slots suited for firing arrows.

"This time, let's not pretend to be diplomats," Fin cautioned, speaking so his voice wouldn't carry to the guard watching the gate. "Let's make it simple and straightforward. We'll tell whoever is in charge what's happening and ask how they want to move forward."

When Fin was done talking, Brando smiled as if whatever Fin said was perfectly logical for something so wrong. "We are technically diplomats now, and we could get in trouble for not mentioning it right away. It worked before, and we have the documentation to support our story this time."

Fin sighed, "Okay, but first, let's just ask to see the king. It couldn't hurt."

Brando shrugged. "Fine, we'll try it your way, but as soon as they tell us to kick rocks, we tell them whatever gets us through the gate."

A dwarf standing in front of the gate looked up to the two men nearly at eye level with the tip of his spear. "State your names and business."

Fin collected himself and offered their names. "We are here to see the king."

"One moment," the dwarf said before walking away.

"See, I told you we didn't need to make up a whole story," Fin beamed. "Simplicity is key."

The dwarf returned, carrying an empty wooden crate. He set it down and stood on top of it. "Sargeant Crispin, at your service," The dwarf offered, "I hope you understand that the king doesn't just see anyone, what business do you have?"

"There is a goblin slave camp south about a four- or five-day journey. We were told to come here and ask for assistance freeing the captives, one of which is a dwarf called Heidle the Hammer."

"That's a whole different story altogether," Crispin said with a look of distaste. "One moment."

When the dwarf came back carrying a second crate, Brando smiled smugly, "It looks like he wants to be able to see the look of disappointment in your eyes when he turns you away."

Crispin stacked the crates and climbed on top, "I haven't heard of this Heidle chap, but that is some grave business indeed. You said he's a dwarf? Are there others?"

Fin nodded even though he had only seen the one. He reasoned that the more this dwarf saw them as trying to save his people, the more likely he would allow them to pass through.

"Unfortunately, this isn't something that can be handled quickly. You'll need to stop by the office of requisitions and put in a request to investigate your claim," Crispin explained. "It could take anywhere from three days to several months, though I'm assuming you'll want this sooner than later. Requisitions will probably want to send a team down to take a look and make a report on their findings before approving the requisition."

"And they report their findings to the king?" Fin asked with a hopeful tone.

"Not quite," the guard responded. "The report goes back to the office of requisitions. Then, if it's deemed a critical matter, which I'm certain it will, the head of, I don't know, someone above my level would look at it."

Brando pointed away from the gated entrance, "Should we go start that process now? That way, we'll be able to help all those people suffering in the slave camp in about a year or two. You don't suppose there's a tried-and-true method of speeding requisitions along, is there?"

"Afraid not," the dwarf responded solemnly, missing the hidden message in the words. "It will probably take even longer since the king declared war against Clive Rae this morning. No, I don't think this issue will be addressed any time in the near future."

"The king what?" Brando asked, unsure he heard correctly.

The dwarf looked over his shoulder before talking. "We got word this morning that the derelict king had a champion defeat whatever violent things were keeping us out of our ancestral mine. As soon as the mine was safe, he made a royal proclamation only allowing you lanks to dig, no offense to you, of course, just the other lanks.

"Since the first report this morning, we've gotten at least twenty more. After Clive broke the treaty, all Lokardale dwarves have been relocating here. The king made an informal declaration of war just today."

"If we are at war," Fin slowly formulated his question. "What happens to delegates of Lokardale?"

"Clive Rae doesn't keep dwarven delegates," the guard nearly spat. "It's a good thing, too; it would make me feel uneasy arresting my own kin and keeping them locked up until the war ended. The king is angry, but I'm unsure what he plans to do."

Fin gave Brando an 'I told you so' look before agreeing with Crispin, "No way of knowing. That's for sure."

"I probably shouldn't be saying this, but you two seem like the best of the tall folk with your mission to rescue my kin from the goblins," the guard nodded his appreciation. "But don't talk about any of this until it's official."

After Fin and Brando promised not to mention a word of it, the guard offered as much help as he could, "If you're just looking for some extra hands, you could visit the mercenary guild. You look like you have some coin between the two of you. They're right behind the old market near the church of Loden. Tell them Crispin sent you."

Brando slapped Fin with the back of his hand, pointed at Crispin, and asked, "Are there any mines around here we could try our hand at? Who knows? We could make enough to where we could buy all the mercenaries."

"You don't strike me as miners," Crispin said uncertainly. "But if you're going to be waiting on requisitions anyway, I suppose there really isn't anything better than uncovering the secrets of the earth, eh?" he cleared his throat. "There's plenty of mines around, but only three main ones that are publicly accessible. I recommend the Dunkle mine. They take a larger cut, but it's better suited for short-term excavations."

Fin was about to ask about its location when a series of sharp sounds came from behind the gate.

The guard glanced over his shoulder, "Changing of the guards. You better shove off. Come find me if you're ever successful, and I'll buy you a whole cask of ale for the story."

The two thanked the guard and left just as the gate started lifting.

"That was a balanced conversation of helpful and disappointing," Brando said with a chipper tone.

Fin agreed, "Yeah, but I feel sorry for anyone who openly admits to being a Clive Rae delegate. Remember, like you wanted to do?"

"We don't talk about that," Brando said with a dark glimmer in his eye.

Fin smirked. "Because of the whole imprisonment thing or because I was right, and you were wrong?"

"Let's forget about all that and go find an armor shop," Brando curtailed the topic, looking around as if he could sense one nearby.

Chapter 46

It took some time, but Fin and Brando eventually found what they were looking for. They opened the door of a small shop with a picture of a helmet on the sign instead of actual words. A makeshift bell above the door alerted their entrance with a single, non-melodic thud.

A young dwarf rounded the corner and startled at the sight of the two humans. "Loden's boots, you surprised me! You don't see too many long leggers in here. I mean, uh, what can I do for you today?"

Fin smiled at the dwarf's discomfort. "We are looking for some armor that will stop a crossbow bolt."

The dwarf considered for a moment and then shook his head. "I don't think we have anything that would fit you, but Master Olhoff has done some work for humans before. I'll get him."

The dwarf left before Fin could protest, so he took the time to look around. Suits of armor lined the walls on racks. Shelves holding various helmets stood over crates of gauntlets, boot covers, and other undiscernible pieces. In the room's focal point hung a complete set of armor that would make the wearer look like a wolf. It was all fascinating to look at. Only everything around was made to fit a dwarf, not a human.

"Hello, hello," an old voice walked into the room and, despite having been clearly told about the stature of the new customers, gave a less-than-subtle third, "Hello."

"I am Master Olhoff, at your service, and this is my apprentice, Tory." The old dwarf had a thick grey beard that he kept around the back of his shoulder like a scarf. A glass monocle stayed wedged in his left eye despite the surprised look on his face. He adjusted it before asking how he could help.

"We are looking for some armor that can stop a crossbow bolt," Fin said, resisting the urge to unstow said crossbow. "One for each of us."

"You're looking for some thick steel then," Master Olhoff considered. "When would you need it by?"

Fin looked to Brando, who said with uncertainty, "One week?"

Olhoff's monocle fell out.

"One week?" he snorted. "I can't put my pants on that fast! I could maybe do it in a month if it was a rush job. If my mother's life depended on it, I could maybe, maybe, do it in two weeks, but that's just for my mother and just for armor for one of you."

"It doesn't need to be pretty," Brando offered, holding up his hands in defense. "It just needs to stop a bolt from impaling my chest, that's all."

Tory cleared his throat. "May I offer a solution?"

Olhoff held his hands in a way that indicated, "You have the floor."

"There might be some pieces we have already made that they can use. Their arms might be longer, but now that I'm looking at them, they are about the same width. If one of them lets me build their armor, I can do it in three weeks. It will also help me complete the certification for my journeyman." Tory sped up his speech before he lost anyone's attention. "He said it himself; they aren't looking for anything pretty. The crude design they probably want cuts at least a week off of the time. I can have it done in less than three weeks. That is if that's okay with them?"

Olhoff glared at Fin.

"Three weeks?" Fin repeated. "We can do that. We'll need that time to dig up the funds for this anyway."

"What do you mean, 'dig up the funds?'" Olhoff interrogated. "I'm not dumping hours of my life on hopes and promises into a shoddy-looking project that I won't be able to sell to anyone else. For this job, I'll need at least half up front."

"For now," Fin reached into his shirt and unstowed his two remaining gems, "All I have are these."

"And that's how you're planning on paying?" Olhoff asked, "With gems?"

Fin and Brando both nodded in unison.

"I don't know anything about gems," Olhoff sighed. "Apprentice, go get my brother."

Tory ran out of the building like his livelihood depended on it. The men left in the room stared silently, uneager to break the silence. When Tory returned, he was followed by a dwarf similar in every way to Olhoff, except cleaner looking.

"Olhoff," the dwarf greeted his brother.

"Kertchel," he greeted back, holding out the two gems. "Can you look at these for me and tell me what they're worth?"

Kertchel took the stones without ceremony and inspected them. "It's got a good weight. I am unsure about the clarity or how well they will cut. Topaz?" He looked around for an answer.

Fin nodded. "They're both topaz."

"That's unexpected," He resumed his inspection. "This blue one could be anywhere from three gold to thirty. And that's based on my limited knowledge of blue topaz. This other one," He whistled. "If it's clear..."

"If it's clear?" Olhoff nearly shouted.

"Two or three hundred, and that's just selling to a merchant." Kertchel looked up from the gems. "Where did you get these?"

"It's a long story," Brando waved the question away and addressed Olhoff. "Will those be good enough for you to start?"

Tory and Olhoff responded with a "Yes" and "No" simultaneously. Everyone looked to Olhoff.

"I don't want to take payment of uncut gems when I don't even know if they'll be worth anything," Olhoff explained. "If I'm going to spend the next three weeks hammering armor that is too ugly to sell, I want assurances."

Kertchel stepped in with a reasonable solution: "Go ahead and start work. I'll cut 'em and have an answer for you in a couple of days. I have some new designs I want to work out, and this stone will be perfect for them. I'll only charge a small fee of twenty silver at a family discount."

Brando leaned down and whispered in Fin's ear, "Find out if he's robbing us."

Knowing what Brando wanted him to do, Fin immediately activated Detect Lies and braced himself as the room exploded in light blue colors. The skill's effect had made him uneasy, so he wanted to use the ability as little as possible. However, it wasn't as bad as the last time. Either he had gotten used to the perpetual movement of everything undulating like blue flames, or he wasn't prepared for it the first time. Either way, whatever Olhoff was trying to tell him was clearly honest.

Olhoff was waiting for a response to something, so Fin recounted the conversation. He looked at Kertchel and asked, "You cut gems for a living?"

"No, I'm a scribe," Kertchel's color showed he was being honest. "I cut gems as more of a hobby, but it does help with the finances."

"Are you good?" Fin pressed, observing for signs of the orange glow that would show if he was lying.

"I am confident that I can give you the most value for the gem as any stone cutter," came the honest response.

"Is your family discount really twenty silver?" Fin asked, almost a little too casually.

Kertchel shuffled his feet a little, and when his color started turning orange, Fin held up a hand and asked the other brother.

"He has done some work for me for as little as two silver," Olhoff replied matter of factly.

"But those gems were significantly smaller than this one," Kertchel cut in before amending his price. "I wouldn't charge you any less than six silver for a gem of this magnitude."

Fin withdrew six silver coins and handed them over. "I'm pleased to do business with both of you."

Kertchel frowned but relented, giving his brother the edge to speak first, "Tory, for your journeyman, pick which twiceling you want to make armor for."

Tory walked over to Brando, asked him to move his arms around, and then approached Fin with the same directions. Finally, after glancing between the two much taller people, he pointed at Fin. "I'll take this one. The bigger one seems like he could use the work of a master."

Before Brando could remark about being called "the bigger one," Olhoff had him take a knee and began the arduous measuring process. When all the measurements were taken, Tory brought out pieces of previously smithed plate. Brando instinctively handed Fin the parts that didn't fit.

Fin found an arm harness that he could fit into but was too short. Tory beamed with joy and explained that the fewer original parts of the armor he had to physically make, the better. He marked each piece that fit or was close to fitting with chalk and set them in an empty crate. He was enjoying the process more than Olhoff, whose frown grew deeper and deeper with each failed fitting.

"Do you think you're going to lose weight in the near future, or are you planning to always be this fat?" Olhoff poked at Brando's belly.

"Are you kidding me?" Brando roared. "This is all muscle. Feel it now."

"That's quite alright," Olhoff protested. "I've lived long enough to know what delusions feel like. We're about done anyway."

Fin looked at Tory, who was writing on a pair of nearly-fitting gauntlets. "Can you make it so my fingers are exposed?"

"Are you sure?" Tory asked skeptically. "If you get your fingers chopped off, you'll be as good as dead."

"It's okay," Fin assured the dwarf, considering how effective the crushing grip and talon abilities work together. "My sword has a good finger guard, and I need to be able to use my fingers."

"Does that mean you don't want a shield?" Tory asked, holding a bit of chalk above the gauntlet.

Fin shook his head, and Tory drew a dissecting line across the fingers of the gantlet. He made sure there were no other special requests and then dismissed him. "Check back in periodically for adjustments. This is the first armor I've made for a human, so I want to ensure it goes well for both of us."

Fin thanked Tory and then walked past Olhoff, who was making inflammatory comments about Brando. He decided just to wait outside.

"That was fun," Fin said offhandedly as Brando walked out the door.

"Sure," Brando scowled, "that was really fun. So much fun that I never want to think about it again. Where to next?"

"Let's go find this Dunkle mine," Fin said after some hesitation. "I have no desire to visit the house of requestions or whatever it's called. Besides, if we can get enough gold to hire all the mercenaries, which we can, I don't see why we can't just handle the whole thing ourselves."

"And get all the gems," Brando added greedily.

Fin intended to return the gems to the people who mined them, but something inside him shuddered in pleasure with the thought of owning a mine he could see through. He could amass enough wealth to sleep on an entire bed of gems. He wondered if cut gems were more comfortable than uncut gems. There was only one way to find out.

Chapter 47

The mine turned out to be a large building called "The Dunkle Mine." To reach the entrance, one needed to traverse through an onslaught of shops, merchants, and hawkers, all selling their wares so randomly that one was likely to pass the same shop multiple times before reaching the end.

It was just as well for Fin and Brando, who were able to find and purchase a map, an extra pickaxe, and several jars of glowing moss. For an extra silver, the moss came with a container of 'super moss fuel' that restored its light when it started dimming.

A cool breeze preceded the mine entrance, which was refreshing in such a dense market. When the mouth of the mine became visible, the sight of it was both comforting and daunting. It was comforting because it was not just big enough for humans, but whole carriages to move through freely if desired. That alleviated the worry of crawling through small holes made for dwarves. It was daunting because of the heavy traffic going in and out of the entrance, with each dwarf sharing unspoken customs and courtesies utterly foreign to Fin and Brando. They watched the circulating traffic for a while, trying to glean as much information as possible to avoid making any grievous customary mistakes being strangers in such a foreign place.

The dwarves coming out of the mine placed their tools and small sacks in a bin. Then, they subjected themselves to a search while someone else went through their items. If they came out of the mine with valuables, they placed them on a small scale, indicating a fee and possibly taxes they would need to pay. Sometimes, the fee would be taken from valuables, and sometimes, coins were exchanged. The pattern was clear: it was no problem entering the mine, but upon leaving, you had to undergo a rigorous search, and you had to pay the price for anything mined.

When Fin and Brando decided they had learned enough, they went inside. Glow moss lined either side of the pathway, making Fin feel foolish for spending money on it. Brando felt similar and pointed out every new patch of the abundantly growing moss as more appeared.

Glowing green lines split as the road periodically diverged into multiple paths. Fortunately, with each new path came clearly demarcated signs that correlated with Brando's map.

Fin was using his Sense Treasure ability, already looking for gold, when they stumbled upon the oldest-looking dwarf they had ever seen. The old dwarf stopped what he was doing, greeted the two humans, and exchanged some small talk. His name was Rasengold Kel. He slapped his arms and boasted about hitting rocks better than anyone younger than him. The conversation and silly anecdotes elicited genuine smiles and laughter from Fin and Brando.

Before walking away, Fin pointed an arm's length to the right of where the old man had been mining. "Try digging here instead. Who knows? You might find something."

Finding enough gold worth the effort of mining took time and patience. Most of the early tunnels had sparse traces of valuable ore, even remotely shallow enough to start digging for. The first group of nuggets Fin found was only a few paces across from where three dwarves were already mining. Fin pointed at a place for Brando, and they both began excavating.

After long hours of digging, they only unearthed half of what was hidden in the walls. So, Brando marked the spot on his map, and they left for the day.

The next day, they checked in at the blacksmith, where they were remeasured in some places and asked questions, some seemingly ambiguous. One of the questions was, "What's your favorite animal?" Brando answered for both of them.

"I like horses and Fin has an uncomfortable obsession with dragons," Brando said with a wry grin. "So much so that he actually thinks he-"

"Thanks, Brando, I got it from here," Fin cut him off. "Dragons are fine. Why do you ask?"

Tory gave a 'wait and see' answer, which probably meant it was for armor decorations.

Before leaving, Fin gave Olhoff seven reasonably sized gold nuggets and promised to bring more. By the look on Olhoff's face, Fin ascertained that, though it wasn't much, it helped build a sense of goodwill with the master smith. Olhoff, in turn, offered to melt down all future gold they found into uniform molds that could generally be used as currency. What he didn't say was how he would keep the uniform parcels of gold in case the gems they brought turned out to be worthless. Fin was fine with the implied agreement because he and Brando still had over twenty gold between them, which was more than enough spending money to tide them over.

Returning to their site, they greeted the old dwarf, who was happy to see them. He offered them lunch as a gesture of gratitude for Fin's mining recommendation, which they accepted graciously. He even took their moss jars and poured in a liquid from a flask, brightening the glow significantly. Brando asked what was in the flask, and Rasengold told him it was water. This infuriated Brando, who had paid a whole silver for the 'super moss fuel' but kept it to himself. Fin felt bamboozled himself, which he also hid. He and Brando had been more or less pooling their funds since they set out on their current quest, and a loss for one of them was a loss for the other.

When they reached the spot they had marked on the map, the three dwarves that had been mining across from them the day prior were now occupying their spot.

Brando cleared his throat and addressed the group, "I noticed you were working down there yesterday, and now you are over here… In our spot."

"Go home, lanks," one of them replied rudely. "Or will you try to kick us out of this mine too?"

Fin was ready to intervene and prevent the situation from escalating when Brando surprised him.

"I guess this has to do with Clive Rae kicking the dwarves out of the mine, huh?" Brando asked but continued when no answer was forthcoming, "If it's any consolation, I apologize on behalf of humans everywhere for your mistreatment. Not all of us are as bad as Clive Rae. Well, his daughter's actually worse, if you can believe it. I was going to kidnap her cat, but, well, things fell through, and I wasn't able to. If it was up to me, we would have let her die in those very mines you were banned from."

Brando noticed the looks of shocked confusion on the young dwarves' faces. It wasn't the response he was going for, so he cleared his throat and backtracked. "I understand your disdain, but not all of us are bad people. I have seen the real enemy and hope one day we can fight them together. For now, I can only offer my condolences for your mistreatment and move along."

One of the dwarves harrumphed, but another got a suspicious look in his eye and asked, "When we go to war, whose side are you going to stand on, the humans or the dwarves?"

"Neither," Brando replied. "We are preparing to fight another war, and I don't want to see the princess again, no matter what side she's standing on."

Fin clarified by explaining their circumstances and plans to fight the goblins. He felt they had wasted enough time already. Still, it seemed important to Brando to curry a sense of amity with this group. So, he sat down and told the same story that he had told a near countless times. By the end of it, the disposition of the group had softened.

"You can have your spot back if you really want it," one of the dwarves offered, eliciting an angry look from another.

"No, that's fine," Fin stood up and brushed his pants off. "There's a few good chunks of gold in there, but we can find more."

The dwarves looked at the stone wall and then back to Fin several times with disbelief.

Fin sighed at the thought of doing a good deed to someone he wanted to pummel only moments earlier.

He walked between them, took his pickaxe, and drew seven circles in the stone. Then he pointed to each circle and gave rapid instructions, apathetic to the possibility that the instructions were not fully comprehended. When he finished, he wished them good fortune and strode onward for a new mining spot.

The next few days came and went with a sense of routine. They visited the smithy, went to the mine, ate breakfast with Rasengold, and mined for gold. The only change was the size of the group waiting for them with Rasengold. It started with the three dwarves who had initially stolen their spot and were now suddenly interested in mending the ties between humans and dwarves. Both Fin and Brando knew they were there for the same reason everyone else was.

The group grew from four people to fifteen overnight. Each person brought food from home to thank Fin for sharing the insights of his 'gold attunement.' The food and drinks were not considered payment. Still, it was generally understood that the donation was a small price to pay for Fin to draw one of his famous circles, signifying the location of hidden gold. The fifteen dwarves were a bigger crowd than either of them would prefer, but the home-cooked meals and drinks were too good to pass up, and Fin was able to stow all the extras for later.

The crowd seemed to double every day. It started getting out of control when they arrived to discover a group with numbers greater than fifty, all holding neatly wrapped lunches and jars of cream, juice, or ale. Fin was about to turn them all away when Brando saw an opportunity.

"Why don't you let them mine for you?" Brando suggested, waving his hand over the neatly organized row of dwarves holding treats and wearing looks of anticipation. "All you have to do is point at the wall, tell them what's in it, and they'll give you part of what they find."

Part of Fin felt weird about taking a portion of someone else's gold, especially since he hadn't paid the mine or the taxes on the gold he had accumulated. After all, what good is a secret storage space if you don't use it to evade taxes and fees? He could argue that it was for a good cause, but he knew he would have avoided the payments no matter what the circumstances would be. He decided to ask the dwarves what they thought about the idea.

Fin led everyone to a larger cavern and had everyone gather around. He spoke with a confidence that he had not known before he set out only months prior.

"Hello, everyone. For those who don't know me, my name is Fin, and this is my friend Brando. Someone has probably told you that I can tell you where to dig if you bring meals. That is not very sustainable with a group this large, so I want you to help me develop a more sustainable plan," Fin allowed the murmurs to grow and then die down before he continued. "We are only here for a limited time. If all I do is go around and tell you where to dig, I won't be able to gather the funds I need. However, if we work together, it is possible that we can find a way that is mutually beneficial. One idea is that I can show you where to dig; in return, you can give me a portion of the gold I directed you to. If we do it this way, I can only guarantee enough gold at your site to afford the cost. However, I do not want this group to grow any bigger. Something tells me that if our operation becomes public knowledge, we all could get in a lot of trouble. In return for your silence, I will not be searching you like they do outside. We will base our agreement on honor, something I have found to be a great strength among the dwarves."

"Tell them what the gold is for!" shouted one of the original members of their mining party from the back of the cavern.

Fin groaned inwardly. He would trade all the meals in his inventory to never have to tell this story again. He looked at Brando with exhaustion and waved him forward.

Brando didn't want to tell the story either, so he invited the helpful dwarf to center stage to retell their story. The story lasted longer than it should have, and the dwarf focused on things that neither Fin nor Brando would have, but the point was made and it seemed to resonate with the crowd.

Fin thanked the dwarf, making a mental note to get his name later, and tried to conclude the speeches as quickly as possible. "I guess that helps you understand what our goal here is. Does anyone have questions or ideas?"

"If I come with you, can I use the mine?" A voice asked from the crowd.

Brando stepped in to answer, "If you fight with us, we will give you full access to the mine once we conquer the encampment. It will be dangerous, but we will gladly welcome all extra swords, hammers, and shields when the time comes."

Questions spilled from the crowd. There were questions about the type of jewels in the mine, the size of the enemy army, and trivial details like travel arrangements. One of them dared to ask if they could mine after the battle. The questions, however, had nothing to do with their current arrangement. Finally, Fin announced there would be time for questions later and directed everyone to form a line behind him. He led a multitude of dwarves through the mine without the slightest clue of what he was doing.

At his first stop, he drew three circles for the first two dwarves immediately behind him. He explained how deep they would have to go for each marked place and asked for one of the pieces of gold in return. The dwarves agreed and got to work. Fin pressed forward and repeated the process of periodically stopping, marking locations with his pickaxe, and directing the miners immediately behind him. Sometimes, he would set a price and other times, he would negotiate based on the quantity of gold. The process went on for long, excruciating hours.

Brando used the map to navigate new areas while Fin worked diligently to get miners dispatched to gold-rich areas. Fin needed time to recover periodically before continuing forward, so they all sat down, ate, and rested. The rest and meals had helped a little, but the constant activation of Sense Treasure made his head hurt. Still, he could not stop while he had miners left following him. After the last dwarf in the line was commissioned, Fin followed Brando to where Rasengold was mining and sat down. He gave one last helpful instruction to the old dwarf before curling up on the cool earth and falling asleep.

Chapter 48

Fin woke in time to witness three dwarves, each giving Brando a chunk of gold and offering a bow of respect. Fin sat up and tilted his head to return their respects. He was happy to see the look of pure joy on each of their faces, but he was unprepared to see them start to form another line. His head felt a little better, but he was in no condition to start the process over again.

Fortunately, Brando informed the dwarves that Fin was too exhausted for anything more today. The speech seemed practiced as if he had been telling people the same thing for hours. He asked Brando about it, and the answer confirmed his suspicions.

"You've been sleeping all day," Brando said, raising his fingertips to indicate that there was some good news, too. "But you wouldn't believe how well my plan worked! Look at this!"

He lifted and set two lunch boxes in front of Fin. The effort to lift the boxes alone signified the massive wealth they held. Brando unlatched and unbuckled the lids, but it dispelled all doubts of the fortune inside when he lifted them. Inside each lunch box sat a heap of rough chunks of gold. The dull green glow of moss light was not enough to dispel the allure of the precious metal.

"My plan worked," Brando reiterated. "I don't even think this is all of it. The dwarves have been finishing and then immediately coming to find you."

Several more dwarves did come to drop off their donations to Fin before He and Brando decided to leave for the day.

Even though Fin had slept all day, he was still tired enough to sleep again. After washing up, he unstowed the wealth in his inventory and dumped it on his bed. It was a ritual that Brando had become accustomed to and even expected. Brando wished he could borrow Treasured Sleep for just one night, but he would settle for any sleep.

The following day, Fin opted to go to the back room of the smithy before upending a lunchbox full of gold. Brando shook his head with distaste when he realized Fin was keeping the second one for himself.

"Am I supposed to believe you two mined this out of the ground yourselves?" Olhoff asked rhetorically. "You're not turning me into some third-party accomplice, are you?"

Brando was, for once, grateful for Fin's propensity to sleep on hoarded treasures. He could imagine Olhoff's reaction if the pile of gold on the desk was doubled, and it wouldn't be good. However, he knew that they were just delaying the inevitable at the pace they were at. At some point, the pile of gold delivered would be double, at least.

"It's nothing like that," Fin cheerfully disregarded Olhoff's concerns. "We've found some investors that want to help us with our cause."

"I'm sure it has to do with rescuing the slaves and not the massive gem mine we would be liberating," Brando added sardonically.

"I see," Olhoff said, slowly looking from Fin's eyes to Brando's. "How many investors have you found so far?"

"We don't need more investors as much as we need fighters, tacticians, and siege equipment," Fin guided the conversation away from the secret mine cult they were cultivating. "If you can help with that, I would count it as a big favor."

Olhoff shook his head with the look of sincerest disappointment that only a child showing empty pockets to a bully could mimic. Before he could formulate a proper rejection, Tory peeked in and informed him that his brother had arrived.

"We will be out in a moment," Olhoff said, placing the gold on a scale, writing down the weight, and producing a receipt. "I cannot assure that the weight will be the same after removing the impurities, but the result should be close enough."

Having tested Olhoff's honesty on multiple occasions, Fin knew that his word was worth the gold in the lunchbox. He took the receipt and thanked him before going back into the display room. There, he was greeted by Kertchel, who produced two velvet sacks that could only contain one thing.

"The gems are done?" Fin asked with excitement. "How do they look?"

"Words cannot explain the absolute majesties these gems turned out to be," Kertchel said with a genuinely joyful smile. "Come look!"

Fin anxiously watched as Kertchel put on a black cloth glove and slowly removed each gem. He placed each gem delicately on top of its respective pouch on the sales counter.

The largest gem had shrunk but still maintained much of its size. The color seemed lighter, too, with a deep burnt orange in the middle that lightened to a near yellow along the edges. The gem was nearly circular with a flat, glossy surface on the top and bottom. The sides of the gem were a culmination of curved gradient angles and the added texture of alternating triangles. Kertchel watched in horror as Brando picked it up with his bare fingers.

Fin ignored Kertchel's chastisements toward Brando as he looked at the blue stone. It was similar to the first shape, like two trapezoids connected at the base, but it was longer vertically. The deep blue color made Fin think of the sky on an absolutely perfect day. However, he had no intention of keeping the gem or selling it. This would be his gift to Heidle as thanks for all his help.

"I have buyers lined up for each of them when you are ready to sell, but," Kertchel sighed longingly at his new creations. "I believe the larger one will be more than sufficient to cover the costs of the armor."

As Kertchel's words registered, Fin plucked the blue gem off the table before realizing he made a mistake. Fortunately, Kertchel's back was turned, and he could replace the gem without notice.

"If that is the case, I don't believe I will be selling the blue gem," Fin said when he was far enough from the table to absolve him from suspicion. "I want to give it back to Heidle. He's the one that funded our trip here."

"Very well then," Olhoff agreed, picking up the gem with his black glove. He eyed Brando suspiciously before wiping it off, putting it in the bag, and handing it to Fin.

"I can sell the bigger one then," Kertchel coughed, bringing the eyes of the room to him. "I may require several small fees to find a buyer, haggle over the price, and make the sale. I believe I can sell it for three thousand gold with no problem at, let's say, ten percent?"

Fin learned how to take percentages once, but the concept was rusty in his head. He grew up a farmer after all, not a wizard. It took him a moment, but he was able to work out what ten percent of three thousand was, and he was not about to pay thirty gold to sell a gem he could sell himself. He made a counteroffer of one percent and refused to budge.

Kertchel tried to haggle the percentage up, but when Fin threatened to sell it himself, he accepted the deal. It wasn't the three hundred gold he had wanted, but thirty gold was decent enough, even for selling such a high-scale gem. Besides, in luxury sales, you paid for the seller's connections more than anything, and he already had two interested buyers lined up.

Kertchel agreed and held out his hand. Fin hesitated before shaking his hand or solidifying the deal. Three gold was still a lot of money just to sell someone else's gem, so he decided to get his money's worth.

"Before I agree, can I also ask one more thing from you?" Fin asked, holding the power of the deal aloft. "Can you get me a list of mercenaries, prices, and availability for when my armor is finished?"

Kertchel shrugged and held out his hand. "I can do that. Do we have a deal?"

"We have a deal, and hopefully, it's the first of many," Fin shook the dwarf's hand before realizing he needed one more thing. "I also need some chalk."

Chapter 49

Despite Fin clearly asking to keep their operation secret, the group of miners waiting for him had increased to around seventy. He didn't dare turn any of them away for fear that the angry dwarves would turn on him, so he took his place in the center of the group and prepared himself to give another speech. This time, he would make it perfectly clear that no one else could join.

The speech was brief and to the point, except for a repeat disruption of a certain dwarf yelling, "Tell them the story!"

This time, Fin got his name before inviting him down to the front to regale the crowd.

Tib's retelling of the goblin slave mine story was better in some ways and worse in others. This time, he breezed through the basics but added parts about starving dwarven children and beds of nails. Fin would have corrected him on the spot, but it was close enough to the truth, he supposed.

He had a big day ahead of him and had to figure out how to make his Sense Treasure ability last even longer. He had spent too much time worrying about costs the day before. If he could minimize that interaction, he could probably get through all seventy or so dwarves without needing a break.

Fin addressed the crowd one last time before telling everyone to line up. He walked to the front of the line and motioned for Brando to lead the way. Brando took a moment to plan the best route, but before long he was moving confidently. His map started showing signs of wear and tear, but it was still serviceable.

Soon, everyone fell into a comfortable rhythm. When Fin spotted an area rich with gold ore, he made quick circles with Tory's chalk, gave the briefest explanations, and moved along. He let the dwarves figure out the rest themselves. He also wasn't worried about setting a price. When he showed up, and there were people he had never seen before with lunches in hand, it meant that everyone who showed up already knew the expectation.

During the past week, Fin had reached the end of the many tunnels in the mine. At the end he found a large cavern with a dense concentration of gold in one corner. Strangely, it was completely devoid of treasures everywhere else. However, the gold vein he saw was over twice what he had accumulated the day before.

He was starting to feel he was at the limit of his ability. Still, with only seven dwarves left trailing behind him, he was in a much better shape than the previous day. He marked the wall and memorized the depth and angle of the vein before disabling the ability.

No sooner did Fin mark the wall that he noticed how uneasy the dwarves around him had become. "What's wrong?" He asked as a solemn murmur broke out among his group.

A dwarf by the name Guile tugged on his sleeve and pointed to the walls, ceiling, and ground. "Do you see those holes and grooves?" He asked with a cautious tone that made the hairs on Fin's body stand up. "It's a bad sign. We should leave now."

Fin looked closer and noticed perfectly round trenches carved into the cavern, like evidence of water corrosion in a dry riverbed. Only the unnaturally curved angles precluded the effects of water, and most of the grooves ended in a hole big enough for a snake or a large rat to fit through.

Brando held his jar of moss up to one of the holes. "What is it?"

Guile waved for everyone to slowly back out of the room before speaking. "They are called many things, satriks, mine devils, and dirt eaters. My grandfather told me that if I saw those grooves or holes in the wall, I should get away as soon as possible. You can't kill it, but if it gets angry, it can kill you."

Fin considered the advice, but not for very long. The massive amount of gold waiting for him just inside the wall was too great to pass up. He would be careful and run away if anything happened, but he would not let the opportunity go.

"I am going to stay for a while," Fin addressed the dwarves. "If you don't want to stay, I can meet you all at the last fork in a few hours. I need to recuperate my gold attunement anyway, and won't be much use until I do."

The dwarves understood and were more than happy to wait elsewhere.

When they were gone, Brando asked, "Are you sure you want to stick around?"

Fin smiled and responded, "Yes, and you would be, too, if you saw the size of that nugget in there."

They took turns hitting rocks loose from where Fin had marked. They were worried that whatever was hiding in the holes could come out at any time, so they pushed through the fatigue and dug deeper into the stone without rest. When the last layer of stone covering the gold came loose, they worked feverishly to dislodge the rest of it. However, the harder they worked, the less progress they made. Fin wondered if the rock had somehow become more dense, but a glance at Brando's next swing explained the truth. He halted everything.

"We're almost there," Brando said between heavy breaths, not ready to quit.

"Look at our pickaxes," Fin said, showing the tip of his own. Or, instead, what was left of it.

Brando's eyebrows lifted as he looked at the tip of his own pickaxe. It was completely dull and seemed shorter somehow, as was Fin's. A closer inspection showed the tips had been cleanly removed. They both looked from their tools to their exposed prize in the wall and took a step back. An orb the size of an orange sat on top of their gold, looking like a continuously glowing spark.

"It's eating the gold," Brando frantically whispered. "We have to do something."

"I think that's the dirt eater they were talking about," Fin explained, "I don't know if there's anything we can do."

"But look at the gold," Brando said with pleading eyes.

Fin considered if there was anything he could do and realized that the spark looked familiar. It had the same glow as the worms had in Clive Rae when they were eating. That meant that it was probably corrosive, but he was probably immune. If he caught it in his hands, he could hold it while Brando gathered the rest of the gold, but then what? He didn't want to make it angry. He wondered if he could stow it. Finally, he devised a plan and warned Brando to stay back as far as possible. If he was right, there was a good reason the dwarves were afraid; this golden ball could probably dissolve skin and bone with a single touch.

Fin approached his rapidly dissolving fortune and gently poked the creature while activating Greater Stow. His finger had not dissolved, but the creature had also not disappeared. He realized he would need to pick it up first, so he reached in to grab it. The spark seemed to wake up, slipped free from his grasp, and hovered around his head like a bee.

"Offer it something," Brando whisper yelled.

Fin unstowed his favorite rock and offered it forward. When nothing happened, the rock disappeared, and a small nugget of gold took its place. This got the orb's attention; it landed on Fin's hand to absorb the treat. Fin immediately activated stow, and the round creature disappeared.

"It worked?" Brando asked, astonished. "I can confidently say I didn't think it would."

"Me neither," Fin admitted. "Since it didn't burn my fingers off, I figured I could just hold it in my hands if all else failed. Help me get the rest of this."

While Brando collected the gold, Fin checked on the creature in his inventory, where the golden energy ball was labeled as an "Earth Sprite." However, the Earth Sprite appeared to be moving freely from one storage space to another. Fin frowned as it landed in the location that held his money. He unstowed his coins, but the sprite unstowed, too. He then stowed the coins, but the sprite seemed to be able to enter and leave his inventory at will, outside of Fin's control.

"Hurry!" He yelled while juggling the sprite and all his wealth in and out of his inventory in a frantic effort to save his wealth.

Brando turned around, holding more gold than he had in his life. "What are you doing?" he asked as various coins, gold nuggets, and an earth sprite reappeared and disappeared in Fin's hands.

"It's eating all the money," Fin said, frantically moving items around and spreading them out.

He unstowed the sprite and one of the elemental cores simultaneously, and the orb momentarily stopped its rampage to investigate the earth-attuned item, seemingly interested. Fin moved the core back and forth the same way he would get a dog excited about a toy before rolling it across the room. The gambit worked, and the sprite followed after it.

"Hold your shirt open," Fin urged, not waiting for Brando to comply before wealth started accumulating in his hands. "When I tell you to, run and go fast."

Brando nodded as Fin dumped as much treasure as he could into Brando's outspread shirt.

Looking at the sprite with either Sense Magic or Discern Earth brought a curious sight. The orb connected golden thread strings from the elemental core to the rocks scattered around the mine floor. Only when the string began compressing and drawing in rocks to create limbs did Fin understand what the sprite was doing. He told Brando to run and immediately stood his ground for another fight against an Earth Elemental.

"Protect the wealth!" came Fin's battle cry as the elemental stood and charged.

Only the limbs of the elemental were very short. They were made from the largest rocks in an area that were consequently all minuscule shards. The charging creature's bulbous head only came to about knee level. A smile broke out across Fin's face as he watched the pathetic thing run towards him. His joy was short-lived when the elemental punched him in the shin. Fin bent over, picked it up, and stowed it. He wasn't playing anymore, even if his pain-resist ability nullified the credibility of the punch.

The earth sprite moved to where its meal was supposed to be. It hovered in circles for a moment and then stopped, turning a piercing color of silver and back to gold. It started attacking Fin, putting holes in his shirt and cutting off one of his sleeves.

Fin flinched as the sprite charged at his face and bumped into him. It felt like getting hit by a dinner roll. When the sprite disappeared, Fin checked his inventory and noticed he still had a silver coin and a blue topaz gem. He immediately unstowed his forgotten treasures and held them tightly in his grip. A moment later, the pathetic elemental appeared in his hand and punched him in the face. He restowed the elemental, and the process repeated several more times. The elemental appeared in his arms, attacked his face, and then got restowed.

Eventually, the earth sprite gave up and reappeared. It looked around the room before moving out into the passageway. Fin did not want it to find Brando or the vast wealth he was carrying. If it got loose in the mine, there was no telling how much damage it would cause. So he charged after it, and with a combination of luck and habit, he called for it to stop. Surprisingly enough, it did.

"Look," Fin held out his silver coin. "I will give you this if you leave us alone."

The sprite squeaked, and a vision of walls flowing with delicious gold popped into Fin's imagination. It squeaked again, and all the gold was gone—no more delicious, buttery gold, just flavorless minerals in the rock. A third squeak showed Fin taking the last morsel from the sprite's mouth and eating it himself.

At first, Fin thought he was losing his mind and imagining random things. That was until the third squeak when he saw the crude caricature of himself with a massive nose eating gold. It wasn't something he would imagine if he was stuck in the mine for a hundred years. The only explanation was his Earth Commune ability; he might have just figured out how to use it, even if it was a vague understanding.

Fin said, "Trade," and held up the silver coin while imagining himself walking in one direction and the sprite floating in another.

The sprite squeaked and portrayed itself taking a small bite to see if it was any good.

Fin relented with the word "small" and showed exactly what he meant.

The sprite floated closer, and Fin held up the coin. It was one thing to believe you were conversing with an earth-plane creature, but it was entirely different to know you were. When the sprite approached the coin and took the smallest of bites, Fin felt wholly vindicated.

Another squeak brought Fin's attention to the fact that while the metal was nice and chewy, it was nowhere near as good as the gold was.

Fin slapped himself on the forehead. All he needed to do was find his little friend a new home. He told it to follow and walked out into the mine. It didn't take long before he was able to find a decent-sized gold deposit. He hit it with the sharp side of his pickaxe a few times before coming up with a better idea. He transferred what he saw to the sprite so it could dig its own hole.

The sprite hung in the air motionless while it processed what the dragonkin was truly showing. It moved cautiously toward the spot indicated on the wall and burrowed into it. It was one thing to say that you could see through walls, but it was entirely different to prove it, and the proof was delicious.

Fin crept away, relieved to have gotten rid of the destroyer of wealth.

He found Brando and the seven dwarves shortly after and almost regretted not listening to them.

"Did everything go okay?" Brando asked with concern, still holding his shirt like he was collecting walnuts.

"It was a close call, but everything's fine," Fin said before waving for him to follow. "We'll be right back."

Fin led Brando around the corner from the dwarves so they wouldn't see the massive transfer of wealth, followed by its disappearance. It wasn't that he distrusted dwarves, but more like he distrusted strangers in general.

"Let me find something to put that in," Fin said, opening his inventory and freezing in place. The mine devil was in his inventory, snooping around. He checked his hand to ensure he was still holding the blue gem and that it hadn't been eaten. Sure enough, he was still holding it and the nibble-bitten silver coin in a white-knuckled death grip. He immediately took a handful of gold nuggets from Brando's shirt and charged for the dwarves. He put a piece of gold in each of their little hands and made them promise to not tell anyone about his preferential treatment. That was to get them to go away.

"It's in my inventory," Fin admitted, feeling a sense of doom creep up his shoulders. "I don't know how, but he's in there. It's in there."

"What do I do?" Brando asked, seemingly ready to bolt at any moment.

"If it sees you, you're dead, so stand on the other side of that corner," Fin pointed to a well-shadowed area hidden from view. "I'm going to drop four lunchboxes and a pillow. When I tell you to, put the gold in the lunch boxes and stuff them in the pillowcase. Wait for me at the usual spot. If I'm not back in two days, just get out of here and pay the taxes. I have to ditch this thing before I can go anywhere."

Brando didn't move or speak. He didn't understand the full extent of Fin's worries, but he knew how worried Fin was, which worried him. When Fin yelled, "Clear!" Brando sprung from his hiding place and picked up the items left for him on the path. He then dumped the valuables from his shirt into two of the lunchboxes, stuffed the lunchboxes in with the pillow, and ran for Rasengold's favorite spot.

When he was back in the sprite's cavern, Fin sighed and pulled out the blue gem. He said, "Trade" again but added that he was not allowing any samples. The gem was the last thing he wanted to lose, but he also knew that Brando wouldn't leave the mine without him and have to pay all those taxes and fees.

The sprite approached the gem and hovered around it, getting close enough to make Fin's fingers twitch. Finally, it told Fin, "Squeak," but instead of them walking in different directions, the sprite followed him to find more gold.

Fin refused, so it made a counter offer. This time Fin was surrounded by piles of gold and blue gems, but the sprite was being good and not leaving Fin's stowage space. It only wanted to "sample" one of each—and one more for good measure, maybe two more. Three at most.

Fin pulled out his favorite rock and offered to trade once more. This time, Fin offered the idea that he had no gold, and this rock was all he had left in the world.

"Is this rock good?" the sprite asked.

"You can sample it if you want, but I have nothing else," Fin answered.

It gently landed on it, creating a slight indent, and commented, "This is different. What is it?"

"It's my favorite rock," Fin replied. "So, do we have a deal or not?" Fin asked.

The sprite squeaked to confirm the deal. It would follow Fin around, finding all the hidden pockets of gold, but they would separate ways when it ate the silver coin and the gem. However, it wanted to use the rock for something, and there was something about moss.

The part where he and the sprite went separately was straightforward, so Fin agreed and held the items out.

The sprite landed on the rock, but instead of dissolving it, it sent tendrils of power through it. The rock looked like it had golden blood vessels pumping energy through it. Fin asked what it was.

"Moss."

Fin shrugged and held up the gem and the silver coin to conclude their deal.

"I'll eat it later," was the only response before the sprite jumped into Fin's inventory.

Chapter 50

Several things happened at once. Fin stowed his rock to see if there were any changes. It was now labeled as an Oath Stone. Before he could investigate further, he noticed a quest notification.

Earth Quest Complete: Enter a bond with an Earth Plane creature. +1 Level, +1 Active ability.

Active ability: Lesser Earth Control

Path Quest Complete: Enter a bond with a higher being. +1 Level. +1 Quest.

Transcendence Quest: Enter syphon sleep. +5 levels, +5 basic stat points, +5 golden stat points, +1 passive ability, +1 active ability.

Affinity Quest Complete: Chaos (1 of 0): Trade everything for CHAOS! +1 Level, +2 Intelligence. Chaos Affinity. Forfeit Further Affinities.

Chaos Quest complete: Enter a bond with the Anthectis Destroyer. -1 Intelligence, -1 Level, +2 Levels, +1 Active Ability, +2 quests, Forfeit all Transcendence quests.

Active Ability: Alter Ability

Chaos Quest: Activate all abilities simultaneously. +1 Active Ability, -1 Random, +2 Random. Forfeit Random.

Chaos Quest: Fuse all abilities with chaos. +1 Passive Ability, +1 Active ability. Forfeit all Random.

Seeing the multiple quest achievements made Fin dizzy with excitement. However, the longer he read through them, the more weary and confused he became. To start, Fin had no idea what one of zero meant. He tried doing the math, but math wasn't his strong suit. He then realized that one percent of three thousand was thirty. He felt disappointed for the mistake but had to push the miserable thought away. He had more pressing things to focus on. On the bright side, he had just gained a point in intelligence, however obscurely, and decided he would never make a deal based on percentages again.

He looked back at his achievements to find something to cheer him up. The transcendence quest looked promising. If he was able to figure out anything about Syphon Sleep, the rewards would be substantial. Then he noticed that he had forfeited all his transcendence quests. There would be no transcending for him.

Three quests were almost identical, and he was able to learn a few things about the Earth Sprite currently sleeping in his inventory. He already assumed it was an earth-plane creature based on the golden glow it emitted. He even risked a finger on that assumption. What was interesting to learn was the sprite was also considered a higher being and was referred to as the Anthectis Destroyer. He didn't know what the first word meant, but he knew the word destroyer, and it made sense. There was no way a dragon could sleep a wink on its piles of treasure with the Anthectis Destroyer around. It would wake up as destitute as the day it was born.

The two chaos quests were interesting, and he was excited to try out his new abilities. He also needed to come up with a plan to get rid of the Anthectis Destroyer before he too became broke.

Fin unstowed the oath stone and a lunch box. He ate while he considered his old favorite rock. There was a reason why the sprite changed it. His inventory wouldn't classify the sprite as a higher being without good cause. Had it tricked him into forming a bond and had no intention of eating the gem or the coin? He considered destroying the Oath Stone but thought better of it. What if it was there to ensure both parties held up their side of the deal? He felt like the stone was on his side, and all he had to do was get the sprite to finish the arrangement and leave.

He unstowed the sprite and shoved the silver coin into its center. However, the coin was not dissolving. He noticed that whenever the coin got close to the creature, it turned silver in those places. Fin learned two things, when the sprite was silver, it was not corrosive, and the sprite had no intention of being corrosive around the two treasures. He was forced to stop when the small elemental appeared in his hands and started hitting him.

Fin immediately began dialogue with the sprite and yelled, "Just eat it and go away!"

The sprite gave him the picture of moss.

Fin's curiosity won out over his rage, "What is moss?"

The sprite pulsed and showed the vision again. This time, Fin concentrated as the scene played out in his imagination. There was moss, but it began growing and receding on a cave floor. The longer he watched, the more the moss fluctuated. Looking closer, he noticed that the moss was dying as it receded and slowly growing back. It took a while, but he realized it was equivalent to an image of the sun spinning overhead at a blurring speed. It meant "For a very long time" or worse, "Forever."

"No," he stated before getting up and sprinting for the exit. The sprite had no trouble keeping up with him as it hovered close behind and even jumped in his inventory to go along for the ride. He tried appeasing it with hidden gold stores in the mine, hiding from it with Stone Vizard, and blasting it with Caustic Breath. When nothing worked, he tried out his new abilities.

To Fin's disappointment, Lesser Earth Control did not allow him to sculpt stone like clay. The ability seemed to irritate the sprite but did not cause harm. Only when he activated Caustic Breath and Lesser Earth Control did he notice he could lengthen, shape, and project the golden mist further than before. He then tried Alter Ability, directing the ability toward Stonespire Wings. It was an ability he couldn't use anyway, so if the alteration was permanent, he wouldn't use it on any of his useful ones. The combination changed the ability to Stone Simulacrum Wings, and it appeared as if it was permanent. He still couldn't use them.

While looking for other abilities to alter, Fin saw that he still had two from affinities he would never have, Dark Sight and Hydro Lung. The first became Inverse Sight, which did everything he assumed Dark Sight would do. The tunnels became bright as day, with pools of shadow coalescing around the glow moss. Hydro Lung became Absorb Ambient Energy, and he was delighted to find the Earth Sprite did not like it, just not to the point where it would agree to leave him alone. But it was a bargaining chip nonetheless. Fin sat down with determination, pulled out the Oath Stone, and began renegotiations. If they were going to be stuck together, it would be better if they could at least be a team.

Near the mine exit, Brando slept despite his many and unconventional efforts to stay awake and guard his pillow. Ultimately, he couldn't resist the lure of the cave's cold and uneven dirt floor. Startling awake to the sound of approaching footsteps, he regripped his dull pickaxe and took an alert posture. Most of his fears were reserved for the danger of taxation more than the danger of theft, a fear that soon diminished as Fin came into view.

"What took you so long?" Brando asked, gathering up his things. "Did you get rid of it?"

Fin sighed and unstowed the golden, gold-eating orb, and after a glare of warning, it turned silver. "It's an Earth Sprite, and I didn't get rid of it as much as I found myself stuck with it."

"What do you mean stuck with it?" Brando said, flinching as the orb investigated him, floating around his head.

"Don't worry," Fin said, trying to calm Brando's nerves. "As long as it's silver in color, it can't hurt you."

"It's always been silver!" Brando protested, "And I don't want it shredding me to pieces like it did your clothes!"

Fin's clothes were shredded and disheveled, and his right sleeve was bunched up around his wrist. As he changed out of them for clothes in his inventory, he explained the predicament he had been in and the resulting negotiations. He then unstowed the small earth elemental from his inventory. The creature made out of the elemental core and various rocks strung together by the sprite made Brando marvel. Having already fought a larger version of the monster in Clive Rae, he knew that it would make a powerful ally.

"Splitting your half of the treasure seems harsh, but this," he gestured at the stationary elemental, "I don't know… This could be good. Will it help us fight?"

"It won't follow my orders, but I think I can get it to work with us somehow," Fin restowed the elemental along with his discarded clothes. "It's too early to tell, and I'm too exhausted to think anymore tonight."

Fin brushed himself off and turned to ask if Brando was ready to leave, only to find him holding out a piece of gold toward the greedy little sprite.

"Don't feed it!" he shouted as it absorbed the gold and settled on Brando's shoulder.

"I think it likes me," Brando beamed, running a finger over the lump.

Fin's lip curled up into a sneer. "Of course, it's going to like you if you feed it! If you had any idea how much gold I've already fed this thing, you wouldn't want to be its friend. It's an endless pit of hunger that sucks all riches into its void. In fact, I'm going to call it Void."

Path Quest Complete: Become named by a higher being. +1 Charisma. +2 quests revealed.

Royal Advantage: Create a kingdom. +1 Passive Ability. +5 Charisma, +5 golden stat points. Nobility Ranking Increased. Forfeit all Royal Conquest quests.

Royal Conquest: Destroy a kingdom. +1 Active Ability. +5 Constitution, +5 basic stat points. Renown Ranking Increased. Forfeit all Royal Advantage quests.

Fin looked at his stat sheet and sure enough, where it used to say, "Name: Lord Finlay of Dragonthrone" now said, "Squee". He shook his head, but he was too tired to comment on it. He stowed the pillow before he, Brando, and the indomitable Void left the mine.

Chapter 51

Fin woke late in the morning and found the pile of gold he woke with was less than what he had fallen asleep with. He glared at Void, who was resting innocently on Brando's chest. In response to Fin's accusations, the silver ball of thievery explained that it was only taking its rightful share. He was about to share his displeasure with the sprite but caught his reflection in the mirror. Some of the hair he had grown on his face was missing in perfectly round patches. He beckoned Void to his hand, and after instructing it to turn gold, he dragged it over his face. It was the smoothest shave he had ever gotten, and Void didn't seem to mind, so he inferred the creature had at least one useful quality.

Soon, Brando was awake, and when they were both ready, they set out on their daily routine. They checked in with the armor smith, dropped off the gold, and went to the mine. The days came and went, each day bringing new surprises. Void showed itself useful, burrowing into the stone and allowing Fin to reach in and pluck out whatever it left behind. However, not all surprises were welcome.

The gathered dwarves waiting for the 'Fin the Gold Scry' had steadily increased, but the amount of gold collected at the end of the day had decreased. Fin directed the dwarves to work together to tunnel further into the rock in various places as the easily accessible veins had all but depleted. This worked in Fin's favor as the team wouldn't need redirecting the next day. There was the problem of purchasing support beams, which Fin would sometimes need to split the cost with the miners who happily installed them in growing mine shafts.

Finally, Fin and Brando's concerns about having such a large following and drawing the wrong attention were realized. One morning, when they were about to enter the mine, they were intercepted by an official surrounded by uniformly dressed guards.

"Good morning, Fin the Gold Scry and Brando the Collector," a dwarf said with a grim look. "The boss would like to have a word with you. Will you follow me?"

Brando took the situation stoically and directed the official to "Lead the way."

They were led around the mine entrance to the left, through a passageway, and up a winding stairway surrounded by weapons pointing menacingly upward. The armed and armored dwarves escorted them to a top-floor office, where a female dwarf sat behind a desk waiting for them.

"I am Marriam Dunkle, the owner of this mine and establishment," she said, pointing at two small chairs in front of the desk. "Please, have a seat."

Fin sat while Brando looked dubiously at the tiny chair. He gingerly lowered himself into a seated position below knee level with an irritated look.

Marriam continued without ceremony, "In the past weeks, the mine has seen a significant increase in production. So much so that I began looking into what was causing the spike in income. Do you know what I discovered? I found you two. I did some digging, so to speak; it turns out that while you were leading the greatest expedition this mine has seen in forty years, you have yet to take even an ounce of gold out of the mines yourself. However, I have it on good authority that you have collected a significant portion of the claimed gold. Hence, the honorific, Brando the Collector. Do one of you care to explain this anomaly?"

The question hung in the air for several palpable heartbeats before Brando spoke, "Are you implying that we have some kind of undetectable pocket we can put gold in that makes us able to sneak past your security without paying your exorbitant fees?"

"I am implying that I could have you arrested at a word," Marriam stated coldly. "However, I am willing to overlook certain unscrupulous deeds if you are willing to solve the riddle of how one of you can find the gold and how the other is making it disappear."

Fin considered the offer before unstowing the oath stone. He didn't know how or if it worked, but it made him feel more comfortable with what he was about to do, if only in a superstitious way. He placed it on the counter, causing the guards to visibly tense.

"What is this?" Marriam asked, looking at the rock.

"Hold it in your hand and swear that whatever I tell you, you will not repeat it to anyone else," Fin said with a serious edge to his voice. "Also, that you will, in fact, absolve us of any potential unscrupulous deeds. After you make the promise, I will tell you and no one else."

"And say that you won't kick us out of the mine," Brando added. "There's a lot of people depending on us down there."

Marriam picked up the oath stone quizzically. "A rock?"

"Yes," Fin stated. "It's an oath stone. I'm certain you will keep any promises you make while holding it."

"I promise not to call you crazy," Marriam said, holding the rock to her forehead. With the next breath, she proclaimed, "You are absolutely insane."

"You didn't call him crazy, though," Brando chimed in with a point of his finger.

Marriam called both of them crazy, which caused Fin to frown. He stood up to reach for the rock, but he was stopped with two spears to his throat.

Marriam waved for the guards to stand down.

"You can wait outside," she said, placing the rock into Fin's waiting hand. "I have sent my guards away and agree to your terms. If you tell me, I will take your secrets to my grave and not stop you from entering my mine. Why would I? You've made me a lot of money."

Without hesitation, Fin confessed everything, "I have a secret pocket where I can carry things around completely undetected, and I can see gold through walls."

Marriam called for the guards. When they rushed in, Fin spoke rapidly to keep from getting skewered. "I swear, I'm not lying," he said, holding his hands up. "Test me, I'll show you."

Marriam held up a hand and addressed her guards, "Go get Genris, have him open the vault. Bring twelve chests, empty half of them, and fill them with rocks. Make sure Genris keeps everything organized."

The guard bowed and left the room. Marriam instructed the other guards to help. When they had left, she leveled her gaze on Fin. "You will find that I do not have the patience for misdirection or glib remarks," she warned, reclaiming her seat. "If you are unable to substantiate your claim, I will have you arrested, and we can repeat this conversation a year from today."

Fin barely registered the threat, as something else had caught his attention. A massive, double-sided war hammer was hanging on the wall of Marriam's office. On one side, the hammer was square and flared out at the end; on the other, it had a round spike. The handle was as long as most swords and was wrapped with old, cracked leather. The weapon looked too gaudy and unwieldy to interest him; the colorless glow from the hammer caught his attention. Fin stood up from his squat chair and walked absent-mindedly toward the hammer. It hung propped up on the wall with a hook.

Marriam watched as Fin brushed his fingers over the simple design work etched into the side of the hammer. "That is a forgery of the Gladrohm Hammer," She said, approaching, taking it off the wall, and giving it several one-handed swings. "My grandfather bought it from a merchant who swore to its authenticity. Only after my grandfather bought it did he learn that the actual Gladrohm Hammer was made from a combination of metals too heavy to allow such a one-handed swing from his granddaughter. I keep it to remind me not to make the same mistake as he did. The hammer was as expensive as it was fake."

"May I?" Fin said, holding out his hand.

Marriam placed the hammer in Fin's hand and gave it several test swings.

"It's lighter than it looks," he marveled.

"Yes, and it would break in half with a breath," Marriam said with dismissal.

Fin wasn't so sure. The magic glow of the hammer indicated that if it wasn't an authentic piece, there was at least something special about it. He searched his stats to find some inkling of what the magic did. His eyes fell to his Strength stat, and his brows lifted ever so slightly. He hung it up on the hook and grasped it again, retaking its full weight. His strength went from negative nine to eleven each time he picked it up. Whatever the Gladrohm Hammer was, this was probably it.

Treasure Quest Complete: Identify treasures with resourceful means. +1 Active Ability

Active Ability: Identify

Fin had already been looking at his status when the notification appeared. He immediately activated the Identify ability on the hammer and found he was, in fact, holding the Gladrohm Hammer. It gave a stat boost of twenty to strength. He did not know how he felt about Marriam yet, so he didn't voice his discovery out loud. Instead, he hung up the hammer and gave it a compliment.

"It looks good," Fin said, returning to his chair. "The grip needs to be replaced."

"I'll take that into consideration next time I use the decoration in battle," Marriam remarked.

The conversation dwindled into silence as the three sat and waited for the chests to arrive. When guards started carrying small, unassuming boxes through the door, Fin nearly sighed in relief. He stood and faced the wall until the guards had set the boxes down. Even without the ability to see the contents, he could tell which ones looked lighter, and he wanted to eliminate any doubts about his abilities.

"Instead of watching the chests for hints of their contents, you turn your back," Marriam said, noticing what Fin was doing. "I am intrigued but not convinced. Go ahead and point to the boxes with gold in them."

Fin turned to inspect the neat row of chests. They were uniformly spread out, so every other box contained neatly stacked gold coins. He couldn't see the contents of the other chests except for one. Inside the second to the last box lay a gold bit as big as the tip of his little finger.

"Every other box has gold starting from the second," Fin said after another brief glance. "Shall I open them?"

Marriam rushed to the first box and snapped the lid open. She then moved down the line of chests, opening every other one. A look of pure shock crossed her face for the briefest moment before she regained composure.

"Can you really see through boxes, or is there some trick that I'm missing?" She asked skeptically.

"What would you be willing to wager that this box also contains gold?" Fin lifted a foot and set it on the second to the last box.

"Impossible," Marriam stated. "You heard me give the order; only half were to contain gold."

"Would you bet the hammer there is no gold in this box?" Fin asked, trying to contain his excitement.

Instead of taking the bet, Marriam pulled the box out from under Fin's foot, unlatched the lid, and dumped the contents on the floor. Grey rocks spilled out over the carpet, and Marriam cocked an eyebrow.

"What were you saying?" She asked, arms folded in front of her petite frame.

Fin plucked a single rock off the floor and held it up in the air, "I'm asking you to wager the hammer that there's gold in this rock."

"If there's gold in that rock," she said, pausing for consideration. "You can keep the hammer, but in return, I need something from you. You have to help me purchase some property that will reimburse the price of it."

Chapter 52

Fin pinched the rock to steady it on the ground and brought the spiked end of the hammer onto it. The strength boost from the hammer combined with its imperceptibly leaden weight made it easy work to unveil the stone's secret treasure. Marriam watched, not with shock or amusement, but something else entirely. Greed? Excitement? She appeared to have abandoned all the principles that once kept her grounded. The lesson of her grandfather's con artist vanished with the hammer on the wall.

Fin looked into her eyes and saw certainty. "I believe we have a deal then?"

"You really are the Gold Scry," she mused as she took the precious metal from Fin's dirt-stained fingers. "The hammer's yours if you'll accompany me to hunt for real estate."

Fin shrugged and looked at Brando, who also shrugged. "Sure, when do you want to meet?"

Instead of answering, she called for Genris. When a meek-looking Dwarf woman entered the room, Marriam started dictating orders, "I need two scribes, six guards, and transportation for the ten of us and our two guests. Be quick; you and I are going shopping."

"You want to go right now?" Fin asked, surprised at the haste.

"You'll have to forgive me for saying this, but you twicelings don't have a..." Marriam paused, reconsidering how to say, "Your reputation for keeping your promises leaves something to be desired. It is better to go now, in case you can't be found in the morning."

Brando clapped his hands together, "Great! I'm sure you will all have a lot of fun. Since you won't be needing me for any of this, I might just sit this one out."

Fin deadpanned, "You don't want to come?"

"Of course I want to come! However, I have a little shopping of my own to do," Brando stated, not at all suspicious. "Besides, if you want me to replace the hammer's grip, I'm going to need supplies. I am a leather worker, after all."

"That's fine," Fin relented after looking at the cracked and crumbling grip on the hammer. "You really think you can fix this?"

"It's what I do best," Brando radiated reassurance. "Keep the hammer for now; I'll gather everything I need in town and craft the grip when you come back."

Soon, they parted ways. Fin followed Marriam out of the building, where three carriages waited for them. There were six dwarves holding spears and two carrying leather satchels. After squeezing into the tight-fitting carriage, Genris and two guards were forced to stay behind.

Fin rode in the tight carriage with dwarves squeezed beside him and against his knees. The trip seemed to take forever, so Fin was impatient to exit the cart and stretch his legs. They were well outside the city. He assumed they were going to all the most affordable plots of land first.

Marriam looked at him expectantly, "This is our first stop. Can you sense anything?"

Fin languidly peered around, "There's nothing here."

"We haven't walked around yet," Marriam protested. "Maybe after you poke around, you will find a vein of gold or something?"

"As much as I hate to say this, I didn't need to leave the cart to tell you there was nothing here," Fin said, shaking his head. "But taking a break from nestling next to Pimly is nice."

Marriam shook her head to one of her scribes, who crossed something off her list. Fin saw how long the list was and lost any residual cheerfulness. There must have been a hundred locations written down.

"Let's try to make this more efficient," Fin said, trying to rekindle his determination. "If you want me to inspect somewhere, just yell out the window and I'll tell you if the property is worth buying."

When they left, Fin allowed himself to fall asleep. Periodically, he was elbowed awake only to activate his ability, lean his head out the window, and yell, "No!" On several occasions, Fin saw enough precious metals underground to call the carriages to a stop and investigate. More often than not, there weren't enough trace metals for it to be worth purchasing the property and setting up a new mine. Once, he saw massive veins of what he assumed was silver, but a farmer already owned the property.

Not wanting to be involved in the attempted swindle to buy the property from the farmer, Fin told him exactly what his property held. This made for a poor start toward building relations with Marriam, but he did not care. He was leaving town soon anyway and wanted to do so with a clean conscience.

Not soon after did Fin find a veritable wealth underground. The area was not on the list of places to visit, but it was overgrown with foliage and in the less expensive outskirts of town. Both scribes worked frantically to mark their location as Fin walked around. He found some low-hanging fruit, so to speak, and unstowed Void for a snack. The deal he made with the sprite was that it would only eat half and allow Fin to have the rest. Soon enough, Fin reached into a perfectly round burrow and retrieved a handful of silver and raw gold.

He frowned at Void. "This doesn't look like half to me."

Behind the golden ball of greed, Fin noticed Marriam, the two scribes, and the guards staring at him with mouths agape. They cautiously stepped back and he saw the looks of horror on their faces.

"He gets hungry sometimes. Or she does? I'm not sure, but there's plenty…" Fin trailed off, realizing no one was as concerned about the potentially missing gold as the thing that ate it. "Don't worry, it's not dangerous; it just kind of follows me around and tries to eat all my gold."

One of the guards started stammering and pointed. However, the words came out of Marriam's mouth first, "That's a mine spirit!"

"Technically, it's a sprite, not a spirit," Fin corrected, inviting Void to rest on his hand and disappear. "It's harmless as long as you don't make friends with it."

"Where did it go?!" The stammering dwarf found his words.

"He carries it around with him?" "It's a curse!" and "I'm not riding with him." came the mutterings of the dwarves around Marriam before she quieted them down. Subconsciously, Marriam knew she was about to sell her dwarven intolerance toward satriks for wealth. Still, she was more than happy about it. She was getting such a good deal for her grandfather's counterfeit hammer that if Fin wanted to make friends with a goblin, she would offer the green savage a mug of her best ale.

"Everyone, calm down," Marriam ordered. "There will be time to discuss the dirt eater later. For now, I need the scribes to come with me while the rest of you safeguard the perimeter."

Marriam gave Fin an odd look as she approached but surprisingly did not mention Void. Instead, she asked if he could describe the locations of the gold and approximate its amount. Fin obliged and began pointing to various locations with brief descriptions as the scribes scribbled rapidly to capture every word he said.

Marriam's heart raced as he told her how much wealth they were standing on. She would buy this land for a pittance and get a return far greater than the original cost of the hammer. She hid her excitement. As long as Fin the Gold Scry didn't think she was satisfied, she would use him as much as possible. When the terrain was correctly mapped, Marriam had everyone back in the carts and moving on with haste.

Chapter 53

Fin was happy to have more room in his carriage. None of the other guards wanted to travel with him, so they opted to squeeze into the other ones. All but for poor Pimly, who drew the short grass and had to share Fin's carriage. He sat wide-eyed and rigid. Sitting next to an uncomfortable dwarf was vastly better than sitting uncomfortably next to three of them.

As time passed, Fin realized that every time Marriam shouted at him through her own window and he replied in the negative, it probably meant the scribes were crossing off another location from the list. He had lost count of how many gold-desolate areas he had demarcated, even though not all had been completely barren. He had seen multiple places with at least some copper, silver, or gold, but it was never enough to stop for. Especially when they could be crossing more places off the list. Then, the unexpected happened. Marriam called something out of the window, but it wasn't directed toward him. Pimly, blatantly ignoring him, perked up at the words and scrambled to get out of the carriage. They were stopped entirely, and the silence of the wheels allowed him to hear boots shuffling in the dirt, the clinking of metal, and the words, "To battle!"

Fin instinctively unstowed his dull sword and got out of the carriage to help if he could. When he saw what was attacking, he froze. It wasn't from cowardice; it was from a mixture of shock, uncertainty, inexperience, or a dozen other reasons, including wisdom. The dwarves stood in formation with spears pointed upward toward the ugliest group of winged creatures he had ever seen. They were maybe twice the size of a vulture but looked like a combination of a mosquito and a bat. Tufts of grey hair outlined skin, webbed wings, and a needlepoint beak longer than his arm.

Instead of running in blindly, he stopped and observed. The dwarves seemed to be holding their own, moving forward and backward together and attacking with powerful thrusts in a coordinated effort. One of the creatures fell out of the air. A dwarf gave an order and stabbed the fallen creature while the others thrust their spears upward to keep the rest at bay. Watching them fight was a presentation of skill and mastery.

Fin wondered if his Identify ability would work on the creature or if it was just for weapons. What he found left him with more questions than answers, at least he discovered what the creature was.

Mammoth Stirge: Lean, stringy, and chewy.

First, he had an odd feeling that the description showed the creature's edibility. He tested the theory by identifying one of the guards.

Dwarf: Small but filling.

He shook his head in disgust and decided not to tell anyone about it. Of all the abilities he had, this one was by far the most incriminating.

The dwarves made short work of the stirges. They kicked the corpses out of the road and walked back to the carriages with smiles. Pimly held up a few strands of grass and said something with a hopeful look on his face. The others laughed at him and directed him toward Fin's carriage. He eventually gave up, threw the grass away, and walked dejectedly toward Fin.

Fin couldn't believe it. The guards all fought what could have been the most frightening-looking monsters he had ever seen, but they didn't want to share a carriage with him because of Void? Furthermore, they were all laughing and smiling as if the fight had been no big deal.

The carts moved again, falling into the same routine. Fin was happy to tour the outskirts of the dwarven city and was only slightly discouraged. Pimly did not want to talk. He considered unstowing Void and having it harass the solemn dwarf when he saw something strange.

He stopped the carts and walked out into an open field. He waded through waist-high grass under a stone hill. Ahead of him, dead trees hanging at obtuse angles sat bundled together at the far end. His destination was nowhere in particular yet everywhere around him. He could see densely sporadic signs of precious metals through his ability, but they looked nothing like the gold veins or gem clusters he was used to.

The ones he could see above ground lay dispersed, shallowly around in an almost uniform pattern. He stopped at a spot with a large enough item to start his investigation. He dug in the ground with his fingers, wishing he had a shovel, to find a clue of what was hiding. Finally, he had dug deep enough to uncover a remnant of what might have been a money pouch and dislodged three coins from the earth. As he tromped back through the grass to show the others, he noticed they were gathered around the base of a grassy hill, eating food from wooden baskets.

"This place is full of odd things spread around the ground," He explained, holding out one of the grubby coins he found. "It might be worthwhile to look into it."

Marriam told him to help himself to the food she brought, which consisted of breads, cheeses, preserved meat, and not one, but two casks of her own "Special reserve." As he started picking through the baskets, Marriam dripped an amber liquid from her cup onto the coin. She repeated the process several times, rubbing the face of the coin with her thumb.

Fin filled a cup and had already taken two drinks before the overwhelmingly unpleasant flavor registered in his mind. A confusing amalgamation of flavors assaulted him from every direction at once. One flavor, in particular, held no mysteries; it was sour! Not "I left the dough out too long," sour, but "This dough was left out when your grandmother was born." It gave him a similar feeling to when he ate a gooseberry; it was a lesson his brain told him he was about to learn again.

He waited for an opportunity to spit it out. Marriam exclaimed something in dwarven, and all attention was on her. He was one second too late before her full attention slammed into him like the executioner's axe.

"Where did you find this?" she asked, holding up the now perfectly visible silver coin.

Fin swallowed, grimaced, and then pointed toward the trail he had made in the grass. "Just over there, this place is full of them. Or, full of something similar."

To make his point, he pushed through his mental exhaustion and peered at the ground around him. Transfixed on an area several paces away, he set down his cup and started digging with his hands. Then, he discreetly unstowed his dagger and used it to dig. When his target was partially uncovered, he gripped it and tore it from the ground, pulling up a handful of debris. When he inspected the item, he saw it was a ring. Unfortunately, it was still attached to the skeletal remains of its late owner's hand. An audible gasp came from the dwarven onlookers, and Fin dropped the hand with a shriek, high pitched enough to disappoint his father.

The dwarves ran to the skeletal hand and began poking it with their spears and toes. Marriam leaned down and picked it up with a calm courage that would have earned Fin's father's respect. She removed the ring and tossed the rest away like the bones on a dinner plate. After dropping a small amount of her private reserve on the ring, she showed everyone the emblem it bore.

"This writing isn't Dwarven," she muttered before attempting to give it to one of the scribes. The scribe ambled backward and leaned in as if Marriam was simply showing it to her.

"It's Elvish, I believe," she said before nodding as if she had seen all there was to see.

"Dark Elvin," the other scribe corrected. "The letters are straight, not curved. That's assuming it's letters at all, but it's not a picture, so what else could it be?"

"Do elves live around here or something?" Fin asked out of curiosity. He had never seen an elf or didn't think he did. All he knew was they had pointy ears, which could probably be hidden under a hat easily enough if he had.

"No," Marriam answered, apparently giving up on trying to offer the ring to anyone else. "That's what makes this so strange. Do you think you can find anything else?"

Fin shrugged and started looking around. He could tell his energy was almost gone. If he was in the mine, he would eat something or lay down for a nap, but they were running out of time; the sun had already begun to set. So, he mustered all his determination, set his jaw, and finished the rest of Marriam's potent drink. He followed it up by throwing berries, bread, and cheese in his mouth to rid himself of the flavor.

"I have been a poor host," Marriam said sincerely. "I should have given you food to travel with, and now you are starving."

If his mouth wasn't full, he would have had to figure out how to say, "I'm just trying to get the taste of your disgusting cider out of my mouth," in a polite way. Instead, he waved to suggest, "It's okay, this is just how I eat," and pushed through his exhaustion to activate his ability.

All of the treasures in the ground gave up their secrets at once. Working quickly, he marked the treasures with bits of bread and instructed the guards to dig in those places. He then turned and faced the grassy hill behind the picnic and stared. There was a faint glow in a very distinct pattern on the face of the hill underneath the foliage. Before he could investigate, his willpower gave out, and his ability faded into normal vision.

Fin sat on the ground, needing a moment to close his eyes and collect himself. Marriam asked about him with concern, but he assured her that he was fine. She soon turned her attention to the others digging in the places indicated by bread. The guards dug out another coin, the rusted remains of what could have been a dagger, and an obscurely large button. When he told them about the odd symbols he had seen in the hill, it was already too late to investigate. So, the scribes wrote quick descriptions and were directed back to the carts.

The trip back was surprisingly quick. The carriage carried lit lanterns, but the light had not been useful until they were stopped outside the Traveler's House.

"Thank you for your help today," Marriam said sweetly. "I will bring breakfast in the morning, and make sure to bring extra travel rations."

Fin was surprised at the implication that he would go with her again in the morning. Hadn't he done enough to satisfy his end of the deal? Hadn't he just shown her a brand-new mining site brimming with precious metals and discovered a potentially lucrative ruin? He was still formulating his response when the carriages pulled away, not giving him a chance to negotiate. His time was valuable, and he had more important things to do than ride around in a carriage couped up with dull company all day. He sighed and walked towards his room. He could deal with it tomorrow.

Chapter 54

Fin found Brando rummaging through and organizing crates of provisions, weapons, and tools.

"I'm glad you're here," Brando stated, removing a burlap sack and a leather bundle from one of the crates. "Can you make all of this disappear?"

"What is all of this?" Fin asked, gingerly approaching the hoard of random supplies.

Brando pointed to bags, crates, and bundles, in turn describing the contents of each. "Meat, vegetables, and some spare weapons for when we get to goblin town. More mining supplies. Oh, I splurged and got some new leather working tools for myself. My old ones are nowhere near this quality. It will also help me put a good grip on the hammer. Are you sure you want to use it? Marriam did say it would break. Probably not against goblins, but why risk it?"

"It's a magic weapon, and it gives a strength boost of twenty," Fin said, unstowing the hammer. "And it's not a forgery. This is the real thing. Whoever Gladrohm was, this was his hammer. It's not going to break."

"Twenty what?" Brando asked, taking the hammer skeptically. "I don't feel stronger."

"Twenty points of strength," Fin shrugged. "I don't know exactly what that equates to, but it's more strength than I've gained since we've met. I think I'm going to learn how to use it."

"Easy, just hit them with one of the ends. Like this," Brando made a few example swings. On his final swing, he failed to stop the hammer's momentum in time before it struck a wooden crate. The crate exploded into a million splinters, spilling bags of potatoes everywhere.

Brando winced as the room fell into abrupt silence. "I'll fix that grip tonight."

"I'll start stowing all of this," Fin said and then remembered something important. "Just one thing, before I forget...."

Human: Flavor varies.

"What?" Brando asked.

Fin shook his head. "If we ever run into a dragon, I'm just going to kill it."

The next day, they visited the armor smith, as usual, but they didn't bring their customary lunch box full of golden nuggets this time. Olhoff had become their unofficial banker. He would take their gold, melt it into uniform bars, and was more than happy to keep it locked away for a fee. This pleased Fin because it kept it out of Void's untrustworthy care. Brando didn't seem to care about the gold as much as he cared for good food and clothing that featured horses.

"Ah, I'm glad you're here," Olhoff said, wiping soot off his face and replacing his monocle. "I think I fixed the arm joints. I need you to wear the armor and wave your arms around."

"Actually, I was hoping we could just take whatever you have and head out," Fin said reluctantly, knowing that Olhoff would not agree.

"What?!" Olhoff demanded, monocle hanging taut against its chain.

"We're almost done; why would you want to stop now?"

Fin sighed and rubbed his eyes. "Marriam Dunkle seems to think I owe her something, and I suspect that she's going to make life difficult if I don't go along with her."

Tory had entered the room and offered, "You probably want to sneak out at night. I can smuggle you out in a hay cart, but it will have to wait until tomorrow."

"What did you do?" Olhoff asked with disappointment in his voice.

"It's a long story," Fin said, unstowing the hammer behind his back - like it wouldn't be noticeable - and showed the two smiths. "Her grandfather bought…"

"The Gladrohm Hammer!" Olhoff said, hands twitching to reach for it.

"That's a cool trick," Tory complimented. "Can you teach me that sometime?"

"Uh, yeah," Fin said, handing the hammer to Olhoff. "What's the story with this thing anyway?"

Olhoff looked over the hammer, which was as long as he was tall. "Some historians noticed that three famous warlords from three different eras all had the same looking hammer. Some believe it's the same one. It's named after the first of them - Gladrohm the Wyvern Slayer. I see the rumors are true; this is too light to be the real one. I like the grip on it, though. I've never seen this pattern before."

Before Brando could brag about his craftsmanship, Fin asked, "Is it lighter than Tory?"

Olhoff was old but not too old to decline a challenge. He grabbed his apprentice by the back of the shirt and hefted him off the ground with one hand. Tory howled in surprise and then let out a string of insults and curses when he was bobbed up and down in the weighing process. Olhoff ignored the insults, and Brando nearly fell over with laughter.

"This can't be right," Olhoff said, confused. "I know I've been feeding you well enough, but you're as light as a baby."

"Put me down, you old coot!" Tory yelled.

"May I?" Fin asked, gently taking the hammer from the old coot. Tory's feet immediately touched the ground as Olhoff's strength gave out. He tried lifting his apprentice again but couldn't. Fin gave him back the hammer, and Tory lifted it off the ground with a curse.

"By Loden, what is this?!" Olhoff exclaimed, dropping Tory and looking at the hammer as if for the first time. "Is this some kind of magic weapon? Is this the real hammer of Gladrohm?!"

Olhoff talked about the history of the hammer while he and Tory dressed Fin and Brando in their respective suits of armor. Fin's set was considerably more decorated than Brando's, even though it was made by an apprentice and not the master himself. The detail and craftsmanship of the armor, paired with the dark circles around Tory's eyes, was enough to know that a considerable amount of time was put into it. A gold trim was around some leading edges, and a gold-etched dragon was on the breastplate, with gold-etched fire streaming out of its mouth. Then, because Tory was romantic, eccentric, or both, he attached a cape to Fin's shoulders through several ribbed spikes.

Brando looked at Fin's armor with jealousy. His armor was basic, metal-looking, and boring. There wasn't even a horse on it. Yes, it had enough functionality, would keep him alive, and even made him look intimidating. He would look like a warlord, however, standing next to Fin in his armor, he looked like the warlord's scribe.

They moved their arms around, bent their knees, and stepped in different directions to test out the joints in the armor. The well-oiled joints moved smoothly in every direction.

"It feels good," Fin said, rotating his arm soundlessly around. "I think we'll take them today."

"What? No!" It was Tory's turn to protest. "I still need to finish decorating your helmet and polish everything!"

"It's okay; we don't need anything decorated or polished," Brando said, not wanting Fin's armor to look any better than it did already. "We're just going to get them dirty. Besides, I think we should get used to wearing them before fighting in them."

"That is true," Olhoff said, handing them a small brown sack and two sets of light brown clothes each. "I was going to tell you to wear them as much as possible to break them in. Wear them while you do mundane things until your body gets used to the extra weight. Do not take them into the mines; if you get dirt in the joints, don't come crawling back to me to clean them out. The most important thing to know is not to run while you are in battle. You'll survive as long as you have the energy to fight, but you'd wring yourself out too fast if you run. So don't do it. Do I make myself clear?"

"Yes, Master Olhoff," Fin and Brando said in unison as if they had been trained.

"Good. Now, I was going to going to polish this first, but seeing how you tall folk don't have enough sense for polishing your armor, I'll give it to you now," Olhoff reached behind the counter and took out a large helmet with a square nose guard and a square mohawk that curved toward the backside into a point. It was exquisitely designed to incite fear in the hearts on the battlefield.

Brando took it with metal-clad fingers. "This is beautiful, I don't know what to say. Thank you."

Olhoff blushed. "I got some help with it. A true master knows how to ask for help."

Fin was eager to see his own helmet. "Where's mine?"

Tory's eyes snapped up. "It's not done yet. Can you wait until tomorrow?"

Olhoff then brought a crossbow from behind the corner and pointed it at Fin's chest. "How about a demonstration, as promised?"

Tory nearly leaped to stand in front of Fin and held out his hands to stop him. "No! If you want a demonstration, shoot your own armor!"

The tip of Olhoff's bolt rotated until it stopped in front of Brando. "Brace yourself, lad."

Before Brando had time to protest, the crossbow clicked, and the sharp metallic twang of a bolt ricocheted off his body and splintered into a shower of little pieces.

His heart nearly came to a stop, and he let out a gasp of surprise.

"I've already taken the payment for the armor out of your personal supply," Olhoff said nonchalantly, replacing the crossbow behind the desk. "Do you want to take your gold now or pick it up tomorrow when you return for the helmet?"

Chapter 55

Fin and Brando stepped outside, looking like generals at war. Their pockets were not as heavy as they could be, given the great expense of the armor. Still, they were wealthier than they ever thought possible. They were making their way to the mercenaries' guild when they noticed the whole square had stopped to stare at them.

"Just keep moving," Brando muttered under his breath. "If we ignore them, they will go away."

Fin took Brando's instruction and kept walking when a familiar-looking dwarf approached them and bowed. "Master Gold Scry, when you did not return to the mines, I offered to see if you were well. Then, some others agreed to accompany me, and then, well," the dwarf gestured around, "We all came to check up on you."

They turned toward the people in the square. It dawned on Fin that the people weren't strangers staring at the well-armored humans; they were their fellow miners. The problem was that it was causing more people to stop and stare. The square was now full of miners and pedestrians standing and staring. They were at the center of attention in a busy square in the center of a foreign city.

"I don't know if I like this Fin," Brando said, crumbling under everyone's attention.

Fin reluctantly stepped forward, cleared his voice, and addressed the crowd. "Thank you for your concern. As you can see, we are well, but we will not be returning to the mines. Instead, we are going to fight for a different mine."

One of the dwarves called out, "You're going to take back the Lokardale mine from Clive Rae?"

"Uh, not exactly, but what Clive Rae did was pretty dumb from what I understand," Fin regained his train of thought. "No, we are going to a mine that is five days west of here. It's inhabited by a group of goblins. What's worse is they have captured humans and dwarves, using them as slaves. We are going to fight the goblins. If any of you want to fight alongside us, you are welcome to join us. We are leaving in the morning, regardless."

"What kind of mine is it?" someone asked from the crowd.

"Topaz," Fin announced. He looked down to the dwarf who had greeted them and used True Name before continuing, "We have to make preparations to leave, but Grimwald here will answer any further questions."

The dwarf blushed and stammered for a refusal, but Fin had already turned to leave. The questions all came at once. Fin had to hand it to the little guy; he was good at pretending to know what he was talking about.

Fin and Brando nearly ran into the group of Marriam's guards, who were also waiting.

"Frome's legs," Brando cussed. "How does everyone know where we are?"

"Because you're the only humans within fifty leagues, and you do the same thing every day," Marriam smiled from the center of her well-armed and armored guards. "May I entice you to join me for a meal?"

"Marriam, I feel like you and I are even." Fin was glad to have the chance to tell her in person. "We both held our ends of the deal, and now I have other pressing matters to see to."

"I see," Marriam said, tracing her eyes over his and Brando's armor. "How about this, then? Let me buy you a meal as a 'thank you,' and we can talk about what I can do to help with your pressing matters."

"I could go for a hot meal," Brando said, clinking his gauntlet on the metal over his stomach.

Fin was hungry, too, and making allies with such a powerful person could be beneficial, so he agreed. Soon, the three of them sat at an alehouse with more food than they could eat without him using a basic stat point, which he had. He waited until everyone was finished eating to use it. His Dexterity went from -5 to -4. Brando gave him a knowing look as the rest of the food vanished from the table.

As the meal progressed, they told Marriam about where they were going and why. The more they said, the more she started getting that look in her eye. When the tale was told, they all sat in comfortable silence under the watchful eye of guards from adjacent tables.

"I will send ten of my best guards with you and purchase all available mercenaries," she said before draining the last of her ale. "Six of my guards alone could handle fifty goblins. But with ten, you, the mercenaries, and any of the miners you've convinced with your speech, I don't doubt you will win."

"Why are you helping us?" Brando asked bluntly.

"Did you know that I make more money from the shops in my mine than I do from the mine itself?" Marriam asked rhetorically. "Those shops were not there before I inherited the place. I put them there because I see the value in people, and right now, I am making an investment in you two. No strings attached other than the promise of good relations… And exclusive rights to incorporate shops, money exchanges, and places to meet general necessities here and there. Mostly for good relations."

Fin agreed to the terms immediately. If Marriam had said, "I want the mine all to myself," he still would have agreed. He had more gold than he knew what to do with and could easily make more. He didn't want to stay in the desert and mine anyway; he might pluck a few gems out for his mother, but he was ready to go home. He just had a friend to rescue first.

"Marriam, I am excited to work with you," Fin said, moving to shake hands. His fingerless gauntlet was in the way, so he put his hand on it, and it disappeared.

"Fin, can you do that to my armor?" Brando asked as he stood and walked around the table. "I really have to, uh," he glanced at Marriam, "relieve myself."

Fin placed his hands on Brando's armor, which disappeared into his inventory a moment later. Brando thanked him and walked out of the room with a casual quickness. Marriam's eyes sparkled with possibilities as she watched Fin sit back down.

She held out her own hand, "I am excited to work with you too."

With dawn came the acrid feeling of change. Trees gave up their dying leaves, husbands kissed their wives goodbye, and Fin discovered that Void had eaten a midnight snack. Thankfully, the hammer and armor were safe; what wasn't safe was the dark elf coin he had found. He made it absolutely clear to the creature that the weapons and armor were completely off-limits. For the price of several years' wages, Void agreed.

Brando paid the bill in the lobby while Fin collected the horses. When he got to the front of the Traveler's House, he saw a sight he had not expected. Twenty dwarves mulled around horses and carts in the middle of the street, waiting for him. Some miners were ready to battle for the promise of wealth. More came by the moment. He was pleased when Rasengold showed up with his entire family. He wished them all a good morning, and they offered him breakfast. Brando was also offered a warm bowl of porridge and an egg when he arrived.

Before leaving, Fin made one last stop at the armor smith. Outside, he saw the ten guards Marriam promised and ten others, all carrying weapons. He directed them all toward the larger group and walked inside. The dull thunk of the doorbell drew Olhoff into the main room.

"You're early," he greeted, then whispered his next words, "He's been up all night putting the final touches on your helmet. This is a big moment for him, getting his journeyman's and all. So, try to be patient. He's almost done."

After a moment, he continued, "Well? Did you bring your armor?"

Fin nodded his head.

"I'll go check on him," Olhoff said and then went into the back.

Fin closed his eyes and concentrated. He had never stowed or unstowed anything at a thought, but he felt he could do it. After nothing happened, he opened his eyes, pulled up his inventory, and focused on his armor. It appeared on his body in the blink of an eye.

Olhoff returned with a startled expression. "Well, you are full of surprises, aren't you?"

Then Tory came out with the helmet. It looked similar to Brando's but different. Instead of a monochrome color, it was trimmed with gold around the eyes and noseguard. Two golden dragon wings flared out from either side, pointing straight up and fanning around to the back with webbed spikes. It didn't look like something a general would wear; it looked like something a king would wear.

Fin reached out and took it gently from Tory's fingers. He placed it on his head. It fit snugly and didn't limit his vision. The leather inlay made it comfortable. He felt absurd wearing such a fine suit of armor but stood proud.

"This is incredible!" Fin said, taking off the helmet to look at it.

"There's just one more thing," Tory said, taking a hammer and the smallest chisel out of his apron pocket. He hammered a small dent on the bottom left of Fin's plate. "It's customary to give you your first dent so you won't die in battle."

Fin smiled and hugged the tired dwarf.

"How come I got shot with a crossbow for my first dent?" Brando asked the uncomfortable-looking dwarves.

Olhoff shrugged. "Builds confidence."

The two said their farewells and rejoined the waiting dwarves. The group had grown to forty, restless to start their journey; they began.

Chapter 56

The trip started out well enough, but was slow. Dwarven legs were short, and not everyone had horses or carts to ride or enough room for more than a few others. One cart lacked a horse, so the owner pulled it. Instead of adopting an even slower pace than walking, Brando gave up his horse, and with a few loops of a rope and some well-tied knots, the horse and cart kept up with the rest of the convoy.

Fin and Brando took turns walking and riding. When one of them walked, they wore their armor. Olhoff had told them to wear it as much as possible to get used to it. Even with the slower pace, the armor was heavy, and despite the chill of the northern winds, it was hot. By the end of the first day, they had stopped wearing the armor altogether because of the heat and exhaustion.

Meals during the day consisted of travel rations, usually dried meat, dried fruit, or dry bread. Only after they had stopped for the evening did they cook a hot meal. Everyone was surprised when Fin produced multiple cooking pots and pans big enough to feed a large group. No one considered where he had kept them. Rasengold insisted that he assumed the cooking duties. His family gathered the wood and built the fires.

The guards and mercenaries developed a watch plan incorporating everyone except Rasengold, Fin, and Brando. With over forty people, almost every person would have to stand a watch once for the whole trip. Fin offered to join the rotation, but the mercenaries refused because he was the customer. So, he slept.

As the next morning's march began, Brando felt increasingly uneasy. At some point, they would be traveling through the village they had fled from not too long ago. He approached Fin, who was walking next to a group of miners, talking about nothing in general. Brando asked if he could have a moment, and the others graciously fell back.

"What are we going to do about Eugal?" He finally asked when he was out of earshot.

"We already solved that problem," Fin answered. "He said he would clear our names and we have some pretty incriminating evidence against him. So I'm not worried."

Brando considered it but shook his head. "I don't trust that Eugal did, in fact, clear our names. He's as crooked as a lopsided snake. Even if he did, we made enemies with the village before we left. If we get there and they make a spectacle, we might lose some very important trust with our travel companions."

"What do you think we should do?" Fin asked.

"I don't know," He floundered. "Go around?"

"That seems like a bad idea. There has to be a better way," Fin stared across the grassy terrain as he thought. "What if I rode ahead, got to the village first, and cleared things up before everyone arrived?"

"That could work," Brando agreed. "But what are you going to do? Walk into the village elder's house and ask him if Eugal cleared our names after we escaped their little jail and fled like a couple of bandits?"

"Actually, that could work," Fin's lips curled into a smile. "But what if Lord Dragonthrone pays the village elder a visit instead of me?"

Fin rode ahead in a gallop. It felt liberating, moving at a faster pace. All too soon, the village boundary came into sight, and he realized he would have to work fast. He unstowed his armor around him and donned his helmet, cautious of the extra weight on the horse. As he approached the center of the village, he saw a group of men stop and gawk at him.

"Correspondence for your village elder," Fin said, hoping the sense of urgency he put in his voice would aid his disguise.

One of the men motioned for him to follow. "This way, young master."

The man had taken ten steps before the constable intercepted him. The closer he had gotten to the village, the more his sense of unease had grown, and now his heart was racing. *Would the constable recognize me*? He hoped not.

The villager explained the situation, and the constable made eye contact.

"Thank you, Folgram. I will take it from here." when the villager left, the constable held out his hand. "I can take the letters if you wish?"

He had a curious look, as if he had recognized Fin but couldn't quite place his face.

"It's a verbal correspondence for your elder alone," Fin decided to say. It was one of many backup plans he had created.

"Very well, sir," the constable nodded. "If you will follow me?"

Fin sighed in relief as the constable introduced himself: "I am Constable S. Seagram. May I ask your name?"

"Lord F. Dragonthrone," Fin said, trying it out. He wasn't sure how he felt about incorporating an initial into his own introduction, but it made Seagram look important. Out of curiosity, he activated True Name to see what the constable's S. stood for. It was also Seagram.

Seagram Seagram led Fin into a normal-looking home. Had he not previously seen other houses in the village, Fin would have thought that it was nothing spectacular. However, he had seen the other houses, and it was quite spectacular. The open-spaced common room had a table, chairs, and a large hearth that was clean but stained black through years of use.

The village elder sat in a chair, smoked a curved stemmed pipe, and greeted them as they entered. While he was old, he had not grown fully grey. He was short, had a short beard, and was dressed like everyone else in the village. Fin wouldn't have guessed his position at a glance.

"Elder Carthage, this is Lord F. Dragonthrone, and he comes bearing correspondence," Seagram announced and stood aside for Fin.

"A lord? In these parts?" Carthage asked with something similar to a scoff. "This must be important to bring the message yourself and not a messenger."

"Yes, quite so. First, I brought my letters of the station so there is no confusion about who I am before I begin." Fin produced pristinely folded papers on expensive parchment from a borrowed satchel. Carthage took the papers and studied them.

"I see," He handed them back. "And the message?"

"First, can you send for your mercer?" Fin asked, placing the papers in his satchel and stowing them. "His name is Eugal, I believe."

Chapter 57

Eugal approached the village elder's home with excitement. Why did a lord from Clive Rae come here to see him out of all people? Did he want to make a trade agreement? Make a large purchase? He had so many questions but composed himself before entering. Inside, he saw the lord speaking to the village elder. He was tall, wearing a suit of armor that cost more than the village itself, and he looked familiar in an odd way. Eugal figured he must have seen the young lord on one of his many trips to Clive Rae, maybe even done some business with him. He bowed and introduced himself.

"Eugal, I want to congratulate you on behalf of the king for aiding his Majesty's efforts in stamping out a plague in our countryside," Fin said with a smile. "You are a true hero."

"I uh, I don't know what to say," Eugal stammered, face turning bright red. "I am but a humble servant to his majesty the king."

"Please, you don't have to be humble in our company," Fin said regally. "Do you want to tell them the story, or shall I?"

"Please, continue. I couldn't possibly," Eugal said, not knowing what he had done.

"Some time ago, I came here under the guise of a commoner to seek out and eliminate certain criminal activity," Fin said carefully so Eugal would know what was about to happen. "I asked Eugal to spread the rumor of two slave traders in hopes of flushing out the real ones. He executed the plan with determination and cunning, and we were able to flush out the criminals we had been hunting."

Fin removed his helmet, "I apologize for misleading you all, but I made you believe Sir Brando, protector of the realm, and myself were the criminals to flush out the real ones."

The room didn't audibly gasp as much as it did physically. Fin had made his gambit, and now it was up to Eugal to make a move. He had Eugal's signed receipts for buying and selling enslaved people if it came down to it, but he hoped it wouldn't. The second part of the plan relied on it.

"Yes, of course," Eugal said somewhere between a smile and a grimace. "I am just glad you found the real ones."

"But you said he broke into your house and stole from you after his escape?" Seagram asked from his nominal spot in the back of the room.

"Yes, that was all part of the plan." Eugal gave Fin an uneasy look. He was sweating.

"And the damage to the prison?"

Fin could tell Eugal was about to crumble, so he answered, "It was all a carefully constructed ploy. If the real slavers knew I was in prison, they would know it was only a matter of time before you found out you had the wrong people. I apologize for the inconvenience, but the trouble was quite necessary."

Fin diverted the conversation to prevent further questions, "Now, I am traveling with around forty dwarven mercenaries to eliminate the rest of the operation. We are traveling to a goblin slave camp due South about a five- or six-day journey, but with our speed, it will probably be double that. Before you ask why we are using dwarven mercenaries over human ones, just know that I caution you against questioning the orders of his Majesty the King. They will be here midday and probably want to stay the night."

This time, the room audibly gasped. Eugal frowned at Fin, wondering if there was a limit to his lies. The village elder stared in shock. Even the constable's stone visage showed its cracks under a wide-eyed expression.

"How can this be?" Carthage asked, holding his extinguished pipe aloft. "The dwarves don't travel outside their own gates but rarely, and for so many?"

"These are desperate times," Fin replied, starting to believe it himself. "They will require food and drinks. Eugal, I hope you will see that the inn is properly stocked and your prices are low."

"Of course!" Eugal bellowed louder than he would have liked.

"Constable, I trust that you will ensure there are no mishaps this evening."

"Yes, my lord," Seagram bowed.

"There's just one more thing," Fin tried to keep the smile off his face. "They all want to try your famous apple pie. I hope you can make enough for everyone on such short notice?"

The dwarves came as promised late into the day. They were directed to an empty street in front of a sign that read, "The Village Inn." Inside, they found Fin arguing with a strange-looking man about pies. He held a paper and said things like, "This says unlimited pie for free, or can you not read your own handwriting?" and "You're a hero now; it's time to start acting like one!" Some of the dwarves wondered what they had got themselves into; others would not wonder until it was too late.

Everyone knew the night in the village was the last semblance of civilization they would see for the remainder of the journey, so they ate heartily and drank deeply into the night. Too soon, the excitement of the road came and went, and the group fell into a routine. They would travel through the day but stop early enough in the evening for a hot meal and formation training.

Marriam's guards took over the training. They taught formations, short verbal communications, and weapon forms. They did not spar as much as they practiced group actions for different scenarios. The guards would demonstrate how it would look, and the rest of the group, mercenaries included, would imitate them. They said that goblins fought by swarming, and the best way to fight against them was to hold your ground and work together.

Fin discovered that four of the dwarves used war hammers and he received special instructions from them. His hammer gave him too much of a benefit to want to go back to the sword. When he held it, his strikes were as powerful as his movement was swift, even while wearing armor. It even gave him a more extended reach, albeit of blunt force. It wasn't until they were attacked that Fin realized how fortunate he was to have it.

On the ninth day, the gradual incline of the mountain pass had dampened the spirits of the group as much as their brows. The wind changed directions, whistling through the trees for a brief gust and bringing an acrid smell of something unpleasant. Fin was deep in his own mind, barely noticing the smell, when Brando stopped him with a hand.

"Something doesn't smell right," he said in a low voice.

Fin's attention snapped to the present, and he looked around warily. Some of the other dwarves looked concerned, too, which heightened his concerned. Brando lifted a hand for everyone to stop, and they did so, happy for the break.

One of the mercenaries approached. "I smelled it, too. I'll send a scout."

"And let you have all the fun?" Brando joked with false bravado. "Besides, you short leggers aren't very good at sneaking around. I'll be back in a bit."

Brando unsheathed his sword, slipped into the trees, and a moment later, he was out of sight. Fin stared into the foliage a good distance off the road, craning his ears for anything out of the ordinary. He was looking and listening so hard that when someone touched him from behind, he was startled and yelped.

"Sorry, I didn't mean to sneak up on you," Rasengold said, holding out a cup of ale. "Drink this; it will help with the altitude."

Fin was halfway finished with the cup when Brando ran out of the bushes yelling, "Formations! Form up! They're coming!"

Fin stowed the cup and unstowed his armor. He instinctively equipped his sword but then switched to the hammer. Some miners were seasoned veterans, while others had learned the various formations only days ago. They took up shields and arms and lined up the same way; the only difference was the confidence in some that others lacked.

Fin placed a hand on Brando's shoulder, and despite the unknown danger, he allowed himself to stop and focus. Several terrible heartbeats passed before Brando's armor appeared around him.

"What's coming?" Fin asked as he took his place on the line.

"Lizard people," Brando replied. "Lots of them."

And lizard people they were. Dozens of shoulder-height, lizard-looking monsters charged the line, walking on feet and tails. Fin identified one of them.

Kobold: Corrupted.

"Kobolds!" he roared as they reached him, hoping the information would help someone.

He stabbed the hammer out to stop their momentum and then brought it down on the first one's head. As it crumbled to the ground, he leaned back to collect his momentum for a powerful swing as the person on either side of him either blocked or attacked. The line worked, and he was able to follow through with his next swing, taking another down.

It wasn't perfect, however, when he noticed that several dwarves had sustained ugly wounds to their arms. The attacks came too fast, and he could hear the claws scratching across his breastplate. He grabbed the kobold's wrist with his bare fingers and pulled down, toppling the lizard to the ground.

As his hammer crushed the fallen creature, Fin realized something. He was stronger than the kobolds, and they couldn't hurt him. He looked down at his chest and saw vague scratch marks but nothing more. He wondered if he could do more damage forward of the line rather than in it. It wasn't battle courage, bloodlust, or hubris. The people around him were bleeding, and he wasn't. So, he looked for his opening and stepped forward.

Kobolds surrounded him, but his whole body was a weapon. He struck with his hammer, snapped elbows back, stabbed, and swung. The creatures' sweating bodies gave a musky scent over the growing smell of blood. Snarls, grunts, and growls permeated the atmosphere.

Fin felt arms around him in an attempt to hold him, but he wiggled and spun free. He broke free but was running out of breath and was beginning to feel the aftereffects of his wild fight. He looked for the line and saw it was just behind him, or rather, a secondary line had formed behind him. He and eight others he recognized as the mercenaries were taking the brunt of the onslaught, and by the look at the bodies surrounding them, they were holding out!

"Fall back!" Fin gasped before spinning the hammer around in a deadly arc, back and forth, clipping some and knocking others down as he retreated. When he was back in the line, he made a minimal effort to fight until he could breathe again. Then he stepped forward, struck two kobolds down, and regained his place.

Repeatedly glancing at the ground littered with corpses, the kobolds ceased their relentless attack and pulled back. The two groups stared across the sloped roadside battlefield in a stalemate for a moment. There were no more reinforcements for the kobolds; they were intelligent enough to know when a battle was futile. The dwarves held their line, neither retreating nor advancing. One of the kobolds gave a harsh order, and they all, albeit reluctantly, abandoned the dead and ran back into the trees.

As soon as the kobolds were gone, some of the dwarves collapsed to the ground either from exhaustion, blood loss, or worse. There was no time for celebration as the injured were treated or given their last rites as warriors.

Chapter 58

Fin wasted no time. He immediately activated Violent Healing and drained the life of the surrounding foliage where each injured dwarf fell. Miniature wastelands expanded outward as the color of death slowly bled into the surrounding tufts of grass. One healed dwarf after another lay in a brittle patch as Fin moved through the battlegrounds. Brando helped by moving the injured dwarves to more nature-dense areas, and soon, there were no more injured to move.

Fin was healing the last injury when he noticed Void pop out from hiding and hover curiously around his hands. Despite his efforts to tell the little ball of destruction to go away, it refused. The dwarf he was healing noticed, scrambled to his feet, and ran away with a shriek, still bleeding from a shallow cut. Void took the opportunity to put itself in the center of the healing energy in Fin's hand. It seemed happy, so he kept the ability active at the cost of more of the surrounding wilderness. Brando cleared his throat, and when Fin looked up, he cut off his ability.

Surrounding him were faces painted with fear, curiosity, and blood. He stood and tried to make up an excuse for everything when a gruff voice cut him off.

"You don't need to explain yourself," Rasengold spoke to the benefit of the people around him. "We all knew you had to have made a pact with one evil or another to be able to spot gold through a mountain of rock. A dirt eater isn't as bad as it could be, but it makes sense."

A murmur of agreement moved through the crowd, and some of their postures relaxed. At once, conversations broke out, sorting the crowd into multiple discussion groups. One of the Kel brothers bellowed with excitement, causing everyone's attention to shift thankfully away from Fin.

"Not only are my wounds healed, but my lungs feel amazing!" He demonstrated by inhaling a full lung of pipe smoke and breathing it up into the air.

Rogard, the de facto leader of the mercenaries, motioned his group forward from the crowd and isolated Fin.

"There's something we need to discuss while the battle is still fresh on our minds," He said solemnly. "Do you know what you did wrong back there?"

After Fin clarified he was talking about the battle, he said he didn't know.

"You deviated from our training and broke formation mid-battle," Rogard said matter-of-factly. "We call that the good idea fairy."

The surrounding mercenaries muttered in agreement.

"The more we train together, the more we fight with cohesion. I can fight more confidently, knowing exactly what to expect from the person beside me. The problem is that we sometimes get a good idea in the heat of the battle. That's the good idea fairy sprinkling her magic dust all over everything. You have to ignore her; otherwise, you'll start doing unexpected things and making the battlegrounds chaotic," Rogard explained, pausing for his words to sink in. "When you had the idea to step out of formation you confused people you were standing next to. They froze up and didn't know what to do. Then the good idea fairy visited Adleweed, who broke formation to go to their aid."

One of the mercenaries, presumably Adleweed, blushed and shrugged.

Rogard looked at him disapprovingly and continued, "When Adleweed broke formation, we all had to break formation. Fortunately, it worked out, and for once, the good idea fairy didn't get everyone killed.

"Starting tomorrow, I want us to train in this new formation. We'll think of a name for it later. We will stand forward of the line, and Fin will stand forward of us. That way, he can step back for a rest when he needs it, and we all can step back when we need it. It will look kind of like a triangle. The Triangle Formation, if you will."

"So, from now on, we don't change what we've trained unless we change how we train and train on the changes we made?" Fin tried reiterating and then added, "To our training plan?"

"Yes," Rogard said, perhaps too quickly, and then it looked like he had changed his mind. "Uh, what?"

Before Fin could devise another ridiculous tongue twister, he noticed a billow of smoke rising behind the mercenaries' heads. It was darker than campfire smoke and had an unnatural smell. He pointed at it and asked if it was normal. Rogard and the other mercenaries turned to look at it. Before long, the whole group moved to the source of the smoke out of novel curiosity.

Approaching, they could see something small and black burning on the ground. A dwarf, Fin recognized as Grimwald, had a guilty look and immediately began explaining himself as he approached.

"The kobolds had these candles. Well, we thought they were candles," he stammered. After the command to "Just get on with it," he said, "So I lit one, and now it's smoking."

"It smells like old boots," Brando's voice came from among the crowd.

"What made you think lighting it would be a good idea?" Rogard scolded, waving insects out of his eyes. "For all we know, it could be poisonous."

"If it was poisonous, I would probably be dead by now," Grimwald admitted, slapping something on the side of his neck. "I was trying to figure out what it smelled like, and I breathed in a lot of it. The closest thing I can think of is corn after it starts decomposing."

"It's attracting flies!" One of the onlookers yelled and pointed.

As smoke bellowed from the black candle, a swarm of flies congregated around the smoke. The more the air became dense with flies, the more insults Grimwald had to endure from the group for lighting such an accursed candle. Finally, they decided to leave and put as much road between them and smelly, fly-attracting candle smoke as possible.

When the bugs were behind them, conversations gradually returned to Fin despite his efforts to change the subject. Fin answered questions and endured compliments, and eventually, everyone left him alone. Void kept asking for healing energy again, but he explained that he was low on energy. So, Void changed their contract and allowed him to use Absorb Ambient Energy, or rather, insisted he use it.

A short time later, for Fin anyway, he felt ready to slip off into the surrounding foliage. He decided he would conduct Void's little experiment away from prying eyes. The group was moving slowly enough that he could always catch up later. When he told Brando what he was going to do, he got a questioning look in return.

"I didn't think Void could get injured," Brando said with a frown. "Why does it want healing?"

"I don't know," Fin replied, walking at a leisurely pace. "I'm hoping the healing power feeds it so it won't eat my gold anymore."

"I'll come with you," Brando said, unmounting the horse. "I'm bored anyway."

The two left the trail and the convoy traveling it and waded into the brush. When they were out of sight, Fin activated Violent Healing and directed the energy towards Void.

"How long do you think it will take for all of this to grow back?" Brando asked, looking at the spreading desolation. "Oh, sorry. Does that take concentration?"

"Not really," Fin replied casually. "And I'm not sure. I hope it will all grow back. We could do some experiments. Drain the life out of a big area and check on it periodically."

"You could also charge people to clear their land. I'm sure there are a lot of people who – " Brando cut off mid-sentence.

Under the current of healing energy, Void started pulsing with green shards of light. The pulsing got faster and faster until a green orb separated from it.

"It's duplicating!" Brando exclaimed, then amended his statement, "It broke into two pieces!"

"I think it just had a baby," Fin said, keeping the ability going.

"A baby?" Brando considered what that meant. "Does that mean it's a she? Huh. Void's a girl."

Fin laughed and agreed. "I guess so."

For a while the two watched the orbs floating and nuzzling each other. Despite not really knowing what was happening, they both smiled at the curiosity of it. Then Brando's smile dropped into a solemn look of comprehension.

"You know what this means, right?" Brando asked, building up to break the news. "It means you're a father now."

Fin's smile remained glued to his face. "That's absolute rubbish. If anything, this tree is its father."

"Don't call your daughter an it," Brando reprimanded. "Imagine that. If you had told me last year that I would be an uncle to a green floating orb, I would have called you crazy. She really is beautiful, though. What are you going to name her?"

"She's not my daughter! All I did was suck the life out of these plants and direct the life energy toward…" Fin trailed off, realizing that he really might be the father. "Oh no. I really am the father."

He checked his notifications and was surprised there wasn't any. Apparently, this situation was too strange for his dragon quests to trigger. He identified the green orb and found it was called a Nature Sprite, or rather, she was a Nature Sprite. He told Brando, whose loving smile wasn't helping to ease the tension.

After a while, the two orbs seemed to finish cuddling or whatever they were doing and broke off from each other. The green one explored the area and, upon reaching the border between Fin's lifeless circle and the outside forest, acted curiously. She floated in and out of the dead zone, observing the dichotomy of life and death, and then spun in a circle over the dead ground. A sprout reached up from the ground and started growing at a rapid pace.

"She made a sprout," Brando smiled. "That's what we should call her."

As soon as the plant grew large enough to be recognized as one of the many flowering bushes in its surroundings, it began to wither and die. The green sprite reversed the growth enchantment and drained the plant of its life. As soon as the sprout matched the plants in Fin's circle of death, the sprite hovered around to drain the life out of other plants.

"More like sprout killer," Fin said, watching the plants wither away one by one.

Brando took slow steps back. "I think we should leave our little sprout killer here; I would hate to find out what would happen if it landed on one of us."

Fin nodded slowly and returned his gaze to the sprite's mother. "Void, can you ask that little ball of joy not to suck the life out of anyone?"

Void did not bob, weave, or otherwise move in acknowledgment, but Fin knew she understood. She flew to her green offspring, who was sucking the life out of a tree, and appeared to start communicating with her. The two sat motionless and conveyed as much emotion as two balls of glowing energy could. Finally, Fin got an image in his head and realized what Void wanted him to do, so he picked a stick off the ground.

The Nature Sprite hovered near the stick and shot colorless energy into it. When she was finished, Fin identified the stick. It was labeled an Oath Twig, which he knew exactly what to do with.

"I name you Sprout. Is that okay?" Fin began, holding the Oath Twig like he would the royal scepter, and tried to convey the idea that she wouldn't suck the energy out of anyone.

Sprout seemed to agree, but there wasn't anything that indicated the Oath Twig worked. Then he got an image of him giving Void a literal mountain of gold in exchange for the deal. Void was using her offspring as a bargaining chip. He frowned and countered with a single gold coin and no more. It wasn't until he agreed to three gold coins that he felt the oath go into effect. He unstowed the gold to solidify the deal, and Void shamelessly devoured the treasure.

Chapter 59

It didn't take long for everyone to become used to Void and Sprout hovering alongside the traveling group. Void generally rested on Fin's shoulder, and Sprout traveled from plant to plant, helping some grow and causing others to shrivel and die. Whether she would help a plant or destroy it was a coin toss.

The rest of the trip resumed as normal. In the evening, Rasengold and his family would cook while the rest of the group practiced their new battle formations. Brando joined in as the tip of a second triangle. With the two triangular formations side-by-side, they looked and acted like a professional fighting force, even if there wasn't a single heart fearless of the coming fight.

After the sharp slope of the mountainous trail broke, the scenery changed. Dense wood made way for dry surroundings with sparse greenery. Some thorny bushes lay sporadically around, looking like defensive constructs rather than decorative ones. The dry surroundings gave Fin grim memories of his escape from the slave camp. The closer he got to the destination, the more uneasy he began to feel. That was until the outline of the goblin camp came into view, and his uneasiness turned into resolve.

The group traveled trusting in Fin and Brando's vague memories of the desert landscape. When their destination came into view, it came with mixed emotions. There was happiness that they had indeed gone the correct way and the opposite feeling for the same reason. Fin raised his hands and motioned everyone to stop, and everyone gathered around him.

"The goblin camp is just down there," Fin said, pointing. "I saw them, which means they probably saw us too. The sun is still high if we want to press our advantage and mount a surprise attack. Our other option is to set up camp and attack in the morning. We'll have more daylight if we wait for morning."

"Can we draw them out?" Adleweed asked, having been briefed on the camp previously.

Brando nodded. "I'd wager I could draw some of them out, but we won't be able to get them all."

"Before we do anything, we need to scout the place out," Rogard said, almost sorrowfully, "and we need siege weapons."

Fin unstowed his second elemental core and smiled. "I think I can handle the siege weapons, but I'm going to need some help."

Fin employed ten dwarves to help him collect and move rocks. There were rocks everywhere, and before long, he gathered enough for his own burial if his plan didn't work. He arranged them into a tall, humanoid figure with long legs, nearly two heads taller than himself.

He hadn't told Void what he was planning, nor had he asked her if she would help for a very specific reason. He had no control over the smaller Earth Elemental in his inventory. If he wanted it to help, he would have to ask Void to control it. With what he was planning, he would need a semblance of control over the new elemental.

When everything was ready, he showed Void the rocks, the elemental core, and a small fortune in gold. His reserves were running low, but he could spare the money if everything worked out as planned. He told Void what he was planning and then prepared himself.

Over the last weeks, he tried to figure out how elementals work. After long inaudible conversations with Void, he only had a basic understanding but felt it was enough. So, when Void started stringing the rocks together and connecting them to the core, he waited for the perfect moment. Just as soon as the golden threads were connected to the core, he reached his mind toward the elemental before Void could. Before he felt or even noticed the connection, he held the Oath Stone in his hand and willed the most brief and basic of agreements.

"Friends?"

Elementals could only be under contract with one individual. It did not matter what that contract was as long as there was one. Void would naturally form her own contract after creating an elemental. To her, it was part of the process. This wasn't good for Fin because he already had a tiny elemental in his inventory that he had no control over. What was worse was Void had actively used the construct against him when they were first working out their differences. So, he followed the advice of an old saying about apologizing and asking permission and formed a contract right from under Void's nose, so to speak. It was a vague contract with countless possibilities of disaster, but it was his, and most importantly, it was not Void's.

He felt the contract solidify and hid the evidence of his betrayal by tossing the Oath Stone into his inventory. He watched the elemental steadily get to its feet. At the same time, Void experienced a peculiar feeling of confusion. Fin reached out to her to see if she suspected him. He got the impression that she was considering destroying her creation and starting over.

Fin got between Void and the elemental and said, "Don't hurt him; he's my friend. Friends don't hurt friends."

He wasn't sure why he referred to the construct as he, but now that he did, he decided to give the elemental a masculine name. Void hesitated, but that's all Fin needed.

"Let's call you Graniteheart Stoneloins," Fin waved for the elemental to follow him. "Actually, let's just call you Grant. Come on, Grant. Let's go meet my other friends."

It was odd having such a dangerous creature following him, but Fin had experienced many odd things since leaving home. What was a giant rock creature compared to a maniacal princess or fathering a nature sprite? He could handle it; he just needed to make sure his other friends could handle it, too.

Most of the group still stood around discussing a plan when Fin approached.

"Listen," Fin addressed the whole group, speaking at a rapid clip. "The rock monster following me is a friend. We haven't exactly defined what a friend is just yet, but I'm sure it will all work out if everyone shows him friendship by being extra friendly and by not attacking."

As soon as the elemental approached, Fin greeted him. "This is my friend Grant. Grant, these are my other friends. When we see friends, we say hello, or in your case, you can wave. Like this," Fin waved a hand in what he hoped was a sincere gesture. "We certainly don't attack other friends."

"Will it help us?" Rogard asked, thinking twice before attempting to touch it.

"I'm not sure," Fin replied honestly. "The contract we have is just, 'friends.' There are no promises not to do harm, obey orders, or anything to stop him from going on a violent rampage if he decides to. All it consisted of was the word, friends. Furthermore, my sprite thinks she made a mistake and is going to try to disassemble my friend Grant as soon as her confusion clears. If we are going to try anything, we have to try it quickly. I vote we send this big guy down to knock on the door."

"We'll need him to do more than just knock on the door…" One of the Kel brothers began before his whole family restrained him from speaking another word.

"If time is of the essence, then send him in," Rasengold said to vindicate the honor of the Kel name. "Let the consequences weigh themselves out."

"I will," Fin decided. "I also better accompany him."

Rogard nodded. "I'll give you a line to pull back to."

"Don't bring anyone within crossbow range until we clear the top of the wall," Fin warned. "All I plan to do is open the gate and fall back."

"I'll show them the line of the crossbow range," Brando offered. "I'll also take my armor now."

Fin put his hand on Brando and unstowed his armor. He then handed over the helmet and motioned Grant forward.

"Come on, Grant," Fin said, walking ahead. "It's time to go pay some non-friends a visit."

The monolith of stone took a direct path to follow Fin. Several dwarves had to jump out of the way of his massive footsteps, avoiding certain death.

Fin sighed with frustration. "Grant, please don't step on any dwarves."

There were no more dwarves to step on as the two started heading toward the slave camp. The elemental moved slowly, but with unnaturally long legs, he more or less kept pace. Behind them followed all the people who accompanied their journey, each with determined expressions filled with menace. Between them and his new friend, he almost felt bad for the goblins, and that thought made him smile.

Chapter 60

When Fin was just outside crossbow range, he donned his armor and slowed his pace. Surprisingly, as he approached, not a single bolt had flown from the battlement. He started to wonder if the goblins had even seen them when bolts and arrows showered down on him in a decisive effort to end his life. The projectiles attempted to push him off balance, but none penetrated his armor. The bolts that targeted Grant bounced off his stone exterior, but he did not break stride.

Fin wondered if the bolts were irritating Grant because he saw the elemental lift his hand as if to swat the projectiles away. To his utter horror, he realized Grant was waving. He briefly considered scolding the stone giant for waving to the enemy but decided to address it later. He had more urgent matters to deal with. The large wooden gates were rapidly approaching and he informed Grant that they needed to knock them down. He then unstowed his hammer and gave the first swing.

The hammer arched through the air and landed on the gate with an astounding blow. Reverberations ran through it, but it was otherwise undamaged. Grant took some experimental swings, but they, too, were ineffectual. The only thing Fin could do was keep hitting it and hoping it would eventually come down. He then considered something else that might work.

He tried to remember how the support rods were set on the other side of the gate. The only image he could recollect was a latch somewhere in the center. He wasn't sure if a wood beam spanned across the middle of the opening like other gates he had seen, but he assumed there was. With nothing to lose, he used Caustic Breath to cut a line down the center of the gate, hoping the ability cut through something important.

His breath, visible to Discern Earth and Discern Magic, cut through the gate like a spoon through an uncooked potato. He had to force the breath out of his lungs over several attempts. It was not easy. He became lightheaded and leaned heavily on the gate to stay on his feet.

A transient blast snapped him out of his daze as Grant took another mighty swing. The gate bowed in farther than before; Fin's efforts were working. Before he could resume cutting through the center, a group of goblins began gathering on the adjacent walls, launching bolts and throwing rocks.

If the goblins wanted to throw rocks, Fin had the perfect rock for them to throw. He positioned himself with his back towards the wall, unstowed the smaller elemental from his inventory, and heaved it to the top of the wall. Whether the elemental hated him or it had been frozen mid-attack, Fin did not know. What he did know was the moment he unstowed the tiny, violent creature, it immediately started attacking. Or it tried to before it was flung to the top of the wall, where it met something else to take its aggression out on. The violent rock creature went into a frenzy, swinging at arms, legs, and little goblin shins.

Shouts of alarm and anger from above paused as Grant landed another mighty strike against the gate. The gate cracked and splintered, but it held.

"Grant, get a running start and ram into it with your shoulder," Fin called above the shouts and cries from above.

Grant backed up, and when he felt he was far enough, he charged for the gate. Just before he formed a battering ram with his shoulder, a goblin fell off the wall and landed directly in his way. Grant shuffled his feet to avoid stepping on the goblin, tripped, and flung toward the gate with destructive clumsiness. The gate exploded inward allowing the elemental in where he gradually slid to a stop.

Fin dispatched the injured goblin as the dust settled inside the gate. Looking in, he saw the staircase to the top of the wall and went for it.

"Grant, you can step on goblins," he corrected and considered the innocent people trapped inside. "But, only goblins. They're the green ones."

After climbing the staircase to the top of the wall, he decided to go in the opposite direction from where Voids' violent elemental had set up residence. It was perfectly content to sit on top of the wall as if it were enjoying a peaceful day on the farm. Fin looked for Void but didn't see her. It would have been nice if she had commanded it to attack the guards on the wall, but without Void, there was no controlling it.

Taking care to reserve his stamina, Fin started moving around the wall. He struck down his goblin and human assailants from the wall one by one. When he had gotten halfway around the track, the guards started running away from him and his catastrophic hammer.

Instead of crossing paths with the territorial elemental, they began devising other ways to get down from the wall. Some jumped, some used ropes, and others were thrown off.

When Fin tried to pass, the elemental also attacked him. He seriously considered going back around or climbing off the side of the wall like everyone else had, but he didn't have the time. Instead, he mustered all his courage and reached for the animated rock cluster. The elemental scratched and swung at him and got a few good punches in before it disappeared safely into his inventory. He made a mental note to drop it down a well if he ever found one.

From his vantage point on top of the wall, he could see his allies had already begun approaching. They were fighting off waves of goblins that seemed to be trying to escape more than to do battle. Upon seeing the triangle formation with Brando in the front, the goblins ran either left or right. To intercept the goblins, the formation morphed into a reverse triangle that funneled goblins to Brando in the back. It was clearly the handy work of the good idea fairy, but Fin had other problems to consider.

Grant had run off somewhere in an effort to step on goblins, and Fin did not know where that was. He knew it was potentially dangerous for Grant to be left to his own devices this early in his life, but it was a risk that would mostly fall to the goblins. He let that consideration ease his discomfort if only a little and joined the formations.

Outside the gate, Fin met Brando standing in the center of the new cone formation and wondered out loud who had come up with the idea. Brando admitted accountability.

"Rogard is going to yell at you after this is done, you know," Fin warned. "He says that changing the plan mid-battle can get people killed. He calls it the good idea fairy."

Brando slashed at a goblin running towards him and turned to Fin. "It was his idea to do a cone formation in the first place. If he yells at me, I'll just tell him he started it and see how he likes a taste of his own medicine."

Fin doubted Brando would win the argument but put it out of his mind. "Let's share the center of the cone. We can switch every now and then, so we don't get tired."

"Now look who the fairy is," Brando chided as he kicked a goblin towards the sideline. "If Rogard yells at me, you got my back, right?"

"To the very end, brother," Fin promised.

The command to move forward brought the formations through the broken gate. There, scores of goblins advanced on them with many mismatched weapons. One of the more prominent weapons, pointed sticks, brushed off Fin and Brando's armor easily. Fin noticed some of the goblins climbing the stairs to regain the wall. Before he had the chance to say anything, Rogard commanded a handful of dwarves to regain the stairs.

"Switch!" Brando yelled and fell back.

Fin immediately took his place at the focal point of the battle and faced the sea of cruel green faces. They charged him with teeth and claws exposed. He caught two of them with his hammer before striking out with his own claws. He activated Sharpened Talons and Crushing Grip and punched finger-sized holes into attacking goblins. He attacked, parried, and struck blindly around for so long that it felt like he was taking on all the goblins alone. He stole a glance behind him and saw Brando hunched over a body on the ground. Fearing the worst, he ran towards his friend when Brando abruptly stood.

"Catch this," Brando said, tossing something small and black into the air before yelling, "Switch!"

Fin caught the item with his fingerless gloves, feeling something warm and wet on his fingertips. A notification came up, and upon reading it, he dropped the item and wiped his hands on the ground.

Blood Quest Complete: Hold the beating heart of an enemy. +1 basic ability point, +1 talon ability.

Active Ability: Cleave

"Did it work?" Brando called out, cutting through more goblins.

Fin hesitated. He couldn't figure out what upset him, the macabre battlefield prank or the fact that he had just completed a quest he intended to ignore. If it was up to him, he would delete his remaining quests so he wouldn't have to look at them. He ignored Brando's question and called for a switch.

When he was front and center of the wholesale onslaught, he decided to try his new ability. He activated Cleave and felt energy gather in his hands. Immediately, he knew two things. He could use this ability with just one or both hands, and he should be very careful if he did. He swung his naked fingertips forward in a half circle. Energy formed from his fingertips to create a series of hairline blades that slashed out. Wood spears, hands, and heads split off and hit the ground in unison. The attacking goblins seemed more surprised than Fin, and, in their hesitation, he and Brando finished them off together.

"It worked," Fin admitted, so no one tried to give him any more battlefield surprises. "And I'm upset about it."

"I'm sorry," Brando apologized. "I thought you would be happy about it. I really did. I'll make it up to you. Cross my heart."

Fin shook his head but thought nothing more of it. Before long, they were marching through the encampment, looking for goblins in hiding. Eventually, they arrived at an old, familiar cast iron gate that led into the mine. Brando pushed it, and it opened freely.

"That doesn't seem right," Brando muttered more to himself than anyone. "It's not like them to keep this gate unlocked."

Fin followed behind, hoping to see some old faces, and he was not disappointed. Just through the gate stood dozens of familiar-looking, dirty-faced people in a big group. In the front of the group stood Heidle the Hammer, but he didn't look his cheerful self.

"Heidle! We came back!" Fin announced, barely containing his excitement.

"Ah, so you did, lad, and it's good to see you." For a brief moment, Heidle's face lit up with a genuine smile, and then it was gone. "I think it's time for us all to go, nice and easy like."

Fin's smile faded. Something didn't seem right, and Brando's grim look suggested he felt the same way.

Brando stepped forward to ask what was wrong, but everyone's face stiffened. Noticing the tension of the group, Fin held out a hand to stop Brando from approaching. He then spoke to the group, trying to keep the mood light.

"Sure, if you all want to leave now, you are welcome to," Fin stepped aside and gestured for them all to pass. "Good luck out there."

The group moved silently past him as if everyone was holding their breath at the same time. He tried frantically to understand why they were all acting so spooked when he saw something that made it all click together. It wasn't what he saw, but what he didn't see, an ear.

When he and Brando were first taken to the camp, they met a woman with a missing ear. She seemed to be the one running the operation. Fin realized that as the camp was being attacked, she must have thought she could disguise herself as a slave and escape with everyone else. By how everyone was acting, he figured she had a weapon against one of their backs.

While he tried frantically to devise a plan, the group of hostages had already made it out of the mine and were almost at the broken gates of the camp's entrance. Movement from the side caught his attention, and he saw something he couldn't believe. While everyone was fighting goblins, Sprout had been busy cultivating the largest weed Fin had seen in his life. Spiked leaves, too heavy to stand up, flopped to the ground around a large, white-seeded flower taller than he was. It was a farmer's worst nightmare.

He reached out to Sprout and asked where Void was. After the equivalent of a mental shrug, he removed the Oath Twig and made her an offer she couldn't refuse.

Fin had noticed a common theme among Sprites: They seemed to operate in terms of deals and contracts. He had only met two, but seeing how rare it was to meet or communicate with them, he could very well be the subject matter expert. The last time he made a deal with Sprout, it was in Void's favor. Sprout was inexperienced enough to make another such deal, but this time in Fin's favor.

"I will give Void this coin and gem," Fin unstowed a silver coin and a blue gem to prove his point, "If you do one little favor for me."

Chapter 61

As Fin watched the hostages leave the gate, he kept his eye on one person, Lady Marsha. She was taller than the rest, better fed, and had premature gray hair. She was significantly younger than she looked, but as she walked, she seemed to get older with each step. Fin had employed Sprout to drain her life away as seamlessly as possible. Hopefully, she wouldn't notice until it was too late. Already, she was starting to hunch while she walked.

In the time it took to drop a knife, everything changed. The woman's shoulders slumped under the weight of her rapidly increasing years, and a soft metallic sound rang out against the desert floor. The surrounding group of people seemed confused, and then all at once scrambled to get away. In the chaos, two people dove for the knife that Lady Marsha dropped. Heidle and Marsha's husband, who had also disguised himself among the captives, reached for the weapon simultaneously. The scuffle was pitifully short and ended with the man fleeing as Heidle lay in the dirt, spilling blood from a fatal wound.

Fin ran to him. As he ran he dismissed his armor and invited the cool air to wash over him. The hard packed dirt had nothing but a rock garden to pull life from; he started his healing ability anyway. He slid on his knees coming to an abrupt stop over Heidle who was in bad shape.

"I almost didn't recognize you," Heidle coughed, spitting blood out of his mouth. "I'm glad I lived long enough to see…"

"Don't worry, I'm going to get you healed up; I just need you to keep your eyes open for a little longer," Fin scooped Heidle into his arms and ran back towards the goblin camp.

He hoped the massive weed Sprout was growing would have enough life energy to heal Heidle or at least prevent him from dying. He saw the green orb following him, and realized she might not like the idea of him draining the life out of her special weed. So, he sent her away. He envisioned the man who stabbed Heidle and the direction he ran in. Sprout chased after the man before he could offer her anything in return. He would have given all the gold in the world to heal his friend, but he was glad not to have to.

"I'm not going to make it," Heidle managed. "Just let me go, lad."

Fin fought back tears as he kept running. He felt the activation of Violent Healing and knew his options were limited. He tucked the dwarf under the left shoulder of his life-giving hand and pressed the other to his own chest. Despite the name of the ability, the life absorption didn't hurt. He could feel his life source drain from him like water through an unplugged hole, but it was absolutely painless. His pace slowed, and he stumbled through the broken gate. It was getting dark. He could see vague shapes around him but couldn't make out their faces. He vaguely remembered calling for someone to take him to the weed when he was overcome by his own frailty. He fell face-first onto the gravel.

Brando heard Fin yell something about the weed, so he turned. He saw him carrying the blood-soaked Heidle and knew what he had to do. The giant weed was a wonder to all but only a mystery to a few. Everyone who was a part of the convoy had, at one point or another, seen the green sprite grow or destroy a plant. Sprout's antics were a point of entertainment and made an otherwise boring trip more bearable. Brando knew that the oversized weed was a source of life to Fin.

He scooped Fin and Heidle into his arms and ran towards the weed. When he arrived, he dropped the two on the ground and ripped open Heidle's shirt. There was a stab wound that had already started knitting together. Brando placed Fin's right hand on the weed and his left hand on Heidle's wound. When he noticed Fin's skin. It was wrinkled and grey as a corpse. Brando directed the healing energy away from Heidle and back into him. When the plant died, the ability cut off, and Brando called for food.

"I know there's a big pot of stew around here somewhere," Brando told the people around him. "Go find Sophia and ask her for three bowls."

Chapter 62

Fin woke up to a pounding headache and a notification.

Precarious Blessing Quest Complete: Heal an ally at the expense of your own life force. +1 Active Ability.

Active Ability: Bestow Ability

He sat up and squinted against the horizontal sunlight.

"You're awake!" He heard Brando exclaim.

"How long have I been out?" He asked, pressing his hand against his beating head and adding, "Did Heidle make it?"

"It's been four days now," Brando said bitterly. "And no, Heidle didn't make it."

"Ah, don't mess with the lad," Heidle's voice pierced the sorrow in Fin's heart. "You passed out five minutes ago, and I'm fine. Or I will be fine after a while. Now, have a taste of this soup before we lose you again. You look like an undead draugr."

"A what?" Fin asked, receiving a bowl of soup in shaky hands.

"Just eat," Brando admonished.

"After you finish, you should unpack the supplies so everyone else doesn't have to eat Sophie's stew. She hasn't gotten better at cooking since we've been gone."

"That reminds me!" Fin exclaimed, feeling dizzy from over-exertion. "I brought you something."

Fin reached forward and produced an apple pie from thin air. "We are farther East than you originally thought; the village with the apple pie is directly North of us. I did some shopping there before coming here and bought you this. It's cut into slices so we can all have a piece."

A feeling of overwhelming joy brought tears to Heidle's eyes, and he took the pie. He thanked Fin sincerely and, without regard for his dirt-covered hands, removed a slice and began savoring each bite. Brando reiterated how they could all share, but Heidle ignored him. He kept him away with his elbows as he took one wonderful bite after another.

Fin unstowed and gave many of his supplies to Sophia and Rasengold, who cooked. At the same time, everyone else took turns sleeping or standing watch. That evening, everyone ate and drank to their hearts' content and greedily slept beneath the stars under the watchful eye of dwarves and freed slaves alike.

The next morning, everyone set out to do one chore or another. Enemy corpses were taken out of the camp and tossed into one of the many ravines; others were buried with ceremony. Exploration parties investigating the camp found supplies, a well, and the last surviving goblin.

Peggy, an older woman verified among the slaves, vouched for the goblin. "This is Hobby, and he was made a slave like the rest of us. You can't kill him! He didn't do anything wrong!"

No one liked the idea of having a rogue goblin roaming around, but Peggy cried and begged them to spare his life. So, reluctantly, they did and were forced to endure a goblin's company for a time. That was until Grant returned, greeted everyone with a wave, and stepped on poor Hobby. Fin, who was sleeping in the late Lady Marsha's bed, woke to an unexpected notification. As he was still not feeling well, he ignored everything except the gold stat points. He allocated one and went back to sleep.

Blood Quest Complete: Defeat all your enemies. +2 levels, +8 gold stat points, +1 Passive Ability.

Passive Ability: Blood Halo

Days turned into weeks before Fin's youthful color returned to his face, but even then, he still didn't feel like his normal self. He helped with the chores the best he could, which mostly meant looking around for more secret stashes of gems. Lady Marsha had one in her room behind a loose brick, and some of the goblins had hiding places around camp. He decided to split the gems among the miners who had stayed, which was most of them. After all, they were the ones to dig them up.

First, he sorted through the gems in his inventory, keeping all the quartz for himself. The quartz was virtually worthless to anyone else, but it served as excellent bargaining chips with a Sprite who didn't know any better or simply didn't care. He ended up with a fortune in quartz, which he used whenever he needed something from Void. Unfortunately, he forgot to ask for the smaller elemental's contract before fulfilling his promise to drop it down a well. The little creature fought the whole way down.

The residents created a kind of economy in the mining camp with the redistributed gems. They were used as an exchange or gifted to Rasengold for cooking. The old dwarf gave some of the gems to Fin, but the rest he sent to town to be used for supplies. Brando drafted a letter to be delivered to Eugal. He would pay him a visit with his appetite for apple pie if they weren't given a fair deal for supplies. He also asked Eugal to send some plants and trees. The massive, overgrown weeds around the camp had started to wear on his nerves.

As Fin explored his new abilities, he could only figure out what one of them did. Bestow Ability was self-explanatory, for the most part. He tried it out on Brando, gifting him an ability he couldn't use anyway. If he lost it forever, it wouldn't matter.

"I think I feel something," Brando admitted. "I'm not sure, though."

Fin looked at his abilities; sure enough, he no longer had Stone Simulacrum Wings. This is what he was afraid of, losing access to an ability once given away. The real test would be to see if the ability ever became available again. While Fin was musing over his abilities, Sprout saw something that made her lose interest in her latest weed. She drifted over to Brando, who had something trying to grow from his back. She loved making things grow, so she helped.

Brando was in the middle of mentioning how something didn't feel right when massive wings sprung from his back. He immediately fell backward.

"I thought you were giving me the ability to see gems," Brando struggled on the ground. "Why do I have wings?"

"I said," Fin took Brando's arm and helped him to his feet. "If everything works out, I will let you borrow Sense Treasure. I just don't want to lose it forever, so we are testing giving you something less valuable."

Brando dusted himself off and tried to get a better look at his wings. They were massive things that appeared to be sculpted with black marble so thin as to break off at any moment. They were smooth in some places and rough in others. Fin touched one of the wings, and it didn't feel like it looked. It felt like leather and bone.

Brando's first instinct was to try flying, but he couldn't seem to flap his wings hard enough. He ran around and tried jumping off the wall. At most, the wings slowed his fall. He would have to do something truly dangerous to test them further, which he looked forward to. He then tried to test how sturdy they were. Fin tried punching and scratching them, but they held up to a decent amount of abuse.

The final test was to see how well they could be folded. Even with the wings folded up as far as they could, they were still very noticeable.

Three black spires rose from behind each shoulder and draped like a sinister cape to the ground.

"Do you think they would let me visit the princess looking like this?" Brando asked, posing with his wings.

"Probably not," Fin admitted. "You look like a storybook villain designed to scare children."

"You have no idea how happy that makes me," Brando admitted. "I think I'll keep them."

"Hang on," Fin said, pulling up his ability page. He had an ability point for a long time, waiting for something useful to spend it on. He purchased Wing Attack and used the Bestow Ability again to see if he could give someone more than one. It went through, which meant he could. It also meant that trying to boot another ability out might not work.

At Fin's prompting, Brando tried a Wing Attack. His wings slashed forward one after the other, causing him to briefly lose balance. It was a powerful attack that would be perfect for a melee fight. It had reach, speed, and power. He then asked him to try deactivating the wings.

"What do you mean, deactivate it?" Brando asked incredulously. "I still want to play around with them."

"Just will the wings to go away," Fin suggested. "Picture a lever that activates your wings, and then pull that lever backward."

Brando pulled every imaginary lever he could think of, and nothing happened. He wished they would go away so Fin would stop using lever analogies, and it worked. The wings seemed to evaporate like smoke. Through the back of his torn shirt, Fin could see two grey scars that ran down the length of his back. Brando willed the wings to return, and they shimmered into existence. He couldn't have been happier.

Eventually, Fin discovered how to take the ability back, but it required the other person to give it back while he activated Bestow Ability. He also tried experimenting with Blood Halo but couldn't figure out what that did other than to decorate his shroud ability.

Below the circular status, ability, inventory, and quest menus that floated above his head now sat a red circular halo. As far as he could tell, it was just for decoration, but he kept it up in case something revealed itself.

Marriam, the owner of the Dunkle mine, made good on her unofficial agreement to profit from the mine. Caravans arrived, bringing food, supplies, and building materials. Shops popped up overnight and sold wares in the morning. Marriam came herself a week later and was disappointed to find she had competition from the Kel family restaurant and general store. Fin and Brando made it abundantly clear that all residents and all those who helped fight the goblins had equal ownership. And so started the Equal Ownership Mine, though most people still referred to it as 'the goblin mine,' 'the mine,' or 'camp.'

Eventually, the plants and trees arrived in a caravan, and Sprout gladly went to work growing them. She also still grew giant weeds, which Brando made go away under the cover of darkness. She didn't seem to notice when the weeds disappeared but floated around, growing things as usual. Soon, the mine was a veritable oasis of greenery in the desert.

New faces arrived to dig up gems, and new shops opened, bringing new ways to make and spend money. Fin and Brando had long since become wealthy on gems, taxes, and fees, but they knew they weren't going to stay forever. Heidle was the first to go. After Fin and Brando drew him a more accurate map from rocks, he made them promise to visit. They did, and after tears, hugs, and promises, Heidle left the mine he had been imprisoned in for years.

The place wasn't the same without Heidle, so Fin and Brando decided to go too. They had already stayed longer than they intended to. They traded their gems for gold, spent as much of it as they could, and said their goodbyes. They left the mine under the glow of the rising sun. The journey home should have been the easiest part of their travels, and it was. The difficult part was going home with the feeling that they would have to explain the two orbs and rock giant following them.

Chapter 63

Lord Finlay of Dragonthrone and Brando Dragonthrone, Protector of the Realm, rode in on some of the largest horses the town had ever seen, wearing dwarven armor and throwing coins the way most farmers threw seeds. At first, no one knew why such eminent people had deigned to grace their town, but one person dreaded the truth. It was too obvious that Brando should arrive the day before the election with such a blatant scheme to buy votes. But it was too little, too late. He would need to buy more than a few rounds of drinks to beat Vice Secretary Tannor Rae for the title of Governor.

"Do you just want me to throw money to the dirty children, or should I toss some to the clean ones as well?" Fin asked, tossing another handful of coins to a group of orphan-looking children. "I'll be happy either way; this is your show, after all."

"You're going to have to follow your heart on this one," Brando said, oblivious to the people following him. "Just try not to throw money at the ones I already threw money at. Unless they look like they really need it."

They had come to Brando's town to make his ex-wives regret leaving him because he was poor. The plan was simple, throw money at orphans, buy everyone a round of drinks, and let the gossip mill take care of the rest. Brando did not seem to care about wealth and would gladly toss everything away for the sweet feeling of revenge. Though having spent time in an orphanage, it felt nice to give something back for a change.

The first tavern they entered was called The Green Bog. It was only a little better than they expected from a place with such a name, but not by much. As Brando entered, everyone stopped and stared at them. Fin suspected they would treat them similarly if they weren't festooned in their fine armor.

"I have an important message from Lord Dragonthrone," Brando belted out to the crowd. "On this day, in the year of his majesty, 14, hence fourth... There will be no empty mugs because the next round of drinks is on me!"

The Green Bog lit up like an outhouse in a forest fire. Not a single face was without a smile, and Brando was at the center of it. He talked and laughed with everyone but did not stay too long. He had a mission, after all. So, he dropped a pile of coins on the bar, and it was off to the next pub.

"I kind of like the important message from Lord Dragonthrone part," Fin began, picking up on the spirit of things. "Can I make the next speech?"

Brando agreed, and at the next tavern they entered, he bought two rounds before addressing the crowd.

"I would like to buy everyone a round!" Fin announced, and when everyone finished cheering, he lifted his mug and toasted it to Brando. "To Brando who was born and raised here. He single-handedly saved the life of the royal princess and was knighted as Protector of the Realm. I will also drink to the health of the poor, poor women living in this town who left him before he was rich!"

A resounding "Here, here!" erupted from the tavern.

They stayed longer than intended as people kept buying drinks for their story. Brando eventually pulled himself away and went outside. He then had to go back and physically pull Fin away from a pair of grabby hands and batting eyelashes. Brando told him there would be time for that later; they had a job to do.

After the fourth ale house, they started drawing a crowd. Many of their followers were from previous taverns trying to get the next free round. After the seventh, the tavern was too crowded, so Brando had the barrels of ale brought outside, where musicians played music, street vendors served food, and the streets were saturated with festivities.

Fin had an idea to host a race where the prizes for first, second, and third place were a gold, silver, and a copper coin respectively. Brando loved the idea so much that he decided to host multiple competitions, which is how the street tournaments began.

Brando found himself sitting on a massive throne in the center of a closed-off square, judging various games like the Highest-Jumping Musician. First, the competitors had to play a song on any instrument. There were some grey areas about the quality of the song or instrument, but that was what Brando was there for. With a raised thumb, the competitors would then attempt to jump over an ever-rising rope.

"How am I doing on money?" Brando asked Fin, as he doled out coins to the previous round's victors.

"You're about halfway there," He said after checking his inventory.

Brando handed his empty mug to whoever kept refilling it and stood to announce the next competition. Before he could, a throaty voice went to such lengths to begin a monologue that it was completely baffling. Brando stayed quiet throughout the entire speech.

"Well, well, well, such a gallant man we have in our midst, or rather, a man having gone through great lengths to appear so," As the man approached, he was followed by others who were dressed in similar robes of office. "There he is, the so-called Protector of the Realm, throwing coins around in a dastardly attempt to buy votes. I don't know who he thinks he is, but I did some research and found out who he really is. Brando, the leather worker, was orphaned as a child, penniless, and twice divorced. He is no Protector of the Realm, and he did not save any princess. He is a fraud and a disturbance of the peace and is unfit to govern this town."

Brando sat in his gaudy oversized chair, completely dumbfounded. He had no idea what he had done to deserve such an insult that he thought it might be a joke. No matter how much he looked, he couldn't see any signs of it being one. The man's features were angry, not jovial. He had a slight lean as if the vein on his forehead weighed him forward. The climate, changing from loud to entirely silent, submerged him further into shock.

Fin was confused but came to his senses first. As he approached Brando, he held up a finger and asked for a moment.

"Brando, who is this guy?" He whispered.

"That's what I'm trying to figure out," Brando replied. "I swear, I've never seen him in my life."

"Ex-wife's husband?" Fin suggested.

"Maybe," Brando guessed. "If he is and he gets us arrested, it will ruin my whole plan. We can't have that happen."

"Do you want me to handle it, or do you want to handle it?" Fin asked.

"I'll handle it," Brando sighed. "If I look like I need help, feel free to jump in." He then cleared his throat and addressed the man so everyone could hear.

"I don't know who you are, but you seem to know a lot about me," Brando's voice did not waver as he stood and addressed the arrogant man. "I was born here. As a matter of fact, I was born just around the corner, on Ridger Street. I grew up a penniless orphan, and although I am not proud of my failed marriages, they have made me who I am today. I was given the title of Protector of the Realm after rescuing Princess Desiree Rae."

Fin held up two pieces of paper that Brando pointed to. "I have the proof right there."

Tannor approached Brando, but he held out his hand to stop him. "I will show everyone except for you. That way, to call me a liar, you have to call everyone else here a liar, and they might not be as forgiving as I am."

"How dare you talk to me that way. Do you know who I am?" Tannor's face was red with anger. "Guards, arrest these men for their insolence!"

"If I am not mistaken, I am the ranking official here," Brando had no idea if this was true, but he believed in the power of the bluff. "Guards, arrest this man instead!"

"Arrest them! I am the king's nephew!" Tannor huffed.

"Arrest him! I am Lord Dragonthrone, and I am courting the royal princess!" Fin declared, feeling disgusted with himself for name-dropping Dezi. He took a drink of his mead to wash the mention of her out of his mouth. It didn't work.

The guards jerked in indecision, hesitant to arrest either of them. Finally, a man wearing robes similar to Tannor introduced himself as Chancellor Cargwen and voiced his concerns.

"This is highly irregular," he said in a soft but authoritative voice. "I propose we settle this matter in a less public forum."

"No, I want to settle this right now!" Tannor demanded. "For the sake of honor and my family name, someone read those falsified documents, so you can arrest them already!"

Chancellor Cargwen approached Fin and held out his hand. Fin handed them over, and he studied them. After a while, he called more of the robed figures to help scrutinize the documents under the public's watchful eye. They muttered quietly to each other, pointed at various details, and held the documents up to the light.

"It appears they are both who they say they are. However, neither Vice Secretary Tannor nor Sir Brando has the power to arrest the other at their own volition," Cargwen cleared his throat. "Lord Finlay, on the other hand, could have him arrested if he so desires..."

Fin declined.

Before Brando could resume the festivities, he saw someone that gave him pause. His ex-wife stood in the crowd with short brown hair, frozen blue eyes, and light freckles, and she had seen the whole thing. She had even seen him verified as Protector of the Realm! His mission was complete.

"You know what, Fin?" Brando asked as he tucked his coin bag away. "I think I'm done here."

"Do you want to plant some grapes in the dragon soil and make wine?" Fin asked, wondering how melon-sized grapes would taste.

Cargwen cleared his voice. "Excuse me, but I thought you would want to run for Governor. If you did, I would be more than happy to help you gain the position."

"Is it a lot of work?" Brando asked.

"Not too much," Cargwen considered. "A meeting or so a week and a few signatures here and there. Nothing too strenuous. All I would ask for in return is approval for one thing or another. Only small things, I'm sure."

In the dying light of the sun, Brando's eyes twinkled with the possibilities of governing his hometown. Fin was still thinking of growing grapes with Sprout's help. He wondered what he would call wine grown by a nature sprite from dragon soil? Maybe he would call it Dragon Berry Wine.

THE END

Acknowledgments

Thanks for reading, and a special thanks to everyone who made this book possible. For starters thanks to my narrator for making this so easy for me. Thanks to Jens, Micah, Gabriel, and Nate (chronologically) for letting me bounce ideas off you. Big thanks to Finlay Potato, Garett Armstrong, and Katie "Catherine" Sweeny. Thanks to all of my alpha, bravo, charlie, and delta readers, you guys are OP. You're not ready for this list: Maudib (Who keeps trying to get me to drop the princess off a cliff), Destiny (with two z's who adamantly agrees with Maudib about the princess), PaulTB, Obsurver, Caladin, Gleg, Chriama, RaccoonLover, Reedweaver, BlazeSpirit, Sirenstorm, Rathgill, BurnthePionex, JM5109, Anon8, SkylarG, Briana StormCloud (Don't worry, it's not THAT Briana), GumpyPants, J. Davis, Steamrolla, Unmaker, VeganPurple, My mom (my actual mom, that's not a user name), Tracat (that's a user name), Dawn Chapman, Stupidcat, Timelord0, and Beth Ruck. Big thanks to everyone at Immersive Ink. If you want more Fin and Brando shenanigans, please rate and review. If it does well, I'll drop my other books and do another one.

About the Author

Evan Kvalvik is an electrical engineer with a certified pinky ring. He was born in Washington and immediately joined the Navy. He drove a submarine, became an ordained internet minister, and officiated about fourteen marriage ceremonies. It's a hobby….

He and his wife live in Tennessee where they raise two hairless cats on something that resembles a farm. He has a miniature chicken who keeps sitting on the eggs. So they give her fertilized, normal sized chicken eggs to hatch. It keeps working, but all her children are bigger than her. It's kind of funny to see that play out. They also raise quail. At the time of this publication, there are approximately 50 quail. They haven't tried giving their little chicken quail eggs yet, so stay tuned in the next addition of "About the Author" with your favorite poultry enthusiast.

www.ingramcontent.com/pod-product-compliance
Lightning Source LLC
Chambersburg PA
CBHW070343010826
48976CB00019B/1514

9798991397650